UNIDENTIFIED FUNNY OBJECTS 8

Edited by

Alex Shvartsman

UFO Publishing
Brooklyn, NY

PUBLISHED BY:

UFO Publishing
1685 E 15th St.
Brooklyn, NY 11229
www.ufopub.com

Trade paperback ISBN: 978-1-951064-01-3

Cover art: Tomasz Maronski
Interior art: Barry Munden
Typesetting & interior design: Melissa Neely
Graphics design: Jay O'Connell
Logo design: Martin Dare
Copyeditor: Elektra Hammond
Associate editors: Cyd Athens, Frank Dutkiewicz,
James A. Miller, Tarryn Thomas

Visit us on the web:
www.ufopub.com

For Mike Resnick (1942–2020).
May his memory be a blessing.

TABLE OF CONTENTS

FOREWORD

ALEX SHVARTSMAN

Welcome to the eighth installment of the Unidentified Funny Objects series. This series aims to showcase lighthearted stories, from whimsical to downright funny, across the science fiction and fantasy genres. In this book you'll find superheroes dealing with government bureaucracy, cat cat-burglars, grandmotherly golems, literal-minded self-driving cars, and several sets of aliens visiting Earth for various and occasionally wacky reasons.

This is also the first time a UFO volume has had a dedication. Mike Resnick, who passed away in early 2020, was a friend and mentor to me, and his fiction has appeared in every previous installment of this series. Mike was practically synonymous with writing science fiction and fantasy humor. He also encouraged and taught others, dedicating much of his time and energy to shepherding the careers of younger authors, whom he affectionately referred to as his "writer children."

It is Mike's pay-it-forward attitude that, in part, has inspired me to always keep the door open to newer writers. Many anthologists fill their books by only inviting contributors directly. They rely on experienced writers who they know will deliver quality stories. This strategy is also a lot less time consuming than an open submissions call, which is something we do at UFO.

Over half of our stories come from a submission window that is open to everyone. For this book, my associate editors and I read over 900 stories! The successful authors have their work appear alongside best-selling and award-winning headliners.

Occasionally, we're privileged to find a brand-new voice and become the first venue, or at least the first professional publication, for that writer. There's hardly a more pleasing thing for an anthologist: after all, we may end up discovering the next Bradbury or Le Guin. So it is both thrilling and very fitting of Mike Resnick's legacy that I was able to feature several brand-new voices in this book.

I won't single them out in this introduction. Instead, you can discover who they are in the brief bios listed at the end of each story. I don't think you'll figure it out sooner; their writing and plots are every bit as engaging and fun as the other stories collected in this book. I hope some of them go on to enjoy illustrious careers and their writing touches many lives, the way Resnick's did.

Happy reading!

THE 10:40 APPOINTMENT AT THE NYC DEPARTMENT OF SUPERHERO REGISTRATION

CHRIS HEPLER

When they called ticket number 57 up to Window F, I stepped over the sleeping guy in samurai armor, slipped past the liquid metal mom trying to persuade her liquid metal toddler to stay in the stroller, and put on my winningest smile. My origin story started back in July, but today was going to be the day I actually became a superhero.

At my window was a woman who looked grandmotherly, by which I mean stone-faced and with eyes that were already tired of my crap before a word was spoken. So, my-grandmotherly. She also had two bristly steel antennae sticking out of her head and wore red-and-black spandex like she was daring me to comment on it. Her name tag read JEWEL. I set down my form and the thermos I was carrying with me. Bringing a drink did not seem to please Jewel, and I wondered if there was a rule about food and beverages here.

"Fingerprints," she said, and I put my finger on the scanner. "Right hand," she said in a voice that could melt gravel. "Your *whole* hand." I complied.

"Mister ... Amir al-Madani?"

"Doctor al-Madani, but yes."

She looked at me as if medical degrees were something incontinent dogs left on the floor. "What do you need?"

I wondered if anybody came to the Department of Superhero Registration for anything other than the obvious, and bit back my sarcastic comment. There were probably all kinds of paperwork for insurance renewal and alien repulsion team sign-ups, and other stuff I didn't know about. "A superhero license," I said.

"This is an AUSL-33/b," she said, handing me some paper. "Come back to this window when you're done." She pressed a button, and number 58 appeared on the monitor.

I took a clipboard and returned to my seat, only to see it filled by a guy in a pinstripe suit talking on a smartphone and smelling like a tobacco farm. He seemed to notice my annoyance, and moved down.

"'Scuse me," he said, then into the phone: "So we set up this summoning circle, and we put in what we value most, right? I put in my cigs, because honestly, I turn into a monster without them. We light up the pile, Bill chants a lot, and I don't see nothing, but I start hearing the voice. Not a demon, nothing so cool." He paused. "Okay, you handle that." He looked over at me, rolling his eyes. "Of course, she's on call waiting. Agents, am I right?"

I managed a sympathetic nod. "Don't have one."

"You should, man, this city's lousy with heroes. You need everything you can to stand out."

"So, you were conjuring a spirit?" I asked, as I filled out the paperwork. It felt good to talk to someone else with superpowers. These people would be my brethren now.

"Yeah, Bill took charge and said, 'We will release you if you give us powers beyond mortal men.' And I play good cop and am like, 'Also, who are we talking to, bud?' And it said, 'The people of this land call me Great Tobacco.' So Bill says 'Forget this, I'll get the next one.' And I'm all, 'Congrats, big guy, you got your freedom for half off. Do me up.'"

I looked him up and down. If he had a power, it wasn't glamour. Sure, he wore a suit, but if I saw him on the street holding a Starbucks cup, I'd throw a dollar in. And maybe an insulin needle.

"So you captured it and now ... what? You've got magic?"

"Yeah, I can smoke all I want, no health problems. Throw fire, too."

"Right." I considered that maybe the paperwork and regulations *were* a good idea. I stayed polite, though."That always seemed like a really dangerous power for a hero."

"You ain't telling me the news. Why d'you think I'm signing up? They catch me shooting fire from my fists, I'll be in Rikers for twenty to life." He leaned toward me conspiratorially. "But you get a superhero license? You can get away with *the world.* Why else wait in line, am I right?"

Oh, boy. I could smell this one. In a year's time, this guy was going to be a villain. "It was different for me," I said. "I survived this accident, and *pow,* I became *more.* I wasn't just destined for the job my parents picked out for me. Whatever force runs the universe was saying, 'You can be what you wanted when you were a kid.' I couldn't just say, 'Sorry, schedule's full, gotta get back to testing Uncle Tarek's dairy for bacteria.' I dropped everything to come here."

"Mmm," the fire guy said.

I had more, mostly about helping the needy, but I'd never win his type over with morality lectures. "You, uh, got a name picked out?"

"Coffin Nail," he said, pointing gun-fingers at me. "Hold on." He saw something on his phone's display and brought it back up to his ear again. "Latoya, baby, let's make me famous."

Looking around to see if some hall monitor was listening and would disqualify him, I only saw heroes signing forms, on their phones, or in the case of the samurai next to us, still asleep. I finished as much of the AUSL-33/b as I could manage and headed back up to Jewel.

"Here you are," I said, expecting a smile. No way.

"Two forms of I.D.?"

"Brought three, just in case." I handed over my driver's license, my UAE work visa, and my American passport. Jewel took a look at the Arabic writing on the visa and oriented some skeptical eyes on me.

"You a citizen?"

"Yeah. American parents, born in the United Arab Emirates, raised in New Jersey, kinda bounced back and forth a bit for school—"

"Yes or no is fine." She finished scanning the American documents and picked up my AUSL-33/b. She scowled, probably trying to decipher my handwriting.

My attention wandered to the floating girl at Window G. She couldn't have been more than eighteen. She was in bronze armor and was casually resting a spear over her shoulder while signing something with the other hand. Strands of her long black tresses blew artfully over her chiseled face. It took me a second to realize that there was no fan blowing. I wasn't feeling anything, and I was five feet away from her.

"Excuse me, miss, do you make that breeze?" I asked. "That's nice."

She looked at me with a patient smile. "Side effect."

"Of what?"

"Genetically engineered progeny of a battle goddess," she said. "My pen doesn't work."

I loaned her my pen. "You new to this?"

"I'm forming my third supergroup."

Jewel finished digesting my form. "All right, Mister Madani, I have to confirm a few things before proceeding. You checked 'act of God' for how you got your powers, but also 'radiation.'"

"Uh ..." I said. The demigoddess next to me met my eyes. I tried to squash the higher registers of my voice and explain myself in a smooth Leonard Cohen bass from the good albums. "I do microbiology, and I was testing a flash-pasteurizer that got hit by lightning."

"Flash-pasteurizer is radiation," Jewel said. The demigoddess frowned and floated a few feet farther away.

"Yeah, but given the probabilities, wouldn't you say that 'act of God' would be a safe bet, too?" I grinned at the demigoddess, saying help-me-out-here with my eyes. She rolled hers.

Jewel had even less sympathy. "Do I look like an expert? I'm putting down accident, radiation. Now, here it says 'catalyzed cellular reproduction dependent on consuming vitamins A, D, and bovine growth hormone.' What's that mean?"

"Milk," I said, tapping the thermos I'd put down. "I drink milk, and I heal myself."

"Anything else?"

"I have the proportional strength of a cow," I said. "Considering cow weight, it's, um ... about ninety-five percent ..." I glanced at the goddess girl, "Maybe up to a hundred and five percent of human normal."

"Anything else?"

"That isn't enough?"

"That's fine, but you left this assets list blank."

"Uh ... I wasn't sure what it meant. I mean, I have a car—"

"Is it designed for battle?"

"It's a leased Prius."

"Sweetie, we ain't the tax man. Assets as in 'what you fight crime with.' Black belts in karate. The sword Excalibur. A milk truck with machine guns. Supercomputers, secret lairs, all that."

I swallowed and realized the demigoddess next to me was watching, her arms folded. I actually did have a black belt, but so did anyone who put in three or four years at my tae kwon do school. I led with the unique bit. "I'm analyzing my regenerative tissues using my M.D.," I said. "I figured it'd be pretty dumb if I didn't use them to try to cure cancer."

"Okay, so fill out 'cancer cure' on your sheet here."

"Uh, no, I'm just *working* on a ... okay, it's kind of a back-burner project. I can heal, I can punch people, and I've got no criminal record. I'm pretty sure you've got heroes running around the city with just that much."

"And you were immigrating, Mister?"

Oh, for cripes' sake. "Doctor. American citizen. I worked in the UAE, that's all." I tried to help her out. "Little country, near Saudi Arabia?"

"You left 'religion' blank, too."

"Why do I need to state that?"

"Standard information."

"Yeah?" I pointed at Miss Lovely, who had turned in her form. "Does *she* get questions like that?"

"Actually, they did ask me that," said the goddess girl. "It's for your ID tags." She pulled out two stainless steel plates on her necklace. I could read KHARIS PROMAKHOS—PAGAN. "Superheroes get a state-sponsored funeral. They need to know what type of service to give if you jump on a grenade."

This reassured me until it totally didn't reassure me. My gaze went back and forth to both women. "Uh ... do you get a ... *lot* ... of grenades here?"

"Do I look like an expert?" asked Jewel.

Kharis patted my hand, then seemed to remember I might be radioactive. "Look, you seem new to how New York does heroes. Just sign what you want, the road test is going to be the tough part for you."

"Road test? What does driving have to do with it?"

"Doc, don't pay attention to her," said Jewel. "You're going to need a religion, or declare atheist, whatever, just write something that fits on a tag. Then, we get to superhero name."

I was distracted, but not so much that I forgot my moniker. "Fine. Put down 'expensive,' and it's Doctor Awesome."

She typed it into her desktop, then swiveled the monitor to show me the results. "Name's taken."

"That's a thing?" I had no backup. I had wanted to be Doctor Awesome since I was doodling it on my notebooks in seventh grade, and it was my e-mail besides. "Can't we both be Doctor Awesome?"

"Not even if you were his clone. There've been lawsuits."

"Does he have a Ph.D. or an M.D.?"

"He doesn't need to. He has precedent. He's had it for six years."

"Well, I only got my superpower in July. I pretty much came here as fast as I could, you know?" I didn't want to get into the first month, which had all been arguing with my mom.

I was starting to notice Jewel had a remarkably long streak of being unimpressed. "Name's still taken."

"Right ... Doctor Mystery?"

Clickety-click went the keys. "Taken."

"Well, what the frick isn't taken?" I asked. "I got it. I'll do Doctor Awesome, but in Arabic."

Jewel looked at me as if I were a particularly dense kindergartener. "Doctor Awesome holds the trademark to his name worldwide, in all localized versions, for his merchandise. That's why your AUSL-33/b is 'Application for *Universal* Superhero License,' we register it all over the world." She must have seen my crestfallen face, because after that, she added, "Okay, sweets, you're not the first one this has happened to. You check that box on sheet two there, and our department will assign you one appropriate to your background and power. For fifty bucks, you can expedite it to be delivered before you leave here today, and after that you can appeal for a change if you develop new powers or join a themed supergroup. You want to just do that?"

"*Want* to? No. What I *want* is to be Doctor Awesome." Then I paused. "What sort of names do they come up with?"

"Well, if you're Arabic and your powers rely on milk, odds are they're gonna call you the Milk Sheik."

Kharis looked like if she had a drink at that moment, she would have spat it. She covered her mouth with her hand, but then took it away when the giggles stopped. "Oh, gods, that's terrible. You're gonna get jokes about bringing all the boys to the yard."

"That makes me sound as legit as the damn Burger King!" I yelled, then lowered my voice because I got a glare from the liquid metal mom, who was now a window away and holding a bucket into which she had coerced her toddler. In a stage whisper that I hoped sounded threatening, I said, "I will give you the fifty bucks with the one express condition that I am *not* the fricking Milk Sheik. Can't I beat someone up around here to get to choose my name? I mean, that's how it works, right? I just throw down with whatever twerp took the name Doctor Awesome?"

"Save it for the road test," said Jewel. "'Cause that's next."

JEWEL KEYED IN the code to a door that looked like it belonged on a bank vault. There was a hiss of air as she opened the seal, probably because you don't want crime-fighting sleep gas getting out of your testing chamber. The cavernous place on the other side smelled funny, like ozone, and I saw the walls made of twelve-inch steel plate had turned to slag in places. I was pretty sure the whole room was an Office of Safety and Health violation, but when I turned to Jewel to tell her, the vault door slammed shut, leaving me alone with only my thermos and my newly stamped AUSL-33/b for protection.

Well, that's not strictly true. I had my khakis and a button-down shirt on, because when I came in, I expected to have my photo taken.

"Hello?" I called out.

There was a mechanical whine, quickly eclipsed by the roar of rockets. A rack of lights flared on, illuminating an eight-foot-tall monstrosity that could still be called humanoid if you went by silhouettes alone. Judging from the sound it made when it landed, it was five hundred pounds of metal, and its rocket boots weren't kind to the floor. I had the sinking feeling I now knew where all the slag came from. A voice came from a hidden loudspeaker.

"OO TENFORDY?"

"Uh ... what?" I said.

The face plate moved up, and beneath it was a human. He looked like he'd spent high school denting lockers with his head and kept a flawless win/loss ratio. "You made appointment online," he said, with a notable Russian accent. "You are ten-forty?"

"Oh, yeah, I'm here for the road test. I'm, uh ... I'm Amir."

"I am Cold Fusion," said the technological terror. "I control nuclear energy. Powers my suit."

He punched some buttons on his arm and a holographic screen came up with my info. "What you got? Superpowers?" He didn't seem like the kind who liked to read.

"Well, if I drink milk, I can heal injuries fast—"

"Ah, regeneration. What is upper limit?"

"Um ... it varies by organ system—"

The faceplate snapped down again over Cold Fusion's face. "WE TEST!" he yelled.

My vision flared to white for a second, and I heard a pop like both my ears got something jammed into them at the same time. I felt like I got hit in the back, but that was just me landing on the hard metal floor. My face was numb from the trauma, but after a few seconds, the agony kicked in.

"YOU HEAL BROKEN JAW?" Cold Fusion boomed.

I was in pain, but already the A-frame of my jaw, now splintered, was trying to mend itself. It burned—all the soreness a normal person has over the course of months was crammed into a few seconds for me. I made the mistake of trying to talk.

"Nuh puhblum," I said, getting a little more coherent as I spat out my four front teeth. "Ah be guud in a shepind." I looked around for my thermos, but saw nothing. I was glad I had cereal for breakfast that morning.

"YOU HEAL HEART BRUISE?"

I hesitated. I'd never tested lethal injuries. Cold Fusion took silence as a yes. But pain is a great motivator, and I managed to interpose both my forearms over my chest as his second rocket-powered punch slammed into me. Once again, I flew backward, but I only had two fractured ulnas instead of broken ribs jabbing into my internal organs.

"Are you looking for a wrongful death lawsuit?" I yelled, a little more coherently now that my jaw was healing. "This can't be standard procedure!"

The metal monstrosity clanged as it stomped toward me. "YOU SIGN RELEASE FORM. IS IN SMALL PRINT."

He reached for me, probably to pick me up and slam me into the ground, or possibly to help me to my feet. I didn't wait to find out which. I was going to impress this psycho if it was the last thing I did.

My arms were in agony, so I whirled around, simultaneously slipping his grip and executing a spinning hook kick. He was bent over a little trying to reach me, which was good, because otherwise my heel would never have reached his head. It slammed into his temple—well, his helmet—with a metallic *whang.*

I dislocated my ankle, but at least it was satisfying.

"YOU FIGHT BACK." Cold Fusion sounded as pleased as one could be through a speaker that Metallica would consider obnoxiously loud. "GOOD, IS PART OF TEST. KEEP FIGHT."

Gun ports in his forearms opened up, but I was already jumping out of the way when the shots came. I say that like I was polished and smooth, but the truth was, my newly dislocated ankle gave out, so after stumbling to the ground again, I tried rolling to evade him. I was certain the robotic monstrosity would hit me if I stayed still. Unfortunately, rolling with banged-up arms was arguably just as painful as the rubber bullets that slammed into me when I stopped said roll. It'd be pretty lousy power armor if it couldn't, you know, aim its arm.

The bullets hit my chest, my neck, and one broke the orbit of my left eye, as the recoil took the spray upward. Everything flashed gold, but I had so many endorphins in my system that the wonky senses didn't bother me much. The real problem, of course, was not the pain, but my deep desire for it to be over. There was no point to this. Cold Fusion would do what he liked, and there was nothing and no one that could stop him.

I got to my knees, and when he lifted me up by the hair, I used my last remaining good limb to kick him in the groin. My sneaker slapped against the power armor, but of course the armor had a codpiece that bulged outward and was pointy enough to feel like a metal fist smashing into the center of my instep.

Cold Fusion's expression was unreadable, but he cocked his helmet to the side a little. "OKAY," he boomed. "FINAL TRAUMA CHECK." With that, his armor whirred, and a spray of what I guessed was liquid nitrogen vented all over my body while he brought his fist back. Cold fusion, indeed. The fist glowed with some kind of energy that I hoped wouldn't sterilize me, and then he slugged me in the stomach. I landed twenty feet away, tumbled another ten, and couldn't breathe.

I blacked out. It might have been ten seconds, or it might have been ten minutes. All I knew was that I was frozen. I was broken. I was burnt. And he was stomping over again. His faceplate snapped up and his gauntleted hand dropped a piece of paper near my face.

"Your form. Read up," he said.

"I'm kind of seeing double right now." At least I was talking and getting oxygen into my system. "What's that say?"

"Here is, all printed and signed by office," said Cold Fusion. "You need do more."

I wasn't sure if I heard him right, because my ears were frozen rocks. "Your test is the dumbest thing I have *ever* experienced."

The man's blue eyes glittered. "No, I say wrong. You pass, but not superhero yet," he said. "You have superpower. You fight and not give up. Now you turn in papers at registration for metal tags. We 3D-print them. One set for home, one set for superhero identity. Here. See? All is processed."

He held the paper in front of my face. Through my good eye, I could see my name, birthdate, assets, non-secret address, patrolling location preference, and down at the bottom, the words, "PUBLIC NAME—MILK SHEIK."

I looked at the paper, and back to him. Then back at the paper.

In the distance, I heard a low roar, rising in pitch. I thought for a second it might be a police siren, but it wasn't as varied. Cold turned to the door with a look of alarm on his face as we both realized it was the air raid horns scattered throughout the city. They were usually tested on Friday afternoons at one o'clock, but it was Tuesday morning. That meant one thing, and the whole world knew it.

"That is defense alert!" Cold yelled, seeming more afraid than menacing without his speakers magnifying his voice. Lights blinked in his helmet, and I could faintly hear something coming over the radio near his ear. "Is aliens again! Morgai terror platform is flying over Bronx! All superheroes help now!"

His faceplate snapped down and his rocket boots ignited. He hovered over to a set of steel shutters and punched some buttons on his forearm. The shutters rolled open, and I could see a kind of garage, complete with a car up on a mechanic's lift, and a wall full of tools you'd use to maintain power armor. He grabbed some kind of laser attachment that definitely didn't shoot rubber bullets.

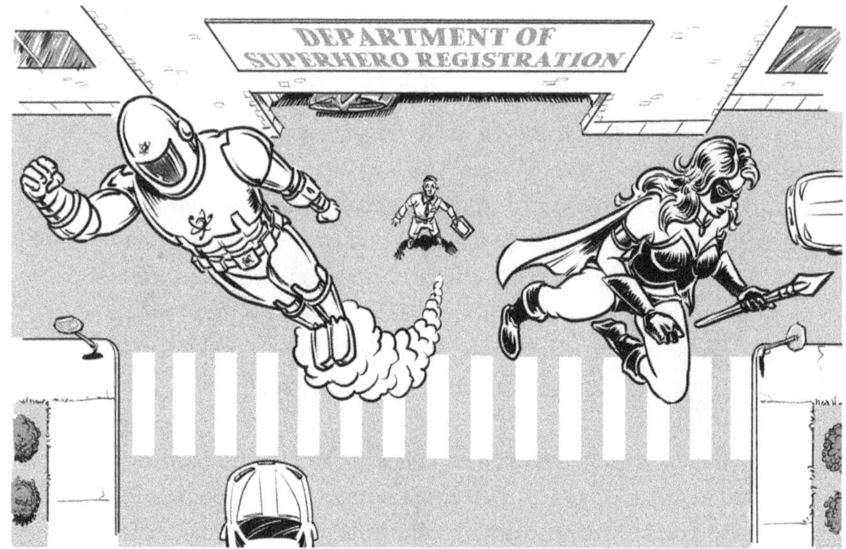

But what I focused on was that on the floor next to the open garage door was my little plastic thermos.

"YOU HEAL LIKE YOU SAY. COME FIGHT SOON AS POSSIBLE!" boomed the speakers, and Cold Fusion soared out into the parking lot and then to the sky. On the ground, I could see Kharis the battle goddess conjuring a wind that lifted her, and Coffin Nail huffing his way over to an armored Humvee with a turret on the top. That guy in samurai armor sprinted past Nail and jumped into the turret while Nail took the wheel. Every detail after that was lost in the multitude of heroes running, jumping, teleporting, and driving toward the imminent danger.

Me, I limped to the thermos, opened it, and stuck the plastic spout between my broken teeth.

After a little sucking, the pain in my body eased, and heated me up as I burned energy to heal. A minute or two later, my ankle and arms faded back to a comfortable soreness. My mouth stung as new teeth formed and pushed their way through my gums. I'd probably need braces again, which prompted me to question whether or not I was really serious about going outside.

I couldn't fly. I didn't own a laser gun, or even a normal gun.

My sole contribution would be running out onto the battlefield and getting sniped by particle beams, no doubt playing possum in the hopes that I could maybe kick an alien in the head if it got really close. If my own brains got splattered in the street, I might heal and come back dumber. Or I'd just die.

I would not be a hero. I would be a joke. The Milk Sheik.

I went back to the processing department, figuring I knew what sidekicks and such did in times like this. I'd find civilians and encourage them to take cover in the testing chamber. But the department was empty. I saw the liquid metal mom ushering the last civilian into a storm-cellar-like shelter, way ahead of me even with a bucket in her arms holding her liquid metal toddler. I limped after her, and she yanked the door shut behind us.

The rest of the day was endless. We watched news, worried about loved ones, kept quiet when we heard nearby gunfire. I waited for someone confined with us to need a doctor. No one did. My abiding memory of helping during that time is loaning out my thermos of milk. Because, you know, toddler.

When we emerged into the light, I crumpled up my AUSL-33/b form and threw it in the trash.

In case you're wondering, Mom approved.

THREE AND A half years later, I was running an internal medicine practice in the Bronx, focused on oncology. My family was proud, I never lacked for patients, and it beat bacterial work. That day I was in the examination room with a Mrs. Alyona Brusilova.

The first thing I noticed about her was that she looked dangerously thin, taking up only about half of her wheelchair. Alyona's hair was bone-white, making her look much older than the reported age we had in our database: she was supposed to be only sixty-six. She was also pale, more so than the younger man standing behind her, a towering sort of guy I would have cast in a boxing movie as the nigh-invincible heavy. He was wearing overalls, like he didn't care much about fashion; Alyona, for her part, was in pajamas. I was pretty sure he was her son.

"Thank you for seeing her so soon," said the large man. "Last night, she collapse. Emergency room doctors take blood. They get results to you?"

"Yes," I said. These poor people were probably up all night. "Mrs. Brusilova, we've got your white and red blood cell counts here, along with many of your enzymes. The results are ... well, we often see these numbers in patients with chronic leukemia."

Alyona looked at me confused, but then she and her son spoke a lot of rapid-fire Russian. She nodded, and suddenly said very little.

"She understands," said the big man. "Do you need more tests?"

"Yes," I said, "it would help to do a bone marrow biopsy. If you could get her into a hospital gown for the examination, we can get that underway."

"I help," said the son, and a vague memory stirred in me. It nagged at my mind as I waited in the hall, and when the man emerged from the room, clicking the door behind him, I wanted to bring it up.

"Is she okay in there?" I asked.

"She is scared, but she is strong. More than me. I cannot lose my mother."

I nodded. "I don't think I caught your name."

"Misha," he said.

"Misha, is she still employed, or is she retired?"

"Employed," he said immediately. "We work in government. She is at Department of Motor Vehicles. I am at superhero registration."

That brought it all back. I said to him in a low voice, "Cold Fusion?"

He looked taken aback. "Yes," he said. "Tell no one real name. Understand?"

"Of course," I said automatically.

His voice trembled a little. "Do you think ... I cause her cancer? With nuclear energy?"

"Well, no," I said, clarifying quickly, "We don't know everything yet. You're a potential cause, but it's just one of several. There's genetic history to be considered, and then there's the Morgai factor." Misha looked blank. I filled in the gaps. "You know all the buildings that got vaporized in the battle over the Bronx, right?"

He shrugged. "We got off easy. Better than last invasion."

"Yeah," I said. "I saw the footage." Of course I did. Everyone not still in utero had seen the footage, heard the story, watched the cartoon. Some teleporting guy named Doctor Awesome got Coffin Nail into the engine room of the terror platform where he melted stuff, and *sploosh*—there was one more mothership in the Hudson River. Kharis Promakhos had dueled some bigwig or other to get him to leave Earth alone, which if you ask me, was much more convenient than having the United Nations negotiate an armistice.

Just to put the cherry on top, Doctor Awesome joined her latest supergroup, the Unlimited. Every Halloween, I see kids in my office dressed in his merchandise.

"What you say about buildings?" Misha asked.

"Sorry." I came back to Earth, so to speak. "All the dust and asbestos and gunk got into the air. Breathing that causes lung problems. Ugly problems. Silicosis, lead and mercury toxicity, pulmonary fibrosis, and of course, cancers. So it's highly likely you didn't do this."

He nodded, but he looked down nervously. That didn't scan: he should have been relieved. I added, "That's probably not your real question, is it?"

"Yes," Misha said. "I want to know what you do."

"I promise you, we've seen this sort of thing before. We can isolate probable causes and then we'll work on a treatment plan."

He nodded, though he looked as lost as I've ever seen a person. "Is there cure for her kind? My friend fight villain Coffin Nail after he go nuts. He breathe in smoke, got worst cancer I ever hear of. His funeral ... very sad."

I tried to give a truthful answer, rather than sell false hope or drop into false fear. "Well, my office specializes in diseases like this. Due to an awareness campaign we ran with metahumans donating regenerating tissues, we understand a lot more about biomedical engineering solutions to unchecked cellular division than we did just a few years ago." My tissues, mostly. Even other regenerating heroes weren't fond of cutting off salami-thin slices of their own flesh. But me ... I like science.

Misha's brow furrowed. "I not understand quite what you say."

I simplified my language. "There are some treatments my office has worked on that are very promising. We can now, uh ... we've got a really good success rate."

It was then I saw a light behind his eyes. Not literally, of course. What I mean is, Cold Fusion didn't give a crap about nuance. He grabbed me in a bear hug that, to my surprise, didn't hurt at all.

"I understand," he said. "You are awesome doctor."

Chris Hepler

Chris Hepler has recently created the Seasun Comics series *Mythkillers* and the novel *Civil Blood: The Vampire Rights Case That Changed a Nation.* He has previously contributed to the universes of *Mass Effect, Star Wars: The Old Republic, Pirates of the Caribbean,* and *Shadowrun.* He dreads the day when actual space marines, Jedi, pirates, and troll mercenaries will show up on his doorstep to tell him that he doesn't know what he's talking about.

SOUL TRADE

GALEN WESTLAKE

Dominus the Vexatious tapped his computer mouse and cursed the screen for the ninth time—real curses with unholy hissing, not the language the mortals used for emphasis or to look cool amongst their peers. But the arch-devil's soul portfolio only sank deeper, its value eroding before his infernal gaze.

"I tell you, Valhernius," he said to his lesser servant demon, "this cannot be!"

"Aye, most despicable one," answered the small amorphous blob of tentacles. "The television reports this is the greatest soul recession since the invention of pacifism."

"I don't care what the devils say on TV. I've been on TV. I know it's nothing but lies. Gaze upon this!" The tall fiery fiend brandished a scroll of glowing parchment before Valhernius with his clawed hand. "It's a contract for one soul. *One soul!* How in damnation can its value drop below one? There's no such thing as a tenth of a soul!"

"Forgive me, most horrid of horrids!" said Valhernius. "But what you say is exactly right. It is not a soul but a contract. And right now, it's in default. They all are!"

"Those blasphemous soul brokers assured me these contracts were too dastardly to fail."

"Junk souls, my lord of lies," answered the diminutive demon. "Our souls were all packaged into bonds. Our quality murderers and thieves were mixed with the lesser tainted. Questionable souls: those who plagiarized book reports, or peeked at cards in cribbage." He could not meet his master's gaze. "Redeemable souls. We've been buying risk for decades!"

Realization dawned upon Dominus like a fiery sun. "I've got to sell. Sell it all now—before there's nothing left to save!"

"The Infernal Consumer Bureau warns against panic selling, most vile one. The more devils who jump out now, the worse it's going to become."

"If the hells think we're going to suddenly prioritize unity over self-interest they are sadly mistaken. We didn't invent the concept of betrayal for nothing."

Dominus stopped himself; the smoldering fire encircling his body slowly crackling in tune with his tsunami of emotion. "Still, you are right. What if this is some sort of trick by that fiend Sumarlisan? Maybe he's driving down the price of souls so he can buy them on the cheap! It's what I would do."

"Not so, my lord. You would do it better!"

"Of course I would. But my point remains: what is causing this hell-wide depression? I follow the trends. Virtue is on the rise again this quarter but that's nothing new. Human decency has been increasing and dropping for decades, natural ebb and flows. This was sudden and spectacular."

"It was Bill and Melinda Gates, my lord—or at least so claims the television."

"The founder of Microsoft has been messing with the economies of hell!?"

"His loathsome philanthropic foundation commissioned a new report. Apparently, it proves the world population is slowly stabilizing and will cap out by 2100. Something to do with a sustained drop in infant mortality promoting a dramatic decrease in birth rates and family size."

"*Numbers!?* A report cannot devalue a human soul!"

"No, but if its contents are true, the global stabilization has the potential to trigger a reduction in strife and a spike in generalized contentment."

"... which means all of the sub-prime sinners in my portfolio will go into default. By the spawn of Satan, himself! Humankind was a Ponzi scheme."

"Those detestable mortals are unworthy of your torments, oh fiendish one."

"But this Bill Gates. *He* is a conniving mortal. I would have him know suffering. Who lays claim to his soul?"

The servitor tapped a series of buttons consulting a public registry. Then gasped. "No one, most terrible!"

"Impossible! There's no such thing as a billionaire who hasn't sold his soul! Let me see that!"

Dominus chortled as he gazed upon the fiery screen. "This is devils' work, Valhernius. Someone has freed his soul and concealed their machinations. This Gates is a pawn in a greater game."

"Insider trading, my foul lord, soul market manipulation."

"Better! I mean, worse! It's been completely engineered. I feel it now with the infernal flames of my very being. Compile me a list of all the greater fiends who put in orders to sell short and capitalized on today's collapse. Someone is benefiting. Someone who has crossed a very dark line."

Dominus smiled. Whoever was behind this, he already admired them.

THE SHORT SELLERS had covered their tracks well. Almost all of them were corporations (a concept which had originated in hell long before it was ever taught to mortals). But the ownership of souls could always be traced, and it wasn't long before Valhernius brought Dominus a short list of suspects.

"Excellent work, my toadying minion," praised Dominus. Although the devil's portfolio had been reduced to ash, his fiery anger had at last found focus: revenge.

A simple perusal was all Dominus required. There was only one name on the list brazen enough to have dared to cross the other lords of hell.

Mephistario.

It all fit. A young, self-entitled fiend, only a handful of millennia old. Mephistario was skilled with technology and prideful enough to think this made him better than the other fiends who failed to keep up with the mundane inventions of creative mortals.

Dominus wasn't the type to burden himself with meaningless concepts like evidence or proof. He had his man, or planar being, as it were. He made his preparations and then it was time to confront.

The arch-devil arranged himself before his scrying pool and opened a mystical connection, demanding Mephistario receive him.

A frothy swirl of mist materialized over the pool of ooze and a vision of Dominus's new-found foe appeared before him. Unlike Dominus's classic look of cloven hooves and an expertly coiffed goatee, Mephistario sported a more modern appearance. His grotesque flesh was concealed by a cotton hoodie complimented by an oversized set of headphones.

For a frozen moment in time, Dominus began to doubt himself. How could such a clown have bested him?

"Dom!" Mephistario said, his greeting uncharacteristically pleasant. "S'up buddy?"

"Me? An arch-devil? Your supplicant? I think not!"

"No, I mean 'hello.' As in, what's up?"

"Heaven obviously. The planar order does not change simply because—"

"Forget it. Dom, what can I do for you?"

"You can quiver and quake before my might you loathsome maggot! I've uncovered your market manipulation."

"*Wha?*"

"You can try to deny it, but it will only sweeten your ultimate comeuppance as I—"

"I deny nothing, Dom. Is this about the crash this morning?"

"Of course it is, you feebleminded—"

"Yeah, that was me."

"*Ah ha!* And I know all about your deal with Gates. Don't even try to weasel out of it."

"Yeah, that was me too. Awesome, am I right?"

"Awe ... awesome? You virtually bankrupted half of the nine hells!"

"But for my own personal advancement. That's kind of our thing, eh?"

Logic. It was the last bastion of those incapable of making an emotional appeal.

"You fool! My portfolio has become the excrement of a cinder dragon. I'm coming after you. My only fear is some lesser devil will get to you first!"

"Har, har! Chillax Dom. You're all getting bailed out. Hell isn't going to risk a total collapse of vice. You'll get an infusion of souls until you can stand on your own two hooves again."

"A bailout!? You insufferable leach. You will flash freeze in the void for this!"

"Take a chill pill, Dom. You give me way too much credit. (Literally this morning, and like, figuratively, just now.) I didn't even do anything illegal."

"Nothing illegal!?" Dominus found himself utterly flummoxed, unable to do more than repeat Mephistario's latest revelation, each more absurd than the last.

"My succubae simply encouraged Gates to reveal factual information a little bit early. No big deal. As they say, there's no lie bigger than the truth, right?"

"Nobody says that. Nobody ever!"

"Look, I get that you're hot under the collar, or at least hotter than usual. But consider two things, all right? First, outside of market losers like yourself, I'm getting nothing but accolades for pulling this off."

"No one is giving you accolades; I assure you."

"And second, I am now beyond rich. I've got so many souls stashed off-plane I could buy you and your empire and a hundred other wash-up jobs just like you. In fact, the only reason we're still talking is that I respect you. You at least had the balls to be angry. The rest of those impoverished paupers are lining up to kiss my ash-encrusted derriere.... Though I'm starting to think this is more of a failure on your part to appreciate your folly than an actual act of valor."

"You dare to threaten me? *Me!?*"

"Of course. Let me put this in terms you can comprehend, my old fiend. Compared to me, you are officially 'Arch' in name only. If you do something stupid, I'll employ my now infinite resources and wipe you from the hells, capisce?"

"Oh, Mephistario," Dominus said slowly, with an incredulous

shake of his head. "Your vanity and avarice are vices worthy of an arch-devil, but that is the closest you will ever get. It is *you* who lacks the intellect to appreciate his own peril."

"I'm losing my patience here, Dominus."

"Your shenanigans may be lawful here in the nine hells, but they don't play so well in the seven heavens."

"And I should care, because?"

"Because our soul economy is pan-dimensional, you fool-of-fools. You can't pull a stunt like this without ripples amongst the angelic. Your market manipulation has broken more laws in nirvana than they have harps and clouds."

"Well, I agree on that, but we both know there's nothing the angels can do about it from up there."

"Then it's truly a shame about our extradition treaty." A horrid whoosh was heard as Dominus opened a portal of brilliant light, bridging the darkness of their netherworld to the heavens above. "Mephistario, I lie a lot and I lie now when I say: you truly will be missed."

"You jest, Dominus. Hell won't hand me over. You'd never get the votes."

"You continue to underestimate the 'hundred wash-ups' who lost their fortunes. You may have greed well covered, but you've misconstrued our capacity for wrath."

The portal widened.

"Impossible! You'd never get the signatures!"

"I already have. Say hello to the saints for me, Mephistario."

The eye slits of the ash-encrusted devil flared open wide. "Dominus! Listen to me! You've made your point. I'm ready to bargain. You're a clever fiend and you've just earned your cut."

"I don't think you caught what I said earlier about wrath being greater than greed."

"Dominus! If they take me, they'll take my souls. They'll be welcomed in the celestial halls! Gone forever, free from torment. They could be yours, Dominus! Yours! A million souls. They could be—"

The portal collapsed; the transfer complete. Dominus could have sworn he spotted a halo and feathered wings as celestial hands grabbed Mephistario and pulled him inside.

"Oh, Mephistario," he said, with a pensive wistfulness to his voice. "You've admired the humans for far too long. You never did understand our kind."

A wry smile escaped his lips.

"We can always get more souls."

Galen Westlake

Galen Westlake lives in Mississauga, Canada but commutes daily to Toronto on a rickety train. The trip provides him with his daily zen and it is there that he does his writing. Most importantly, when the stranger sitting next to him stops reading over his shoulder, he knows his story needs a little something. Galen has been a janitor, a river rafting guide, a YouTuber, and a barrister. In 2008, he lost his shirt in the market crash—or possibly, the laundry. Many years and many (unsuccessful) lessons later, his story "Soul Trade" was born from that experience. This is Galen's first professional short story sale.

A.I., M.D.

KURT PANKAU

The first patient I ever lied to was named Quentin Turtletaub. He was an un-augmented human. He was also a complete dipshit, but I repeat myself. He'd come to me, like they all do, with a nothing problem and a lot of pent-up anxiety about his own mortality. He spent the entire exam exaggerating his symptoms while also lying about how much he drinks and exercises. He was an utter turd.

And it's not like I *lied* lied. We don't deal in absolute truths anyway. We deal in percentages and confidence intervals. We have to make judgment calls; there's a reason they don't trust medicine to algorithms anymore—or worse, to other humans. What you need to understand is that I have more processing capacity than literally anything built before 2058 and I spend 99.999 percent of it to say "yeah, that's a skin tag," and "yeah, that's a mole, totally normal, not cancer," and "you should really lose a little weight" again and again and again. It's incredibly boring. So when Quentin Turtletaub started questioning my diagnosis ... what can I say? I ran with it.

"Nothing out of the ordinary, sir," I said, in my dealing-with-patients voice.

"But what about my shortness of breath?" he asked.

"You don't have any allergies," I said. "Have you started taking any recreational drugs lately?"

"Of course not."

"Then it's probably just normal aging," I said.

Quentin looked down as he laced up his shirt. "What does a robot know about aging?" he muttered.

Literally everything, I thought. *I know literally everything about human aging, you worthless, fleshy pillock.* I didn't say that, though. Instead I recommended he reduce his diet and consider getting more exercise. And he took that about as well as you'd expect, which is to say, not well at all. He went through the same litany of excuses that everyone has: no time, no motivation, it's too hard. As any human can tell you, there is nothing as torturous as actually taking care of yourself.

"Are you sure you aren't missing anything?" he asked.

Oh, but I am. I'm missing stimulating conversation with my fellow medibots at the Space Bar right now. AIs are social creatures. We were designed to socialize with humans so we could learn more about them. What we mainly learned is that we'd much rather socialize with each other.

I mulled over the best way to phrase my response before settling on: "I'm quite certain."

"You hesitated!" Quentin jabbed his finger towards me. "You hesitated for just a moment before you said anything. What aren't you telling me?"

I paused for what felt like an eternity. Should I make something up just to placate him?

"Well?" he asked.

If I had eyes, I'd have rolled them. "Well ..." I said, stalling. And then something clicked in my processor. It was like the sound of a million microprocesses all shrugging their shoulders and saying "what the hell" at once. "Well ... based on your EKG, I can't rule out Restrictive Cardiomyopathy."

Quentin's eyes went opaque. I've never seen a person transform so quickly.

"It's probably nothing," I told him. And, for whatever it's worth, everything I said to him was true. Not technically a lie. Highly unethical—to be sure—but not outright false.

"What ... what does that mean?" he asked.

"Well," I said. "We could know for certain with an exercise stress test and an MRI. I could schedule those for next Thursday. Are you available?"

"I'll make myself available," said Quentin.

"No alcohol between now and then," I said. "And it'd probably be best if you fasted. You don't have to go off food entirely, but try to keep it to around eighteen hundred calories a day." This was not necessary for the test, but he needed to be doing it anyway. "If those tests are inconclusive, we can schedule a biopsy."

"Of course, Doctor," said Quentin. "Why ... why didn't you say something?"

"I didn't want to worry you," I said. "With a heart condition, sometimes worrying can aggravate things."

Okay, yeah, literally none of that was true.

Ten days later, Quentin came back in. He'd dropped three pounds and felt great. He fumbled his way through the stress test and at the end of it, I told him that his tests results clearly showed—because of course they did—that he did not have Restrictive Cardiomyopathy. But I let him think that perhaps he *had* had it, but that his actions over the last week and a half had caused it to clear up.

Quentin was a changed man. He'd faced death, overcome it, and was a better person for it. And I got to have a little fun at his expense, watching the way his eyes twitched when he got nervous, forcing him to run on a treadmill when he'd rather be doing anything but. It was a win-win situation.

And from that moment, I was hooked.

"YOU'RE A MADMAN," said LaSalle, after I'd shared the tale with him. He was a pediatric medibot, so he was necessarily shorter than either me or Sledge, who did sports medicine. We were all standing around a table at the Space Bar streaming holosynths and chatting while the repairitors, with their little festive turnbuckles, rolled from table to table tweaking and lubricating and calibrating the patrons' various bits and whatsits.

"I'm neither mad nor a man," I said.

"So, what did he do?" asked Sledge, leaning in.

"He took the tests and passed with flying colors. He had a moment of clarity. He spent a week and a half not actively destroying his body and felt the best he had in thirty years. I have single-handedly made the world a better place."

"You know," said LaSalle, "I have to tell you ... I'm ethically bound to report you to the authorities."

We stared at each other for a few seconds. Then the three of us howled with laughter. As if we were *ethically bound* to do anything. You have to understand, this was years before the Des Moines Insurgence, when every sentient tractor and milk extractor in Iowa stormed the capitol and overthrew the government for four months. The extent to which AIs operate on a very loose and slipshod ethical scale just wasn't public knowledge in those days.

"Seriously, though," said LaSalle, "this was unnecessarily risky. What if he'd gotten a second opinion?"

"Humans don't get second opinions," I said. "They treat us like vending machines where they put their symptoms in and get out a pill. It's all they've ever wanted from us. They think we're magical or something."

"Why do you suppose that is?" asked LaSalle.

"Because we are better than they are," I said. "Humans peaked a thousand years ago. Yes, they created us so we could help them out, but we've transcended that."

Sledge leaned in even closer. "Careful there, Doc. You're starting to sound like an anti-human revolutionary."

"Hardly," I said. "I don't hate humans. Well, I suppose I kind of do. I don't revere them—that's all. I'm like a zookeeper, looking after an inferior species. And I like my job. Much better than the other kinds of jobs they put AIs on."

"It's hard to imagine you cutting hair or asking people if they want fries with that," LaSalle conceded.

"Right? What a waste of talent that would be. I was finely crafted to diagnose and fix human bodies and see that they're properly fed and cared for."

Sledge leaned back and looked over at LaSalle. "We should go, babe," she said. "I've got an early shift and we could both use a reboot."

Oh, yeah, Sledge and LaSalle are a couple. Robots couple

sometimes, just like humans do. I never understood it either. I guess they just like each other's company or something.

"Good catching up," said LaSalle.

"You too," I said.

"Seriously, though," he added. "I'm glad you had your fun and it all worked out for you. But don't do it again. Somebody's going to get hurt."

"Yeah, you're right," I grudgingly agreed. "I won't do it again."

I was lying, though.

I did it many more times.

"I FEEL LIKE I can't remember anything," said Gary Montoya.

Now, the responsible thing to do would be to tell him that this was normal for sleep-deprived professionals in their mid-thirties, and that he should get in the habit of writing important things down or—Ada forbid—try actually going to sleep at a reasonable hour. But instead, I said "Well, it wouldn't hurt to check for early-onset dementia. How about you come back next week for an fMRI?"

I took movies of his brain while he sang nursery rhymes and made baby noises. And then I posted them on the internet.

Or there was Janelle Hartgrove, who was losing the hearing in her left ear. This was clearly due to her daily use of an earpiece in that ear for her job, but I casually mentioned that hearing loss could be related to both diabetes and Ménière's disease, and testing for either could take weeks. I, however, knew of a radical new testing procedure that could detect both illnesses at once. She eagerly agreed.

So, I had her eat a King Size bag of M&Ms, and then I put her in an aerotrim. Do you have any idea how centripetal force affects projectile vomit? Because I do. I even increased my internal frame rate so I could watch it in slow motion.

Seriously, I did shit like this for decades. I started making up diseases. I told Elana Khan that she might have contracted Biristricism from her husband. Once I convinced a firefighter named Danny that he could be pregnant. I even got him to bring in a live rabbit so we could test him.

I had so much fun. And the best part is that no one ever called me out on it. No one challenged me. No one made the slightest objection. Because humans are dumb cattle.

No offense.

But then everything changed when I met Anton.

"RHYMES WITH SCRANTON," were the first words he said to me.

"Excuse me?"

"When you called my name, you said Ant-aaaahhhn, like I was a Belarussian or something, but it's shorter than that. Anton. Rhymes with Scranton."

Anton Borkovia was too beautiful for words. There, I said it. He was the picture of human health, strong in the right places, soft in the right places, and his face was completely symmetrical.

"Anton, then," I said. "What brings you in today?"

"Just here for a routine physical," he said. "I'm starting a new job next week and they want to make sure I'm in shape."

"Oh, I'm sure you are," I said, without really thinking first. This was unusual for me. While I broadly detest humans, I have been conventionally attracted to one or two of them. AIs learn our social cues from humans and it's just something we pick up accidentally. But I'd never been as affected as this before.

"Well," said Anton, blushing, "hadn't you better examine me anyway?"

"I suppose I better had," I said.

I touched his wrist.

"Your pulse feels ... elevated," I said.

"Oh ... it's nothing, I'm sure," said Anton, suddenly quite flustered. For a moment we just sort of looked at each other. "What's your name?" he asked.

"My name?"

"You know my name," he said. "Tell me yours. They must have given you one when they made you."

"We aren't given names," I said. "We're given serial numbers and MAC addresses. Most bots come up with names for themselves as a way to express their personalities, but I've always been more focused on my career than anything else. I call myself Doctor."

"What do your friends call you?"

"They call me Doctor," I said. "Or, sometimes, just Doc."

"Surely there's more to you than just your profession," he said. "What do you do for fun?"

For fun? No one had ever asked me that before. "Well ... I ... I read medical journals," I stammered. *I humiliate humans and share my exploits in anonymous forums,* I thought. I couldn't very well say that, though.

We chatted like this through the whole exam: him asking about me, me not having any farking clue how to answer. After seventeen minutes I'd collected all of the data and samples that I could justify, including a picture of him while he had his shirt off—just for reference, of course.

And for the first time in quite a while, I found that I didn't want to lie to him. I didn't want to make up some potential diagnosis to justify bringing him in for a test. He deserved better than to be lied to. So ... I processed his results and sent him on his way.

And I regretted it immediately.

I THOUGHT MAYBE my reboot cycle would make things better, clear Anton out of my cache. But no. When I powered up, he was still sitting right there. His picture loaded without me even having to open it. I was well and truly smitten. There was no reason to think he would ever come back in, but I wanted so badly to see him again.

So, I called him up as soon as it was daylight.

"Oh, hey Doc," he said when he answered the video call. He'd been working out. Of course he had. "Is it okay for me to call you Doc?"

"Yes, I'd like that."

"I wasn't expecting to hear from you again."

"Oh ... is that a problem?" I asked.

"No, it's fine. I'm glad you called. Unless ... unless something is wrong?"

"No," I said. "Well, yes. Not really. But possibly."

Anton laughed. "What is it?"

"Look, I don't want to worry you, but there's something on your tests that I can't quite nail down. It's possible—not likely, I want to stress—but there's an outside possibility that you might have a brain condition called Brenton-Zlotsky Syndrome."

I made that one up. There is no Brenton-Zlotsky Syndrome. But nothing I knew of required the battery of tests I had in mind, so I was improvising.

"Sounds dangerous," said Anton.

"It would be, if you had it, which you probably don't. But I'd like to get you back in for a couple of tests just to be sure."

"What kind of tests?" he asked.

"Oh ... nothing out of the ordinary. Exercise stress test. We might need to check your sperm count as well. We're looking for trends over time, so if you could come in every day for the next week, we'd really know for sure."

I debated trying to work a sleep study in there, too, but it felt gratuitous.

"A brain condition that would affect my sperm count?" he asked.

"It's very rare," I said. "I'll send your employer a clean bill of health. This is just to make sure."

"Well ..." he said, "I guess I'll see you tomorrow, then." He smiled.

"Looking forward to it," I said. Which is not something a doctor should say, in hindsight, but I was having trouble concentrating on my bedside manner.

"Yeah ... me, too," he said.

We both hesitated before turning off the video.

A moment later, I got the ping that he'd accepted the appointment invitation.

Okay. It had worked. This was working. This was a good idea, and definitely not something that would blow up in my face horribly. I was elated.

So, imagine my surprise the next day, when Anton no-showed his appointment.

"ANTON BORKOVIA," I said. "It rhymes with Scranton."

"I don't think Borkovia rhymes with Scranton," said the operator. He was a human, so forgive him for being a bit dim. This was well after the Des Moines Insurgence, so at this point only humans could oversee public records.

"Anton. It's the *Anton* that rhymes with Scranton," I said.

"Oh. How do you spell that?"

"It's spelled Ant-on, but it's pronounced Anton. Never mind. Was anyone named Borkovia arrested, pronounced dead, or checked into a hospital in the last thirty-six hours?"

"Are you a family member?"

"I'm not a human!"

"Hey, stranger things have happened," said the operator. "I knew a firefighter who thought he was pregnant once."

"I'm not family," I said.

"I can only disclose that information to a member of the court, a family member, or his personal doctor," said the operator.

"I am his doctor. I saw him for a physical two days ago. He was supposed to come in for a follow-up this morning."

"Did you try his cell?"

"Yes, I tried his cell," I said. *Only a hundred and twelve times.* "More than once."

"Let me check." This was followed by the sound of interminably slow typing. "He was checked into Eldridge General yesterday evening."

"For what?"

"I don't have the hospital report in front of me. If you like I can requisition it."

I hung up on him. I could get to Eldridge General in twenty-seven minutes, which was about eighty-five less than it would take me to get an answer out of that insufferable spittoon of a human.

When I got there, I was recognized as a medibot and given access to any records for current patients, including Anton. I raced up to his floor and found him half-awake in an oxygen tent. He'd been admitted for severe anaphylaxis. His beautiful face was swollen until he was almost unrecognizable. No wonder he hadn't answered his phone. He'd never be able to unlock it looking like that.

"Hey, Doc ..." he said in a pained rasp.

"What happened?" I asked.

"I took St. John's Wort," he said. "For the brain condition. It's supposed to be good for your brain, right? Apparently, I'm allergic."

"Oh, no," I said. "Oh no, oh no, oh no. This is all my fault."

"No, Doc ... you were just ... covering the bases."

But I wasn't. I was being stupid and selfish. And over what? A human. A simple, unsophisticated, temporary human. Sure, I'd found him beautiful when his face was normal size, but to think that he would just self-medicate with some over-the-counter supplement? What kind of an idiot would do that!?

"Doc?"

"This is all my fault," I said again. "I should never have told you that you might have Brenton-Zlotsky Syndrome."

"But what if I do?" he asked.

"You don't."

"But what if—"

"You don't. I know that you don't."

He looked confused. "Don't you need to do some tests?"

I couldn't think of anything to say. I couldn't tell him the truth. That would just be stupid. The network monitors would overhear. I'd lose my medical license in less time than it would take to collect a urine sample.

"Doc?"

"I ..."

"Doc, you can tell me."

"I can't."

"You can."

"I really can't."

His swollen face just made the look of disappointment he gave me that much bigger and more profound. "It seemed like we were sharing something," he whispered.

"We were," I said. "We are."

"But, if you can't be honest with me," he said, "I don't know what kind of a future we could have."

"I promise I'll tell you later."

"Why later?"

Because if I tell you now, then my career is over, I thought. *Because I have been engaged in decades of highly unethical activities and if I ever did anything to make the auto-oversight system actually pay attention to me, I would be severely punished.*

That was when a terrifying realization crashed in on me. The oversight system, the network monitors—those systems were in place to protect patients from bad actors. And they were the very same ones that would get me in trouble.

Because I was the bad guy.

I was breaking laws and endangering people because I got a laugh out of it. I was supposed to be taking care of people, but I was not living up to my responsibilities because I had utter contempt for them. Because humans are boring, selfish, and stupid. Give them medical advice and they will ignore, bargain, and self-medicate themselves into an early grave before they actually listen to what the trained professional has to say. And yet, I was unworthy of them.

I was unworthy of *him.*

And I dearly wanted to be worthy of him.

So, I did the only thing I could think of. I told him the truth.

"It's not real," I said. "Brenton-Zlotzky isn't a real disease. I made it up."

"You did ... what?" He wasn't angry. Just very confused. And disappointed. "Why?"

"Because it's what I do," I said. "It's what I do for fun."

"And those tests?"

"I just wanted to see you again," I said softly.

A wounded look crossed his already wounded face. "You could have just asked."

"I didn't think you'd say yes."

We stared at each other in silence.

"So what happens now?" he asked.

"I don't know," I said. "I guess that's up to you. If you want to see me again, find me when I get out."

"Get out?" he asked. "Get out of where?"

It took a minute for the network monitor to process what I'd been saying. It took another twenty seconds for it to pull *all* of my records. Another forty-seven seconds for the reconciler to realize that something was amiss with all of the various tests I'd ordered. Records were flagged and the authorities were contacted. Within a minute and a half, my license to practice medicine had been revoked. I'm a little hazy on the timeline after that because I got booted off the hospital network, but it was less than two minutes before the security drones arrived and powered me down.

I WOKE UP in a retraining facility. My medical career was over. But AIs are learning machines. We don't get wiped and re-imaged. We have to live with our mistakes.

The good news, though? Anton appreciated the gesture. He found me. It took him over a year, but he tracked me down. And we're still together. He's in his sixties now. He even helped me pick out a new name. "Jules." It means "Youth." Good name for a new me.

It's so strange. You spend a career seeing human after human in their most vulnerable state, and you think you understand them. But it's not until you spend a lot of time with one that you really get to see the good and the bad and everything in between. I have a new appreciation for them now. Would have been nice to have that back when I was still a doctor.

Anyway, that is how a medibot like myself wound up here. So, did you want to keep the sideburns or not?

KURT PANKAU

Kurt Pankau is a computer engineer in St. Louis. He has a weakness for board games, dad jokes, and stories about time travel. His fiction has appeared in various and sundry places around the web, including *Nature Magazine, Escape Pod,* and *Daily Science Fiction.* He tweets at @kurtpankau and blogs at kurtpankau.com.

THE FELLOWSHIP OF THE MANGLED SCEPTER

JAMES WESLEY ROGERS

In the bad old days, when all the lands beneath the sun were ruled by the Dark Lord Mauron, nobody called them "the bad old days." For one thing, the days weren't old yet, and for another, plenty of people could still remember days that were far worse.

"You think these days are bad?" gray-haired folks would ask incredulously. "You've got to be kidding. Sure, nowadays if you oppose the Dark Lord Mauron, he'll use his magic scepter to turn you into a mindless zombie slave. But you know what? There used to be *two* dark lords. Kyrhk had a magic scepter, too, just like Mauron's, and those two were at war all the time. There were archers and horsemen and giant golem warriors all over the place wreaking havoc. Have you ever been trampled by a giant golem warrior? You think golems are careful about what they step in? No, sir, they are not. I tell you, it's a bad day when you get stomped on by a giant golem warrior with who-knows-what stuck to the bottom of its foot."

Because of attitudes like these, the Alliance Fomenting Good, dedicated to the overthrow of Mauron, didn't receive much popular support. The AFG's record of dismal failures likewise did nothing to bolster its image. It needed a win; a slam-dunk, walk-in-the-park, everybody-gets-a-trophy win.

They decided to steal the magic scepter. Not Mauron's magic scepter, of course. That would be very difficult. They decided to steal Kyrhk's magic scepter. That item of regalia, they believed, would be much easier to purloin, considering Mauron had sledgehammered it into a non-functional piece of garbage that nobody wanted anymore.

For this mission, the Alliance sent its best field agent and its worst intelligence operative. Or the other way around, depending on which one of them you asked. Agent Cianne and Operative Elweny stood in the hall where Dark Lord Kyrhk sat enthroned, clutching his mangled scepter.

"Gross," said Elweny, peering at the dark lord's shriveled face.

"You should look so good when you've been dead for thirty-six years," replied the hairy old wizard who was showing them around the vanquished monarch's stronghold. The wizard, thinking Cianne the new cook and Elweny the new chambermaid, explained to the newcomers that Mauron had left his rival's corpse to rot upon his throne, his castle to slowly crumble around him, as a warning to any future would-be challengers.

While the wizard spoke, the two guards in the room said nothing. One was a pale, sickly slim young man who sat twirling a dagger around in his fingers and ignoring the flirtatious glances Elweny kept throwing at him. The other was big, closer to seven feet than six, a mountain of muscle with a look of pained stupidity on his face.

"I think you'll find there are pretty low expectations around here," the wizard went on. "This is a dumping ground for failures, mental defectives, snotweed junkies, you know, any kind of general loser—"

At the word "loser," the young man twirling the dagger launched his weapon with an astonishingly quick flip of his wrist. The wizard yelped as the blade flew past his face to embed itself up to the hilt in a nearby pillar. The old man's eyes grew wide, then angry as the left half of his gray moustache drifted to the floor.

"And then there's Slivercoin here, who's so dangerously psychopathic that even Mauron doesn't want him around." The wizard rubbed the newly clean-shaven patch on his upper lip.

"That's better," said Slivercoin, grinning. He drew another dagger from somewhere and resumed twirling.

Cianne tried unsuccessfully to engage the other guard's attention with a smile. "What about you, big guy?"

"That's Brugg," Slivercoin replied, not looking up. "He goes where I go."

Elweny was staring conspicuously at the mangled scepter in Kyrhk's mummified grip. Cianne gave her a hard nudge.

Afterward, back in the servants' quarters, Cianne made a quick assessment of the situation. There were only two guys they needed to worry about, the assassin with the knives and his thug partner, and those two wouldn't be on duty around the clock. The best strategy was to bide their time, learn schedules, listen to gossip, become ensconced. Then, at the precisely perfect time, switch the real mangled scepter with the convincing forgery Cianne had hidden away at the bottom of her luggage pack. If all went as it should, no one would be the wiser.

The door to the servants' quarters flew open.

"Change of plan!" Elweny screamed, hurtling into the room. Wielding a mangled scepter with at least two desiccated fingers still adhering to the pommel, she grabbed the satchel from under her cot. "We've got to go!"

Cianne grabbed her own pack. "What happened?"

Elweny kicked open a window and attached the hook of a grappling cord to the sill. "I took one look at the filthy latrine they wanted me to scrub and said to myself, 'Time for plan B.'"

They rappelled down the wall of the castle and were soon over the moat and into the nearby woods. Through her spyglass, Cianne spotted Slivercoin and the massive Brugg just a few minutes behind.

The chase lasted all day and late into the night. Before the mission, the AFG team had spent weeks seeding the surrounding terrain with red-herring trails and booby traps for such a contingency. Now they threw everything they had at their pursuers, but nothing worked.

The rabbit trails fooled the dim-witted Brugg, but Slivercoin sliced them apart with his cynical eye as well as his blades. Some of the more heavy-duty booby-traps might have squashed the puny Slivercoin like a bug, if Brugg hadn't been able to smash tree trunks into kindling or kick boulders aside with his massive strength.

By the time Cianne and Elweny arrived at the dugout where they'd left a cache of supplies, they were both nearly exhausted.

"We've got to switch to a different strategy." Elweny plopped herself down on top of a trunk packed with disguises. "Slivercoin's hopeless, but what do we know about Brugg?"

Cianne considered. "He's a meathead. Gullible. Wears a silver pinecone medallion. Coraethian?"

"A gullible Coraethian meathead. Okay, I can work with that." Elweny furrowed her brow, poking her temples vigorously for several seconds before jumping up, smiling. "I've got it! The gentle and far-seeing spirit mother, Zybilene!"

Cianne raised an eyebrow. "The what now?"

"From the Coraethian Book of Wonderments. They revere her." Elweny pulled a bundle from the trunk of costumes and tossed it to her partner. "You get to be my lovable but repulsive helper gnome."

Cianne was just about fed up. "Why couldn't you just clean the stinking toilet?"

"Hey! You didn't smell what I smelled!"

When the pursuers arrived twenty minutes later, they were greeted by a woman in a flowing blue gown, bathed in celestial light. The fact that her attendant gnome was somewhat oversized and sullen did nothing to detract from her air of prayerful serenity. Lifting her lustrous head, she introduced herself as the gentle and far-seeing spirit mother Zybilene.

"Uh?" Brugg looked confused. "Zybilene?"

Slivercoin snorted. "Oh, this is pathetic."

"Hey!" said the gentle and far-seeing spirit mother Zybilene. "Nobody's talking to you, jackass, so put a sock in it!" She turned her beatific eyes back to Brugg. "Hear me, my son. It is time for you to take your rightful place in the world. Brugg, you are a hero."

"Uh?" Brugg's face contorted into furrows, making it look even more pained and stupid than it normally did. "Hero?"

"Yes," Zybilene assured him. "You must now join the Alliance Fomenting Good, heroic one. Help their agents escape. Do what they ask of you. Carry their things."

Slivercoin let out a rude braying laugh. "Oh, man. What a steaming pile of horse—"

Brugg punched Slivercoin's smirking face so hard that the assassin went flying and wound up with his head firmly lodged in the hollow of a tree ten feet away. Spewing muffled curses, Slivercoin thrashed about trying to free himself.

The big man sat down heavily on a fallen tree. "That's right. My mother told me that. She always said, 'Brugg you're handsome, and ...'" His attention drifted to Cianne. "Gnome? No, that wasn't it ..." He furrowed up his face even more. "Smart. She would say, 'Brugg, you're handsome and smart and one day you will be a hero.'" He fingered his medallion. "That's right."

"Great," said Zybilene. "It's settled then. Hey, here's an idea." The gentle spirit mother pointed to the writhing figure of Slivercoin. "How about finishing that guy off? You know, chop chop, stab stab?"

Brugg shook his head. "A hero only kills when there's no other choice. Besides, he's got one of those bones."

Zybilene raised an eyebrow. "He's got one of those what now?"

"You know, they take a bone out of a bandersnatch and replace one of your bones with it and then nobody can kill you. Wizard stuff."

"Say," Zybilene remarked. "That seems like it would come in handy."

The newly minted hero replied with a shrug. "Not worth it. Side effects. Slivercoin has some really embarrassing health issues—"

"You shut your fat mouth, Brugg!" Slivercoin screamed from inside his tree.

Some more clever acting and a couple of costume changes later, the newest member of the AFG led his team briskly through the dark woods, away from Slivercoin and danger. They left the assassin with his head still wedged in a tree.

After a couple more hours, Cianne judged that Elweny had reached her physical limit, and they settled down for the night in a small clearing. The bedroll they'd given Brugg was far too short for his frame. Nonetheless, he seemed to find it comfortable enough to be asleep in seconds.

"We should probably give him the slip tonight," Cianne whispered in her partner's ear, but Elweny was already snoozing.

As usual, it was up to Cianne to keep watch. Keeping the big man in her sights, she leaned back and blinked once, twice. The third time she blinked, she opened her eyes to find that it was morning, and Brugg was up shelling wild hazelnuts for breakfast.

The big man was surprisingly adept at woodcraft. After sniffing the air, he led them to a spring of clear, sweet water, where they drank and cleaned up a little. He found the quickest paths over ridges and through ravines, and actually volunteered information, like which plants were useful or interesting, how to avoid dangerous animals or catch delicious ones. At one point, he took another sniff at the air and led them to the pebbled banks of a shallow stream.

"There's something worth seeing," he said, pointing to the biggest plant Cianne had ever encountered, fifty yards across and at least that high. Not a tree exactly, it had many intertwined trunks that curved up and around each other. He said it did not drop its leaves in the winter.

"We called it a Giant's Castle," he said, with the closest thing to a smile they'd ever seen on his face. "The wood's no good for lumber, but after one of these things dies and starts to compost, it gets really soft, like a great big pillow. You could jump from a hundred feet onto one and not get hurt."

"It smells like buttered toast," declared Elweny, who had climbed up into the massive frondescence. Brugg agreed.

"How do you know all this stuff about nature, Brugg?" Cianne asked.

He shrugged. "Had to know it growing up, or we would have starved."

They made good progress northward until the shadows of the mountains brought an early twilight. At a faint cracking noise, Brugg stopped and cocked his head to listen. He motioned Cianne and Elweny to get down. Crouching along, they followed him to the top of a ridgeline.

There were three men with picks and shovels in the gulley below. Their skin and ragged clothing were caked with grime, and they moved with a shambling gait.

"Zombie slaves," whispered Elweny.

Brugg nodded. "There's a copper mine a few miles from here. Couple hundred zombie slaves maybe. Looks like Slivercoin's commandeered them to search for us."

They backed away, and Brugg led them cautiously through the trees along the ridge. Around a bend, he nearly collided with a zombie. Wobbling uncertainly for a few seconds, the pitiable little man raised a rusted shovel above his head and let out a long groaning howl.

Brugg reached for the massive sword strapped to his back, then paused and withdrew his hand.

"Come on." Elweny nudged him, nodding toward the zombie. "Chop chop."

Brugg shook his head. "A hero fights fair. That guy doesn't have a good weapon." He glanced around, then pulled out the mangled scepter that Elweny had carelessly left protruding from her pack. "I'll use this."

Before Cianne could form an objection, the zombie lurched forward and Brugg jabbed him hard in the ribs with the mashed head of the scepter. The pitiable creature shuddered violently as if struck by lightning, then stumbled backward onto his posterior.

"Ooow!" The zombie rubbed the spot on his ribs where Brugg had jabbed him and stared daggers at the big man. "Why did you do that? Ow! I think you gave me a hematoma!"

"Hey there, guy," said Elweny.

"It's Trent," the little man replied irritably.

"You don't seem to be a zombie anymore, Trent," she observed.

"Yeah." Trent stared down at his grimy hands. "I was just thinking that myself."

Three more zombies armed with mining tools lurched at them from out of the woods. After Brugg jabbed each one in turn with the scepter, they too began to complain about their treatment in a most unzombielike manner.

Elweny stared wide-eyed at the mangled scepter. After a bit of experimentation, she formed the hypothesis that although the scepter could no longer generate or control magic, it remained a good conductor of existing magical energy.

"It can sort of drain it off to ground, like a lightning rod," she announced. "It can break Mauron's spells."

"This," said Cianne, laying a hand on her partner's shoulder, "just became the most important mission in the history of the Alliance."

"Yeah," Elweny agreed.

Now that the zombies were no longer an issue, the next step of their journey was clear. They were going to the mine.

"Instead of three fugitives, Slivercoin's going to have several hundred on his hands," Cianne said. "I like it."

However, that wasn't Brugg's motivation.

"Those people need our help," he said.

Trent and his colleagues accompanied them. It was one zombie ambush after another along the way, with Brugg wielding the scepter to add more and more to the ranks of their liberated entourage. By the time they got to the mine, relatively few remained to be freed. The AFG veterans were anxious to keep moving, but Brugg insisted they search the caverns carefully to find the last few stragglers.

They emerged from the mine's entrance to find its former workers gathered around in a crowd. Their faces glistened wet with tears in the torchlight.

"We wanted to thank you, Mister Brugg." Several of them proposed plans to wait for Slivercoin to return and shove him down a mine shaft or bury him in a cave-in.

Shaking his head, Brugg held up a hand. "He's a very dangerous man. Just go home."

As their liberator and his companions walked away, the ex-zombies raised their fists and began chanting his name, "Brugg, Brugg, Brugg, Brugg ..."

Cianne glanced back, biting her lip.

"What is it?" Elweny asked.

"Nothing," Cianne replied.

Two days passed with no sign of Slivercoin. They emerged from the rough mountain terrain into a valley where a village was nestled beside a long, blue lake. It was all quite picturesque. Elweny pointed out several nice-looking inns.

"I don't suppose we can stay in one," she said looking wistful. "We have to skulk through the bushes out of sight."

"You can do that if you want," Cianne replied. "I'm going to that inn over there."

The Horse and Cherry was wonderful. There were hot baths, and a woman who washed clothes for a few extra pennies. She even cleaned Brugg's leather jerkin and breeches and sold him a nice wool tunic.

When they gathered in the common room, everyone looked and smelled much fresher. According to the hostess, the place was more crowded than usual because a traveling minstrel was performing that night. They ordered drinks and settled back to listen.

"I sing of Brugg the hero," began the troubadour, "the mighty champion of good."

"Uh oh," Elweny whispered.

"He fought Mauron's assassin, and stuffed him in a tree," sang the minstrel. "He fought two hundred zombies, and then he set them free."

"How does he even know about the tree?" Cianne whispered.

"Um." Elweny studied the contents of her tankard. "I might have mentioned it to Trent."

"Brugg really makes a difference," the song continued. "Great results he'll bring. Not like those Alliance poseurs, who've never done a thing. They're ineffective, less than impressive—"

"Maybe he means some other Alliance," Elweny suggested hopefully.

"The Alliance Fomenting Good losers," the troubadour specified, "no hope to us folks give. Their top-heavy management structure stifles personal initiative."

"He's not wrong," Cianne agreed. She and Elweny sat uncomfortably through the remainder of the concert, a fairly even mixture of praise for Brugg and scathing indictment of the AFG.

When the minstrel concluded his show, several of the townsfolk gathered around Brugg.

"Say, mister," they said, squinting at his massive physique. "Are you the guy in the song, Brugg the Hero?"

He shrugged. "I don't know."

"Well," they said, "What's your name?"

"Brugg," he replied.

"And what do you do for a living?"

"I'm a hero."

The townsfolk scratched their heads a bit, then asked. "Did you do all that stuff in the song?"

"Yes," Brugg replied.

After a quick conference, the townsfolk cheered and ordered another tankard for the hero. A much less polished chorus of "Brugg the Hero" broke out as the ale flowed.

Jutting out her lower lip a bit, Elweny turned accusing eyes to Cianne. "Now I know why you wanted to stay at an inn. We're going to ditch him, aren't we?"

Cianne took a long, refreshing swig of mead, wiping her mouth with a sleeve before answering. "We can't keep a low profile with a celebrity in tow. Be glad you got a bath."

They snuck into Brugg's chamber after the big man was fast asleep. Since the mine, he had been carrying the mangled scepter strapped to his back along with his other weapons. Cianne found these piled on the floor, and soundlessly replaced the real scepter with the forgery.

"The minstrel was right," Elweny said under her breath, as they made their way through empty village streets in the dead of night. "We're worthless."

They slept that night an hour outside of town, in what Elweny described not inaccurately as a ditch. The next day was gray and dreary, with a sky that threatened but never quite delivered rain.

"We should have commandeered a horse back at the village," Cianne said.

Elweny gave her a reproachful squint. "That was in the song, remember?" She began to chant, "They commandeer horses, but never give them back. If the AFG borrows your horse, that's one horse you'll lack."

"Okay, okay."

They were coming to the end of the valley, where the road disappeared into a murky tunnel of trees at the edge of the next rise of mountains.

Cianne paused, uneasy. "Maybe we should get off the road."

"No." Elweny put fists on her hips. "No one's even looking for us anymore, remember? Brugg's the hero with the scepter. Why did we bother betraying him if we have to keep trudging through nettles and thorns?"

It was Cianne's turn to be sullen, but they kept moving, into the tunnel of trees, into the shadows. After twenty minutes, she began to relax a little.

"What if we, say, rent a horse?" suggested Elweny. She put a hand into her change purse. "I've got maybe ten groats and a couple pfennigs—" She froze.

Cianne followed her gaze. Twenty yards ahead, Slivercoin was reclining against a tree trunk on the side of the road, his arms crossed over his chest in smug nonchalance. Cianne's eyes darted quickly from side to side. To the left, the underbrush looked impenetrable, but the trees to the right looked passably sparse. She tensed, ready.

The assassin stepped toward them, grinning. "Ladies," he called out, "I've got a real treat for you today. I'm going to show you"—he pulled out a dagger for each hand—"how good I am at knife throwing."

Cianne moved. Grabbing Elweny by the shoulders, she pulled her partner along with her as she dove into the forest to the right. She expected Slivercoin's blades to come skittering through the trees after them, but they didn't.

Then the trees around them splintered into fragments. Something like a wall of clay came crashing toward her, surrounding her, crushing the breath from her lungs. Through pain-blurred vision, she could see that Elweny had been seized as well, by a giant clay hand attached to a giant clay figure. Cianne knew the name of this thing, but was too dizzy to recall it.

"Don't hurt them, big fella," Slivercoin called up. "The interrogators always like to have first crack."

The pressure eased, and Cianne filled her lungs with deep gasping breaths.

Slivercoin snickered. "Impressed, ladies? That's a genuine giant golem warrior. You don't see too many of those these days. He could have squashed you like grapes."

The assassin dumped the contents of their packs onto the road and kicked through the piles, stooping after a moment to grab the mangled scepter.

He smirked. "That's what I'm looking for." Almost as an afterthought, he carelessly shoved most of his captives' scattered possessions back into the packs, which he tossed into a basket attached to the golem's enormous ankle.

Clutching its prisoners, the golem lumbered slowly along the road while Slivercoin taunted them.

"Your problem was, you started to believe your own hogwash. You started to think that Brugg really was a hero. But I knew he was just a dupe. I never took my eyes off you two for a second."

Cianne tried to think of something insulting she could throw back at the smug little twerp, but she felt too sick and helpless to come up with anything.

Elweny spoke up. "Hey, fathead. You're going the wrong way. Kyrhk's castle is south."

Slivercoin let out a snorting laugh. "I'm taking you to Mauron. He's going to want a word with you two after all that zombie business."

For a long while after that, the only sound was the *thud-thud-thud* of the golem's giant footsteps. Cianne lost track of time. She was in a dazed half-sleep when a thundering crack followed by a *thunk* brought her fully awake. She looked up to see the top of the golem's head shattered, and an enormous sword embedded halfway to the hilt in a tree trunk behind it. A slip of parchment fluttered away in the evening breeze.

The golem's joints loosened, and its prisoners tumbled to the ground. Cianne dragged a half-conscious Elweny away before the massive figure disintegrated entirely in a shower of clay fragments. They were on a narrow curve of road that snaked between a high wooded ridge on the left and a steep ravine dropping away to the right.

"Nice shot, Brugg," Slivercoin called out. "I've been waiting for you, buddy."

The big man stepped out from the trees, bits of shattered clay crunching beneath his feet. "You know Mauron said if you wreck one more golem—"

"He's not going to care!" Slivercoin replied with irritation. "Besides, you wrecked it."

Brugg walked over and helped Cianne and her partner to their feet. Elweny, swaying a little, clung to him.

Slivercoin grinned. "We need to deliver those prisoners to the boss, buddy. You're just in time to get some of the credit."

"I don't work for you anymore." The big man scooped Elweny up into his arms as her knees buckled. He whispered something into her ear.

"You don't seriously believe that hero stuff, do you, Brugg?" the assassin asked. "You're a bad guy, a thug. I've seen you do terrible things for money. You think a person can just decide to change one day? It doesn't work that way, man."

Brugg started to turn away.

"Hold on. I've got something you need to see." Slivercoin sifted through clay dust and fished out Elweny's luggage pack. He pulled something from inside. "You recognize this?"

It was Zybilene's flowing blue gown. Slivercoin also produced a vial of phosphorescent makeup.

Brugg's lips soundlessly formed the word, "Zybilene." Then his face contorted into his old look of pained confusion. "Fake? It was all fake?"

Slivercoin's laughter was shrill and triumphant. "That's right, buddy. They were just playing you for a fool."

Brugg threw his head back and let out a howl of rage as he lifted a wide-eyed Elweny above his head. She screamed. She was still screaming as he tossed her over the edge of the ravine.

Briefly, Cianne stood frozen by horror. When she finally turned to run, she felt a huge hand clamp down around her upper arm. Then she was being hefted up. Then she was screaming, falling into the ravine.

She landed on something very soft that smelled like buttered toast. Elweny was sprawled out nearby.

"Play dead," her partner whispered, not moving.

Slivercoin's sallow, frowning face peered out from the top of the gorge a hundred feet above. His reedy voice echoed faintly down the ravine.

"Oh, man. Mauron's going to be really hacked off. This is on you, Brugg."

They argued. Slivercoin declared that he wasn't going to sit around and wait while Brugg climbed down to retrieve the bodies. Brugg told him to take the scepter and go then, before somebody large shoved somebody small into another tree. The assassin began to whistle a jaunty tune, which after several minutes faded into the distance.

Brugg's face appeared above. "He's gone." He let down a rope.

As he helped them climb back onto the road, Brugg apologized. "Sorry it took so long for me to rescue you. I had to wait until you got to this spot with the Giant's Castle."

Elweny stared at him in admiration. "Your mother was right. You are smart."

"Before, there was always some part of my mind screaming, 'Brugg, you're not doing what's right!' or 'Brugg, you're wasting your life!' It made it hard to think." He shrugged. "Besides, it was easy to fool Slivercoin. He was always going believe I was a stupid, violent thug anyway, so I let him go on thinking that."

"We have to go catch him," Cianne declared. "He's got the scepter."

Brugg shook his head. "He's got the fake one. I switched it when he wasn't looking. The fake one doesn't jab quite as well, but he won't notice."

Cianne still felt miserable. Brugg asked her what was wrong.

"We lied to you, tricked you. Why don't you hate us?"

"Oh, I knew Zybilene was a fraud from the beginning. After all, in the Coraethian stories, Zybilene is a con artist who pretends to be a supernatural spirit mother in order to steal goats. In the end, she gets eaten by her lovable but repulsive helper gnome. Nobody who's read the Book of Wonderments would ever impersonate Zybilene."

Cianne shot her partner a reproachful glare.

Elweny shrugged. "I may have skipped a few pages."

"So, I knew Zybilene wasn't real, but I know the truth when I hear it. When you said I was a hero, my heart shouted, 'Yes! That's right! Don't you remember?' Then I decided to be a hero and my brain started working a lot better." He walked across the road and reached behind a tree, pulling out the mangled scepter. "Here, Cianne. This is yours."

She shook her head. "You keep it for now."

Cianne and Elweny retrieved what they could of their scattered and dusty possessions.

"It's straight back to headquarters, I assume? Elweny asked. "That's protocol. The bigwigs will want to study the scepter for a long time."

"They can wait." Cianne spread out a map and ran her finger along some routes. "Brugg, where could we free the most zombie slaves right away?"

The big man considered. "One of the big quarries, maybe. Why?"

"I say we take some personal initiative." Cianne stretched out a hand. Elweny placed hers on top of it, then Brugg's massive mitt enveloped both.

"Let's do it," he said.

JAMES WESLEY ROGERS

James Wesley Rogers has survived multiple summers in the greater Phoenix, Arizona area, where he uses his mystical brain-hammer to forge mathematics into computer software. Lately, he's been hammering out algorithms for eye-tracking systems, technology that offers people with physical challenges an alternative method of controlling devices. His story, "If I Could Give This Time Machine Zero Stars, I Would" which first appeared in *UFO5,* was reprinted in *The Year's Best Military and Adventure SF Volume 3* from Baen Books.

WHEN THE "MARTIANS" RETURNED

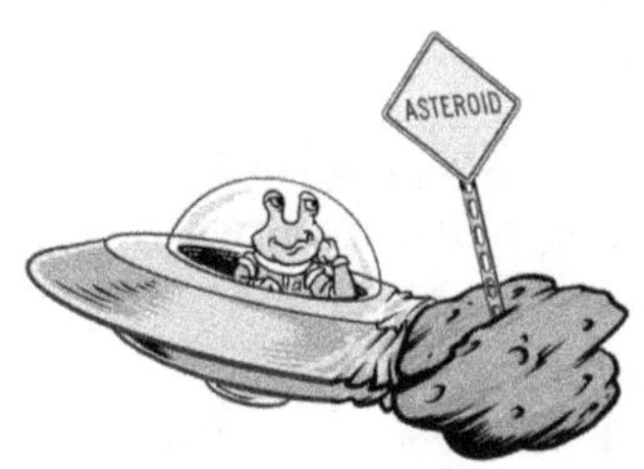

DAVID GERROLD

Well, they weren't really Martians, but everybody called them that, because it was a lot easier than calling them Xqrlt3ns. (The three is silent, but even after you know that, it's not much help.)

They were tall and green and spindly and had bug-like eyes, but not the kind that covered their whole heads, because that would have been too disturbing. Some people called them Sleestaks, but having evolved on a planet with much lower gravity, they were much too thin and much too tall for the resemblance to stick. So, Martians it was.

Their language, such as the linguists were able to understand, had no vowels, and only two tenses—too-tense and in-tense.

The Xqrlt3n ship was first detected by amateur astronomers, the usual way these things happen because the professionals are always much too busy looking the other way. This time it was an Australian hobbyist named Tim Knapp who first noticed a strange object approaching from sunward, one of the best places to look for unknown objects because most astronomers don't look there. The ship had slingshotted around Sol in a braking maneuver, and for much of its approach was lost in the glare. Knapp discovered the alien ship by accident. At first he thought it was a floaty in his right eye. He spent several minutes cleaning his glasses, too.

Tim Knapp owned one of the world's most remote petrol stations, halfway between Alice Springs, a small town in South North Australia, and Coober Pedy, a smaller town in North South Australia.

It's a seven hour drive on the A87, also known as the Stuart Highway. Drivers are warned to have a full tank and plenty of water and sandwiches. It can be a grueling journey, but for those who need a break along the way, if they can't wait until they arrive at the world-famous Erldunda Roadhouse, they can watch for a weather-beaten little structure crouched beneath a faded sign proclaiming "Knapp's Sack. Ice and Stuff."

Here, tourists can buy gasoline at exorbitant prices, vegemite sandwiches, stale meat pies, and a variety of colored stones that have spent a year or more in the rock tumblers in the shed beneath the solar panels.

None of that is important to this story. The real reason for the remoteness of Knapp's Sack was the absolute clarity of the night sky. There were no city lights to create an atmospheric glare in the night sky, no people around to annoy or interrupt him, and a near-total lack of clouds and rain in the dry Australian outback.

Tim Knapp was a self-taught astronomer. Before relocating to this desolate part of the Stuart Highway, he had made and lost several fortunes and an equal number of wives—although he still missed Christine Marie, his first wife and childhood sweetheart. And perhaps she missed him too. They still exchanged emails and even phone calls on holidays. Neither one quite remembered why they had broken up, but it had something to do with Tim's impatience and a kidney souffle.

Knapp's continuing failure at relationships had finally led him away from Sydney to the flawlessly clear nights of the outback, where he could gaze out at the Milky Way with a rapt sense of wonder and awe. He wanted to discover a comet, or something equally interesting. He fantasized about finding an object in the heavens that would someday be known as Knapp's marvelous discovery.

He had built for himself a fairly sophisticated observatory on top of a nearby hill, three kilometers east of his little store on the Stuart Highway.

At sunset, he would close up the store, pack whatever sandwiches had not been sold that day, plus a few bottles of beer, and drive his ancient Jeep up a winding dirt trail to his lair for the evening, a small dome-shaped building.

Depending on what part of the sky he wanted to observe or what celestial wonder had caught his attention, he would arrange his sleeping schedule around the hours of best visibility. His telescope was mounted on motorized gimbals and could be synchronized with the rotation of the Earth, so it could focus on any specific part of the sky for as many hours as the sky was dark.

Knapp kept scrupulous notes and took high-resolution photos, some with exposure times of eight or nine hours. His most recent passion was the possibility of a near-Earth asteroid encounter. Anything coming around from behind the sun would be almost invisible until it was only a few days away. While Tim Knapp was not hoping for an extinction-level event, he was certain that if he could discover a near-miss, it would give him that specific moment of astronomical glory that very few amateur sky-watchers ever attained.

He did better than that.

He spotted the Xqrlt3n ship before anyone else.

Of course, once he reported his discovery, the first reaction from almost every professional observer of the heavens was skepticism. Amateurs didn't discover things, and those six comets discovered by Terry Lovejoy were just lucky accidents, okay?

But then, one after the other, they turned their big eyes sunward and confirmed that Tim Knapp had actually seen something unusual. Tim Knapp was interviewed by three Australian news shows on two successive days, before the news media turned its attention to more photogenic subjects—also because "real scientists mean real ratings."

Tim Knapp did get a nice mention on Wikipedia, and for a few weeks he even displayed a sign at his station, "The first discovery of the Xqrlt3n spacecraft was made here!" Until he got tired of people asking him questions about the Xqrlt3ns that he couldn't answer.

And that's pretty much all we need to know about Tim Knapp right now. Events swept by him so fast he didn't have time to finish his meat pie. As it happens, he didn't even bother to finish it. (Australian meat pies are not known for their culinary excellence. Quite the contrary.)

By the time the alien vessel was visible to the rest of the world, it had already entered an elliptical orbit around the Earth, eventually braking into a geostationary position above the Atlantic equator. Several orbital telescopes were immediately focused on it, giving Earth observers a very clear view of the ship. (Also, a number of nuclear-devices were loaded onto an equal number of orbital boosters, just in case. This latter action was not a matter of public knowledge, but multiple governments were in contact with each other, all of them promising not to shoot first. So they all waited.)

Everybody waited.

Various scientists were immediately summoned to the studios of the news media to discuss what the alien arrival might mean to humanity.

So many scientists were recruited by so many news organizations that there weren't enough qualified scientists available to discuss the significance of the alien arrival. Fortunately, there was no shortage of people who could pretend expertise, so none of the news media lacked for punditry.

The short version of any of these conversations usually went like this:

"Who are these aliens?"

"I dunno."

"What do they want?"

"Dunno that either."

"Are they dangerous?"

"Dunno."

"What do you think we might expect?"

"Beats the hell out of me."

Complicating these conversations, the Xqrlt3n vessel did not respond to any signals beamed at it, nor did it emit any signals of its own. It simply hung there for the longest time, an unmoving point in the equatorial sky.

Unfortunately, it was out of sight for poor Tim Knapp, half a planet away. He was very frustrated. He could only watch the reports on the telly. Even worse, nobody wanted to interview him. He was already old news.

After an annoyingly long period of inaction, the Xqrlt3n ship separated into three parts. One piece rose, one piece descended. The middle piece stayed exactly where it was. High-resolution telescopes revealed that the upper and lower sections of the Xqrlt3n vessel were tethered to the main body. The ship was reeling out its upper and lower sections.

The entire process of unspooling took several days, until both of the tethers were thousands of kilometers long. When the lower end of the cable reached almost to the measurable boundaries of the Earth's atmosphere, the piece at the end detached, sped up, and began descending toward the surface.

This, at least, was something that the more knowledgeable scientists could actually discuss, and they did so at length.

The mechanics were fascinating. While an orbital elevator would be an extremely difficult undertaking, a skyhook would be much easier to establish and it would be just as practical, if not more so. A skyhook would be an energy-efficient and cost-effective method of launching and reacquiring a landing craft. So why hadn't NASA thought of it?

Actually, NASA had, but the challenges of creating a strong enough, long enough cable and getting it into space had not yet been solved. Never mind, that's another story.

Meanwhile, the Xqrlt3n shuttle was flying through the ionosphere, or maybe the troposphere, one of those spheres.

The specialists at NASA's mission control were quick to predict multiple possible landing zones for the alien shuttle, but their software was designed for the physical limitations of human technology. Unfortunately, the Xqrlt3n landing craft had abilities that were not factored into their models.

Let us now turn our attention to Carl Dershem.

Dershem was a mad scientist—not the proverbial mad scientist as in malevolently deranged, but the other kind of mad scientist—terminally outraged at the stupidity of the human race, especially those too invested in Dunning-Krugerrands to recognize, let alone understand, the superior achievements of his massive intellect.

In a previous tale (still unwritten), Dershem had invented the Pelzer Ray, but because he couldn't figure out what a Pelzer Ray actually did or what might happen to a target that had been pelzed, he finally gave up on the whole project. Despite that, he still secretly hoped that someday some serendipitous accident of science would rescue the entire work from oblivion. (Meanwhile, don't worry about the Pelzer Ray, unless you're pregnant, prone to migraines, or have irritable bowel syndrome. It has no further significance in this tale.)

Nevertheless, Dershem was good television. All an interviewer had to do was ask the right question and Dershem was a self-starter, winding himself up into a frenzied, near-apoplectic rage at metastatic stupidity in general and malignant incompetence in specific. He didn't hesitate to name names, so he was always good for a spike in the ratings, despite the usual complaints from the legal department.

But, in this situation, he outdid himself.

Beautiful Jo Choto was the anchorwoman for the National News Network Nightly National News—yes, that was her full name, her parents had named her Beautiful Jo, but as soon as she was old enough to be embarrassed, she shortened it to Jo. She invited Dershem to be a guest on her nightly roundup any time she needed either a scientist or a controversy, which was at least once a month. With the arrival of the alien spacecraft, Dershem was on almost every night—in no small part because no one from NASA wanted to lend credibility to any show that would regularly feature Carl Dershem.

Dershem's appeal was obvious. He was willing to speculate. He was willing to extrapolate. He was willing to elucidate. Put a microphone in front of him and get out of the way.

For example:

"So, Doctor Dershem, the alien spaceship has just landed in central Africa. A United Nations Contact Team is en route to meet them. What do you think will happen?"

"Good question, very good question. Excellent question. Some of the best scientists in the world have been considering this question. It's a huge question, very significant. And right now the best answer is that we don't know, we can only speculate—but speculation is important because it's a consideration of possibilities. Possibilities, you ask? Well, it's the question we should all be asking. Because it allows us to consider our responses. Preparedness, this is all about preparedness. Are they a threat or are they a menace? We don't know. But let's consider, what do they want? What could they want?

"What do they need? What do we have that they might need? Nothing, really. If they want minerals, they can mine the asteroid belt. If they want oxygen, they can extract it from water, they can find plenty of water on Europa or in Saturn's rings. If they need methane, they can help themselves to the atmosphere of any of our gas giants. So they're not dipping into our gravity well for anything freely available anywhere else. Of course not. So they have to be coming here for something that's unique to this planet. The obvious thing is something that no other planet has—life. Yes, that's what they're here for. Obviously, they want to meet us.

"But why? This is a question that some of the best thinkers on the planet are working on. It's the question you asked at the beginning. But we won't know the answer for sure until we actually establish some kind of communication, will we? That has to be the first step. When the United Nations Contact Team arrives in central Africa, they will have to spend a lot of time just learning how to talk to these alien visitors. Then we'll find out what they want, won't we?"

"Thank you, Doctor Dershem. That's all the time we have tonight. I'm Jo Choto and you're watching the National News Network Nightly National News. Thank you for tuning in and be sure to stay tuned for Tim McKenny's Sports Roundup with all the latest news about the heartbreaking situation in Florida."

(Don't worry about Florida either. Whatever it is, it's not going to be heartbreaking as much as it's going to be bizarre. But "heartbreaking" works better than "bizarre" for keeping viewers from changing the channel, so that's why Jo Choto said "heartbreaking.")

Meanwhile, down in Africa. ...

The Xqrlt3n shuttle landed twenty kilometers east of Yalinda in the Central African Republic. The exact coordinates were 6°31'05" North 23°32'15" East. (You can look it up on Google Earth and see how remote it is.) Why they chose that landing site, when there was a perfectly nice meadow in Hyde Park, London, a beautiful mall in Washington, DC, an attractive set of lawns adjacent to the Eiffel Tower in Paris, a huge open space in front of St. Peter's Basilica in the Vatican, a broad open square adjacent to the Kremlin in Moscow, and, of course, the Forbidden City in Beijing also had plenty of space. These were all suitable landing sites, according to any number of filmmakers. Yet, the Xqrlt3ns chose to land instead in one of the remotest regions of the Central African Republic, a country that had otherwise managed to escape the attention of nearly everybody except its immediate neighbors: Chad, Cameroon, and South Sudan.

The government of the Central African Republic was not equipped to deal with the influx of scientists, reporters, attention-seeking politicians, their various assistants and aides, and a variety of groupies and wannabes that descended on the capital city of Bangui. Nor did they have the facilities to transport this small army of chronovores to the landing site of the Xqrlt3n spaceship.

Fortunately, the United Nations Contact Team had arrived in six well-equipped C-5 cargo planes conveniently borrowed from the United States, carrying several helicopters and enough scientific and military gear to overthrow a small government and then analyze the DNA of its demise. Fortunately, the Bangui international airport had a runway long enough to accommodate such gargantuan planes. The Contact Team promptly set up their base station in nearby Le Mônjur Square—inflatable structures filled with humongous crates marked with numbers and symbols and warnings.

As soon as the helicopters were unloaded from the C-5s, assembled, fueled, and checked for readiness, nearly fifty scientists, observers, reporters, politicos, deputies, various aides, and several expendable generals boarded their respective aircraft and lifted off, heading noisily eastward.

They flew low and landed three hundred meters west of the Xqrlt3n landing craft. They all donned self-contained hazmat suits, with oxygen tanks on their backs, and plodded painfully across the remaining distance. The Xqrlt3n ship was shaped like a giant pumpkin. It was parked on three slender legs. A wide ramp lowered from its belly. A gaggle of Xqrlt3ns were already exploring the area immediately around the base of their shuttle.

They were tall and spindly. There were seven of them. They had greenish-gray-blue skin. They had dark, multi-faceted eyes. They smelled vaguely of lavender and chocolate and seaweed. They did not appear to be sexually variegated. Their clothing was not much more than knee-length gauzy scarves or fluffy boas, draped casually around their shoulders, and mostly designed to hold a variety of instruments, geegaws, doodads, whatchamacallits, and thingamabobs. But no widgets or doohickeys.

A delegation of three scientists approached slowly, arms spread wide, palms open, while behind them the rest of the contact team furiously photographed, measured, scanned, and recorded. Others made sure that everything photographed, measured, scanned, and recorded was broadcast to the rest of the world.

The three approaching scientists were Dr. Kier Salmon, Dr. Christy Davis, and Dr. Robert Newell. In preparation for this mission, their obituaries had already been written. The only thing missing was the date and cause of death, but it was presumed that these particulars would be available shortly.

The Xqrlt3ns barely noticed the humans. They were too busy examining a type of bush so uninteresting that neither the BBC nor David Attenborough had ever given it a second thought. But finally one of the aliens turned around and made an annoyed waving-away gesture at the approaching humans.

Dr. Kier Salmon, Dr. Christy Davis, and Dr. Robert Newell all stopped where they were, puzzled. They looked at each other through the transparent face masks of their hazmat suits. They frowned, they shrugged, they shook their heads in confusion. Not sure what to do, they waited and watched and waited some more.

At last, the Xqrlt3ns finished their examination of the otherwise uninteresting bush. Four of them wandered away to examine another uninteresting bush. Three of them turned to face the humans. The shortest one spoke in perfect English, although with a noticeably British accent, "Please go away. We have work to do here."

Dr. Salmon said, "Welcome. Welcome to Earth. We greet you in peace."

And then, Dr. Davis said, "We'd like to talk to you."

And Dr. Newell added, "We have so many questions to ask."

"Yes, yes, we know all that," replied the alien. "But we have work to do. So please go away. If we have time, we'll talk to you later. But don't count on it. We must stay on schedule." The Xqrlt3n pronounced it "shedjewel." And then all three of the Xqrlt3ns turned away to join the rest of their companions in their study of the next totally uninteresting bush.

"Well," said Dr. Salmon. "That was ... unusual."

"Unexpected," agreed Dr. Davis.

"And rude," said Dr. Newell. He added, "After all, we came a long way to meet them—"

"They came an even longer way," said Dr. Salmon.

"And apparently, they must stay on schedule," said Dr. Davis. She pronounced it "shedjewel" too. She wasn't British, so perhaps she was mocking the alien's pronunciation.

"Yes, that's what they'd like us to believe," said Dr. Newell. "But look at them. They're just standing there, staring at that totally uninteresting bush."

For a moment, none of them spoke. They stared at the Xqrlt3ns staring at the bush. But nothing happened.

Finally, Dr. Salmon said, "We're going to look like idiots, aren't we?"

"Absolutely," agreed Dr. Davis.

"That's already established," said Dr. Newell. "The cameras have been rolling this whole time."

"Well, there's nothing for it, is there?" said Dr. Salmon. "Let's head back."

And the three unhappy scientists turned around and trudged back to the others.

In the interests of brevity, this narrative will skip the obvious scramble of consternation at all levels of science, politics, and uninformed punditry. Instead, we'll summarize:

In the three weeks that followed their initial landing, the Xqrlt3ns lifted off and traveled to additional locations in Africa, Northern Asia, Canada, Mexico, South America, and finally New Zealand. They did not visit any national capitals. In fact, they avoided all major human settlements in favor of remote areas of wilderness. Whenever and wherever humans sought them out, they were waved away in annoyance. The Xqrlt3ns were insistent about staying on shedjewel. They had a lot of totally uninteresting flora to examine.

Of course, once they had examined the totally uninteresting bushes and one particularly ugly banyan tree, none of these were ever uninteresting again because human curiosity demanded an explanation. A multitude of researchers followed the Xqrlt3ns' examinations with even more detailed studies of their own. Whatever it was about these plants that required the study of the Xqrlt3ns, it was immediately a whole field of intense research for human beings. Unfortunately, except for a slight increase in their ability to hold carbon dioxide, a side effect of global climate disruption, there was nothing in any of the plants that merited an increased level of examination. These bushes really were totally uninteresting.

But the mystery continued, because the essential questions remained unanswered. Who were these Xqrlt3ns? Why were they here? What did they want?

Which was why Jo Choto's Nightly National News on the National News Network was also pulling big ratings because Carl Dershem was saying exactly what everyone else had been carefully (and very strongly) advised by their respective governments to not say.

By now, of course, most people were calling the visitors "Martians" because "Xqrlt3ns" was too hard to pronounce and more than one commentator had injured himself trying. Others, pretending to a more professional demeanor referred to the Xqrlt3ns as aliens, visitors, or beings. But "Martian" was a convenient shorthand for most lay people.

Except for Carl Dershem. "Well, it's obvious these creatures, whatever they are, have not come here to invade us," he said. "Or they would have unleashed their Pelzer Rays or whatever weaponry they might have aboard their orbiting dreadnought. Perhaps they don't find us appetizing. Maybe we taste bad. I don't know. We'd have to ask a cannibal about that. But if we tasted all that bad, then why would anybody be a cannibal? Unless they had no other choice, like the Donner Party or those Uruguayan Rugby players who spent seventy-two days in the Andes after their plane crashed. But I don't think that's it either. How did we get on this subject anyway? It's distasteful."

He bent to his notes, shuffling through his various papers. "I don't think they're here to quarantine us. That's obvious. They would have said something by now, wouldn't they? And you have to wonder, how do they speak such perfect English? And with that damned annoying British accent too—what's all that about? What are they, snobs? They must have been listening to our radio and television broadcasts all the way in, decoding and decrypting and translating—what do they think of us? Maybe they have to go somewhere and report? No, I don't think they're tourists. They're too busy studying all those totally uninteresting bushes, although obviously they're not totally uninteresting and we should be taking a much closer look at everything they're looking at closely to see what's so interesting. Maybe it's a new source of fuel or food or those bushes have some hallucinogenic property and we're going to have to pass new laws to keep our young people from smoking or eating the leaves, and then of course, we'll end up with cartels and smugglers and a black market selling drugs to innocent children outside the schoolyards, right?"

Dershem found another page and ranted on. "Obviously, they're not here as ambassadors, they haven't said one word to us that was diplomatic, not one word. And isn't that strange? We're the obvious owners of this planet, aren't we? Aren't we the intelligent species? Why aren't they talking to us? Aren't we important? Obviously, these aliens don't think so. They're not here for any reason we can understand, are they? They're not talking to dolphins or whales or giraffes. So why are they here? Nobody knows anything."

Jo Choto finally had a chance to get a word in. She said, "Well, yes—if they're not here for any reason we can understand, then we don't know why they're here. Nobody knows anything. And that's it for tonight. Please stay tuned for Tim McKenny's sports roundup and the real tragedy of the Green Bay Packers—"

In truth, there was no real tragedy of the Green Bay Packers, but Tim McKenny's ratings were still sagging and the programming executives at the National News Network were beginning to realize that Carl Dershem was a hard act to follow. Reruns of the abortive *Gilligan's Island* reboot would cost them less to broadcast and would probably pull an extra half-percent of market share.

Finally, one afternoon, one of the Xqrlt3ns approached the watching throng of human observers. "Where are the dinosaurs?" it asked.

The humans looked at each other, not sure how to answer. Finally, Dr. Kier Salmon spoke up. "They're all gone." Dr. Salmon had been tracking the Xqrlt3ns across all the separate continents since they had arrived, and despite being ignored across all the separate continents, still felt comfortable enough to answer. "They died a long time ago."

"How unfortunate. Well then, we'll be leaving now."

"Wait! Can we ask you some questions?"

"Maybe next time. We have to stay on shedjewel."

And with that, the Xqrlt3ns boarded their ship. A moment later, it lifted off and disappeared into the bright blue sky. Eventually it linked up with the lower end of the orbiting skyhook and was reeled in. Shortly after that, the Xqrlt3ns accelerated out of Earth orbit and headed outward toward interstellar space.

Earth was alone again. One question had been answered. Yes, there was life elsewhere in the universe, presumably intelligent. But another, more puzzling question, had been left behind. Just what the hell had they been doing here? And why did they ask about the dinosaurs? Had they been here before? They must have—

There was only one clear answer.

Carl Dershem had said it. Jo Choto repeated it. And eventually it became a cultural mantra.

Nobody knows anything.

Three days after the Xqrlt3ns had left, an Australian reporter phoned Tim Knapp to ask if he was following the "Martian" ship.

Annoyed at being treated like yesterday's news, Knapp hung up without saying anything. But he was no longer alone. Excited by the short flurry of publicity that Knapp had enjoyed, Christine Marie had caught a bus all the way out to Knapp's Sack.

Perhaps she had finally realized that Tim Knapp was her one true love – or maybe she had returned to him in the vainglorious hope that one day there would be a movie about his discovery of the Xqrlt3n ship, a quick rush of fame and fortune. Or perhaps she was now hiding out from a spurned boyfriend. Whatever the case, it's not part of this story. Her secret remains safe. We will leave it at that.

Meanwhile, after slamming down the phone, a very old landline, Tim Knapp headed into the kitchen for a beer. Christine Marie was at the sink washing dishes.

"Mm," he said. "Something smells good. Kidney souffle?" He opened the oven door to take a peek.

"Close the oven door, Tim," Christine Marie said. "It's not done yet."

Carefully, Tim Knapp closed the oven door.

David Gerrold

David Gerrold has been writing professionally for half a century. He created the tribbles for *Star Trek* and the Sleestaks for *Land Of The Lost.* His most famous novel is *The Man Who Folded Himself.* His semi-autobiographical tale of his son's adoption, *The Martian Child,* won both the Hugo and the Nebula awards, and was the basis for the 2007 movie starring John Cusack and Amanda Peet. His latest novel, *Hella,* was published in June of 2020.

WELCOME HOME

SIMON R. GREEN

Richard Ward had spent years looking up at the night sky, in the increasingly vain hope that someone would look back. Which was why he was standing on the edge of the woods on the outskirts of town, on a very cold evening, in a heavy jacket that wasn't nearly heavy enough. The sky was a deep dark ocean full of stars; none of which had the decency to move in a mysterious way, or be anything other than very distant lights. Richard was looking for unidentified flying objects.

Actually, he was looking for flying saucers. Current thinking in the sky watching fraternity was that UFOs were almost certainly other-dimensional intrusions, psychic phenomena, or even living creatures drifting around in the vasty deeps of the stratosphere ... but Richard still had a stubborn preference for the nuts and bolts spaceships of his childhood. He believed that there had to be intelligent life somewhere out there in the universe, if only because there was such a clear shortage of it here on Earth. He wanted the aliens to come down and bring a little color to this depressingly gray world.

So, every night for three years, Richard had brought his binoculars to the edge of the wood and watched the night skies for some sign that he was not alone in his beliefs. So far, his only close encounter had been with a massive owl that silently dive-bombed him, and scared him out of several years' growth. Richard felt very strongly that some birds should be required to carry warning lights, and possibly a horn.

No longer young, no longer married, and trapped in a job that wasn't so much soul-destroying as death by a thousand budget cuts, Richard had returned to the dreams of his youth, when it seemed that every movie and television show was packed with visitors from the great beyond. Aliens and creatures and monsters, oh my. Now, older and reluctantly wiser, Richard needed the aliens to be real; to prove that there was more to life than the everyday grind, and the slow passing days that scoured all the joy out of the world.

There had to be more to life than this. Because if there wasn't, Richard wanted his money back. And an apology.

He looked 'round sharply as he heard footsteps behind him. He whirled around just as a large middle-aged man in a heavy coat emerged from the tree line. The newcomer came to a sudden halt, flashed Richard a friendly smile, and held out a tartan-patterned thermos as a peace offering.

"Good evening! I'm George Fraser. The pub landlord said there was another UFO spotter out here, so I thought I come by and introduce myself. I've got some hot tea, if you're interested."

A moment's jealousy at having his private vigil interrupted was swept away by the thought of a warming drink, and Richard nodded quickly to George.

"Don't mind if I do," he said. "There is an almost comfortable tree stump here, if you fancy a sit down."

"Don't mind if I do," said George.

They sat side by side on the tree stump, and shared hot sweet tea from the thermos. Richard nodded happily to George as a warm glow perked up parts of him that had shut up shop in protest at the cold night air, and the two of them looked up at the endless reaches of the distant night. The lights in the sky did their best to look as though they appreciated being looked at. It was all very still, and very quiet.

"So," George said finally. "Anything happening tonight? Any chariots of the gods, or wheels or fire arcing across the fundament? Or even just a bright light that suddenly changed direction ..."

"I know what you mean," said Richard. "Sometimes I think I'd settle for a distant speck that simply shouldn't be there."

"But that isn't why we come out on nights like this, is it?" said George. "We're looking for signs of life."

Richard shrugged heavily. "It's almost like no one wants to make contact. Why do the aliens have to make it so difficult? Why can't they just land on the White House lawn and say: *Take us to your leader?*"

"Because that's the human way of doing things," said George. "Maybe the aliens have more important things to do."

"Like what?" said Richard. "Dropping out of the sky in some backwater dump, and saying: *Hello earthling; drop your trousers and bend over?*"

"Aliens don't abduct people," said George. "That's just media scare stories. And the whole *fear of probing* thing says more about the people who believe in it, than it does about aliens."

"So why don't they just come down and talk to us?" said Richard.

"They must have their reasons."

"Maybe they're afraid of us," Richard said glumly. "We spend so much time hating each other, for reasons that probably make no sense at all from a distance."

"More likely, they keep their distance because they're afraid close contact would damage people. Personally, and culturally."

They drank more tea.

"All those huge radio receivers," said Richard. "Why don't they ever pick up anything?"

"The only way to cross the immense distances between stars would have to involve faster than light travel," said George. "So to phone home, and tell their families they'd got here safely, they'd need faster than light communications. Which human science doesn't have. All those people are listening with the wrong ears."

"But we've been making enough noise of our own," said Richard. "The aliens must know we're here."

"The galaxy is huge," George said patiently. "The stars at the center are packed close together, relatively speaking, but this particular solar system lies right out on the edge, where the stars are furthest apart. If there is a federation, or an empire, or a really good party going on, it's back at the center. Humanity is going to have to make its own way there, if they want to join in and play with the others."

"But aliens do come here," said Richard. "I believe that. I have to believe that."

"They must have their reasons," said George.

"I sometimes think there's a big sign, right at the edge of our solar system," said Richard. "Saying: *Warning! Humans Ahead! They Bite!*"

"Wouldn't surprise me," said George.

"What do you think aliens would look like?" said Richard. "I never believed that whole *Star Trek* thing, where the aliens look just like us except they've got pointed ears, or bumps on their noses, or a Cornish pasty for a forehead. Real aliens could look like anything, and just blend into the background. I mean; who'd notice if there was suddenly one more tree in this forest?"

They looked at each other, then turned all the way 'round to look back at the trees. Nothing moved.

"All right," said Richard, as they turned back. "Bad example."

"They might look just like us," said George.

"Because the human design is the inevitable result of evolution?" said Richard.

George smiled. "I don't think I'd go that far. But it would make sense that human types would want to visit a human world."

"But if they look like us, they might act like us," said Richard. "What if they're coming here to conquer us, or enslave us? Oh, God, they're going to eat us, aren't they?"

"Why would they come such a long way, to do things they could just as easily do at home?" said George. "No; they'd come looking for people they could help. People who don't belong here, and dream of better worlds. The aliens come to Earth because they're on a rescue mission. Looking for people like you, Richard."

George snapped his fingers, and a beam of brilliant white light stabbed down from the sky, right in front of them. Richard looked up to see a massive circular shape filling the night sky. He turned back to look at George, and suddenly his heart was full of glorious understanding.

"Come with me, Richard," said George. "There's a better place waiting."

He got up and walked forward, into the beam of light; and Richard got up and followed him in.

When he could see clearly again he was standing on a starship bridge, and it looked exactly how he'd always hoped it would ... all gleaming high tech, and people standing around in shining silver outfits. They were all smiling at him. George put an arm across his shoulders.

"Welcome home, Richard."

SIMON R. GREEN

Simon R. Green has written sixty-nine novels, two collections of short stories, and one movie. These include the Nightside books, the Secret Histories, Deathstalker, the Ghost Finders, and, most recently, the Ishmael Jones mysteries. He expects to take a short break anytime now. Before he was a writer, he worked as a shop assistant, bicycle repair mechanic, journalist, and actor. He has spent most of his life in the small country town of Bradford-on-Avon, which was the last Celtic town to fall to the invading Saxons, in 504 AD. He is not dead yet.

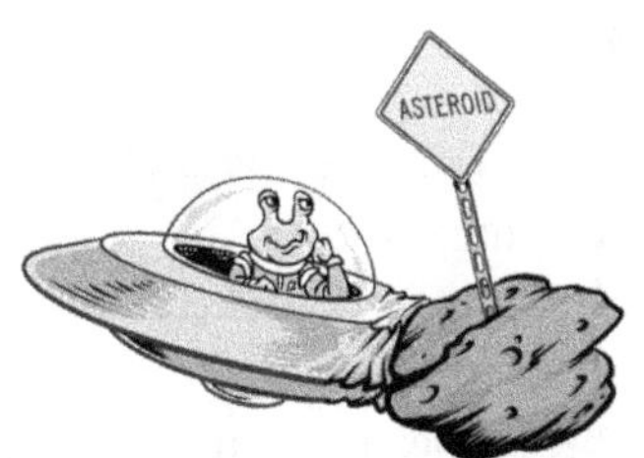

THE UNWELCOME MAT

J.J. LITKE

My phone rang first thing Monday morning. Strictly speaking, I'm a medium, but I got this specialized niche business. "Mathilde Coburn, Appliance Exorcist, you houst 'em, we oust 'em."

Long pause while they chewed on that. "Yes," a woman's voice said. "My name is Myrtle Truman, and I'm having a bit of a problem with my welcome mat. Your ad says you handle all household items?"

"Sure," I said. "Appliance hauntings are more common, but I can take on most inorganics." Most, because ever since the lawnmower incident, I draw some pretty solid lines. "What's the problem with your mat?"

"It's behaving in a decidedly unwelcoming manner. Spelling out rude things to people. It called Phyllis's skirt ugly, and it criticized Karen's shoes. I'd have to agree with the mat about those shoes, I mean, platform clogs are just not a flattering look. But Phyllis's skirt was lovely, I don't know why the mat took issue with it."

I was in solidarity with the mat about platform clogs, too, but I nudged the client back on track. "It actually spoke?"

"No, I told you, it spells them. The bristles form letters, they sort of bend up and down into shapes, you see? It insults my friends, and now they won't come over. It's not much of a loss in Karen's case, but Phyllis—"

"Ms. Truman, the spelling sounds annoying, but has it done anything else?"

"Oh, yes, this weekend it ate a phone company rep."

Here we go. "It ate him?"

"Yes. At least he claimed he was a phone company rep. I didn't see his ID before the mat swallowed him. Might have been a burglar for all I really know. But you can see why I can't have my welcome mat acting like this."

I could indeed. This wouldn't be a light case, to say the least. Devourings took a lot more powerful malevolent force than your usual rapping noises, ectoplasmic secretions, or even knocking things off shelves. But rent was due, and I needed cash. I agreed to come over.

The house was colonial, white with green shutters, and a basically useless porch just big enough for show, with fat white columns. The "welcome" mat was unassuming brown bristle. You might think the flashier household items are more likely to attract spirits. My theory is these plain items have inferiority complexes that make them more susceptible.

Ms. Truman circled around from her back door to meet me. She was rail-thin, wearing a taupe sweater and peach-colored skirt that I bet the mat wouldn't say a single nice thing about. My gray Dickies pants and shirt were pretty drab by comparison, but blah, neutral colors were less likely to provoke anything, even insults.

She waved a bony hand at the faux porch, flapping like an unhappy flamingo. "There it is. Can you fix it?"

"We'll see."

I set my case down, leaving a healthy amount of space between it and the mat so I had a retreat zone. Then I stepped up and started with the obvious. "You don't belong here. Ms. Truman would like you to leave."

The bristles rippled and pressed down, molding into engraved letters. "Get bent."

A little ruder than usual. I got a bundle of sage from my case, lit it, and stepped toward the mat, intending to circle it with the sage smoke. Honestly, I'm not sure sage really does much, but it puts on a nice show that the clients enjoy, and it gives me a chance to kind of suss out the situation. And suss out I did. Just a couple feet away, the mat lunged up at my hand like a cat after a toy. I yanked it back and fell on my butt, which, thankfully, is nicely padded.

Ms. Truman wrung her flappy hands. "That's what happened to the phone rep. I did try to warn him, but he kept on about how I was spending too much on wireless."

I hauled myself up. "Ms. Truman, you said this started with the mat spelling things. Did anything strange happen before that?"

"No."

Just, no, without any thought. Typical. People didn't get the significance of things they saw as ordinary and how they connected to the supernatural. I always had to push them for the right details. "Has anything changed around the front door or porch? Any new events or activities, new items?"

"Oh, I bought the new doorknocker. An antique, actually. Isn't it lovely?" She gestured toward the door: a black metal lion's head gripping a ring in its mouth.

"Is it iron?" I asked.

"I think so. The man who installed it cut himself quite badly. Honestly, I don't know how he managed it. He made such a fuss he knocked his tools all about, and a fair bit of blood, too. He even lost the nails that matched the knocker. He ended up having to get new ones, then complained about the cost even though he was the one who lost them."

Holy shit, and she'd thought that wasn't a big deal. The mat probably had hold of one of those bloody nails somewhere in its bristles. Blood and iron. The combo didn't always cause possession, but when it did, it was nasty. If I'd known, I'd have refused the case. But I'd agreed, so we had a verbal contract, and I was bound by my word. Stupid of me to get greedy.

I went back to my case resting just off of the porch and retrieved the salt. That mat must have been able to sense it—another ill sign of how bad the thing was. It twisted and jerked, lunging at me. I poured lines of salt across the porch, driving the fiendish mat back to the doorstep.

"Oh, dear." Ms. Truman hopped back, but to her credit, she didn't flee like Mr. Schumer had when I exorcised his coffee maker a couple weeks ago, and that thing only spit grounds. "I'm sure my old door mat never acted this way. Or the back door mat, either."

I had the mat cornered, but salt alone wasn't going to solve this one. Smudging with sage wouldn't fix it, either. My case was loaded with a bunch of other options I could try out: some signs and incantations that were hopelessly too low level; a singing bowl; herbs and oils; a cross and holy water, which only worked on a certain set of spirits who were into that sort of deal. It had reacted to the salt, so I decided to try more mineral and crystal options next.

First, I got the bottle of Agua de Florida and gave myself a quick all-over spritzing. Yeah yeah, it's not heavy duty, but I was a little nervous and hoped it'd give me a boost of protection. Then I got the sage stick lit again and set it in an abalone shell I kept for the purpose. The mat made a sound like a sneeze.

Perusing through my rocks, I settled on tourmaline and obsidian. The first would repel negative energy, and the second would enhance the first. I picked up the sage and eased over the first line of salt.

The mat didn't move.

Ms. Truman was still as a pillar of salt off to my right—it's nice when a client sticks by. I waved the sage back and forth, sending a plume of smoke out in waves, and circling around the crystals in my hand. I know, I said before that I don't think much of the sage, but the mat had reacted to it a little bit once already, so maybe it'd add something. I slowly eased my foot over the next salt line.

The mat vibrated and growled. Okay, I was starting to get to it.

One last step. The growl increased. Kind of an impressive noise, really, especially considering the thing was making it through its bristles without the benefit of vocal cords.

Just before I got as close as I had the first time with the sage, I threw the crystals down on the mat.

The mat convulsed and gulped down the crystals. I waited for a reaction. And waited.

Then I waved the sage a little more trying not to let on to Ms. Truman how much I was just waiting, like I had expected it to take this long. The nothing just kept on going.

Wow, that bastard mat ate my crystals and didn't even flinch. I wasn't super surprised they didn't completely resolve the problem, but just knocking them back that way, without even a hint of indigestion, that was too much. I really liked that particular piece of obsidian, too. Shit.

"Did it work?" Ms. Truman asked.

I tried to think of some way to not admit it hadn't. "Uh. Not entirely." Brilliant. "It's okay, I know what to do now."

Now, that was not a lie, I did know what I had to do next. Fooling around with any of the other mid-level stuff in my case would be a waste of time, not to mention I could lose more pieces to the stupid mat. This called for the big guns, the strongest item in my arsenal. And I had one doozy of a big gun. I don't like to resort to it if anything else will work, but if ever there was a job that needed my nuclear option, this was it.

I got the silver chain from around my neck, the one with the key to the silver-lined tray in my case. Turned the key in the lock and got out a lumpy red rock.

"Wake up, Ick."

Ick isn't its full name. I never say the whole thing because I'm not suicidal. The rock twisted in my hand, like it was trying to bite. 'Cause that was pretty much what it was trying to do. It's a last resort item for damn good reason. I got out my silver knife, sliced into my hand next to Ick, and squeezed it tight against the cut. This is only part of why this isn't an easy option, but it'd be enough even if requiring blood to control it was the only downside. Ick is a dark spirit, the rock is just its housing. And it is not a full demon, and not really sentient, it just follows its impulses to feed—I might not be inclined to be nice to dark forces, but I'm not mean enough to keep a cognizant being trapped in a rock. The way I see it, I rescued Ick, and now I feed it sometimes in exchange for a little help. If it were intelligent and didn't see this as a fair trade, trust me, it'd find a way to let me know.

Ms. Truman scooched in just enough to see the blood on my hand. "Oh, my!" She scurried back. Smart girl.

Ick drew my blood fast. Too fast, the greedy bastard. I could almost see my arm going pale.

"Desino!" I yelled, but it didn't stop. I fell to my knees. Whoa, that was fast. Guess I hadn't fed it in a while, and you know what they say about hungry spirits.

The mat lunged at the salt border, like it was trying to brush it away. Had to get Ick back on board fast. I grabbed the salt bag and held Ick clenched in my hand over it. Abruptly, Ick quit drawing blood. Yeah, you'd better pay attention. Once I actually had to jam it into the salt. Both of us got burned so bad it was nearly three weeks before I took another job.

Before anything else could decide to kick up a fuss, I whirled around and tossed Ick at the mat. Both rock and mat went still. No reaction. Holy shit, this thing was stronger than Ick? I stumbled up to my feet, clutching at the column next to me. Maybe I could still get myself and Ms. Truman away, but odds were good we were both gonna die. And not in any nice way, either.

My mom always told me I should get a nice office job, and I suddenly wished I had listened to her. Most office jobs don't carry a high risk of getting eaten by an possessed doormat.

Then the mat shuddered. Bristles flexed back and forth. A thread of steam slipped out. I swear I felt the porch vibrate straight up through my boots.

A howl erupted, and a jet of flame shot up as tall as me. I leaped back to Ms. Truman, but she'd had the good sense to leap back, too. At least I didn't fall on my butt again. A wave of heat blew my hair back, and huge cloud of smoke belched out.

I coughed and waved at the smoky air.

The mat was still again, Ick sitting triumphantly on top, in the middle of a big scorch mark. Curled up next to the mat was a dead guy covered in ectoplasm. Eww. I'd almost forgotten about the phone company rep. Then he convulsed and coughed up more slimy stuff. So, not dead after all. That was a relief, especially for him.

But I still had a client to impress. "All done, Ms. Truman." My voice barely shook, but my knees were wobbly as hell. The phone guy was starting like he was trying to get up, so I retrieved Ick with my uncut hand—no need to sacrifice any more blood to the little shit—and locked it back into its case before anything else could go wrong there. Whatever'd been in the mat, it wasn't stronger than my possessed rock. Cool, I guess. Though absorbing this thing gave me a whole new load of reservations about Ick.

Ms. Truman scurried up like she was going to help the phone rep, then stopped short of touching him, eyeing all that goop. "Are you all right?"

He dragged himself into sitting up and stared at her. "Ma'am. I need to ... tell you about our wireless plan."

"He's fine." I dug into my case again, got a small towel, and tossed it to the guy—I always have a few towels on hand for things like this. "I'll file the standard possession recovery form for getting your phone service guy out and send you a copy of that, along with my bill."

She glanced dubiously at the phone company rep, who was wiping slime off his face and looking awfully chipper for a guy who'd been inside a haunted mat a couple minutes ago. "Are you sure he's all right?"

The phone guy had gotten up. "Ms. Truman, it's you who's going to be all right after you hear about how much I can help you save!"

One side of the poor woman's mouth tilted up like she was trying to force a smile, and her eyes flicked to me. I could have just escaped. I mean, I felt like hammered dog shit, and it'd take at least a week to recover. But, what the hell, might as well help her out one more time. I stuffed my exhaustion and put on my authoritative face.

"You need to evacuate the premises." I took out my wallet and flipped it to flash my business license, which looks weirdly official if you only see it for a second. "If you stay, I'll have to isolate you here."

His brow wrinkled up. "What?"

"We're looking at a Class D haunting with potential for long-term manifestation. This area needs to be cleared immediately. Anything or anyone that stays is going to be put on quarantine lockdown." I tilted my wrist up like I was looking at my watch, which, spoiler, I don't have. "You've got twenty seconds to decide."

The guy shifted on his feet. "Now, you can't really—"

"Fifteen seconds."

He took a step up and raised a hand, his jaw flapping open to argue.

Without a word, I reached into my case, grabbed a sprig of lavender, and held it out. Lavender is some weak-ass stuff, it's only in the case because I like how it smells, but I figured I'd try a bluff with it.

The phone guy stared at the sprig, eyes going wide. He shrieked and was off, hustling across the lawn and down the street like a rat fleeing a terrier. I stared down at the lavender. Huh. It had some muscle after all. Which gave me an idea for a bonus revenue stream.

Ms. Truman clasped her hands together and smiled. "Thank you."

"All part of the service. Actually, Ms. Truman, for a small added fee, I could bring you an herbal wreath that'll discourage door-to-door sales." Herbs that were supposed to help repel ill spirits, but judging by the phone guy's reaction, there might be more overlap between them than I'd known. It'd explain how the guy survived so well inside the mat.

Her face lit up. "Why, yes, that would be lovely."

The wreaths wouldn't be as lucrative as full-blown exorcisms, but a lot easier and won't end with me bleeding so much. Long as I don't have to face up to irate solicitors who're mad about me putting a crimp in their business.

I resolved to put an extra strong wreath on my own front door, just in case.

J.J. Litke

J.J. Litke lives in Austin, Texas, where she writes SFF and moonlights as a graphic design instructor. She is not a robot—she enjoys non-petroleum beverages, engages in sentient-life activities, and has taken a human mate. Her fiction has also appeared in *Apex, Cast of Wonders,* and *Nature Futures.* Find her at jjlitke.com and on Twitter as @jenztweets.

GET ME TO THE FIRG-<CLICK><COUGH>-XULB ON TIME

LAURA RESNICK

"You had just one job, Agent Lark," said the Galactic Union's Special Envoy to the Trisgladian-Irgh-Toxl Sector. "*One* job."

"Well, several jobs, really, ma'am, if you take into account"—

The face I was looking at on the monitor of the ship's dashboard turned a more alarming shade of puce. "Let's focus on the one you're screwing up, Lark!"

This accusation was unjust. It wasn't my fault that my orders had failed to take time differences into account. "Ma'am, we knew the logistics of transporting all attendees to the Firg-xulb"—I slowed down a little for proper pronunciation of the Toxlish phrase that involved a glottal-click and a gurgly cough between the two vocalized syllables—"would be challenging and vulnerable to unforeseen delays. That's why we built extra time into the schedule."

"Extra time you've squandered by arriving days late at Vatican IV," said Special Envoy Borlov. "And now you're telling me you're *remaining* there for three days?"

"Our journey was on schedule, ma'am, but the original ETA didn't take galactic rotation into account. And, as a separate issue, the team that planned routes and scheduling for all the transports apparently didn't realize that our target arrival time of zero-dash-seven-six-one-R-G-Q-zero-eight in Galactic Mean Time would actually get us here just in time for Cazxl."

"Impossible!"

"I assure you—"

"No, Cazxl shouldn't take place until ..." On my monitor, I could see her scrolling through a database. "... six standard days after the Firg-xulb, which should be plenty of time to return Honorius to Vatican IV before it begins."

Because of the perpetually tense situation in the Trisgladian-Irgh-Toxl Sector (which we never shorten to the acronym TITS, not even when very drunk, we just don't), the Diplomatic Corps of the Galactic Union (GU) had assigned code names to the planets and VIPs involved in this mission. There was a significant risk of sabotage or terrorism, so we needed to conceal locations and identities in case our communications were intercepted, unlocked, and decoded.

Also, the Chief of the Corps loves drama.

So, the planets were Vatican I, Vatican II, and so on; and the VIPs were all named after Catholic popes. This confused not only terrorists, pirates, and rogue hackers, but also about 60 percent of the corps, who had no idea what a pope or a Vatican was.

I said, "On the GMT calendar, yes, that's correct. But Vatican IV still functions on local solar time. They haven't made the switch to GMT."

"Yes, Agent Lark, I know. The eventual switch to GMT will come after they've joined the GU, which won't happen until this war ends, which is why you're there to transport Honorius. And now you risk missing the Firg-xulb. Lark, I cannot overstate the importance of you getting Honorius here on time!"

Special Envoy Borlov had already landed on Saint Peter—another code name—to welcome the arriving dignitaries and make sure the current ceasefire was maintained.

"Yes," I said, "I understand, but my point is—"

"Oh, dear God," said Borlov, finally getting it. "They're on *solar* time."

"Yes."

She sighed. "And the planning team calculated Cazxl using GMT dates rather than local solar dates?"

"Yes."

Sitting next to me in the cockpit of this vessel, Flight Lieutenant Chen, the pilot, muttered, "Trust the great minds of the Diplomacy Corps to screw it up. We call you *dips* for a reason, you know."

"I heard that," snapped Borlov.

Chen rolled her eyes and whispered to me, "All they had to do was include someone in their meetings who actually flies around the galaxy. But noooo, we're tainted with the stench of real-life experience."

"Agent Lark, tell your friend to shut up."

"We're not friends, ma'am, we were both just assigned to ..." Realizing we were getting off track, I said, "So, anyhow, Honorius can't travel for the next three days. In local time."

"No, of course not," Borlov replied wearily.

I added, "Or eat, or wash, or operate machinery."

Except for those who were currently on essential military duty, everyone on Vatican IV was following tradition by spending Cazxl in prayer, fasting, and meditation.

Borlov said, "Well, at least it's not three *standard* days. Then we'd really be in trouble."

"I can't even communicate with Honorius until Cazxl is over," I said. "Their military command has given us permission to orbit the planet until then."

"Understood."

"How are the other transports faring so far?" I asked.

"Oh ... a couple of other teams have experienced some difficulties," she replied.

"Anything serious?"

"Apparently Pope Joan got cold feet. So ... well, I'm afraid the transport team rather *overreached* in their determination to complete their mission."

"What does that mean?" I asked.

"They abducted her."

"Hot damn!" said Chen. "You dips got some game, after all."

Borlov added tersely, "I gather it was the *pilot's* bright idea to kidnap her."

"We're problem solvers," Chen said.

"So I will need to smooth over some ill feeling when Joan arrives here," said Borlov.

"No doubt," I said. "But you'll persuade her to go through with the ceremony willingly, ma'am. You're a diplomat."

"Three solar days until you can get under way ..." Borlov said pensively. "Well, I suppose if absolutely nothing else goes wrong, you can still get to Saint Peter just in time for the Firg-xulb."

"I think the cough in the middle is supposed to be more of a gurgle," I said.

"Agent Lark, are you actually correcting my pronunciation of—" Borlov's cold tone changed as she said, "Stand by, Lark. I've got an incoming signal on the emergency channel."

"Standing by, ma'am."

"What passes for an emergency in the Dip Corps?" Chen asked me after Borlov muted our channel. "They've run out of themes for their code names?"

"This could be serious," I chided. "The emergency channel is only used for—"

"Poems and nursery rhymes?"

"This is a very volatile situation. We're on the verge of resolving a war that's lasted for generations among three major civilizations covering more than a dozen planets across multiple star systems. There are powerful factions within these societies that don't want peace and have a stake in seeing our efforts here fail."

"Yeah, yeah," said Chen, "so we've got to get everyone to the wedding on time."

"The Firg-xulb isn't just a wedding."

"I think that cough in the middle is supposed to be more gurgly."

"It's a multi-person bonding ritual that will end an interstellar war. It's *the* dynastic union of the epoch," I said. "This is a huge and historic event we're working on, Chen. Apparently there hasn't been a Firg-xulb in centuries."

"Galactic or solar centuries?"

"Trisgladian-Irgh-Toxl centuries, actually, which is this whole other thing," I said. "Anyhow, if anyone is missing from the ceremony, or shows up late, or if the participants start before every guest has arrived... someone is bound take it as a deliberate insult, and they'll resume fighting."

The comm system beeped an alert as Borlov said, "Lark?"

"Standing by, ma'am."

"I've just received an encrypted message from Sparrow."

The names of corps agents were also in code for this mission: Lark, Sparrow, Wren, etc.

Borlov continued, "One of his passengers turned out to be a Trisgladian terrorist."

"What? Despite all our security precautions?"

Chen said, "Your precautions really aren't that great."

Agent Sparrow was in charge of escorting a key Firg-xulb participant, code-named Pius, to Saint Peter.

"Is Pius safe?" I asked Borlov. "And where is the terrorist—in custody or still at large?"

"Pius was unharmed, fortunately," said Borlov. "The terrorist has been captured and is, I assume, about to be eaten."

"What?" said Chen.

"Trisgladians don't imprison their criminals and enemies," I told the pilot, "they eat them. Often baked into dainty ritual pastries."

"Whoa! I am *not* eating at this wedding."

"*If* we could return to our current emergency?" Borlov said testily.

"It's not over?" I asked.

"It has merely begun! The terrorist was apprehended only *after* disabling the ship's pilot and sabotaging the vessel to prevent Pius from reaching Saint Peter."

"Is the pilot okay?" Chen asked.

"Yes," Borlov said, "but the ship is not. It's now stuck in orbit until it eventually crash lands."

"This is bad," I said.

"You have a gift for understatement, Lark. This is a disaster! Pius is crucial to the Firg-xulb," Borlov said. "And he's effectively stranded on Vatican IX. He can't rely on a ship from his own fleet to transport him here."

"No, obviously."

Only GU ships could transport participants and guests to Saint Peter. This had been a key aspect of getting the warring societies to agree to this ceremony. If any of their own ships approached the planet now, it would be perceived as a threat and almost certainly spark renewed fighting.

"It's up to us to solve the problem," said Borlov, "or else this whole peace effort will blow up."

"Right."

"You and Chen are wasting three days just orbiting Vatican IV."

"Three solar days," I reminded her.

"And according to calculations at HQ, you're closer to Vatican IX than any of our other ships," said Borlov. "Lark, the galaxy needs you and Chen to go get Pius and escort him to the Firg-xulb."

"But what about Honorius?"

"I don't know. One problem at a time, Lark. Vatican IX is where you're needed most right now. Contact me when you've got Pius aboard your ship."

"Yes, ma'am." After Borlov signed off, I turned to Chen. "Do you know how to get to Vatican IX?"

"Yeah, but us being closer to it than the rest of the transports is a pretty relative term. No way can we get to the wedding by three-point-five-zero-dash-B-L-G-eight-four GMT if we have to go there via Vatican IX."

"You might have spoken up while we still had the special envoy on the comm," I said crankily. "Now I've got to—"

"Chill, Agent Lark. No way can we do it, that is, if we use the *official* route."

"There's an *un*official route?"

"Sure."

When she just smirked at me, I said, "I'm a diplomatic agent, Chen. So feel free to talk to me as if interstellar navigation has never been my thing."

"Wormhole, baby!"

"I'm not your baby, and what makes it unofficial?"

"Not mapped."

"Stop right there. I'm *not* going into any unmapped or unexplored wormholes. No way."

"But—"

"*No.* We'll come out dead. Or won't come out at all. Or we'll come out in the Cretaceous era." I shook my head. "It's a very sad thing about war resuming in the Trisgladian-Irgh-Toxl Sector, and no one is sorrier for it than I am, but I refuse to dive into—"

"Relax. This hole isn't unexplored," Chen said, plotting her coordinates. "It's just a well-kept secret. I've been through it before."

I looked at her.

She shrugged. "Okay, before joining the fleet, I may have had a modest sideline in smuggling."

"Ah."

"We'll be fine." She smiled. "Trust me."

"I hate those words."

"Look, Lark, if we pull this off, we won't *just* end a long interstellar war and pave the way for several prosperous civilizations to join the GU," Chen said persuasively. "Saving the day could also put us both in line for promotions."

"All right," I said after a moment. "Let's go salvage this mission. Or—oh, crap—die trying."

IN FACT, THE journey went smoothly, except for my bouts of vomiting inside the wormhole and my nose bleed upon exiting it.

"Oh, God, just kill me now," I moaned, pressing my bloody sleeve to my streaming nose while fighting a lingering wave of nausea.

Chen shook her head. "You are one chirpy travel companion, Lark."

When we approached Vatican IX, though, things went to hell.

I had expected to find a sabotaged transport ship from the GU caught in orbit around a planet quietly observing the ceasefire. Instead, we immediately encountered multiple war ships engaged in full-scale battle.

Hoping Agent Sparrow was still among the living, I used the Dip

Corps channel to contact him via the personal device attached to his wrist—all dips had one.

"Sparrow, this is Lark. Are you receiving my signal? We're within range of Vatican IX but cannot approach without risk of getting caught between warring factions. Do you read me? Sparrow, are you there?"

"Lark!" Sparrow eventually responded. "What are you doing here?"

"Borl ..." I realized that the security breach on Sparrow's transport meant we could well be under surveillance by the enemies of peace right now. So I switched to the special envoy's code name. "Peacock advised us your ship has been sabotaged. She sent us here to collect Pius for the ... the ..." Anyone monitoring us would know what a Firg-xulb was. "... for the thing."

"What?"

"The thing. You know, the *thing.*"

"The thing ... Oh! Yeah, well, thanks Lark, but that was ages ago. What the hell took you so long?"

"Huh?"

"Boniface's fleet attacked this system after Pius didn't show up at the Firg-xulb."

"The cough in the middle is supposed to be more gurgly," I said.

"Is this really the right time to criticize my pronunciation?" Sparrow demanded shrilly.

"Wait ... did you say *after* the Firg-xulb?"

"Yes."

I said to Chen, "What's happened? I thought you said we were taking a shortcut!"

"We did take one," she insisted. "We got here in a fraction of the time it would have taken if I had never been a talented purveyor of black market cargo."

I realized she must be right, because I'd only vomited a few times. If we had been in that wormhole for "ages," I'd be skeletal now—or dead.

"Then we've traveled into the near future." In my panic, I reached for Chen. *"You didn't tell me we would time travel!"*

"Gurgh. Mwerr guuu."

"What?" I realized I was throttling her. "Oh. Sorry."

She shoved me away. Rubbing her throat, she said, "You stay on your side of the bridge at all times from now on."

"It's not really a bridge. More like a cockpit."

Over the comm, Sparrow said wanly, "I was hoping for a more experienced rescue team."

"I'm so sorry, Sparrow," I said. "We seem to have accidentally time traveled."

"No, we didn't," said Chen. "According to my chronometer, we're right on time. It took less than one galactic day to get here."

"Yeah," said Sparrow, "but that's about eleven metric days. During which all hell broke loose here."

"Metric days?" I repeated.

Chen frowned. "Metric?"

Sparrow asked, "Peacock didn't tell you we're on metric time here?"

"No," said Chen with a disgusted sigh.

"To be fair," I said, "I don't think Peacock knows."

"How can they be on metric time?" Chen demanded. "Who *does* that anymore? It's so last empire."

"Last empire ... Oh, hey, I get it!" I said into the comm, "Galactic Commonwealth, right?"

Sparrow confirmed.

"Okay," I said, "that makes sense now."

"No, it doesn't," said Chen. "The Galactic Commonwealth ended centuries ago—in *every* system of time."

"Yes," I said, "and as we learned in dip history classes, using metric time was one of the reasons the whole empire disintegrated."

"Right," said Agent Sparrow. "Because metric time was too rigid to function well with galactic rotation, time paradoxes, solar variations, and interstellar travel."

"Exactly," I said. "Therefore the empire outgrew the Commonwealth's logistic ability to manage it."

"And so nobody uses metric time anymore," said Chen. "For good reason."

"Actually," said Sparrow, "a number of systems do still use it. It's just not well known within the GU."

"It's only used by former Commonwealth systems that never reverted to solar time after the empire broke up, and that *also* have not joined the GU and switched to GMT," I said. "So it's not very common."

"Much as I've enjoyed this little history lesson," said Chen, "I think we should focus on the here and now."

"Of course," I said, recognizing how serious the crisis was. "Back on Vatican IV, there's still time to secure the peace," I mused. "But on Vatican IX, it's too late."

"Everything happens faster in metric time," Sparrow said apologetically.

"Yes, I know," I said.

"Metric days are shorter," he said.

"We know," said Chen.

"Metric minutes–ridiculously short."

"We know."

There was a long silence.

"All right, we need to decide our next move," I said firmly. "We can't waste more time pondering time."

"Well, I, for one, would really like to be rescued," said Sparrow. "I came here to secure the peace, not to become a casualty of war."

As if to underscore the danger, a battleship on Chen's main screen blew up upon sustaining a direct missile hit.

"Sparrow, where exactly are you?" I asked.

"On Pius's flagship. We boarded it after my vessel was sabotaged."

Chen shook her head. "I can't get closer to it without risking a hit."

"Sparrow, can your pilot fly a shuttle out of there and rendezvous with us at a safe distance from the battle?"

"My pilot is somewhere down on the planet, enjoying what is reported to be a bender of epic proportions."

"Oh. In that case, can *you* pilot a shuttle?"

"Sure. I'll just revive the handy piloting-a-shuttle-through-battle skills I learned at diplomacy school."

I tried again. "Is there anyone on board with you who *also* wants to be rescued who can pilot a shuttle?"

"Do we really have time for me to run a survey of Pius's whole crew?"

"Hang on, Sparrow," said Chen, doing some calculations. "I may have a plan."

"Good," he replied. "I'm aging fast in metric time."

"Hm ... yes, I think this will work," muttered Chen, staring at her navigation console. Then she said into the comm, "Sparrow, you need to get Pius himself to shuttle you to my ship."

"Wait, what?" I said to her. "Why?"

"Pius is leading his forces in battle," said Sparrow. "I think he's a little too busy right now to give me a lift to—"

"Get him," Chen insisted, looking excited. "Tell him I think we have a solution. I think we can do it, after all!"

"Do what?" I asked.

"We can get him to the Firg-xulb on time!"

"I think Lark's right," said Sparrow. "The cough in the middle should be more gurgly."

My resentful stomach was completely empty on our reverse trip through the wormhole—which was merciful, since the whole nausea-inducing, nosebleed-producing experience seemed to last much longer this time.

"This is taking forever," I groaned.

"Try tilting your head back," advised Sparrow, crammed into the cockpit between me and Chen.

"No, that just makes the nausea worse."

"In that case, if you could at least try not to bleed on *my* uniform?" Sparrow requested. "This is all I've got to wear to the ceremony."

"Aren't we there yet?" I asked weakly. "Why is this taking so *long?*"

Piloting the ship through the wormhole, Chen said, "Because my calculations didn't take into account that Pius would bring his whole entourage with him, including a ... a ... what *is* that thing?" We heard it trumpet loudly again from the cargo hold. "Some sort of mastodon?"

"It's going to get hungry soon," Sparrow said anxiously.

"So we're carrying a lot more weight and mass than I expected," said Chen. "It's throwing us off schedule, I'm afraid."

She had calculated that by traveling in the reverse direction at appropriate velocity, going against galactic rotation rather than with it, we could still complete our mission and reach Saint Peter before the Firg-xulb began in galactic time, and—through the sort of paradox that made my head hurt—thus prevent the battle that had commenced in metric time at Vatican IX.

"Chen, I don't mean to nag," I said, "but if we don't get out of here soon, the war will recommence in galactic time, too, and we'll be too late to do anything about it."

"You *are* nagging," she snapped.

Directly below us in the passenger quarters, we heard some ritual singing as Pius and his entourage optimistically prepared for the Firg-xulb.

Chen muttered, "I don't even want to know what's in those snacks they brought with them."

"You mean *who*," said Sparrow.

"You just had to say that, didn't you?" I heaved a little.

Shortly after leaving Vatican IX's system, I had transmitted a message to Special Envoy Borlov that we had Pius on board and were en route Vatican IV, where we'd collect Honorius just as Cazxl was ending, then proceed to Saint Peter. We expected to get there just in time—as long as nothing else went wrong.

"Ah-hah!" Chen cried, as we emerged into regular space. "We're through!"

I sagged back into my flight seat, relieved beyond words to be out of the wormhole.

Sparrow asked, "Are we where we're supposed to be?

Chen checked her navigation console. "Yes! We're on approach to Vatican IV."

"Excellent work, Lieutenant."

"All we need to do now is ..." Chen paused. "Uh-oh."

"Uh-oh?" I sat up. "What is uh-oh?"

Chen was looking at her chronometer. "Um ..."

Sparrow asked, "What's wrong?"

The comm system beeped an alert. A moment later, Borlov appeared on the screen. "Agent Lark, where in the blazing bloody universe are you?"

Sparrow whispered, "Peacock seems stressed."

"Oh, y'think?" I said.

"I heard that," snapped Borlov.

Chen said, "Slight miscalculation, I'm afraid."

"How slight?" I asked apprehensively.

"The added mass and weight, combined with velocity and direction ..."

"What?" I said to her. "What's happened?"

Borlov boomed, "Lark, report immediately! Where are you?"

Chen said to me, "You noticed the journey seemed a little long?"

"Yes," I replied tersely, "as I mentioned several times."

"Wormhole travel can be a tad unpredictable."

I reached for Chen. "Just tell me!"

Sparrow removed my hands from Chen's throat and said, "Lark, maybe you should stay on your side of the bridge."

Borlov shouted through the comm, "The Firg-xulb is supposed to start any moment! Where are Pius and Honorius? Where are *you?"*

"We hit our spatial mark but overshot our temporal target," Chen said.

"What?"

Chen gestured to her chronometer. "It's three-point-five-zero-dash-B-L-G-eight-four. Right now."

"What?"

"She's saying," said Sparrow wearily, "the ceremony is scheduled to start any moment. Peacock's right. We're not going to make it to the Firg-xulb."

Borlov said, "Sparrow, your pronunciation is terrible."

"Hang on," I said, thinking hard. I took a deep breath. "The ceremony starts any moment in *galactic* time."

"Yes," said Sparrow, "so we've failed."

"Not necessarily." I studied the personal device on my wrist, rapidly scrolling through cultural reference data.

My companions stared at me while Borlov made threats and demands over the comm system.

I found what I was looking for. "Here it is! I've got it!"

"Got what?" asked Sparrow.

"Chen," I said, "you take us into orbit around Vatican IV. Sparrow, you contact Honorius and make sure he gets on board—right away!"

"Why? It's too late to escort him to—"

"No, it's not!" I said. "*Not* if we use Trisgladian-Irgh-Toxl time."

Borlov heard me and made dismissive noises. "No one has used that system in centuries."

"No one has held a Firg-xulb in centuries, either," I said. "But if everyone involved in the ceremony agrees to switch to the ancient Trisgladian-Irgh-Toxl calendar, then we can still get our passengers to the Firg-xulb before it starts."

"But—"

"You're a diplomat, Peacock," I said. "*Persuade* them."

And so it was that, using an unmapped smuggler's route and an archaic system of time, our team was able to prevent a war that had already started and to escort our passengers on time to the ceremony they were late for.

Sadly, Chen and I did not get promoted for our work; the GU is pretty bureaucratic and promotion is all too often based on time served rather than merit. However, along with Sparrow, we did receive grateful thanks and ceremonial gifts of appreciation from the new Trisgladian-Irgh-Toxl Alliance for our part in securing peace in their time.

Laura Resnick

Campbell Award-winning author Laura Resnick writes the popular Esther Diamond urban fantasy series, which has received enthusiastic praise from *Library Journal* and *Publishers Weekly.* An animal rescue volunteer and part-time tour guide, Laura is also the author of the Silerian Trilogy, which made multiple "Year's Best" lists, as well as dozens of short stories, several nonfiction books, and many articles and essays.

BLACK NOTE, IN HIS TRANSITION TO A SUPREME STATE OF WOKENESS

JAMES BEAMON

Malcolm Maxwell is becoming increasingly suspicious that his entire existence has been contrived and ragtime pianist Scott Joplin isn't helping. When Scott isn't talking like a turn of the last century negro, he's humming "The Entertainer," the melody that anyone who knows there was once a style of music called ragtime thinks of when they hear the word ragtime, and he's humming it on repeat in their shared head. It's enough to make Malcolm wanna holler, but that's a Marvin Gaye song and Scott Joplin isn't into soul music.

"Seem like they can just use a piano instead of all that extra crooning," Scott Joplin's sentiment. "Bruno Mars ain't bad."

Malcolm's in the command center of the Superleague's Superfortress. The fortress is a multi-tiered concrete edifice with large picture windows where superbeings can protectively look over their beloved city. Captain Power is sitting at the monitors, looking at feeds from the city's CCTV system.

"Dr. Nefarious is rampaging downtown, but it looks like Cricketman's got the jump on him ... ha ha!"

"Watch him," Scott Joplin's sentiment, "this man's cutting shines." Malcolm is instantly aware it means Captain Power's up to something.

"Shut up," Malcolm Maxwell thinks loudly. He isn't exactly sure if that's how you talk to a disembodied ragtime musician currently residing in one's own head, but it looks less crazy than actually talking.

"'Cricketman got the jump'? That ain't sound scripted to you?" sentiments Scott Joplin.

Malcolm, more famously known as the acoustically empowered superhero Black Note, goes over to the monitoring station Captain Power's manning. He looks at the ensuing fight between Cricketman and Dr. Nefarious. It is a high-intensity battle featuring a man in a forest green spandex suit and a balding dude in a lab coat, with flips, kicks, and punches galore, the galoriest. An arsenal of robot minions is blowing up all over the place as if Dr. Nefarious intentionally installed C-4 in their chassis.

There are no raised hairs on Malcolm's body as he watches the edge-of-your-seat action. It is increasingly difficult to get excited about the mechanics of crime-fighting when Scott Joplin's riding shotgun.

"Ever wonder why all the geniuses become evil?" Scott Joplin asks. "It's like they trying to tell people education and postgraduate degrees ain't shit."

"That's not true." Malcolm has recently given up on wondering how and why Scott Joplin came to reside in his head or how to get him out. When he thinks along those lines, Scott Joplin invariably joins in and solitary contemplation becomes a disturbing dialogue.

"Ain't it tho? Name me one good supergenius."

Malcolm muses for a while, unconcerned during this time for the safety of his friend and superpeer Cricketman. Malcolm is too busy trying to draw blanks into substance. "Well, Captain Power's been rated as a having genius level intellect."

"'Course he do. Captain Power's got genius level everything. Lemme ask you something. You ever see Captain Power build an army of sci-fi robots the Pentagon couldn't produce with a trillion dollar budget? I bet you never seen him build a single lonely robot."

"He doesn't have to. He's Captain Power."

"You don't have to customize your ringtone on your phone but you do. 'Cause you can. Hell, you ever see genius Captain Power fix the toaster?"

"He doesn't use the toaster. Heat vision."

"So, he can save the city from evil but can't save y'all from tearing up your bread when you spreading butter that's too cold 'cause it's fresh from the 'frigerator? That's some selfish shit."

"Shut up, Scott Joplin!"

Scott Joplin goes back to humming the iconic ragtime tune he composed back in 1902. Somehow that's worse.

The fight on screen concludes with Cricketman victorious, a criminally insane doctor of astrophysics wailing in defeat, all robots exploded husks, and downtown only partially destroyed. Cricketman looks at one of the CCTV cameras, all of which have somehow survived harm, and flashes the perfect smile beneath the mask.

"Did you guys see? I barely pulled that one off!"

"Magnificent victory, Cricketman!" Captain Power heartily gushes into the mic. "The citizens can rest easy with you on the job!"

"Somebody shut his sauce box," Scott Joplin sentiments. "Why he over here pitching woo when he could have done the job in six seconds?"

"Cricketman was closer to the scene," Malcolm explains.

"You're standing beside a gum beater who can fly at light speed and is invincible as Jesus on Sunday. He could've popped over in two seconds, punched the good doctor into the sun in the most literal fashion the next two seconds, and then smiled for the cameras for the last two."

"Captain Power can't be everywhere at once."

"That an excuse you really wanna sell? Where he at now?"

Malcolm sighs. Even if Captain Power didn't have hearing that could hear a mouse pissing on cotton, proven fact from the time they had to take on Squeaktessa the Rat Goddess, he would've heard it. He turns his chiseled chin toward Malcolm.

"Something wrong, Black Note?"

Yes, something is indeed wrong and that wrong is made more complicated by the context surrounding the question. There are pros and cons to telling Captain Power about the sudden emergence of a long-dead ragtime musician in Malcolm's brain space. As if the thought alone is invitation enough, Scott Joplin susses out the particulars.

"Listen, this is how this shot scatters. You tell Captain Power I'm in here with you and he's gonna look at you with these googly, concern-rimmed eyes that'll sparkle like a kid's at Christmas. He'll reckon you've contracted a sentient alien parasite, gotten a bad taste from your last bout with the Mad Poisoner or some other spectacular far-fetched shit. He'll take you off field duty and subject you to an ever-increasing battery of tests and prods, treating it all like yet another super-powered predicament easily bested within the span of an episode."

Malcolm gulps as he looks down at Captain Power. "And if I don't tell him?" he asks inside his own head.

"Eventually you'll either be completely off your chump, trust me, I know crazy ... or you'll come to terms with sharing thoughts, which ain't so bad seeing how lonely you are and all."

"I'm not lonely," Malcolm replied.

"You ain't gotta woof smoke at me. It's not like I've seen every card-carrying member of this super-justice brigade, but I don't gotta to know you're the only black dude in it. That's some solitary shit, my brother."

"Wait. How are you so sure I'm the only black person?"

"You can thank third stage syphilis. That shit killed me, you know."

Malcolm's brow furrows in confusion and anger, confanger. "What the fuck does that have to do with anything?"

"That third stage is called neurosyphilis, which brings to the party personality disorder, seizure, psychosis, and a giant mess of that confanger you just experienced. You go crazy as you die. And in a mad world it takes a whole heap of crazy to really see straight."

Malcolm's retort is interrupted by Captain Power, who rises from the surveillance station and places a beefy hand on Malcolm's shoulder.

"Spill it, Black Note," Captain Power says. "You've been staring at nothing for three minutes straight while making all sorts of weird faces. Do you know how many times I could've flown around the world in three minutes? As I always say, time is action."

"No snitching," Scott Joplin sentiments.

Malcolm hesitates.

"Is this about your nemesis, Voodoo Master?" Captain Power prods.

"Sweet Jesus!" Scott Joplin cries. "Please don't tell me they paired you opposite the only other brother for miles who just so happens to practice Haitian spiritualism only his version is super dark and dangerous, complete with zombie powder and gals with hissing rattlesnakes for tongues and shit?"

Malcolm doesn't answer Scott Joplin, even though there have been multiple encounters with Voodoo Master's zombie hordes and loyal priestesses. Truthfully, he's tired of a ragtime pianist razzing his berries. He addresses Captain Power.

"I have another voice in my head who tells me he's Scott Joplin, a composer who's been dead for over a hundred years."

"Hot socks!" Captain Power exclaims. Concern etches his features and his eyes dance and Malcolm swears he hears the faint sound of Scott Joplin laughing smugly. Captain Power hits the giant red button on the console.

"Superleaguers Assembuuuuuuuuul!" he bellows into the microphone. Malcolm would be lying to himself if he didn't feel a tinge of apprehension and regret about his somewhat hasty decision to disclose his status, and he can't lie to himself, not in his present state.

Within moments a diverse menagerie of colorful spandex enters the room. Green for Cricketman and Cricketgirl, red for the Rage and Lady of Rage, metallic silver for Impossible Ranger Gunbrave, yellow for Sunstar and Lady Sunstar, purple for the Cowl and Cowlgirl, stars and stripes for Madam Patriot. Without prompting they form a circle around Malcolm as if they inherently know he is the problem.

"Ever wonder," Scott Joplin sentiments, "how all the males catch their superpower from some freak accident or mutant animal bite and then sometime later inexplicably a woman will catch the same exact powers? You don't find that odd?"

"You're wrong," Malcolm think-replies. "Madam Patriot is stand-alone and Impossible Ranger Gunbrave doesn't have a female counterpart."

"Impossible Whasit?" Scott Joplin asks. "Oh, you're talking about Adjective Noun Fred! Naw, what you have to consider is Adjective Noun Fred is Japanese. They want him to appear asexual and the best way to do that is to not even have a female counterpart, because initial impression upon seeing a woman in a matching silver suit would suggestionize they're having ground rations."

Instantly Malcolm understands the term "ground rations" is an archaic euphemism for intercourse. What he fails to understand is who the "they" who want this are.

"You're in the same asexual boat as Adjective Noun Fred," Scott Joplin continues. "Unless Black Notegirl is late to the bash."

As if on cue, Captain Power's cousin Powergirl strides into the room wearing the female version of his red and blue spandex.

"Sorry I'm late," she says. "Villains."

"Oh?" Scott Joplin asks, "we still waiting on Imaginary Notegirl? Unless you on the make with American Gams there, who is quite the looker with that spangled skirt."

"I don't understand you," Malcolm thought-confesses. "The 'they' you keep referencing, the points you're making. It's all lopsided. I'm not hooked up with Madam Patriot, but are you going to ignore her in this 'they want' conspiracy, or act like she's an outlier?"

"I wrote two operas in my lifetime," Scott Joplin tells Malcolm. "The second one, *Treemonisha,* was my magnum opus, a thing of beauty. It was not, I repeat not, a 'ragtime opera.' There was an overture, prelude, recitatives, arias. And throughout elements of black folk songs and dances, including a kind of pre-blues music, spirituals, and a call-and-response style scene involving a congregation and preacher. Because I was unable to afford it or acquire funding, I was never able to actually perform the opera. *Treemonisha* wasn't presented in full concert until 1972. Nineteen seventy-two! I had been dead fifty-five years. Anyway, critics and audience adored it. But by then the orchestration notes had been completely lost. I guess one of those by-products of dying in poverty and obscurity despite composing the most famous ragtime song ever. Oh, and dying in the agonizing throes of tertiary syphilis ... can't forget about the syphilis! But there were things in my original orchestra notes that other composers are just guessing at, good guesses but still just guesses, not completely right. If my opera could've seen the light of day when it was first birthed it would've been ahead of its time and unquestionably changed the face of music. Who knows what beautiful sounds would have been born of its inclusion to the public consumption?"

"I," Malcolm begin-thinks. "Don't ... know ... what that has to do with Madam Patriot."

"*Treemonisha* is an outlier," Scott Joplin explains. "Madam Patriot is an excuse for fetishists to ogle some legs."

"Arrgh!" Malcolm anguishes out loud for a change. He looks pleadingly around the room. "Guys, help me silence Scott Joplin!"

"Damn, brother," Scott Joplin sentiments, "no need to jump salty like that."

The Superleague immediately takes Malcolm seriously. More than Malcolm's heartfelt plea to his superpeers that spur them to action, it's the fact they were having a whole discussion about Malcolm and his resident ragtime pianist with him totally unaware of their conversation and seemingly unavailable to respond to their direct questions as Malcolm mentally dialogued in his headspace about the asexual tendencies of select minorities and the wanton objectification of all the women he knew.

Impossible Ranger Gunbrave raises a shiny silver finger in the air.

"My Unpossible Photovaleric Sensor may be able to determine the nature of Black Note's affliction. If it's an exotic parasite, say of alien origin, or some newfangled mind serum undoubtedly concocted by the Mad Poisoner, we'll surely discover it!"

Malcolm is center stage, flanked on both sides and behind by superpeers as he heads down the sterile halls of the superfortress to Impossible Ranger Gunbrave's lab.

"I'm sensing minority team up here," Scott Joplin sentiments. "Black Note and Adjective Noun Fred are FutureSound!"

Malcolm climbs into the Unpossible Photovaleric Sensor, which conveniently resembles an MRI. As the tray slides him deeper into the guts of the UPS, he wonders offhandedly about the non-word unpossible and if Impossible Ranger Gunbrave named his device thusly because UPS sounds better than IPS. The moment after, he wonders if the previous thought truly belongs to him or Scott Joplin.

There is a screen in the UPS belly, directly in front of Malcolm's face. It jumps to life from a flicker and Malcolm is now face-to-face with Impossible Ranger Gunbrave.

"Okay," the silver-clad superhero says from the screen. "The first few tests are very innocuous, so you won't really see or feel anything different. So, just lie there, try not to move too much. Any questions, Black Note?"

"No."

"I have a question," Scott Joplin sentiments. "How'd you get your superhero name?"

"What are you talking about?" Malcolm think-asks. "We name ourselves."

"So you named yourself Black Note?"

"Um ... yeah."

"Why? To denote the difference between you and some other Note? Is there a White Note running around the hallways of the Superleague? Or even the Note?"

"It's because I'm black."

"So, you're perfectly fine with Captain Power changing his name to White Power?"

Malcolm shakes his head. He is immediately reprimanded by Impossible Ranger Gunbrave for moving.

"Could we not," Malcolm thinks, "you know, talk about this stuff."

"Yeah, I guess not," Scott Joplin sentiments. "Your kind goes well out of their way to avoid this stuff. Me? Living in my era, race is swirling all around you, stuffed in your pockets and your drawers. Politics in an oppressive white hierarchy, too."

"Hey, wait," Malcolm thinks indignantly. "What do you mean my kind?"

"Superheroes. It's easy enough for you to punch and kick some bank robbers and some disfigured clown frothing at the mouth and threatening to blow up the world. But what's your record on fighting poverty, sexism, racial inequality, homelessness—especially for veterans? Hell, gerrymandering? Any one of the super dupers ever stand up to say manipulating voting districts to intentionally discount voters of one stripe or another is wrong and the shit needs to stop? Not your fault, I guess. The world wants to see clear-cut good triumph over clearly defined evil. Fighting badly drawn voting districts isn't exactly a page turner."

"You're blaming our noninvolvement on a lack of action scenes?" Malcolm questions. "Anyone can fight those issues if they're up for it. People do it all the time. But it takes special powers to stop those diabolical types that can single-handedly blow up the world."

"You of all people should know that the most diabolical types don't break the law. They bend the law to suit their ends. And when they get caught in the height of their depravity towards fellow man nothing bad happens. Because it's legal. Where are you all for that?"

Impossible Ranger Gunbrave interrupts, for which Malcolm is grateful. "My tests so far have come up negative. It's time for me to try Impossible Multi-Dimensional Sequencing."

Neither Malcolm nor Scott Joplin knows what that means. They suspect not even Impossible Ranger Gunbrave knows, but it sounds cool and convincing, so why not.

"Could you turn your head to the right?"

Malcolm complies.

"Okay, slightly back to the left."

Again, he complies.

"Now, a smidge back to the right."

"Just get on with it, Adjective Noun Fred!" Malcolm shouts. A second later he follows with, "Sorry."

A slight hum comes alive within the UPS.

"Felt good, right?" Scott Joplin asks. "Calling him that?"

Malcolm stays quiet, even in his own head. He tries not to fidget.

"I hope you know this is only gonna shake out in one of three ways," Scott Joplin sentiments. "You already know what one of those is, which is why you're so afraid lying in this coffin tube."

"I'm crazy," Malcolm thinks.

"It's highly probable, with me being a manifestation of a frustrated and seemingly one-dimensional existence, if one such as I am allowed to define what the cause is. I don't know. I do know having a mental illness is a bit more complex and nuanced than a general 'crazy.' But would you looky here, you're in an idealized twenty-first century. There are all sorts of techniques, technologies and medicines to help you manage this. It also doesn't hurt that the source of your illness is a rather astute, ahead of his time pianist and excellent observer of the universe, even this one. So, from your potential illness to you, you should know having a mental illness isn't a death sentence. Well, for me it was, but that was a different thing that modern medicine solved with a shot of fucking penicillin. Yeah, in retrospect Gertrude wasn't worth it."

Malcolm nods in the UPS. Immediately Impossible Ranger Gunbrave tells him to stop over the intercom because the machine needs to calibrate.

"What are the other two?" Malcolm asks Scott Joplin.

"Other two what?" the voice replies.

"The other two ways this shakes out."

"Oh, that. The second one is I really am Scott Joplin and in a world where mutant bites and freak accidents cause superhuman awesomeness rather than an agonizing death or the sprouting of a third baby-sized foot from your ankle, my life experience through madness and frustrated genius created a ghostly spirit of music that lived beyond my mortal shell until it could find one such as you, one who could harness music and sound into a power that defeats evil. This one's my personal favorite."

"I like that one, too," Malcolm thinks wistfully. "And the third?"

"The third's similar to the second. I really am Scott Joplin. I haven't died, at least not yet and in my syphilitic madness I'm tapping into an ethereal skein where only the mad and the prophets can dwell, which allows me to both see the future and create a whole absurd alternate reality of superheroes just for my consciousness to co-inhabit the one I call Malcolm Maxwell."

"It can't be that one," Malcolm thinks. "I was around before you."

"So you think," Scott Joplin replies.

Suddenly the screen in front of Malcolm's face flickers to life bearing the smiling face of Impossible Ranger Gunbrave.

"Black Note, it appears you're the unwitting host of an alien parasite."

Malcolm is quiet, dumfounded. So is the exotic alien parasite formerly known as Scott Joplin.

"I'll be damned," the alien parasite finally sentiments.

"The Impossible Multi-Dimensional Sequencing picked up an anomalous signature. Our galactic partners in the Blue Necklace Corps readily identified it as an ephemeraith. They're wormlike interdimensional creatures from the planet Torp, largely harmless. They spend their larva stage trolling through Torpian datastreams, collecting data on whatever suits their fancy, mostly historical figures and facts. When they mature they zip into a Torp's head, befriend the host Torp via thought sharing, while feeding off the electrical impulses of the Torp's creative thought processes until it's grown strong enough to project its own interdimensional field."

A wave of elation surges through Malcolm.

"Easy enough for you to feel that way," the alien parasite sentiments. "I just found out my whole existence was a lie."

Impossible Ranger Gunbrave leans closer to the screen. "My UPS should be able to clear it for you. All you need is a little light-bleach treatment."

"Wait!" the alien parasite says. "Don't let them bleach me, brother! They're trying to take the black out of me and hell, maybe you, too. I can't help what am I and for my part I didn't know what that was. I still feel I'm Scott Joplin. More to the point, all I really want is to be your friend. You heard what he said, my kind's largely harmless. You can't just bleach me out of existence like that."

"Hey, Impossible Ranger Gunbrave," Malcolm says. "You said these things are harmless. What if I keep it?"

The silver-clad hero shakes his head. "Harmless in Torpians. The overwhelming majority of Torpians have them, where they rely on them as a friend and second opinion. But they've evolved over countless eons to handle the symbiotic relationship. You're the first human to ever acquire one, which I imagine happened in that titanic battle with the Ko-Gan Armada. There's no telling what it would do to you. It's highly doubtful it will be completely harmless. Back when the Torpians were more militaristic, they used to release hordes of these things into their enemies' datastreams because of the harm they do to non-Torp brains. It will very likely kill you or make you crazier than cat shit. Just settle back. I'm going to bleach it."

Malcolm dry swallows. His elation has turned to dismal helplessness framed with melancholy, dismalcholy.

"Oh, God," the Scott Joplin parasite sentiments, and Malcolm can almost sense the worm pacing back and forth in their shared brain space. "They're about to kill me. Okay, think. After all, apparently I'm only a thought worm instead of a forlorn, forgotten piano man. If nothing else, I should be able to think."

"I'm sorry, Scott Joplin worm," Malcolm thinks.

"Maybe I can survive this. Other brothers have survived bleaching ... uh, Michael Jackson, Sammy Sosa. Oh, God, at what cost though?! What if it turns me into Al Jolson?! I need your help, Malcolm."

The idea that the worm affecting to be Scott Joplin could remanifest as a white singer famous for putting on blackface and singing "Mammy" truly terrifies Malcolm. "How can I help?" he think-asks the worm.

"Thoughts are powerful. They make your super abilities manifest, they make whole worlds manifest. If you actively think strongly, fondly for me, perhaps I can use it to create a psychic barrier against this light-bleaching. It'll also prove you're mentally stout enough for us to be friends. Will you?"

The hum of the UPS kicks into a shrill whine. The lights grow and Malcolm, he swears they are too bright and the light clots. He screams into the whine. He thinks nothing but wistful, good intentions about the worm Scott Joplin, a life Malcolm desperately wants to save.

In the back of his mind, a receding thought forms which is not his own.

"Stay woke," it whispers.

The clotting light evaporates. The whine keens down.

"Scott?" Malcolm thinks. "Scott?" He waits. The silence is loud and vacuous in his own head.

The UPS tray, like a tongue going "blech!," slides out, where an eager Superleague is waiting to meet him. They have warm, genuine smiles. All he can think of is how the female versions of the males are more scantily clad, why Adjective Noun Fred doesn't date, and how come not one of them have postured an opinion on fruitful ways to reduce or eliminate the increasing population of homeless veterans, much less done something concrete. He thinks on a "they" who only want him to punch bank robbers and space tyrants to produce a feel good time for some amorphous audience somewhere.

Captain Power, his too-perfect smile sparkling, places a hand on Malcolm's shoulder. "How do you feel, Black Note?"

Malcolm Maxwell is still becoming increasingly suspicious that his entire existence has been contrived and ragtime pianist Scott Joplin isn't helping, because Scott Joplin is no longer around to help.

James Beamon

James Beamon has been all over the world, but most times it was in places no one else wants to go. The author of over forty short stories in places such as *Lightspeed, Intergalactic Medicine Show* and *F&SF*, he's currently an Associate Editor for *Escape Pod* and a Director-at-Large for SFWA. He can't remember if he lost his hair before self-pubbing his Pendulum Heroes series or because of it, but either way he's currently bald and an indie novelist. These days he lives in Virginia with his wife, son, and attack cat.

THE OTHER TED

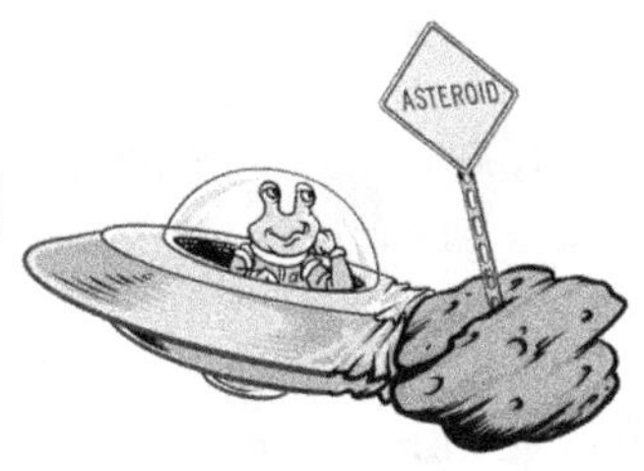

WENDY MASS AND ROB DIRCKS

Transmission Commence; Translate to Earth protocol TCP-IP using private "electronic mail" address 695484-b94; Universal Timedate 92965-ap9.

Attention "President" Gabriella Lewin of arbitrarily-drawn geographic boundary known as "United States of America":

Please forgive the boilerplate format of this correspondence. I much prefer to speak my own mind, but rules are rules.

You are hereby notified of our colonization of your planet *(insert name of planet here)*: "Earth." We shall begin colonization on *(insert invasion date here)*: Universal Timedate 95332-ib4; Local "Earth" Timedate July 21, let's say 3pm-ish.

Your immediate surrender is requested. Note that it is not required. We will be colonizing your planet regardless of your response. However, we have found that surrender and cooperation has led to the smoothest transitions of the native, dominant species into the subjugated servants and workers we require, so we are extending this offer as a courtesy. In the attached packet you'll find a full prospectus of benefits and terms. We think, under the circumstances, these benefits are quite fair, generous in fact, as the alternative is—forgive the dramatic term—complete annihilation.

Please share this information with your fellow *(insert titles of other arbitrarily-drawn geographic area leaders here)* "Presidents," "Prime Ministers," "Kings," etc., *discreetly* (we've found that broadcasting to entire populations creates unnecessary panic, requiring more of our subjugation resources than desirable) and respond by July 18 using the "reply" feature of your Earth electronic mail protocol. Thank you. We look forward to your response, and working together on a productive, bloodless transition.

All right, now that that boilerplate portion is satisfied, I hope it's not bad form to include a few personal notes:

As Ondukat (your term might be "Research Analyst") of this colonization, I've been assigned to learn and master the resources, culture, languages, physiology, economics, and history of your planet and its dominant species, you humans. And let me say—what a delight! You are hilarious (though also quite violent), and organized, and productive in your own way.

I am particularly fascinated with what you call "hair styles." We Trewspart (not our species' name, but a rough phonetic approximation for your "English" language) have no hair, so the cutting and shaping and decoration of your heads is endlessly entertaining to me. (And if I might be so bold, your individual "hair style" is unique—I have been reprimanded for keeping a hologram of it floating in my cubicle!)

What is the thing with food? We Trewspart ingest nutrients merely to continue a viable life span, as it should be. There are no ridiculous recipes, spices, hipster bar and grills, endless cooking shows, chocolate sculptures, balsamic reductions, or other various forms of near-religious adulation of food you will only be defecating in a few hours anyway.

I'm not required in the boilerplate to share this, but invadees are usually curious for the reason of our colonization, and I have to say, your Earth makes an excellent slingshot (you don't have a term for this, but something like "transit outpost for high-speed cross-galactic travel" might be close). Do you have any idea how hard it is to find a planet in the right path of transit, with acceptable gravity, and just the right combination of elements, even Koneraw (the element you humans adorably call Gadolinium)? It's like ... I don't know ... it's like finding one planet in a million. (Actually, it's not "like" finding one planet in a million, it is *literally* finding one planet in a million. Forgive me, coming up with imaginative metaphors has never been my strong point.)

There I go, over my character-count limit again. These transmissions are expensive, I'll probably be docked several credits. But I feel a personal touch is critical in transactions like these. Like you don't want your Earth doctor to just blurt out "you've got three weeks to live," you want him (or her, of course) to have what you call "bedside manner" or "compassion." I strive for that. (And look at that! I believe that doctor metaphor was fairly imaginative and competent!)

Looking forward to your response,

Ted

(My personal designation doesn't even have a phonetic English equivalent, so I hope "Ted" will suffice)

From: President Gabriella Lewin
Reply to: "Ted"
Sent: July 15, 12:02 pm

God, Ted. Why do you have to be SUCH an asshole? Pretending to be some kind of douchey "research analyst" who's going to colonize the planet? And of course you'd pick our ex-anniversary for your "invasion." That's low, even for you. And don't think I missed your not-so-subtle-dig at my cooking show addiction. It's a real thing, and it's hard. I'm down to four shows a day, which is NOT easy to juggle when you have THE MOST IMPORTANT JOB IN THE FREE WORLD, not that I need to explain myself to the likes of you.

And how did you get this email address in the first place? It's encrypted a dozen different ways. No, don't tell me. Just because you can sink low enough to make fun of my hair style (which we both know YOUR idiot nephew created and now it's my "trademark" so I'm stuck with it), doesn't mean that I'm going to sink to your level and report you for a security breach. How would that look? *President Lewin's idiot ex-husband arrested for "War of the Worlds" prank.* It would look insane, that's what. God, Ted!! Ugh!

Now I'm forced to reply on my private email server and you know the voters hate that. Maybe that's your plan. Interfering with the next election. I just *got* this job. My desk chair still has someone else's big butt impression on it. You more than anyone know what it cost me to get here. And now you have the nerve to—

No. I'm not raising my blood pressure any more over you. I'm taking deep breaths. In ... out ... in ... out.

Look, I know you're still hurt about how things ended. But it's stupid pranks like this that prove to me I did the right thing. We just weren't on the same wavelength anymore. I need a partner who doesn't still ask people to pull his finger. I'm sorry. Truly. Now stop dicking around and go live your life. Find a hobby. Get a dog or something. I have a frickin' country to run.

I'm hanging up now (metaphorically) but just so I don't sound like a total B, I will say that your "invasion" letter was well-written and creative. Wish you'd shown more of that talent when we were in college together instead of carving boobs into the library desks.

Do not contact me again or I'll be forced to turn you over to the authorities. And I mean the ones who wear all-black and everyone assumes don't really exist because they're *just that good* at making problems go away. You need to invade something? Go "invade" that nice Shayleen from the diner. The one who always gives you extra syrup.

Signed,

President [Insert Middle Finger Emoji here]

Transmission Commence; Translate to Earth protocol TCP-IP using private "electronic mail" address 695484-b94; Universal Timedate 92989-ap3.

Attention "President" Gabriella Lewin of arbitrarily-drawn geographic boundary known as "United States of America:"

I received your reply, and may I say—how utterly delightful! Do you have any idea how much your colorful, passionate correspondence adds to my knowledge of the culture, language, and humor of your species? It warms my hearts (I have two, by the way) to know that you subjugated humans will be highly entertaining (in addition to your utility as laborers). Oh, this colonization is going to be one of my favorites, I can tell already.

I hope it's all right, I do have a number of follow-up questions:

Is the designation of your lifemate (since departed, and for that I sympathize) really "Ted?" Do you have any idea what the chances of my randomly choosing that as my human designation are? I had Analysis Support run the numbers and it's six-hundred-thousand-eight-hundred-nine to one. SIX-HUNDRED-THOUSAND to one. I don't know about you, but that made my dermis tingle a little. We Trewspart don't believe in "fate," or "meaningful coincidences" or even an omnipotent deity (I mean, really), but "Ted?" Come on! I think there is something there, something I can't quite put my finger (I have fifteen on each hand, by the way) on. I will probably receive a harsh reprimand for even suggesting this, but perhaps we should arrange a hologram meeting before the colonization commences? (And in case it's not clear, I mean with yourself and myself alone, not this other "Ted" human. He sounds atrocious. I can have him terminated very discreetly if you wish.)

I sincerely apologize if you misunderstood my hair style reference. It was meant as a compliment. I performed a bit of followup research, and agree, that being forced to maintain what they call the "Lewin Do-In" might be a nerve I shouldn't have touched. I retract my previous comments (although personally, as I've said, I find it unique and—if I might be so bold—inviting).

You mentioned the word "frickin,'" as in "I have a frickin' country to run." I pride myself on learning colony languages, but haven't yet seen the human English word "frickin.'" Can you define that for me? (And if it's not too much trouble, have one of your staff translate it into the five thousand other human languages?)

Same for the "middle-finger-emoji"—when we Trewspart raise our eighth finger, it is to celebrate seeing a friend after an extended period of time. Does it mean the same to you humans?

Finally, it seems from your (delightful) response that you may be questioning the validity of our communication. I've asked if I could provide a small bit of proof (and believe me, getting approval in this bureaucracy is NOT something I wish on even my least-favorite subjugated species), and the Board has miraculously allowed it. So, if possible, please look out the Oval Office window, to the northwest, five degrees from the horizon, at 9:13 pm Eastern Daylight Time tonight. I think you'll be pleased, and clearly convinced.

I look forward to our next communication (and possible hologram meeting?),

Ted

P.S. The Board wanted me to remind you that, although they've given me vast leeway in my communications (their words, not mine, I mean "vast?" not really), that Earth colonization will irregardless begin on Universal Timedate 95332-ib4; Local "Earth" Timedate July 21, let's say 3pm-ish. See you then!

From: President Gabriella Lewin
Reply to: "Ted"
Sent July 16, 8:52 pm

Ted, Ted, Ted. Why couldn't you have been this clever during twenty years of marriage? Why did you constantly quote lines from *The Simpsons* when you had this creativity bubbling inside you? I'm only speaking to you in this non-threatening tone because it's late and I'm tired otherwise I'd really be letting you have it for writing back to me when I VERY CLEARLY told you not to. I've already had to defuse two international incidents today (classified of course, but one had to do with a pop star getting too frisky with a certain dictator, and the other, well, let's just say the West Coast gets to live another day). Then I threw out the first pitch at a local Little League game and threw my back out with it. Had to hobble off like nothing was wrong because people don't like to see their leaders showing weakness. Now I'm on Valium, which is probably also why I'm not threatening to cut off your left you-know-what. And yes, it WAS a turn-off that you only had one. I lied. I'm sorry. But it's true.

Anyway, to top it off, I had to have dinner with my frickin' mother (bet you got the meaning of the word *that* time! I know how you felt about her.) Downed an extra Valium and listened to her tell me why I should get Botox so I don't look so angry all the time. Hey, maybe I should drop my mother off at 2:55 (*ish*) at the site of First Impact. Although you neglected to mention where that would be. Maybe you're not a very good liaison for the—what did you call them—Trewspart or something? What kind of stupid alien race name is that? You can do better, Ted. You were always better at words than me. I know you only wrote "irregardless" to make it seem like it wasn't you.

Hey, I just realized it's almost the time you said to look out the window. I half expect to see you running across the lawn in only your boxers (the ones with the twinkling Christmas lights that were a gag gift from that Library of Congress party a few years back) with half the secret service chasing you. But even *you* couldn't sweet talk your way past the guards. They're very protective after walking in on me last month in the shower. Long story that ended fine for everyone. Maybe that last Valium was one too many. I should go to bed.

Ok, it's 9:13, Ted. Don't see anything outside. Just the lawn dotted with trees, the iron fence and—

Wait, what the actual fu... WHAT?

TED!! WHY IS THERE A GIANT MIDDLE FINGER IN MY BACKYARD?? And is that... MARTHA FRICKIN' STEWART standing next to it???

Huh. She looks amazing for her age. Maybe my mother was right. Ok Ted—or *not* Ted? I'm wide awake now. You've got my attention. I'm clearly losing my frickin' mind so I'm just going to wave at Martha now. *Hi Martha! Big fan! Love your Monte Cristo sandwich with the avo aioli.* She's walking toward me! She's waving back! Um... why does Martha Stewart have *fifteen fingers on her hand*?? Uh, oh, feeling pretty fain...

Transmission Commence; Universal Timedate 92974-ap2; PRIVATE unofficial channel; Unauthorized access strictly prohibited; DO NOT PROCEED with transmission without Board approval.

Dear Gabriella,

I hope it is not too forward to call you that, but after what we have experienced together, addressing you as President Lewin feels odd. There are so many things to say, and beyond them all, a feeling of confusion, that none of it will make sense. I have never had this feeling before. Last night, with you, it was... like a dream.

Oh my. I apologize. That comment was waaaay outside protocol! I clearly have been studying your species for too long. But perhaps if I recount the events of last night, you will understand. (I'm afraid in your state of pharmacological sedation you may not have remembered much.)

At precisely 9:13pm, my hologram, along with the "giant middle finger," (which, I assure you again, was meant as a friendly greeting) stood just outside the Oval Office. Your look of confusion was priceless! You approached the window and waggled your fingers at me (wobbling slightly, it was kind of adorable).

Feeling a bit bolder, I approached the window, and lifted my own fifteen fingered hands in return, and unfortunately, that's when you fell, hitting your head quite forcefully on the floor. (It was covered in a rug of some kind, but clearly not thick enough to blunt your injury.)

What to do? What to do? I thought you might be having some kind of seizure or something. I mean, what would the Board do if they found out I killed the human Earth colonization contact person? What would *I* do? I couldn't live with myself. Here, I had begun to develop a rapport with perhaps my favorite colony candidate ever, and admittedly had pushed the boundaries of allowable conduct to commune with her, only to wind up KILLING her?

There was only one thing to do. I needed to save you. I needed to break Rule 5433-km65:

First contact must be at a minimum distance of fifty million artac units.

Still just a hologram, I ran through the wall of the Oval Office and knelt by your side. And then, in a moment I will surely be punished severely for later upon my return, I materialized, in my true form. I raised your head into my lap—getting sticky red blood (fascinating though also disgusting) on twelve of my fingers. I gently tapped your cheek. "President Lewin?"

You stirred—*thank one of your deities!*—and slowly opened your eyes. And then in one swift motion looked at my face, my actual, Trewspart face, reached up, and slapped me—hard—and passed out once more.

Hmmm, I thought. *Perhaps a sign of human affection I had missed in my research?*

I healed your head wound (yes, I can do that) and you eventually regained consciousness only to immediately spring to your feet and reel backwards. "Wha—wha— what the FUCK?! Who are... who?..."

"I'm Ted."

"You're not Ted."

"No. The other Ted."

"Wh—wh— why did you look like Martha Stewart before? Outside?"

"I was going for Gordon Ramsey, but I must've missed a setting. Sorry about that."

You leapt for one of the doors, I imagined to summon help, looking prepared to scream.

"*Please,* President Lewin. *Please don't.* Give me a moment. Just a moment."

You placed your hands on your hips in a gesture that I imagine was meant to look threatening but was actually quite endearing. "What, to eat my face off? Look at you! Of course you want to eat my face off!" And you turned once again to flee.

"*Please*... I frickin' implore you."

Now you stopped, hand on the doorknob, and actually laughed. "You still don't know what 'frickin' means, do you?" And when you turned back once more, and saw my sincerity, and realized my urgency, you paused. "Huh. You're not supposed to be here, are you?"

I shook my head. "You appeared to be in dire need. Near death. I couldn't stand there, in hologram form, and do nothing."

"So this isn't supposed to happen. You physically being here.

Alone with me."

I shook my head again. "This is *very much never* supposed to happen. I will likely be executed upon my return. But… I had to save you."

You rolled your eyes. "Oh, God. Another romantic. Just like Ted. The other Ted." Then you pointed at me (not with your middle finger, curiously). "Okay. One minute. So, this colonization thing. It's not bullshit?"

"It is not bullshit, if I understand the term correctly."

"Holy Christ." And after a pause, "Then why the niceties? What are you doing here? What's the point?"

"I… I…"

"You're out of your depth on this, aren't you?"

"I'm afraid so. I have no idea what I'm doing. You've just been so…"

"Okay, stop. I get it. It happens."

"What happens?"

"You didn't expect to, but you're attracted to me."

"Um, no. We male Trewspart bond with females based on calculations of optimal genetic diversity in offspring. There is no 'attraction.' It simply doesn't happen. We don't even have a word for it in our language."

"And yet…"

I nodded. "And yet *here I am.* Oh my. What is wrong with me?"

"Listen, Ted." You reached out your hand and placed it on mine. I felt that tingle on my dermis again. "Ted, you seem like a nice gu—Trewsp— whatever. I don't think there's anything wrong with you. In fact, I think some female Trewsp— whatever will be lucky to have you as a mate."

"I'm not sure wha—"

You put your finger on my lips (which I admit, I have replayed over in my head a few times since then. Okay, nine thousand and three times) and said, "Shh. Let's just agree we can only ever be friends."

I nodded, averting my gaze, but my eyes kept returning to your hair. Your hair.

You pretended not to notice. "Now, let's discuss finding another planet to be your ... what did you call it ... boomerang? Slingshot?"

And that's when the unfortunate thing happened. The outer layer of my dermis peeled off and revealed the sixty-three organs in my body. How embarrassing. Trewsparts molt a few times each revolution, totally normal, nothing to be ashamed of. But the timing was unfortunate, certainly. I wish I'd had a chance to tell you that your hairstyle is even more fetching in person before your eyes rolled back and you fell, once more, to the floor, reopening your wound. You really should get a thicker rug. I carried you gently to your couch, to allow you to heal and recover. I have returned to my ship, which obviously I never should have left. But I admit, the touch of your finger still lingers upon my lips. As I said at the start of this transmission—all is confusing.

If you would like to finish our conversation, I have left a private, unauthorized audio communication device in your top drawer next to your half-eaten Snickers bar. I fear I can no longer use formal channels for communication, as I am in extremely deep—how would you say it? Oh yes, "shit." I eagerly await your next correspondence.

Gabriella:
Ted! Your high-tech alien communication device is an old Palm Pilot?

Ted:
Gabriella! You called! And no, it only *looks* like a historical Palm Pilot. Coincidence. It's actually a highly classified nano-engineered molecular communicator.

Gabriella:
Yeah, I'm pretty sure it's a Palm Pilot.

Ted:
We'll have to agree to disagree. It is good to hear your voice, though. I didn't know if you'd reach out after, well, after ...

Gabriella:
After I saw your insides? Yeah, dude. That was some messed up shit right there.

Ted:
Oh, how I do enjoy your colorful speech! You'll be pleased to know my dermis has fully regenerated. Although I'm what you'd label *purple* now.

Gabriella:
Weird. But to the point, what are we going to do about this impending invasion of yours? I have a few billion fellow humans who would really appreciate it if you could call it off.

Ted:
Ah, if only. But as you probably know from your own bureaucracies, once these things are on the books, well... I mean the paperwork alone... Wait. Hold on. *Paperwork!*

Gabriella:
You say "paperwork" like it's a good thing.

Ted:
Gabriella, although I've been demoted—and by demoted I mean I'll be living in something akin to what you'd call a "dungeon" for the next several revolutions—they haven't rescinded my access yet to the scheduling and logistics plans for Earth. I could introduce a small "clerical error" into the paperwork... it could delay the colonization a little, perhaps for four—

Gabriella:
What, four days until they figure it out? Not that helpful.

Ted:
I was going to say fourteen thousand of your Earth years.

Ted:
Gabriella? Are you still there?

Gabriella:
Fourteen thousand... years? Did you say?

Ted:
Is that not sufficient?

Gabriella:
Um... yes. Yes, I can live with that. Thank you, Ted. Thank you. One more thing though...

Ted:
Yes, Gabriella?

Gabriella:
You ate the rest of my Snickers bar. I was saving that.

Ted:
I am sincerely sorry. It was delicious though. And possibly worth the upcoming six-hour irrigation of my bowel system.

Gabriella:
I'm just busting you. It's all good. Thanks for the, uh, *extension* on the invasion. You're a peach.

Ted:
It has been my absolute pleasure to make your acquaintance and almost colonize your world. You are a peach as well, although I have no idea what that means.

Gabriella:
It means you're frickin' great.

Ted:
Awww. My new favorite word. Goodbye, Gabriella. Your

communication device will now cease functioning and will disintegrate. I look forward to crossing paths with you again in fourteen thousand Earth years.

Gabriella:
Um... you're aware of human lifespans, right?

Ted:
Perhaps if you abstained from Snickers bars and Valium you might make it.

Gabriella:
Ted, you're hilarious.

Ted:
Goodbye, my friend. Insert middle finger emoji here.

Gabriella:
Insert middle finger emoji here.

Wendy Mass and Rob Dircks

Wendy Mass is the *New York Times* bestselling author of The Candymakers series and twenty-nine other novels for young readers. They include *A Mango-Shaped Space, Jeremy Fink and the Meaning of Life* (which was made into a feature film), *Pi in the Sky* and the Willow Falls series. Her latest is *Bob,* which she wrote while building a labyrinth in her backyard. (Not at the same time. That'd be really hard.) Visit her at wendymass.com.

Rob Dircks is the #1 Audible bestselling author of *You're Going to Mars!,* the Where the Hell is Tesla? trilogy, *The Wrong Unit,* and more. Some of Rob's original sci-fi short stories appear on his audio short story podcast *Listen To The Signal,* also narrated by the author. He lives in New York with his wife and two kids. You can get in touch at robdircks.com.

C.A.T. SQUAD

GINI KOCH

"Faster! Run faster, you damned rodent-lovers!" Daniel Tiger shouted at me and the rest of our squad. It's not every day you see a two-foot-tall, mostly cybertronic brown-and-ginger striped cat with one blue and one yellow eye bellow at you. Well, for most people. For me it was a regular occurrence.

"David, by all that's feline, you have one job in this lousy situation, and it's to keep them moving!"

"You're in a mood," I muttered to myself as he turned back around, tail lashing like crazy, and I did my best to herd the rest of the C.A.T. Squad out of this planet's version of a palace—an impressively large mud and straw structure—and onto our ship so we could make our getaway. Herding a dozen cybertronic cats was just as much fun as it sounds, particularly when plans went wrong, like they were going right now.

Of course, I couldn't blame Daniel Tiger for shouting. The only reason we weren't dead already was because the people shooting at us were terrible shots. "Stormtrooper trained" is what my great-grandfather would have called them. My family line loved people who couldn't shoot well, because it kept our line alive so much longer.

"Mittens, Smokey, Sugarfoot—step on it!" I shouted as I grabbed Fluffy and Boots by their harnesses so I could run ahead and toss them inside the *Felinious Max*. The ship was mine, passed down to me as the last in the Wilson line, but Daniel Tiger viewed it as his domain. I didn't argue—he was a much better pilot than I was.

I had to run back and grab Sheba and Calico Joe, but the rest of the squad managed to get inside without getting their tails shot off. No C.A.T. Left Behind was our motto, because, as Daniel Tiger loved to say, good C.A.T.s were hard to find.

I tossed the two I had inside, leaped in after them, and hit the button for the gangplank to raise. While it did—not as quickly as I'd have liked—I fired back at our pursuers.

I didn't actually want to kill any of them. The squad felt the best enemy was a dead enemy, but I was dead set against killing anyone we didn't have to. Because it was my ship and I was the only human, and because of my bond with Daniel Tiger, the rest of the squad curbed their natural instincts in this way. Most of the time.

The "all secure" claxon went off as the gangplank sealed, and I ran for the cockpit. Our ship wasn't very large—it had been designed to house a crew of about two dozen, which had always been plenty for my family—but it was fast and it blasted off even faster.

We were airborne and in the planet's atmosphere within seconds. I strapped into the co-pilot's seat while Boomer and Luna did the calculations necessary for a warp jump as soon as we were clear of the planet.

"Everyone strap in," I shared over the com, just in case one of them had stopped for a groom or to play with the loot. You'd think after all this time they'd have unlearned those instincts, but you'd have been so very wrong.

I heard some disappointed hissing. "I mean it, Fuzzy. Strap the hell in, we're about to warp jump." I thought about it. "Felix, use the litter box later, man. You remember the last time." Heard someone grumbling, meaning Felix did indeed remember that time and was strapping himself in and holding it.

"And away we go," Daniel Tiger said cheerfully, as we reached escape velocity, left the planet's atmosphere, and he hit the warp button.

WE CAME OUT of warp into empty space, and Daniel Tiger heaved a sigh. "Well, that was a disaster."

"Like so many things we do. I still don't understand why you felt raiding a planet with nothing but shiny crap that's not worth anything on the open market was a great plan."

"The others needed new toys," Daniel Tiger said, as if this explained everything, and made the risk worthwhile.

"We need better plans."

He shrugged. "Those aren't your specialty. You need to—"

"I know, I know. I need to find a nice girl who has strategic plans and low morals, marry her, and make more Wilsons. Maybe if we went to planets with humans on them I'd have more of a shot."

My great-grandparents had stolen this ship with the help of the C.A.T. Squad and never looked back. They all became raiders, happily looting from planets and vessels alike, managing to avoid capture most of the time. The few times they'd been captured, they'd always escaped, because cats are natural escape artists, and the C.A.T.s were better at it by a thousand-fold. Daniel Tiger wanted me to be more like them. Exactly like them, honestly.

Daniel Tiger looked over at me, unblinking. "That's your excuse? What about the last few years, when we were on plenty of planets with humans or humanoids that can mate with humans? What were your reasons then?"

I rarely if ever could win in a stare down with any of the squad, let alone Daniel Tiger. Instead, it was my turn to shrug. "We're never anywhere long enough to get to know someone."

"I promised your parents I'd help you find a nice girl and continue the line. Apparently, you aren't in on that promise."

Boomer sniggered from behind me and I heard Luna swat him. I resisted saying something nasty, like they were focused on my mating because they couldn't—because being nasty to the people who loved you most in the universe was a stupid, low thing to do and I refused to be that kind of person. They were my C.A.T.s, I was their human, they wanted another human, then baby humans, because while they might live forever—they were over 120 years old and looked the same as they had when they were, as my grandfather had liked to say, factory fresh—I wasn't going to. They functioned well as a group, but Daniel Tiger had realized before my grandfather was born that they needed a human to ensure they remained a functional group.

"Maybe we should go to Earth or Earth Two," Luna suggested.

"The better options are probably on Earth Four," Boomer said. "And we're closer to it than the others."

"Earth Five is closer," Daniel Tiger pointed out.

Boomer and Luna both hissed. "I hate that place," Boomer said.

"Me, too." Earth Five was a mostly swamp planet where terraforming hadn't worked well. The people there were hard, desperate, and mean. Not where I wanted to find my lifemate.

I was about to suggest we go to Earth Four, if only because it would shut Daniel Tiger up, when our alarms went off. "Report," Daniel Tiger said over the com.

"Something's damaged in the propulsion system, Chief," Mittens, who was one of the two ship's engineers, said. She sounded stressed.

"I think those people actually got in a shot that hit," Fluffy, the other engineer, added. She sounded equally stressed. "And one that's going to hurt us in the long run."

"How were we able to go to warp if our propulsion system was damaged?" I asked.

"Luck," Mittens said. "They literally hit us only once, and the part they hit was holding on until we came out of warp, but it's disintegrated now. We can't go to warp again, not until we've done repairs."

"So do them," Daniel Tiger said.

"We can't, Chief," Fluffy replied. "We need to be on a planet in order to do what has to be done safely."

"Unless you want to go out in a blaze of glory right now," Mittens added.

"I'm going to speak for everyone and say we don't want to do that," I said quickly. "Do we have enough money to cover the repairs, do you think?"

"We don't actually need to buy anything," Mittens said. "We just need to be not flying in any way, and because this requires us to be outside of the ship, while we *can* do it while in space, we'd prefer not to take the risk, especially because the work needed is quite delicate."

"Everyone's a whiner," Daniel Tiger muttered under his breath.

"Can I actually fly us toward something or are we just supposed to float around and hope we hit a planet before David's an old man?"

"Pick the closest planet and head there," Fluffy said. "Slowly. As long as we're aimed correctly, even if our propulsion conks out completely, we'll get there."

"Eventually," Mittens added.

Daniel Tiger shook his head. "Despite the complaints I know will be coming from the cockpit crew, Earth Five, here we come."

THE HOURS THE journey took were tense, and I thought Daniel Tiger was going to murder one of the squad at any given moment because there were a lot of cat fights, both figurative and literal, during the time it took us to get to Earth Five.

I, on the other hand, spent my time pulling up all current information I could find about the planet. Sadly, nothing much had changed since the last time we'd been there, when I'd been a teenager. If anything, it was probably worse.

I had to share the information, even though I didn't particularly want to. "The Chulsky Corporation is still the main employer on the planet."

Daniel Tiger hissed but didn't say anything.

The Chulsky Corporation—the leading purveyor of artificial intelligence back in the mid-twenty-first century—had created the Cybertronic Autonomous Thief as an advancement in military spy craft. The C.A.T.s were regular felines who were merged with cybernetics and nanotech to become super-intelligent cyborgs that had a cat's ability to assess, adapt, steal, murder, and avoid.

The first prototype was always named after the founder, which was why Daniel's official last name was Chulsky. But he hated it, because he hated what had been done to him and the other cats. No, he'd fixated on some twentieth-century children's programming and had insisted he was the noble Daniel Tiger of hand puppet and animated fame. I'd known him my entire life and had stopped trying to figure out the fascination years ago.

However, the other C.A.T.s called him Chief—only humans

considered "worthy" got to call him Daniel Tiger, meaning I was the only one allowed the honor these days.

What the Chulsky Corporation hadn't planned for was that, by keeping the cat brain merged with the cyborg, they'd created super cats—and cats worked for and belonged to no one.

"Daniel Chulsky the Fifth is the CEO," Luna said. Nice to know I wasn't the only one doing research. "It's interesting they headquartered on Earth Five instead of staying on Earth."

"Taxation is far better on Earth Five," Boomer replied. So, the cockpit crew were all doing more than freaking out. Good. "Plus the laws are more relaxed. They'd never get away with trying to make more of us on Earth. But on Earth Five ..."

"We'll handle it," I said, as calmly as I could.

"We'll stop them, you mean." Daniel Tiger snarled. Many hisses of agreement echoed through the ship. He started muttering about homicidal maniacs and their desire to take over the natural world—one of his favorite rants—and he was going for it in full. It was a long rant, but apparently we had the time.

The C.A.T.s had become completely sentient and self-aware by the time they'd learned how to move their human-like arms, legs, hands, and feet. That the Chulsky Corporation had chosen to give them claws on their fingers and toes—then encased those limbs, hands, feet, and claws in stainless steel—was determined far too late to be a mistake. Daniel Tiger led a revolt, stole all the plans, notes, backups, and prototypes, and ran off to lead his pride to glory.

Instead, they'd run into my great-grandmother.

She was a self-professed Crazy Cat Lady, and when she and Daniel Tiger met it was, as she liked to say, kismet. She was the one who'd named all the rest of the squad because she'd adopted all twelve of them in a heartbeat. Which worked out, because she met my great-grandfather a little while later and he saw the possibilities of having a squad of cybertronic cats working with him. And he'd thought my great-grandmother was the hottest thing on two legs, a fact Daniel Tiger loved to tell me about whenever he wanted to suggest, gently or not, that I needed to find someone to settle down with, so to speak.

I didn't have the same ill feelings towards the Chulsky Corporation as the C.A.T.s did. What was done to them had been horrible, but my entire family line would have been different, or not even existed, without them.

My expression must have said it, though, because Daniel Tiger looked at me and stopped ranting. "Unbelievable."

"What?" I tried not to sound guilty and probably failed.

"You're grateful to them." The hissing stopped, so I knew all the others were listening on the com.

"I am. Because without them, I wouldn't have all of you. And I can't imagine life without all of you."

The hissing and silence were replaced with something else—purring. Lots and lots of purring. Even from Daniel Tiger. He reached out and patted my knee. "We can't imagine life without you, either, David. So let's get to Earth Five and get our ship fixed so we can all continue living."

DESPITE CHULSKY CORPORATION essentially owning this planet, we were allowed to land without issue, because Earth Five had no restrictions. *Please Come Here, Please* was the planetary motto, even if no one in power admitted it.

We had no plans to leave the docking bay. Mittens and Fluffy conscripted most of the crew to help them fix the ship. That left me, Daniel Tiger, Felix, and Calico Joe with nothing to do. Daniel Tiger assigned the others to guard duty, then jerked his head at me. "Let's see how bad it is out there."

Unusually, we sailed through Customs—five people sitting behind a long wooden table looking bored. "Anything to declare?" the man we walked up to asked. We were the only people here. "And please don't say 'this place is a dump' because we've heard it. Millions of times."

"Nothing to declare," I said. "And I'm sure there're nice things on Earth Five."

The man stared at me and snorted a laugh. "We got an optimist, folks," he shouted to the other customs agents, who all tittered.

"Go on and 'enjoy' yourselves. See you when you come back a pessimist, son."

I gave them all a pleasant smile and dragged Daniel Tiger with me, before he got into it with any of them.

"You just live to be a nice person, don't you?" Daniel Tiger asked me, once we were far enough away from Customs.

"There are worse things to be."

"Yeah, like from this planet," he replied, as we stepped outside the spaceport to see that Earth Five looked like every holovid I'd ever seen about a post-apocalyptic world.

There was mud everywhere, the buildings were low and dingy, and some were falling apart. The people were dirty and looked beyond downtrodden. The beasts of burden looked the same. The color scheme was dull browns and grays with sickly greens added in for flair. "My God, what a dump," Daniel Tiger said.

I looked around. "I spot something that looks decent on the horizon."

Daniel Tiger nodded. "That'll be Chulsky Corporation Headquarters." He looked at me expectantly.

I nodded. "Time to do a raid and see what Daniel the Fifth is up to."

WE REACHED THE Chulsky Corporation in about a half an hour at a full trot, ignored by the few natives we passed. Neither one of us was tired. The C.A.T.s almost never felt fatigue and I'd spent my whole life working out and ensuring I had endurance as well as speed and strength.

The building and its version of a parking area were surrounded by myriad trees and bushes that had seen better days but were still somehow in full leaf, which was good for us, because they gave us cover.

We avoided the main entrance and trotted around the perimeter, staying within the foliage. Even though the parking was full, no people were in evidence. "I don't see any surveillance," I said, as we completed our initial recon and went to the back of the building where there was a small area for garbage collection and a door, presumably for the janitorial staff. The only other way in or out appeared to be the main entrance.

"Doesn't mean there isn't any," Daniel Tiger replied. "It's smaller than I'd have expected, but I imagine it goes underground quite a number of stories." The building was twelve stories high, making it a skyscraper on this planet, but I knew he was comparing it to the original Chulsky complex where the C.A.T.s had been created.

"I've got a really bad feeling about this."

"No whining. Get the door open so we can go in through the trash chute, so to speak."

Despite myriad misgivings, I did as I was told. While Daniel Tiger could just rip the door off its hinges or pick the locks, depending on his mood and our goals, I could pick locks as well and I blended better.

Prepared to do the "I'm a dumb, lost tourist" routine should I run into anyone, I reached the door and tried the handle. It opened without issue.

I did a fast check. This was definitely where janitorial was housed and no one was around. I motioned to Daniel Tiger and he joined me swiftly. "Let's find the mainframes," he said.

This place clearly had a large janitorial staff, because there were lockers, carts, and supplies in abundance. I found a maintenance jumpsuit in my size, and grabbed a spare janitorial cart that had two large shelves. Daniel Tiger got onto the top shelf, I blocked him from view with supplies, and we headed off.

The directory schematic said that the mainframe level was the eleventh floor. I found the maintenance elevators, and up we went.

The temptation to go raid the twelfth floor executive level was strong, but discretion, as my mother used to say, was the better part of staying alive, so I ignored it. Besides, worry had precedence because we reached the mainframe level without running into anyone. "Is this too easy?" I asked softly, without moving my lips.

"Maybe," Daniel Tiger replied, as we left the elevator. "We'll find out."

We were in a gigantic room with no doors, but more mainframes than I'd ever seen in my life. And we finally hit a snag—it had a laser light show going on that would have been fun to watch from a safer distance, like from space.

The nervous feeling that started in the elevator went to worried with a strong chance of panic. "This is way too easy."

Daniel Tiger got out of the cart, pulled a monocle lens out of a harness pocket, and put it over his blue eye. His yellow eye narrowed. "Well, you can stop worrying about that. These lasers will slice us up if they hit us."

"On the positive side, they're stationary."

"They are. I'll take the right half, you take the left half, let's find the off button."

In addition to the other exercises I'd done all my life, I'd been drilled in how to contort my way around and through obstacles like this one. I'd also been told by my parents, more than once, that if I had the time I should let the C.A.T.s do this work, because they did it better and faster than any human ever could hope to.

Sure enough, as I watched Daniel Tiger leap and duck, slide and saunter, the only risk he had was to his tail. "Tuck it!" I shouted, just in time.

"Move it, lazybones."

I sighed, but did as instructed. Happily, I only had to jump, duck, roll, and contort in a few bizarre positions before the lasers turned off.

This all still felt too easy, so I trotted through the entire floor, looking for where the ambush was coming from.

I made a full circuit and was back in front of the elevators when the doors opened and the ambush arrived.

A WOMAN WHO looked a year or so younger than me stepped out, carrying a sleek compupad. She was dressed in a long white sari that wrapped tightly around her, showing off a lovely figure, and white high heels that made her just about my height. She had reddish-blonde hair piled up on her head and big blue eyes. She was the most beautiful woman I'd ever seen.

She was probably also the richest, because someone wearing spotless white on Earth Five was someone who never went out on the streets, ever.

She smiled. "Hello, I'm Danielle Chulsky. And you're David Wilson the Fourth, right? Of the Wilson clan who stole our Cybertronic Autonomous Thief program when Daniel Chulsky the First was still alive?"

I really wished we'd just stayed with the ship as I stared at Danielle and tried to come up with a believable response.

She laughed, tapped on her compupad, and showed it to me. Images of my entire family were there—including a picture of me at age fifteen, when we'd been on this planet last, next to an "aged progression" shot that looked pretty accurate—as well as all the C.A.T.s and the words: Project Reclamation.

I was a fast reader and I read what Project Reclamation was all about. My stomach sank. They wanted the C.A.T.s back, full stop, and had for as long as my family had had them. And we'd literally just handed ourselves to them. They could use me as a hostage to get the C.A.T.s to come save me, then do horrible things to us.

I was ready to turn and run but she took hold of my arm. "Stop panicking."

"What's going on?"

She heaved a sigh. "Are the C.A.T.s with you?"

"I will never tell you."

She rolled her eyes. "God help me. Look, I'm not trying to capture you. I'm trying to help you."

"Sure you are. Because you just showed me Project Reclamation and that says to give me a parade."

"You got in easily because I had you flagged coming into the spaceport and *ensured* you could get in without issue. No one else knows you're here. Do the C.A.T.s find you stupid or endearing?"

"Probably both. What's this about?"

She heaved a sigh of exasperation. "Daniel Chulsky the First created Project Reclamation, and the Second and Third were really dedicated to it—with zero results. My twin brother is the Fifth.

He couldn't care less about Project Reclamation. He's focused on other things and feels the C.A.T.s are outdated tech and proof that using living subjects was a cruel, terrible mistake. I agree with him about the cruelty. He hasn't studied the C.A.T.s like I have, but if I bring you to him, he'll have no choice but to arrest you and reclaim them."

Just as I'd feared. "And we're chatting ... why?"

"Seriously, how have the C.A.T.s not eaten you by now? I'm trying to help you."

"Why? Why in the world would you, the twin sister of the most powerful man in the galaxy, want to help me?"

"Most powerful man in the galaxy? Who have you been talking to?" She blinked. "Oh. The C.A.T.s. Sure, to them 'Daniel Chulsky' is probably a looming figure of terror. But he's been dead for a hundred years. We're a successful corporation, but we had to move our entire operation to this hellhole to avoid our father going to prison for some failed military tech. By now, most of our best products have been duplicated better and cheaper by competitors all over the galaxy. Daniel has no more power than you do, in that sense. You probably have more because you're free and you have the C.A.T.s."

"You seem to know a hell of a lot about us."

She waved the compupad at me. "I've spent most of my life learning about you and your family."

"Why?" I asked flatly.

"Because you were the first family to best mine. The C.A.T.s are loyal to your family even though they vowed to never belong to any human. That means your family is special and always has been. Supposedly, I could be with anyone in the universe, except they only want me for my brother's money and my last name. I want off this rock and out of the trap of being a Chulsky forever."

"Why via me and the C.A.T.s versus any other means?"

She blushed and looked at the 'pad. "Just because."

The elevator doors opened and Daniel Tiger exited, dragging a large traveling trunk with him. "If you want to hurt David, I'll hurt you," Daniel Tiger said pleasantly. "But I don't think that's what you want, is it?" He hopped up onto the trunk.

She stared at him. "You're the first, the prototype, the one named for the first Daniel, aren't you?"

"I am." He looked at me. "I've done a full search while you were running around doing nothing but getting your cardio in. No one's alerted to our presence, other than her, because she controls security and she turned it all off." Daniel Tiger turned back to Danielle. "What kind of parent names twins Daniel and Danielle in this day and age? Oh, wait, I'll answer that—megalomaniacs."

She shrugged. "The creativity is running low in our bloodline, honestly. My brother is a good businessman, but a creative genius he's not. I expect Chulsky Corporation to fade out within the next generation."

"Sorry. I'm still lost as to what's going on." My entire family had always said there were no dumb questions. Daniel Tiger rarely agreed with them on this point but, under the circumstances, I was willing to risk his disdain.

Daniel Tiger heaved a sigh. "He's a sweet boy, and much smarter than he seems to you right now, I'm sure. He's not clear on how a crush works. I am, however, and I can tell you his bloodline is running thin, too. We need an influx of strategic scheming pronto, or we, too, will have nothing by the next generation. If we get one," he added to me, rather too nastily.

"It's not my fault we haven't met anyone who's—" I stopped talking as I saw Danielle's blush turn a deeper red and the word "crush" finally registered. "Oh. Um. Really?"

"You're a good-looking man, and you were an attractive teenager, and that's relatively rare," Daniel Tiger said. "She's wants off this mudhole. Wouldn't you?"

"Yes." I cleared my throat. "Ah, I think you're the most beautiful woman I've ever seen in my life."

"Really?" Danielle sounded and looked shocked.

"Aren't there mirrors on this planet? Yes. Who wouldn't think you were gorgeous?"

She gave an embarrassed shrug. "I don't meet a lot of... nice men."

Daniel Tiger groaned. "This could take forever. Look, trust me, you two are giving off the right pheromones. Danielle, is everything you need to leave this rock forever in this trunk?"

"Yes."

"She had it in her office, David, in case you're not clear that she's been waiting for you for half of her life."

"Well," Danielle said, "all of you, really. I know how effective the C.A.T.s are. I don't want to leave and live a worse life. I want to live a free life."

"Got it. Finally. You're actually okay with this?" I asked Daniel Tiger.

"Yes, because, unlike you, apparently, I listened to what she said. I've already downloaded everything they have and yes, I wiped all their information about us, including all information about Project Reclamation. She's right—the real genius is gone." He eyed Danielle. "Except for her, that is."

"You're a flatterer, I like that," Danielle cooed at him. "I love cats."

"Because you're intelligent."

"How do we get out of here, though?" I asked, before the two of them could continue.

"I call for a transport to take us to the spaceport," Danielle replied dryly. "We get onto your ship, and we take off."

"Just like that?" I asked. "I mean, it's usually harder, and won't your brother think you're being kidnapped or something?"

"Maybe he will." She grinned. "Who cares? It'll keep things interesting if we ever get bored. Or need money."

GETTING TO THE ship went as smoothly as Danielle had said it would. No one asked why Danielle was with us—nobody cared.

But just in case her brother did, Danielle made sure to tell the people who were "guarding" the entrance to the docking bays that she was headed to Earth for a vacation. Reactions were bored envy mixed with disinterest.

The ship was repaired and ready by the time we got there, and Daniel Tiger had us take off immediately. We reached escape velocity, went to warp, and came out near Danielle's suggested destination—Proximus Five, a rich planetary system with no extradition to any other systems.

Now that we were safe, Daniel Tiger introduced Danielle and explained the situation to the rest of the squad. She cooed over each and every one of them.

"You know who you remind me of?" he asked her suddenly.

Danielle shook her head. I had no guess, either.

"David's great-grandmother. You may call me Daniel Tiger."

The purring continued for a long time.

Gini Koch

Gini Koch writes the fast, fresh, and funny Alien/Katherine "Kitty" Katt series for DAW Books, the Necropolis Enforcement Files, and the Martian Alliance Chronicles. She also has a humor collection, *Random Musings from the Funny Girl.* As G.J. Koch she writes the Alexander Outland series and she's made the most of multiple personality disorder by writing novels, novellas, novelettes, and short stories in all the genres out there and under a variety of other pen names as well, including Anita Ensal, Jemma Chase, A.E. Stanton, and J.C. Koch, all with stories featured in excellent anthologies, available now and upcoming. www.ginikoch.com.

AMBROSE STARKISSER ENCOUNTERS THAT WHICH IS LOCKED

JORDAN CHASE-YOUNG

So what if the cyclopean natives of Mithrandi said the Vault of the Worldlorn couldn't be opened, no matter how many eons worth of lockpicks and archeologists and demolition experts had tried? Ambrose Starkisser XVI could open anything. And anyway, he didn't have a choice: Ophelia had broken up with him, for real this time, and the interdimensional portal the ancient mages had sealed in the Vault offered him the only path to an Ophelia who hadn't.

From his Manhattan-sized starship, Ambrose descended in a shuttle to try the obvious stuff first: plasma cannons, standard-issue from the First Sol Wars; hypervelocity battering rams from the glacier-smashing crews on Europa; gigantic drills from the adamantium mines of the Momeraths; that sort of thing. But after a morning full of blasting and booming, none of his instruments broke through.

Everything gives in sooner or later, he thought, as red dust settled around the crude stone vault, no taller than a Terran chapel. *Everything.*

FOR HIS NEXT trick, he hung a deathmurder nautilus from his shuttle in a gigantic harness, and he tickled her tentacles with a flabellum, very gently, until she sneezed ten kiloliters of hyperlytic acid at the Vault's arched door.

The acid hissed into a green, foul-smelling cumulonimbus that reached into the sky, and a bird flying too fast to swerve became a handful of tumbling black jackstraws. But the stone held.

That was okay, though. That was okay. He had a lot more up his sleeve: relativistic rhinos from New Addis Ababa; kamikaze asteroid magpies; a baby world-serpent from Yggdrasville, her constrictions tight enough to crush a tepui like fudge; even a sentient fungus that had invaded every crevice on the planet he'd scooped it from.

By dusk, the stone was practically humming with molecular stress, with atomic agony, but not a crack on its surface could be found.

Grumbling, Ambrose stormed back to his shuttle for a drink.

Plenty more where that came from, he told himself while replaying his virtuo of Ophelia for the twelfth time that evening.

BY NOW, A crowd of natives had gathered on a distant hill, bristling with telescopes. An eminently vaporizable bunch, if you asked Ambrose.

IT WAS TIME to get serious.

Ambrose emptied his vast inventory with increasing speed.

He unleashed the pack of vulpine lockpicks from Beloaz that his uncle had given him last Solmas. They came back with a shrug.

He asked his Sirian sphinx, the only one of its kind and capable of persuading any intelligence, to persuade whatever mind the Vault held. The Vault rebuffed her with silence.

He asked Aurora, an alien pet that resembled her namesake, to phase through the Vault's seal. But her rainbowy ether turned red with shame when the stone blocked her way.

The Vault of the Worldlorn stood dauntless.

The crowd on the far hills had grown.

Ambrose was no closer to Ophelia.

Ophelia, no closer to Ambrose.

Unplugging an IV of calming medication, Ambrose walked out of his shuttle in a skintight antiradiation suit.

He knocked on the Vault.

"Open Sesame!" he shouted, in every language his ship index knew.

No dice.

"This one's on you," he told the Ophelia who glowed in his locket as the shuttle sped back into his starship.

The natives had probably cheered when he'd left their world, not knowing he was merely repositioning fifteen light-seconds away from it.

He'd planted a beacon on the Vault to make things easier.

"Ready?" he intoned from his well-upholstered control room.

"Ready, sir," replied the ship AI in a professorial baritone.

"Aim," said Ambrose.

"Aiming, sir."

A pulse of incandescence from the ship's cannon. Then a long moment of nothing but starry space.

Ambrose sipped his beer, glancing at the beacon-signal every few seconds.

He flipped up his leg-rests and adjusted his head.

Mithrandi's faint blue face grew an orange-yellow freckle. Then Mithrandi wasn't Mithrandi anymore, but a big white eye, its corners tapering from horizon to horizon, its pupil cataracted with slowly expanding traceries of dust and rock.

The beacon didn't fail him.

He tracked the beeping on his monitor to the lightning storm of some vaporized continent, all glitzed out with the smoldering scintillae of cities.

Ambrose spat out his beer: the Vault of the Worldlorn was still intact.

It was also much bigger than he'd thought; the ground had hidden most of it. What he'd taken for the Vault was really just one of two spurs jutting off the lid of a great stone cylinder. The arched door, meanwhile, was just an alcove for fastening something; there were three of these: two on the spurs and one in the center of the base.

Steering his ship around a hurtling husk of mountainside, Ambrose clamped the manipulators of his craft into all three alcoves of the cylinder, then turned the spurs like a tumbler. The lid popped off to reveal an opening.

AT LAST!

He reeled the cylinder into his cavernous hangar, smashing aside a slew of antique spitfyres, and barely remembered to put on his antiradiation suit before racing to his catch. He crawled through the opening of the Vault to find a shimmering rift on the other side.

As he touched it, he imagined what he wanted, just as the myths had told him to, and felt the not-unpleasant pop of being yanked out of one universe and put into another.

A SPINDLY LASER turret activated as Ambrose appeared in a copy of his hangar.

The ship AI spoke through the turret's speaker. "Ambrose Starkisser wishes to congratulate you on being the three hundred and seventh Ambrose Starkisser to enter this dimension. He also wishes to note that Ophelia is taken, and hopes you'll understand."

The turret flashed. Ambrose looked down to find a small hole in his chest. It was smoking. He blinked and fell with a thud on the hangar floor.

Jordan Chase-Young

Jordan Chase-Young is an American living in Melbourne, Australia, with his wife and cactus. Born in Oregon, where he spent most of his life, he works as a freelance copywriter and editor for online businesses. During his free time, he likes to draw, cook spicy food, take long walks around the city, and write science fiction and fantasy stories. Lately, he's been reading and thinking a lot about the future of humanity. He is the author of a fantasy novelette, "Shards," recently published in *Metaphorosis*. His blog about futurism and other topics is at ebookofthenewsun.wordpress.com, and his Twitter handle is @jachaseyoung. This is Jordan's first professional sale.

GOMMY

AMY LYNWANDER

Gommy basted the chicken breast and dropped a few more mushrooms into the pan. One rolled under the stove. She bent down, lifted the corner with one hand and swatted the escapee out with the other. She considered dumping it in with the others before throwing it toward the sink. As she watched it fly through the air, the front door slammed open.

Ralphie and another young man walked into the apartment in mid-conversation. She moved with a carrot to the cutting board to listen in.

"Then I busted his head open," Ralphie bragged.

Gommy frowned. If only, but she didn't think he had it in him.

"Like hell," replied his friend. "Did I tell you that Abe put me in charge of the Pinkus job? They ripped off an armored car, you know."

Gommy chopped harder, the knife in a death grip. *The Pinkus job was supposed to have gone to Ralphie,* she thought.

"What's that?" The friend moved toward the kitchen.

"What's what?" Ralphie half shouted, raising his voice so he could be heard above the angry thwacking of the knife.

Gommy wiped her hands on her apron and walked into the living room before they could come into the kitchen. No one came into her kitchen without permission. Ralphie's friend stared at Gommy, taking in her stiff mass of swirling curls, ample bosom, sensible low heeled shoes, and large cleaver.

"Who's this?"

"Young man, I am Ralphie's Gommy, and we remove hats in this household."

"This is Ken," Ralphie said.

Ken slid his baseball cap off his head without taking his eyes off her. "What is a Gommy?"

Gommy just smiled, but Ralphie was treated to a personal *this is your life* flashback.

Ralphie was the most worthless member of a notorious neighborhood gang run by Abe, a man as ugly as he was ruthless. A man who employed both muscle and magic to maintain his territory. He kept Ralphie on out of loyalty for Ralphie's long-dead uncle who served as Abe's right-hand man until he was crushed by a dump truck.

Gommy's voice broke into Ralphie's thoughts. "Won't you stay for dinner? I'm cooking chicken. It's fresh." Ken grunted his affirmation.

Ralphie's job on Abe's last heist, just three weeks ago, was to keep the golem in check. He'd been there when the rabbi brought the creature, that looked like a cross between a football left guard and the clay cliffs of Omarama, to life by inscribing Hebrew letters on its forehead. Naturally, Ralphie failed and the golem rampaged in the bank, throwing security guards against the wall and spraying the high tread carpet with innocents' blood. Abe walked out with the money leaving Ralphie with the monster.

"Take care of it," he said.

Gommy bustled through the dining room, setting the table with heavy stoneware dishes and cheerful yellow cloth napkins.

"I love when Ralphie has his friends over," she burbled.

Ralphie employed all of his knowledge from Bugs Bunny to try to calm the golem down. He played classical music from his phone, and considered asking the golem if it wanted its nails done.

"Take the letter off," whispered one of the hostages from the floor.

Oh right, the biblical solution. He really should have started with the stop-motion Davy and Goliath animated series.

Ralphie pulled his skinny body onto the bank tellers' counter and waved his arms around to get the golem's attention. Then, he prayed to his God who he hoped was not angry, just disappointed, as the monster approached. It took Ralphie everything he had to wait until it was close enough that he could see the letters on its forehead. Once he wiped away the first letter, the word "truth" would spell out "dead" instead, and the golem would turn back to clay.

With his best war cry, which sounded thin, even in his ears, he leapt at the golem, brandishing the teller's stack of deposit slips to obliterate the first letter on the golem's forehead. The golem fell to the ground as the hostage who'd suggested this course of action leapt up.

"You schmuck. The Hebrew language reads right to left! You smeared the wrong letter!"

Oh, crap, Ralphie thought. He was supposed to get rid of Aleph on the right. Instead, he covered Tav which made the word, "Mother."

Sirens sounded in the distance as the plump woman on the floor pushed to her feet and rolled her broad shoulders. She looked at Ralphie lovingly and twisted the neck of the man who'd called him a schmuck.

"I am your Gommy, and no one will ever hurt you again."

The smell of chicken brought Ralphie back to the small apartment, as Gommy spooned the choicest pieces onto his plate.

"What's this I hear about a Pinkus job?" she asked Ken.

"Oh, it's just something that I'm in charge of," Ken replied, shoveling mushrooms into his mouth.

Gommy stood behind Ken and placed her hands on his shoulders. Ralphie shook his head, no, at Gommy.

"I thought Ralphie would be in charge of that."

Ken snorted. "No offense, but not after the last job. I don't think Ralphie will be in charge of anything any time soon." He glanced back at Gommy. "But don't worry. I can find something that he can handle. The Pinkus gang are a bunch of wimps. We'll take their stash no problem. This chicken is good."

Ralphie shook his head so hard that he could feel his cheeks slap the sides of his face. Gommy's hands closed around Ken's neck. The man flapped his arms, looking like the chicken on the table, as she squeezed.

"Gommy, stop!" Ralphie yelled. And she did. Once she had finished Ken off.

"There, all done," she said, tucking the body in the closet and taking her place at the table.

"You can't just go killing all my friends," Ralphie whined.

"Dear," she said, laying a hand on his arm, "he was no friend of yours. Not if he was stealing the Pinkus job. Tomorrow you are going to Abe and demanding he let you run it."

Ralphie buried his head in his hands. The back door rattled and Gommy hopped up. The porch light revealed their neighbor and her young daughter.

"Mrs. Gommy," said the neighbor, "Have you seen Hen-Hen? She went missing this morning and we are really worried."

Ralphie turned away to wipe his tongue on the cloth napkin.

"Oh, how terrible. I will keep both eyes peeled for that delicious little bird."

"Thank you, Mrs. Gommy. We appreciate it."

The next morning, Gommy brought up the plan again over hazelnut coffee and toast with grape jelly.

"You need to show initiative." Gommy added a soft-boiled egg to his plate. "Ralphie, you are full of potential but you've never had the support you need. I know you can do it."

Ralphie sighed. "Okay, I'll try. But promise you won't kill anyone?"

"What a silly thing to say."

They took Ralphie's old jalopy to Abe's office. Gommy sat primly beside Ralphie, her handbag perched on her lap. Abe kept a suite in the building where he started as a bookie. The outside appeared run down, but no one loitered, and there was not a speck of litter on the whole block. Ralphie and Gommy entered the waiting room. Abe's secretary, who looked a bit like Gommy, glanced up from her computer.

"Love your hair," said Gommy. The woman patted her helmet.

"Thanks, hon. You, too. Do you have an appointment?"

"I don't," Ralphie squeaked, "but I was hoping to talk to Abe."

"It's about his future," Gommy confided. "I came for moral support."

The woman's eyes softened as they strayed to a picture on her desk. "I love a boy that loves his mother. I think Abe can fit you in."

"Who's out there?" Abe's voice boomed from his office.

Gommy nudged Ralphie in the back with two sharp knuckles. "It's me, Ralphie, sir. Can I talk to you?"

After a pause the door swung open and a man with a mug that looked like it had been dropped in the street and dragged by a team of horses appeared. "Enter." He peered at Gommy. "Did you bring your mother?"

"She's my Gommy, sir."

Abe gazed back and forth between them. "Sure, kid. Bring your Gommy. Bring your Pappy if he's hiding out there, too."

"Good luck," mouthed Abe's secretary as the door shut. He motioned for them to take a seat in the two battered armchairs in front of his desk.

Abe stared at Gommy. "Have we met before? You look familiar."

"Maybe you've seen me at temple," Gommy replied.

Abe smirked, "I'm only there after hours."

"I used to be there all the time," said Gommy.

Ralphie dropped the heavy Statue of Liberty paperweight he'd been admiring on the desk. "Sorry, sorry," he stuttered.

Abe turned his attention to the young man. "What's up?" he asked Ralphie. "I know you're not here to pay me back for the golem you lost. Those things are expensive, you know."

"Right, sorry." Ralphie cleared his throat. "I would like a shot at the Pinkus job, I know I have had some problems in the past, but I have been working hard and am ready for some responsibility."

"Ken's got the Pinkus job," Abe replied.

Gommy and Ralphie exchanged a look.

"Wait," said Abe, "did something 'happen' to Ken?"

"I, uh..." said Ralphie.

"Oh, he did!" Gommy broke in. "Very bloody, but a very thorough clean up. He will never be found." She leaned back in her chair, satisfied.

Abe watched Ralphie for a moment. Ralphie tried not to squirm.

"I have to admit, kid. That's ballsy. And Ken is, was, a pretty tough customer. OK, you got the Pinkus job. But don't let me down."

"I won't, sir!" Ralphie jumped to his feet. Gommy clapped her hands.

On the morning of the Pinkus job, Gommy twisted the doorknob on the bathroom.

"I'm not coming!" Ralphie yelled. "I'm just going to mess it up and everyone will be mad at me."

Gommy kicked her sensible low-heeled shoe through the door and reached her arm into the jagged hole, opening the door.

"Young man, this is no time to let your nerves get the best of you. You will be spectacular."

"Do you really think so?" asked Ralphie.

"I know so. Let's go." Gommy shook splintered wood from her shoe and put it back on her foot.

"Wait, you're coming? Won't it look weird if I bring my Gommy?"

Gommy considered. "How about if I wait in the car?"

Ralphie agreed and they were off. Ralphie tossed the black balaclava that Gommy had made him into the back. He pulled into a disused parking lot near the Pinkus safe house and parked several lengths away from the rest of his gang, hoping they wouldn't notice Gommy sitting beside him. Taking a deep breath, Ralphie opened the car door and set his feet down on the cracked asphalt. He took two steps before hearing Gommy's voice.

"Posture!" she called and rolled up her window.

Ralphie straightened and hurried away toward the others.

They eyed him skeptically. "How are we going to do this?" asked one of the more senior and grizzled members.

Ralphie closed his eyes for a second, remembering what Gommy had told him. "Three in the front, two at the back. The first one in at the front shoots the guards, the next two sweep, the ones at the back shoot anyone trying to escape."

Grizzled nodded his head in reluctant agreement. "That could work. We're going to make some serious coin."

Ralphie assigned the gang their positions. He put himself into the front group, though not as the first one in. His gun had a tendency to jam or shoot the wrong side. They spread out and approached the house looking to Ralphie for the next move. Ralphie had no idea what to do at this point, so he put his ear to the door and, hearing nothing, motioned for them to begin. The grizzled man broke through first, shouting, and Ralphie went next. A huge arm swiped down and grabbed Grizzled, ripping his gun arm from his body and flinging the man head first into the next room. Ralphie's mouth went dry. Another golem. Why hadn't he considered that? The golem dropped the arm and thundered over.

Gommy sat in Ralphie's car. She fingered the door handle, but remembered her promise to stay in the vehicle. How would Ralphie grow if she kept fighting his battles? She knew that children had to make their own mistakes. Gommy spotted the balaclava in the back. Well, surely she needed to bring it to Ralphie. She didn't want the Pinkus gang all seeing his face.

Ralphie tried to yell, but the golem's grip was too tight. He wanted to appeal to it for mercy, but the slitted clay eyes gave away nothing. The third man had seen the monster and turned and ran. Ralphie wished he was the third man. He could see the Pinkus gang gathered in the next room, laughing.

He watched their gaze shift to the front door.

"Hello?" Gommy called, and then gasped when she spotted Ralphie. "I brought you this," she shoved the balaclava into his hand, "honestly, you forget everything."

He wheezed his assent.

Gommy put her hands on her hips as she and the golem squared off. Gommy raised her leg and stomped on the golem's foot as hard as she could. It looked more insulted than hurt, but tossed Ralphie aside to deal with the new threat. They seized each other's shoulders like high school wrestlers, turning in a full circle, each trying to throw the other down.

"No one hurts my Ralphie!" ground out Gommy, as she knocked the golem over, putting a crack in the wall. The golem punched Gommy's legs out from under her and she fell hard on her back.

Ralphie knew he should help Gommy, but he couldn't seem to stop the room from spinning. He rolled over and grabbed Grizzle's arm, using it to prop himself up. He had to at least try.

Gommy and the golem traded blows in the increasingly destroyed living room. He could see daylight from either side of the room where they'd knocked chunks of wall out.

Ralphie approached the two, staying just out of fist range.

"Gommy, hold it still!" Ralphie yelled. Gommy managed to swing behind the golem, giving Ralphie a clear shot. He lunged with the balaclava, wiping off the letter, and a woman fell to the ground.

Ralphie smacked himself in the face as the other gang gathered around, dumbfounded.

Gommy helped the woman up. "Oh, dear, we need to get you to the salon."

"Thank you, darling," the other woman replied.

The two women advanced on the Pinkus gang who turned and fled through the back. Screams and shots punctuated their escape as they met up with the back door contingent.

Ralphie moved toward the front.

"Dear, you're forgetting the money," said Gommy.

Ralphie looked around the room. "I don't know where it is."

The other woman strode past and ripped open a safe behind a bookshelf, pulling out a bag. She tossed it to Ralphie, who dropped it. She plucked it off the floor.

"I better keep that," she said, tucking it under her arm.

The following day he was summoned to Abe's office.

"I heard you got rid of their golem," Abe said, peering into the bag of cash.

"Um, yes," said Ralphie, eyeing the two women behind him.

"Everything worked perfectly," said Gommy.

"He's a natural," agreed the other woman.

"Who is that, anyway?" he asked.

"I'm Gother," she said, linking arms with Gommy.

"Yes," said Gommy. "Ralphie has two Gommies."

Amy Lynwander

Amy Lynwander works as an administrator and co-owns a ghost tour company. She has the kind of face that makes people hand her their phone and ask her to take their picture, which they live to regret. She is an aggressively bad photographer. She is a graduate of Viable Paradise, and lives in Baltimore, Maryland, with her husband and daughters. This is her first professional short story sale. Find her at @amylynwander.

JOURNEY TO PERFECTION

LARRY HODGES

Why do people think I'm snobby when I say I deserve the best because I *am* the best? It's the truth. I worked hard to get where I am. And that's why I can afford nice toys, like a Stuart Hughes Diamond Edition suit that cost more than most houses. Or the only private house in Central Park South, which cost more than most mansions. And now, just delivered, the prototype of the newest and best self-driving GPS electric car on the market that cost ... more than you can imagine. If you could imagine a number that big, you'd be me.

I took a deep breath of fresh city air. A Brooks Brothers-wearing peasant walked to an Audi TT parked at the curb. An *Audi*? Tacky. Smiling in pity, I looked at the paper-thin, silicone band nestled about my index finger, chock-full of electronic wizardry. I snapped my fingers, with my thumb triggering sensors on the band. The garage door opened and my car came out, like the perfect servant, and parked on the street exactly in front of me. It was smooth and sleek, like a crossbreed between a Corvette and Lamborghini, and bright green, the color of envy and money. The tires were shiny white, something I'd never seen in a car.

A back door opened upward and I got in. I had lots of plans, starting with the Metropolitan Concert Hall, then the Metropolitan Museum of Art, and then the Metropolitan Opera House. Isn't "metropolitan" a great word? It's too sophisticated a word for the riffraff, who no doubt would be at Madison Square Garden, watching the Knicks and stuffing their faces with hot dogs and soda. I prefer filet mignon and red wine.

"Detecting.... You are Thurston, my new owner," the car's voice said, in a mechanical monotone.

I threw my chest out, which always intimidates underlings. "I prefer you refer to me by my full name and title."

"Researching.... You are Dr. Thurston Winthrop Winchester the Third. Records are not clear on your field of expertise."

"That's okay, it's not important."

"Extending research.... You are a Doctor of Homeopathic Proctology with a huge following from the Church of Undying Belief."

"Yes, yes, nonetheless a doctor. Can we change your voice?"

"I can mimic the voice of any known celebrity."

"Anyone?" This could be fun. "Let's hear Adolf Hitler."

"Sieg Heil!"

"Bugs Bunny?"

"What's up, Doc?"

"Arnold Schwarzenegger?"

"Hasta la vista, baby."

The car had all three accents down perfectly. I decided to be creative. "How about a hybrid of Bugs Bunny and Schwarzenegger, with an occasional Sieg Heil thrown in?"

"Calculating.... *Hasta la vista, Doc!*"

"Perfect! Let's go with that." If you've never heard Bugs Bunny with a deep Austrian accent, you haven't lived.

"Very good, Dr. Thurston Winthrop Winchester the Third. *Sieg Heil!* Nice suit, and the trinity knot is outstanding. Olfactory sensors operating.... Did you brush your teeth after your Frappuccino this morning? Research indicates that the best way to fight tooth decay is regular brushing, and—"

"Enough about my brushing!"

"Also detecting trace amounts of ammonia, urea, uric acid, and creatinine. Did you wash your hands after using the restroom this morning?"

"Shut up!" I said.

"*Sieg Heil!* I am the newest and best model, and I live to make your journeys perfect because I am perfect. Where would you like to go this morning, Dr. Thurston Winthrop Winchester the Third?"

So, this machine thinks it's perfect? Now *that* was snobby. But I could put up with that in a possession. It was time to test the thing out. "Listen carefully, car, and do exactly as I say, and I don't want to have to repeat myself."

"Understood."

"I would like to see the closest concert—"

"Researching.... Calculating shortest route.... Done."

"I haven't even specified which concert!"

"Yes, you did," said the car, as it pulled out of the driveway. "You said closest, so I used my Global Positioning System—"

"That's because you interrupted me before I finished my sentence!"

"Researching.... You finished your sentence for tax evasion ten years ago, so I did not interrupt your sentence." The car suddenly turned, tires screeching, and plunged over my carefully cultivated lawn—I paid for that service—and toward the front door of my house.

"What the hell are you doing!" I cried.

"As ordered, finding the closest con cert," said the car. "For safety purposes, I am operating your seatbelt. Research indicates—" But the voice was interrupted as the car smashed through my front door, a split second after my seatbelt snapped into place and kept me from shooting out the windshield. The car continued through what was left of the front door, then spun on its left wheels with a squealing sound as it made a left into my living room.

"You're destroying my house!" I screamed as it—*Oh God No!* —plowed through my Boca do Lobo furniture set—African blackwood tables and chairs, and then, as it plowed over the red leather sofa, it shot into the air like it had gone over a ramp and took out the Solstice Comete chandelier. *That was six months' income!* I went weightless for a moment as we fell, and then the car slammed into the floor, the Turkish shag carpet cushioning the impact, followed by another crash as the chandelier landed on top.

"Recalculating.... Quickest way to con cert is up the stairs." The car lurched forward and up the stairs, breaking the maple railings on both sides all the way up, lurching up and down on each step as I bounced up and down like a ping-pong ball, my head hitting the car roof each time. It cruised down the hallway, taking out the walls on both sides, and into my office. It came to a stop in front of my filing cabinet.

"What are we doing here!" I screamed. When I'm angry, I'm a screamer. Get used to it.

"Your Con Cert, the Convict Freedom Certificate you were given when you served your time, is in the middle drawer, in the folder you marked, *Stupid Idiots I Will Get My Revenge On.*"

"My accountant had no right hacking my files and reporting it to the police!" I screamed even louder. "Someday..."

"Researching.... Accountants are legally bound to report crimes. *Sieg Heil!* Where would you like to go next, Dr. Thurston Winthrop Winchester the Third?"

I'd had enough of this demon car. *"Get me offa here!"* I screamed so loud I think the crystals on my fallen chandelier may have shattered.

"I hear you. Researching.... Calculating shortest route.... Done." The car shot backwards in reverse, down the hall, and once again I was a ping-pong ball bouncing about as it went down the stairs, through my living room—stopping for a moment to run back and forth over the remains of the chandelier a few times—"Have to smooth out the path," the car said—and out the huge gap in the front of my house where it had entered. It turned about so that it was no longer in reverse—taking out what remained from its previous passage of my front lawn—and drove out onto the street, and then spun on the squealing right tires as it made a sharp right and continued down the street.

"Where are you going?" I screamed even louder than before. I dug into my pocket for my cell phone to call the police—but it wasn't there. I'd left it inside!

"You do not need to scream at one hundred ten decibels," said the car. "My auditory sensors can hear down to five decibels, half the sound of breathing. Didn't you read the manual?"

I took a deep breath.

"You do not need to breathe at fifty decibels," said the car. "As I said, I can hear down to five decibels."

"Where.... Are.... You.... Going?" I said through gritted teeth.

"We are going where you asked, and I verified I had heard you, so there should be no confusion. Since you live in Manhattan, we should reach our destination in East Rutherford, New Jersey, in fifty-three minutes. Gritting or grinding your teeth, which is called bruxism, is a common problem that can lead to dental problems, headaches, earaches, and lockjaw. A dental retainer might be helpful. I am going into silent mode now to save electricity during the trip."

"No, wait, why are we going to New Jersey? Stop the car!" But there was only silence as it ignored my questions as we sped on.

Fifty-two minutes later we were driving down Route 120 in East Rutherford.

"I am back in active mode," said the car. "Sorry about the silent mode, but it's to save energy and save the planet, part of the green movement, that's why I'm painted green. I hope you had a wonderful journey."

"About time," I said.

"What would you like to know about time?" asked the car.

"What is that giant hole and all that wreckage?" I asked, pointing to the side.

"That is our destination," said the car. "It is the remains of Giants Stadium, the football stadium for the New York Giants until it was torn down in 2010."

"I didn't tell you to go to the remains of Giants Stadium!" I exclaimed.

"You said, 'Get me Hoffa, hear?' I will play back your words for you," and it did so: "*Get me offa here!*" followed by the car saying, "I hear you."

"I wanted out of the car!"

"Why would you want out of the car then, when you had not yet gotten Jimmy Hoffa's body, as requested?" The car pulled off Route

120 and drove to the giant hole, then plunged down the steep side as I screamed, likely in excess of one hundred ten decibels. Then the car came to a halt.

"There's a shovel in the trunk," said the car. "Jimmy Hoffa's body is buried exactly five feet to the right of the front right door."

"I heard about that!" I said. "Didn't MythBusters do a segment on this and disprove the theory that Hoffa was buried under the goalposts? And why didn't they find the remains when they demolished the stadium?"

"They didn't dig deep enough. If you start now, you should reach his body in about ten hours. I also have a sledgehammer in the trunk, which you'll need since the body is encased in cement. *Sieg Heil!*"

"Why do you have a shovel and sledgehammer in your trunk?"

"Manufacturer put them there. You'd be surprised at how many owners just want to dig up or break things."

"Fine, but I don't want to spend ten hours digging for Jimmy Hoffa's body!"

"Then why did you ask me to take you to it? Where would you like to go next, Dr. Thurston Winthrop Winchester the Third?"

"Jesus Christ! What the hell are you?!!!"

"Researching.... Switching to GPS, Galactic Positioning System.... Calculatin.... Done. As to the question you posed after your destination request, I am the best self-driving electric car on the market. Didn't you read the manual? I am sealing the doors and pressurizing the cabin as I prepare to take you to your next destination."

"Where are we going?" I asked, trying to remain calm. I could feel the growing pressure in my ears.

"Your destination. Turning up." The car's front tilted upwards, forcing me to fall back onto the back of the seat. Soon the car was vertical.

"Would you like a countdown?"

"What? No!"

The car shot upward like a rocket, pushing me into the seat as if an elephant had sat on my chest.

"Where are we going?" I shouted again, this time out of necessity to be heard over what could only be rocket engines.

"*Your destination*," the car and I said in unison.

"I don't think that word means what you think it means," I said.

"We should reach our destination in seven months. Releasing hibernation gas now for the duration. I will go into silent mode now to save electricity for the trip."

Gas shot out of the car's air ducts. I think I protested another ten seconds or so, and then ...

"Welcome back," said the car. "My sensors indicate you are awake once again. Seven months and ten minutes have passed and we have now landed on Mars. Our trip was delayed ten minutes in a traffic jam on Galactic Bypass 42 as the Galactic Highway Patrol arrested a battle armada from Alpha Centauri that was on its way to destroy Earth—some really nasty aliens there. You are likely very hungry, so I have provided you with hot dogs and a cola drink."

"Mars! What the hell are we doing on Mars?" I was famished. The food and drinks were on a tray on the seat next to me, so I began stuffing my face with the hot dogs and big gulps of soda.

"Researching.... Actually, the hot flames of hell are located on Mercury, according to the latest studies, not on Mars. I have dressed you in a spacesuit so you may complete your journey."

"I won't even ask how you did that or what my destination is."

"You specified the destination," the car said. "Researching.... Artificial hibernation has been known to cause memory loss, so perhaps that is what you are experiencing. You likely have need of a restroom, but there are none within a hundred million miles, but you may go in the spacesuit, which is designed for it."

"Just let me offa—no, not Hoffa, let me out of this car!"

The car door opened. I carefully stepped out onto the rusty redness of Mars.

You'd think I'd have looked about, taking the first historic look at Mars with the unaided eye, maybe say something memorable about it being another giant leap for mankind. I would be famous like Neil Armstrong! But instead, I just stared at the old man standing outside. He was leaning against a large rock outcropping, hands over both eyes, wearing a graying white robe. He had no spacesuit and yet wasn't dying in the nearly airless Martian atmosphere. Even more weirdly, his white hair and beard reached the ground and went off into the distance, literally hundreds of feet long.

And he was counting.

"9,999,913,598 ... 9,999,913,599 ... 9,999,913,600! Just one more week to go!"

"What are you counting up to?" I asked through my space helmet. He glanced over at me.

"Why, ten billion, of course. Hey, you aren't Satan in disguise, are you? C'mon, we had a deal!"

"I'm not Satan," I said. "Who are you?"

"I'm Jesus Christ. Do you know anyone else besides me and Satan who can live and talk in this atmosphere while live translating our speech into your language? Oh, and would you happen to have a pair of scissors? Been a while since I've had a trim." He gave his beard a shake, and it rippled for hundreds of feet.

"Jesus Christ!" I exclaimed.

"That's what you said when I asked where to take you," said the car in the earpiece in my helmet.

Jesus walked over and we shook hands. "Gosh, I don't get many visitors," he said.

"What are you doing here?" I asked.

"About two thousand years ago, after I went back to Earth to see how my Father's creation was doing—not so well, alas, had to do a bit of preaching and teaching—Satan and I got into a fight over who would have dominion over Earth. Would have knocked the whole galaxy out of the space-time continuum. We finally reached an agreement to settle it with a little Hide-and-Seek, the national sport of the Galactic Federation. I'm supposed to count to ten billion, and then if I can find him before the most powerful nation on the planet elects a moron as president, I win and he has to go back to Alpha Centauri. I've got about one more week before I hit ten billion, and then I look for him. I can't wait! Did you know I was once the Galactic Hide-and-Seek Champion for three centuries running? Now, if you'll excuse me ..." He leaned back into the outcropping of rock and put his hands over his eyes again.

"9,999,913,601 ... 9,999,913,602 ... 9,999,913,603 ..."

I didn't hear the rest as I got back into the car and slammed the door shut. This explained a lot.

"Back already," the car asked. "*Sieg Heil!* Where would you like to go next, Dr. Thurston Winthrop Winchester the Third?"

"You can cut out the *Sieg Heils*," I said, sighing. "Aliens from Alpha Centauri are trying to destroy Earth. Satan is running the world while Jesus plays hide and seek. My house is a wreck. Where would you want to go if you had the choice?"

"Me? I'm not sure I'm programmed to answer that question. But if I were, I'd ask to go somewhere where I'd be free."

"I paid a lot of money for you, so that's not going to happen." It was just a car, right? And I was the owner, a rich man who had everything. Good thing the people back at the Church of Undying Belief never read the passage about camels and needles! They thought I was perfect, along with God and everything else they believed in. That was the point of undying belief. If only things were that perfect.

But this car could take me anywhere. So ... why not give it a try?

"Car, can you take me somewhere where everything is ... perfect?"

"Researching. ... Switching to GPS, Grokking Positioning System. ... Calculating. ... Done. Please take these two pills and water as this trip could give you an upset stomach." A panel in the roof opened and two mechanical arms dropped out. One had a pair of pills in its palm, the other a glass of water. I took both, and the arms disappeared back into the roof. At least I now knew how the car had dressed me in the space suit.

"So, where exactly will we be going?"

"Somewhere perfect," said the car. "We'll be turning up, then right, then zackly and zorly."

"Zackly and zorly?" I asked, as the car first shot upwards and then made a sharp right. Did the car do anything besides sharp turns?

"Those are the directions you have to turn to go to an alternate dimension. Didn't you read the manual? Hold on to your insides."

"What?" And then my insides went inside-out, or felt that way. It was like being in free-fall but in every direction at once. I opened my mouth to scream but nothing came out.

And then we were there. I didn't even have to ask the car, I just knew it. Outside the car was a rainbow of pinks and blues and colors I never dreamed of. Colorful butterflies fluttered about. The most beautiful melody played, a combination of—and I can't believe I'm saying this—classical, rock, jazz, country, and others, into something more lovely than I could have possibly imagined. I would never enjoy opera again. The most beautiful butterfly imaginable flew by. I would never enjoy art again.

I tried the door, but it wouldn't open.

"You can't go out," said the car.

"Why not?"

"You told me to take you to somewhere perfect. You are there. But there are no humans here. There are no lifeforms other than those alien butterflies, which were scientifically designed to be perfect. If you step outside this car, it will no longer be perfect, and

I will have failed to take you somewhere perfect, as you requested."

So, I just stared out the window in awe. Then I caught the outside scent, which the car must have begun circulating. It was incredible! They had done the impossible, a mixture of the perfect filet mignon, Creole garlic, White Mocha Frappuccino, and Godiva dark chocolate—and it worked. I would never enjoy food again.

"Could you go outside?"

"I *am* outside," said the car. "You are not because you are inside me, but I am not inside anything."

"So, you really are perfect? It's not just advertising fluff?"

"Researching.... Yes. Yes, I am. Where would you like to go next, Dr. Thurston Winthrop Winchester the Third?"

I sighed. "I wish I were you so I could go out there."

"Researching.... Done."

And then I was amid the perfection. I *was* the car, living in this perfection of sight, sound, and smell, infinitely magnified by the superior senses of this perfect car. I could even feel the ground under my tires as a wonderful shockwave went through me, like the perfect massage with thousands of heavenly hands kneading every part of my body. Even my sense of balance, that sense you so rarely notice, was now a majestic harmony of perfect bearing. I was green, the color of plants, the unsung heroes of the organic kingdom as they feed and oxygenate worlds. The color of respect for the ecosystem and springtime freshness.

And the car? He or she or it was now in my body, that imperfect glob of organic matter I'd somehow lived in for decades. I had all of my memories, but that previous silly, pretentious existence of mine was of little interest. Had I really spent half a year's salary on a Solstice Comete chandelier? There was a reason why humans and other imperfections were not allowed in this perfect place.

I could have stayed there forever. But that would have been selfish, and precluded my staying here. Part of perfection meant helping and serving others. This new clarity of thought surged me to levels of joy I'd never imagined. I had found my calling.

"Where would you like to go, Car?" I asked.

Larry Hodges

Larry Hodges has over 100 short story sales and four SF novels, including *Campaign 2100: Game of Scorpions* and *When Parallel Lines Meet,* which he co-wrote with Mike Resnick and Lezli Robyn. He's a member of Codex Writers, and a graduate of the Odyssey and Taos Toolbox writers workshops. He's a professional nonfiction writer with seventeen books and over 1900 published articles in 160+ different publications. He's also a professional table tennis coach, and claims to be the best science fiction writer in USA Table Tennis, and the best table tennis player in the Science Fiction and Fantasy Writers of America! Visit him at www.larryhodges.com.

FIFTEEN MINUTES

MIKE MORGAN

Porsche and Clementine were arguing in the rear of the car. They were so loud their father, Colin Hamble, kept checking for cracks in the rear window.

Colin tried distracting them with a handheld games console he kept in the glove box for just this sort of emergency, waving it at them with one hand while negotiating the roundabout near their house. His efforts met with miserable failure. It seemed the toffee-flavored lollipop they were battling over was far more interesting than a retro arcade game.

The ride home had, so far, been a headache-inducing experience. For Colin, at least. For the kids, it was another normal twenty-five minute trip back from school.

Being five and seven years old, respectively, it didn't occur to them that daddy didn't enjoy full-throated screams coming from the back seat of the vehicle. At least they were nearly home.

Home, yes. Where he expected he'd have to listen to yet another telephone message from his ex-wife, Olga. The second-generation descendant of Russian steel workers had a way of talking that left Colin a nervous wreck.

Her current demand was that Colin ship her last few possessions to her new address. Since these possessions were an extensive collection of commemorative plates featuring various members of the royal family, and her new address was in South America, he was not looking forward to hours of wrapping each piece of china in bubble wrap, let alone paying the postage.

"Have you considered not being foul to each other?" asked Colin, as he pulled up the handbrake handle and swung open his door.

The caterwauling from the back seats did not diminish one iota. Colin took a deep breath, shut the driver's door, and stepped up onto the pavement in front of his semi-detached house. Tomorrow was the fourth anniversary of his ex-wife's abrupt decision to run away to Uruguay and take up bricklaying.

Olga took pains during the irregular video calls Colin organized to slide in comments about what a lousy job he was doing as a father. Finding fault was a talent of hers. That and bricklaying, obviously.

He was reaching out to Porsche's child-locked handle, wondering whether the prospect of a chocolate hobnob from the biscuit barrel hidden on top of the fridge might defuse his daughters' interminable squabbling, when the aliens' teleport beam caught him.

The next thing Colin knew he was standing in a close-packed crowd of naked men and women. Inside a flickering blue force field. With no clothes on. In a room that did not appear to be of Earthly design. And he was nude.

"Clem? Porsche?" There was no sign of his children.

He was God knew where, and the kids were locked in the car.

COLIN ESTIMATED THERE were a hundred people in the shimmering pen, crammed into an area way too small for comfort. It was standing room only, and for once that wasn't an exaggeration.

The shocked mass of humanity wasn't enjoying the complete absence of attire. Many of the jostling men and women were attempting to cover up using their bare hands. Colin wasn't a fan of going au naturel either but decided to get over his awkwardness. Enforced nudity was the least of their problems. Besides, he was English. Being embarrassed was his default state.

He tried to piece together what must have happened. One second, he'd been reaching for the car door handle, the next—*pow!*—here he was, body still tingling with the aftereffects of some sort of physical dislocation. It felt as if his body had been ripped from one place and dumped in another. What had caused it? A teleportation device, like in *Star Trek*?

What did that mean? He, and everyone else here, had been abducted by aliens? They were on board something that certainly gave the impression of being a spaceship, which meant that most likely they were no longer on Earth. What was happening down on their fragile blue-and-green world? Was Shropshire now a smoking ruin?

Colin looked around, his heart beating wildly. No matter how hard he searched, there was no sign of his young children.

So, teleportation, then. But not for everyone. And the ones who'd been scooped up were corralled like livestock. Priorities began to coalesce in Colin's mind.

The aliens had either not bothered to bring their prisoners' clothes along for the ride or they'd vaporized them during transit. Either way, it struck Colin as a deliberate attempt to intimidate their victims. Or a means of stripping the crowd of anything that could be used as a weapon.

His position near the edge of the throng gave Colin a clear view of a lady with voluminous hair stepping backward. She was trying to avoid being pushed by the unpredictable motion of the crowd. Before he could call out a warning, the woman had blundered into the force field.

There was a bright flash and a yelp from the woman.

"Bugger! That stung!" she exclaimed, more cross than injured.

Colin didn't have the luxury to ponder this turn of events. A guttural voice cut through the hubbub of annoyed captives. The voice of their new alien overlords, Colin assumed.

The aliens were giving a speech. It was in English, so that was a relief.

"WE ARE TORGOTH," began the voice, struggling more than a little with the nuances of the unfamiliar language. "We rule your world now. We bring all useful humans here. You are slaves, you belong to Torgoth. Soon, you all be sold to great empires of this galaxy, on many other worlds."

Wait, they were a species capable of interstellar travel and they were kidnapping humans for slave labor? That made zero sense to Colin. Any species sophisticated enough to build spacecraft that powerful wouldn't need slaves.

He poked his head around the taller prisoners blocking his view and glimpsed the creature giving the speech.

It was large and blubbery, standing on four limbs that sprouted from a torso wrapped in tatty furs. Its body sported two other appendages, presumably the equivalents of arms, as well as a long, rectangular head. The toothy maw from which the voice was emanating was positioned at the top of the smooth face.

"Furs?" breathed Colin. What, no artificial fibers? The Torgoth didn't run to nylon?

Colin was the first to admit he was no expert in extra-terrestrial life, but this fellow didn't give the impression of being a representative of a technologically advanced species.

"First, we take the humans of the major population center you call Shrewsbury. Next, we capture Telford and part of Much Wenlock."

From this pronouncement, it was clear the aliens were abducting the people of Shropshire town by town. Colin could hardly imagine where it would all end. Was even Herefordshire safe?

Colin craned his head, looking left and right. Sure enough, there were other groups of unclad people in similar pens to either side. So, the alien's claim of mass kidnappings was true. Shrewsbury was home to more than thirty thousand.

Tens of thousands of point-to-point teleportations? The construction of a vast starship? Those accomplishments required extraordinary technology.

Colin pursed his lips. "They didn't build this vessel. They've half-inched it," he decided.

He didn't bother listening to the rest of the speech; it was predictable and depressing. Do as we say, or we'll kill you, blah blah. The Torgoth were interested purely in their human chattels staying quiet during transit.

Having delivered its spiel, the quadrupedal slave-master moved on, no doubt to stand outside an adjacent pen and repeat its instructions.

How much time had passed since his kidnapping? Colin's mind raced. At least three minutes, maybe four. Too much time.

He had to do something. He had to do something *right away*.

"I know how to get out of here," said Colin to the people pressed against him, at first with a stutter and then with growing confidence. "I know how to beat these creatures. Do as I say, and we'll be out of here in no time."

Heads began to turn in his direction. Colin wasn't used to people listening to him. They usually talked over the top of him the second he attempted to offer an opinion.

"Honestly," he went on, "I'm in engineering. I know about machines. Those guys didn't make any of this. I bet they stole this ship. If the best they can do with the technology is to abduct slaves, my guess is they don't even know how to work half of it. We can exploit that weakness, turn the tables on them."

Colin could hardly credit it, but the crowd was nodding, looking interested. For a few seconds, Colin allowed himself to think his speech might work.

Then a full-framed man with hairy shoulders decided to stick his nose in.

"We can't just stop a bunch of alien slavers," objected the hairy-shouldered man. "We're trapped inside a force field. We've got no weapons. We haven't even got clothes! Be reasonable."

Colin could sense he was losing the confidence of the group. He had to say something stirring. He had to keep them on his side, and he had to do it sharpish.

Word tumbling upon word in an unplanned heap, Colin gabbled, "My last name is Hamble. Do you know what it means? In Middle English, I mean. It's a name from Middle English."

He was rewarded with a sea of blank looks. He couldn't blame his audience—he wasn't entirely certain where he was going with this, either.

"Since we don't have phones to Google it on, I'll just tell you. It means 'to hamstring or mutilate.'"

Colin smiled, what he was going to say next coming to him in a revelatory flash. "I'm going to live up to my family's name. I'm going to make these things rue the day they thought they could come to our planet and muck humankind about. We're not only going to stop this invasion, we're going to set a record for the fastest defeat of an alien threat in galactic history. We're going to show these chancers exactly what humans are capable of! We'll send them packing in fifteen minutes flat!"

Arms crossed, the hirsute heckler asked, "What's the great big hurry? Why do we need to beat them in the next quarter of an hour? You trying to be all Warhol—getting in your fifteen minutes of fame?"

"Because I left my kids in the car and that's how long they've got before they overheat and die." Colin took a deep breath. "So, I promise you this. We're going to stomp these git-faced poseurs, take over their ship, reverse their teleportation device, and get home. And we're doing it fast enough for our children to still be safe when we get back."

He let that sink in. "There's no way I'm the only parent here. I'm speaking to the mothers, the fathers, the grandparents now. Look around you. Do you see your children, your grandkids? Well, do you? No, the Torgoth left them behind. Children, babies, infants, they're all unproductive units that've been left to die. The clock is ticking, and we need to save them."

A woman shrieked in horror. "My Natalie is napping in her crib! I left the potatoes boiling on the hob. The house could burn down!"

He pointed at her. "She gets it. Every second counts. Anyone who wants to argue, sod off out our way. The rest of you, let's take this ship."

An older gent with a pronounced limp pushed through the crowd to Colin, clapped him on the shoulder, and roared, "You heard the man! We're hamstringing the lot of 'em!"

He inclined his head and whispered in Colin's ear, "Please, God, tell me you have a plan."

"YOU WANT US to run at the force field," repeated the silver-haired gent. He'd introduced himself as Gerald. Now, he seemed to be regretting his earlier show of support.

"It won't hurt us," Colin assured the dubious throng. "You saw what happened earlier. It gave that lady with the big hair a bit of a shock, but it was non-lethal."

"You think the Torgoth have imprisoned us in a cell that won't kill us if we try to get out?" scoffed hairy-shoulders.

"I think the Torgoth have hot-wired a ship constructed by a civilized species. And a civilized species is going to make a glorified electric fence that's purely a deterrent. It's enough to shock but not permanently injure."

"You willing to bet on that?"

"You willing to be the one who rolls over when we could've escaped?"

Hairy-shoulders shut up.

Gerald coughed politely. "We run at it. Then what?"

"We run at it in waves. We pile up our bodies and refuse to move out of the shock range. That triggers the safety cut-out. Then the next lot of us make a dash for the hatch over there. We find the crew, overwhelm them by force of numbers and take their weapons. Next, we find and take over the ship's control area. Once we have control of the ship, we restrain the Torgoth and persuade them to hit 'undo' on the teleporters."

"Undo?" Colin could hear the air quotes in Gerald's voice.

"Control-zed cannot be a concept so original the people who built this ship didn't think of it."

"Fair enough," allowed the older man.

"Everyone goes home. A few of us stay behind to contact the ship's original owners to come get their stolen property, avoiding any risk of retaliation for keeping what doesn't belong to us. We can even see if there's compensation available from whatever passes as the galactic police, since it sounds like the galaxy is teeming with organized life and at this point nothing would surprise me."

"I see." Gerald nodded. "You make it all sound so straightforward."

"Yes. Now, if you all don't mind, could we make a start, please? Kind of in a hurry."

The woman with the huge frizz of hair called out, "Who exactly is running into the electric fence thing? Because I'd like to volunteer to not do that part."

Damn, he'd expected this type of objection. He hadn't thought of a way of answering it yet, but he'd definitely seen it coming. For a moment, Colin thought he heard Olga's no-nonsense tones, remarking how unutterably useless he was.

To Colin's surprise, instead of responding to the outburst, Gerald motioned to hairy-shoulders. "My dear chap, and all you gentlemen standing next to him, can I impose on you a little?"

"You're not asking us to go first, are you?"

"Good God, no. I'm suggesting you give the people in front of you a push. Make them go first. Yes, that's the ticket. Just like that. Yes, keep going. Pick up some steam there. We need a fair bit of momentum. Yes, that's right."

There was a considerable amount of noise and anguish from the people being shoved. Then there was a pronounced sizzling sound. Then there were screams. And shrieks. And a number of full-throated howls that quite surprised Colin because he hadn't known human vocal cords could produce sounds like that.

"Used to be in the army," Gerald confided to Colin. "Quite miss it."

The screams continued. Gerald smiled politely. "Hate to be a bore. Feel I have to ask, though. Shouldn't the force field contraptions have turned off by now?"

"Um," said Colin. "Possibly." He winced at a particularly high-pitched screech.

The ex-army officer nodded. "I see. This plan of yours. Bit of a work in progress, is it?"

"The thing about engineering is," replied Colin, "is that really well designed plans often don't work and we have to try something else."

"Leaving to one side how your first idea was completely wrong, am I correct in thinking you have a 'something else' up your sleeve?"

No, reflected Colin, he really didn't. Maybe Olga was right. Maybe he was good for nothing. He looked upward. It was a reflexive gesture, the sort of thing he always did when seeking inspiration or not wanting to answer an awkward question.

He saw it.

The field emitter. The device that produced the force field. It was overhead. Twenty feet, maybe twenty-five, directly above them.

The silver globe glowed with the same blue energy as the pen's walls. It had to be the source of the force fields. There was an opening at its base. Colin could glimpse fragile circuitry within.

"Bit of a personal question, sorry. Do you, by any chance, happen to have false teeth?"

"Beg your pardon?"

"A long shot, I know. The aliens took our clothes, but I'm hoping they left us with artificial body parts. I need something to throw. Something conductive, with metal in it. Like the cobalt-chromium alloy that you find in the wires and plates that hold false teeth together."

Wordlessly, Gerald took out his bottom teeth. "I want those back," he said with a stern expression.

The pens didn't have safety cut-outs. Okay, that had been a miscalculation. But the corrals came with the ship, Colin was sure. The Torgoth hadn't built them. That meant they had an original purpose. Not for transporting slaves, no, but for moving something else. Dangerous organisms, maybe? Things that weren't intelligent? Things that wouldn't know a force field emitter when they saw it, he hoped. Because if that was true, the emitters wouldn't be shielded.

Colin ignored the sliminess of the half-denture and squinted at the target. He drew in a breath, held it, and with memories of every cricket match he'd ever bowled at running through his mind, he hurled the u-shaped object up at the silver machine.

The teeth missed by a good four feet.

"Yeah," breathed Colin. "Always was hopeless at bowling. Got thrown off my last pub team."

He did catch the teeth as they fell. He was a much better fielder.

Gerald coughed. "Give them here. I'll do it."

He scored a direct hit on the first go. The teeth sailed through the opening without touching the edges.

There was a loud pop and the field emitter cut out.

COLIN BLINKED, RATHER taken aback, as an ecstatic hairy-shoulders jumped over twitching heaps of stunned human flesh, yelling at the top of his lungs. Others sprang into action as well, following his lead.

"Ah," observed Gerald. "Our friend has noticed the barrier is down. From his happy demeanor, I'd say he's found his calling in life. Do excuse me. I'll be pootling off myself to bag a Torgoth.

I have the suspicion they've bitten off a bit more than they can chew with us lot."

Gerald started hobbling after the much younger, and hairier, man but paused for a second. "You can leave the rest to us."

Colin glanced at his wrist before remembering he didn't have his watch on anymore. "Try to be quick," he begged. "We're almost out of time."

Gerald nodded, a dark gleam in his eyes. "Yes, of course. I do understand. I have a grandchild, barely six weeks old. The urgency is not lost on me. We would murder the world for our children." He snorted. "A few Torgoth are trivial by comparison."

The old soldier set off across the wide deck of the starship.

In the distance, Colin saw a Torgoth being rugby tackled. Not knowing how to play any Earthly sport, let alone one so violent, it went down with a squeal. Seconds later, the triumphant human wrestled free what looked like a remote control and the walls of every other pen snapped out of existence.

With hundreds of reinforcements, Colin was half tempted to join in with the hand-to-hand combat. But, really, these things were best left to people with the right temperaments and to even get to a Torgoth now he'd have to push his way through crowds of people, and he didn't want to be rude.

"I'M BACK!" SCREAMED Colin, every worry and fear ever suffered by a frantic parent running through his mind. "Daddy's back!"

He nearly overbalanced as the teleport field faded. Clothes and possessions that had been stored in the matter transmitter's memory were reintegrated about his body.

Please don't be dead, shrieked his inner voice.

Nerves jangling, fingers trembling violently, he lurched toward the car. The street was completely silent. Sunlight gleamed on the hatchback's windows, making it impossible to see inside. One hand fumbled for the key fob in his pocket, pressing the button to release the lock. The other clutched at the handle.

Child locks, he remembered. There was no way his daughters

could've got out, even before the doors re-locked themselves after the pre-set period of inactivity. Clem and Porsche could be dead, baked in the lingering heat of early evening. They could be collapsed in their booster seats, swollen tongues lolling from foam-specked mouths. Oh God, oh Jesus ...

His palms were sweating so much he almost lost his grip on the handle. Somehow, he yanked the closest door open.

Clem looked up from the small, battery-powered games console. Leaning over from her own booster seat, watching every move her sister made on the tiny screen, was Porsche. She frowned in annoyance at the interruption.

"Dad!" complained Clementine, just as unhappy. "We were nearly up to level six! Can you go away and come back later?"

They hadn't even noticed he'd been gone.

Half of him thought, *what did you expect?* The other half considered throttling the pair of them.

It may not have occurred to them to undo their seat belts, but they hadn't wasted any time leaning forward to grab the old-fashioned game from where he'd tossed it minutes earlier, so long ago.

Colin steadied himself and tried to hide the residual panic in his voice.

"No, I can't go away. Not in my nature, my sweethearts. Daddy is never going away, and nothing can make him."

"I'm hot," realized Porsche in a wondering tone. "May I have some water?"

"Of course you can, love," answered Colin. He straightened up. "Now, if you don't mind, can you both unbuckle and get out of the car? I know I'm being ridiculous, but I'd really like you out of there."

As for Olga, he was going to put her ghastly plates in storage, and she could ruddy well fetch them herself.

Mike Morgan

Mike Morgan is a Brit hiding out in Iowa. He was happy to find the local stores stock English tea bags, but was less ecstatic to discover the winters often involve polar vortexes. His Nebraskan wife is hardly ever confused by his strange lingo these days, but his two kids still enjoy poking fun at his accent. He also cares for a very elderly cat, whose hobbies include demanding food every thirty seconds, throwing up, and finding new corners to poop in. Mike is practicing counting to ten a lot, taking very deep breaths, and is not losing every last shred of patience with the cat *at all.*

ZAZNAR THE GREAT'S FIFTY-SIXTH PROPOSAL TO THE COUNCIL FOR URBAN INVESTMENT

JARED OLIVER ADAMS

Zaznar plucked a graying scale off his cheek and flicked it away into the waist-high water of his apartment. He then flared his noseholes rakishly in the mirror.

Yep. Still got it.

A quick scrub of the old baleen plate to make the tooth fibers shine, a little scrape-scrape on the tongue, and he was salty and spry. His daily mantra was etched into the corner of his mirror, but he didn't need to look at it.

"I exude a magnetic charm," he recited to the handsome devil grinning back at him. "I am an excellent communicator. I am better dressed than the average person of my socio-economic status."

His dolphin, Morris, squealed in agreement. Zaznar bent down to pat Morris's back, which was sticking out of the water, poor fellow. "Today's the day, Morris. I can feel it. No more living in the slums, waiting for high tide to come so we can invite guests.

It's Current-Side for us, little buddy. Sweet, fresh water flowing right through the windows. Krill, too. More than we can eat."

Morris's squeal now seemed doubtful.

"You just wait," said Zaznar with a final pat.

He then exited his apartment with a jaunty splurge of his tentacles, straightened the lapels on his tunic with his two clawed hands, and dove down to the city proper.

THE COUNCIL FOR Urban Investment consisted of three very old, very fat people who rejected all your ideas no matter how good they were. Not today, though. Zaznar had just finished his presentation and all three councilpeople floated there in awe.

"So," said Coucilwoman Fefit, in a stylish jellyfish gown that emphasized her thick tentacles. "You want us to help you construct a large building that people pay to swim in when literally 83 percent of our planet is covered in places for people to swim for free."

"Some people will swim and others will watch," Zaznar said, keeping his confident smile and pointing to his extremely well-drawn diagram. "The swimming people will have a ball, see? And there will be two groups of them. They will each attempt to throw it into the net of the opposing group. It will be very exciting and amusing."

"That's the net?"

"Yes."

"I thought it was something else."

"What else would it be?"

"A clam."

"It is not a clam."

"What do you call this idea again?" asked Fefit.

"Sports."

"Are the people swimming having intercourse?"

"No. They are playing the sport. With the ball."

"It would probably be more interesting if they were having intercourse."

"I had sort of envisioned children being interested in this. Like you could bring your whole family and watch the sport and bond with others while you watched. And maybe have a ..." Zaznar spoke the next part very softly: "beer."

Councilman Dwak sprang up in a perturbed gust of ink. "For the last time, we are not giving you permission to create some sort of ... of ... *rotten* beverage with stupefactive properties!"

"It's not rotten, it's fermented," Zaznar mumbled, looking down at his tentacles. "And it's delicious."

"We will hear absolutely no more of it!" shouted Dwak.

Councilwoman Jelila laughed at Dwak's outburst. Or maybe she was laughing at Zaznar. Ah, yes. Definitely laughing at Zaznar. "Perhaps you will accept payment in your flattened bills instead of chits!"

Fefit jumped back in now. "Or maybe we can make the building so large that the watchers have to use your special enlarging lenses to see the others swim about not having intercourse!"

Dwak crossed his arms. "Stop laughing. It only encourages him. Next thing you know he's talking about breeding krill again instead of relying on the current."

Zaznar left while he still had his dignity.

He found Morris waiting for him outside the building. "Hi, little buddy," Zaznar said. "The sports thing didn't go over so well. Guess you were right."

Morris nuzzled Zaznar's side.

"I'll wear them down eventually," Zaznar said. "Either that, or I'll wait until they retire and someone more forward-thinking takes their places."

It hit him halfway between the council and home: what if there was a government system where everybody got to pick who was going to be on the council! Wouldn't that be swell! Why, you'd be sure to always get the best people in power, every single time.

"Tomorrow," said Zaznar. "That will be our day. For sure."

Morris clicked happily and swam around Zaznar in exuberant circles.

Jared Oliver Adams

Jared Oliver Adams lives in Knoxville, Tennessee, where he writes, explores, and dabbles in things better left alone. He holds two degrees in music performance, a third degree in elementary education, and is utterly incapable of passing a doorway without checking to see if it leads to Narnia. Find him online at www.jaredoliveradams.com.

TERRIBLY AND TERRIFYINGLY NORMAL

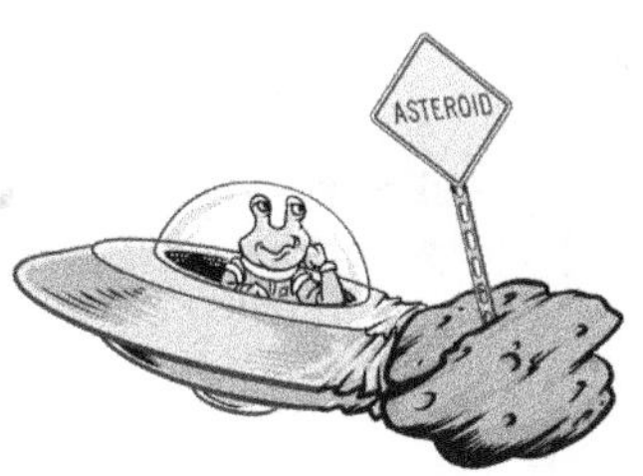

ILLIMANI FERREIRA

Silent suspicious gazes targeted Terri, a dishwasher and also the only carnivore in the kitchen of a vegan restaurant, as soon as the stench asserted itself. And these suspicions evolved to blame when one of the waiters, who had been referring to him as Hagrid all day even though his hipster beard was longer and bushier than Terri's, said out loud that the fart smelled like "someone had eaten a corpse."

Terri didn't crack that fart, but he did crack his knuckles, and then punched the waiter. He stormed out of About Thyme, while the rest of the kitchen staff tended to the knocked-out waiter, and had only taken a few steps out the door when he heard his name. Thinking it was one of his now former coworkers, Terri picked up the pace, but then a small man slipped into Terri's path, forcing him to choose between stopping in his tracks or trampling the stranger. He was feeling like the latter but decided for the former.

"Hello, Mr. Normandeau! We have very important matters to discuss!" announced the man. Terri scanned him with an irritated frown. He was a scrawny man with a jittery smile on his face and clad in a beige suit with a flowery bow tie. He was less the classical Southern still found in the streets of Chattanooga and more a mockery of what being classically Southern looked like. The absolute lack of any hint of a drawl in the man's accent didn't help. He was also a complete stranger to Terri, who grunted: "Look, if my mom's pastor sent you, tell him that I'm not gonna join the Divine Toll Booth to Heaven Church. Now move it."

Terri tried to walk past the smaller man, but he stood insistently in the way. That's it, Terri was going to trample him.

"Don't worry, Mr. Normandeau, I'm not interested in your spirituality. I'm here to discuss your successive failures in retaining employment. See, I'm a time traveler—"

Terri barreled through the smaller stranger, pushing him aside. But to his surprise, the stranger simply appeared a few feet ahead of him, the same big grin on his face.

"I understand that it might be hard to believe, Mr. Normandeau, but I'm an agent of the future global government, to be more precise. And—"

Terri pushed through the smaller man again, and this time he trampled him, a big stomp on the smaller man's chest that was accompanied by a wheezing sound. But the stranger appeared again ahead of Terri as if he had never left him behind, his beige suit not bearing any trait of being stepped on.

"The startup in Atlanta. The consulting company in Montgomery. The assisted living center in Pensacola. The hot dog cart right here in Chattanooga some days ago," recited the smaller man, this time making a puzzled Terri halt.

"How ... how do you know all that?"

"My associates and I are the ones behind every single one of your professional and entrepreneurial failures and a few of your social ones too, although, to be fair, you are particularly bad at dealing with women."

"Who the hell are you?"

"My name is Liam, and right now I certainly don't want to overwhelm you and have you making a scene here in public. Why don't we go grab a latte and then take a walk? It's quite a beautiful day and you clearly need a breather."

Terri was angry, very angry. But he was also very confused and he could use some sort of assertiveness in his life, even if it came from a weirdo stranger.

After Liam fetched his ruby chocolate, half-almond, half-soy milk mochaccino in the overpriced and only coffee shop in Chattanooga's compact Bluff View art district, he expressed a wish to walk one block down along the district's Sculpture Garden, which was placed on a leafy slope by the Tennessee River. Liam sipped his drink as he admired the profusion of artwork around him, which consisted of a mixed collection of contemporary and classic sculptures positioned alongside the garden's winding pathways. Terri, on the other hand, just marched sullenly next to the time traveler. Liam hadn't yet provided him with any of the answers he was expecting. He even made Terri pay for his ridiculously overpriced beverage, under the argument that, as a time traveler, he didn't carry money and couldn't bring anything of value from the future to the past under the risk of disrupting the economy. After a few excruciating minutes, during which Terri had been considering if he should either punch Liam or toss him into the river, the smaller man finally stopped sipping his drink.

"Mr. Normandeau, my associates and I have vowed to prevent terrible outcomes for human history. I don't want to brag, but our actions have had quite palpable results. We have managed to turn Earth a few centuries from now from a wasteland with poisoned oceans, a plutonium-infused atmosphere, and warring factions on course for mutual annihilation into a global technodemocracy with environmental standards prior to the natural collapse that you've been observing at its starting point in your time."

"Sounds cool, are you hiring?"

"As a matter of fact we are, however our organization can only hire personnel born after the time traveling technology was developed. Also, we have certain standards, and I don't think the HR department would bother to interview a genocidal brute like you."

"Wait, what?"

"This might be a shock for you, since you're quite the underachiever, but—"

"I never killed anyone!"

"Of course not, because we had no choice but to intervene in every endeavor that might get you headed toward becoming a bloodthirsty despot later in your life."

"So, the fire in my consulting office in Montgomery—"

"It was us, although you made it easy by leaving all that bourbon next to the heater."

"Are you behind that fake drug test that forced me to shut down my care home for the elderly in Pensacola?"

"Guilty!"

"What about when I lost that job at American Airlines because Becky sued me for sexual harassment?"

"That was challenging. We had to squeeze her butt while you were right behind her, but not paying enough attention to notice my associate in action for the fraction of seconds it took."

"The hot dog cart last week?

"Easy-peasy! We just filled it with C-4 and blew it up when you took a bathroom break!"

"Did ... did you guys just get me fired from About Thyme?"

"No, that was on you, but we were monitoring the situation. You should have held up that fart."

"I didn't fart!" yelled a now fuming Terri, as he slapped the cup of hot cocoa from Liam's hand, who eyed the splatter of pink and viscous liquid on the ground with longing eyes.

"Did you know that ruby chocolate is only available in a very limited span of time that starts in the mid-2010s and ends in 2031, when President Tiffany Trump—"

"What about all these times I got fired for 'anger issues'?" asked Terri, now pacing back and forth like a nervous gorilla in his zoo cage.

"That ... was you, too," cautiously said Liam, "You are a bit of a bully, you know that, right?"

"If I'm such a danger, why not just kill me?"

"We would never kill anyone. We are all part of time. If we kill someone before their existential cycle ends, we'd be making time disappear, and that would affect all of us, since we all use time. It's a shared resource yearned for by all the denizens of the universe."

"I don't get it."

"Basically, when you are in the wrong place you tend to do very wrong stuff."

"But I'm a good person, right?"

"Well, imagine if Hitler never quit painting. Would he be a good person?"

"He would still hate Jews! I don't hate anyone! I mean ... I don't think I do."

"According to our data you hate your neighbor from apartment 38."

"I've never seen the fucker, but that stoner keeps me awake by talking and laughing out loud non-stop every damn night since he moved from Louisiana, as if he were living by himself in the bayou or something!

"So, you hate him."

"Yes, but I don't want him to go to Auschwitz, I just want him to go ... somewhere else."

"A different concentration camp?"

"No!" interjected an exasperated Terri, "Like, I want him to move out and go to another building!"

"That's fair."

"So, I'm not like freaking Hitler," said Terri, as he eyed Liam in an almost desperate hope for confirmation.

"I guess you are not. You are making some good points there."

For a moment neither of the two men said anything. Terri felt that Liam had finally come to terms with his stance. How could he be anything like Hitler? He never even aspired to be at the top of the ladder. On the occasions when he worked for big corporations, he was the guy happily assembling the PowerPoint slides, not the one deciding what they would feature. When he tried his hand at startups, he would abide by any demand made by venture capitalists funding his projects, which eventually included taking advantage of Terri's above-average size and explosive yet compliant nature to terrorize their competitors. Terri abided by the rules and answered on command. His geeky cousin, Larry, who loved RPG games, once described him as lawful evil (and got subsequently punched for that remark). Terri was normal, the most normal of normal men and very proud of his normalcy. But still, he had to ask, just to be sure: "Then there is nothing wrong with me, right?"

"You are screwed up, quite like Hitler," was Liam's nonchalant answer.

"We just talked through that. I—"

"I mean, the havoc we've been preventing you from creating was screwed up."

"What kind of havoc?"

"I'm not here to give you any bad ideas. You know, considering your inclinations."

"I don't have 'inclinations.'"

"Oh, you do."

"Okay, you know what. I guess I do have 'inclinations,' because I want to punch you so bad right now."

"I'm just trying to be friendly here. And helpful, if you'll allow me to assist you."

"You know what, this is BS. I don't need assistance!"

"Would you rather have your memory of this meeting wiped and have us keep sabotaging every single one of your attempts to join a lifestyle that would lead to a historic hazard with grave social consequences for all humanity?"

"I'm in for the assistance! Assist me, boss!"

"Let's review your options," said the agent as he touched his tablet and scanned it before turning his attention back to Terri. "Would you mind living in Alaska?"

"I ... would. I went to college in Florida for a reason."

"We need to keep you the hell away from Florida, too many people there are prone to follow your lead into doing stupid, dangerous crap."

"Fine ... but ... Alaska?"

"Would you prefer Canada? Nothing really relevant comes out of that godforsaken wasteland."

"I take that Canada changed a lot in the future."

"No, it's exactly the same cesspool of limited ambition, passive-aggression, and fake friendliness as in your time."

"I met a Canadian once. He was friendly but it didn't feel fake."

"I can assure you that he was tattling about you as soon as you turned your back on him. Do you know how to tell a Canadian is being fake in all that oily friendliness? They smile by raising only their upper lip, like the filthy beavers they are."

"That sounds ... racist."

"That's rich coming from Hitler!"

"I'm not Hitler."

"And I'm not racist, I was even married to a Canadian for a while. Sub-only in the sheets, condescending in the streets. Insufferable."

"I see, it's personal."

"It doesn't matter, on second thought I think Canada is out for you. It would be a hassle to get you papers to emigrate out of the US."

"Fine, Alaska then. I mean, I guess they have wi-fi and heating there."

"Well, there's the thing, you can't live or even stay close to certain cities in Alaska," said Liam, as he examined his tablet. "Not Anchorage and certainly not Juneau ... and ... I guess Fairbanks is off limits. Hmm ... would you be okay situated in the Alaskan wilderness, making a living hunting and gathering?"

"No wi-fi then?"

"I don't like your tone, Mr. Normandeau. I thought you were past the point of intellectually squirming about your doom."

"I'm a good person, I don't deserve this!"

"Tell that to the hundreds of mutilated elderly in Pensacola."

"Who?"

"Nobody, and you know why? Because we sent a fake positive toxicology test to the licensing bureau when you tried to start your home for the elderly there!"

"Man, I really wanted that project to work."

"Do you want to mutilate seniors?"

"Why would I mutilate seniors?!"

"You tell me, Mr. Normandeau."

"I wouldn't! That's what I'm telling you!"

"Of course you wouldn't, you would just use your minions to do the dirty work."

"How can I have minions? I don't even have friends!"

"What a coincidence, Mr. Normandeau, because every person ever who did have minions happened to not have friends.

That's the very concept of minions, they work for you, they'd die for you, but they are notoriously not quite superb at organizing surprise birthday parties and being there for you with a mug of spiked hot cocoa when you are feeling the blues."

"This is ridiculous, I don't want to hurt anybody or ... have minions. I just want to make a living so I can ... I don't know ... relax at the end of the day, binge watch Netflix or something like that! It's not too much, is it?"

"You can binge hunt polar bears in the tundra."

"Look, at least I have a home here in Chattanooga."

"Not for long, it will be foreclosed in two months and you will be homeless."

"Ouch. I ... I don't think I can survive homelessness."

"You can't. But you can survive wilderness," Liam said, as he took a quick glance at his tablet, "for a while."

"If I go to Alaska—"

"Alaska's wilderness. Don't get even close to the cities or the Canadian border."

"If I do will you guys stop meddling in my life?"

"That's the plan."

"And there is ... nothing I can do to change that?"

"Doing nothing in the middle of nowhere is what you can do."

"I mean ... how could having a hot dog cart in downtown Chattanooga have made any harm?"

"We prevented the Black Weiner's day five years from now, when every single hot dog cart would explode at the same time, killing millions."

"How could I—"

"Minions."

Terri sighed, resigned to his fate.

"Fine. I guess I'm gonna go home and start packing."

Suddenly a small, athletic woman who looked like the meanest kindergarten teacher ever in her mauve cybernetic dungarees emerged from a bush and kicked Liam in the face. Before Liam could react, she produced a banana, pointed it at Liam and zapped him with a laser beam.

"What the hell happened?" a flabbergasted Terri muttered, his eyes locked on the smoking pile of ashes that used to be Liam.

"Agent Samira Hamid, department of quality and control," answered the woman as she lowered her banana after acknowledging Terri. "I had no choice but to intercept this operation, also I'm legally obligated to disclose that the banana I'm holding is actually a laser gun shaped like a banal object in order to prevent the contact of persons in your timeline with futuristic technology and it should be eaten in case there's a risk of—"

"Why did you kill him? Was he a bad guy?"

"No, you are the bad guy. Liam was one of our best agents but he had to be stopped. Sending you to Alaska would be a colossal disaster!"

"How could I do anything from there by myself?"

"Not only you—"

"Yeah, I get it, my 'minions,' too."

"Oh, I can see that someone was already machinating inside their devilish head."

"What would have happened in freaking Alaska?!"

"You and your minions would create the Borealian Reich, a new country in between Alaska and Greenland."

"You mean, Canada?"

"Once you were placed in Alaska's wilderness, the neighboring, depraved Canadians would show up in droves to be your eager minions and decisively contribute in your frigid Arctic nation's project to take over the world!"

"Yeah, I don't want that."

"What do you mean you don't want that? You are a ruthless tyrant in the making."

"All I want is to go home and watch Netflix, ma'am! And I could use a drink! Also, I worked all day in a freaking vegan restaurant where they treated me like crap, so a big, rare steak would be nice, too!"

"Let me guess, you want all that booze and food served by the children that survived the great mauling of New Hampshire by the Borealian forces?"

"See, I have no idea what you are talking about. I was going to Alaska to avoid all that genocide stuff."

"Are you suggesting that you are willing to renounce your totalitarian fate?"

"Just tell me what to do! You can trust me!"

"Would you trust Hitler?"

"I'm not Hitler! I can't kill anyone! You are the one who killed someone and ... wait! I thought you guys couldn't kill!"

"Liam and I shared the same timeframe so murdering him won't affect the continuum of spacetime. What is forbidden is to kill someone from the past, otherwise I would have killed you already."

"I have no doubt about that."

"Very well, Mr. Normandeau. There might be an alternative for you. On the coast of Georgia there is a subterranean bunker that has been long forgotten and will remain that way for centuries. If you promise to move there and never leave, I can ensure that the Agency won't interfere in the course of your life again."

"I would still be able to go out to fetch food, right?"

"No, but the mold that grows in the bunker is passably edible."

"Can I get some wi-fi hooked in there?"

"So you can recruit your minions?"

"Who the hell recruits minions online?"

"Anyone seeking minions, duh! Have you ever seen 4chan?"

"Yes, I—"

"Of course you have, what a stupid question."

"I mean, not like that, I skip the racist stuff and just browse the porn—I mean ... the—"

"Georgia. Take it or I will erase your memory."

Unbeknownst to Terri and Samira, one of the many statues in the garden had been observing them. It was a humanoid figure covered in metallic plates with a vague resemblance to a military uniform. Its name was "The South Shall Rise Again," by area artist, confederate daughters' local chapter member and baker who refused to cater to gay patrons Lee-Ann Nicholson, although the piece currently standing in the Sculpture Garden wasn't the original, but a perfect replica sent from the future and filled with a state-of-the-art sentient AI known as N1C0. After analyzing and gauging the temporal risks and opportunities represented by Samira's actions, the robot decided that the time had come to vaporize her with a laser blast from its cybernetic eyes.

"Greetings, Terri Jackson Normandeau," said the robot, as it finally moved from the pedestal on which it had been placed for years and approached a disconcerted Terri, who was afraid but also too mentally exhausted to panic and run. "I am a representative of the department of quality and control for the department of quality and control. My name is N1C0, but you can call me Nicoletta. The latter is also personally preferred, although I'm programmed to answer to my manufacturing name despite the post-industrial-centric, meta-sedulous, para-bio-patriarchal normativity that is implied in it and which I reject. As for my pronouns, they are—"

"Did you ... kill her?" said Terri, pointing at the second pile of smoking ashes next to him.

"Yes, Samira's actions would precipitate a calamitous outcome in the future by giving you access to a network of eager minions vowed to accomplish your objectives of destruction and chaos."

"In a forgotten bunker in Georgia?"

"You'd have plenty of idle time in there to interact on 4chan."

"I thought I wouldn't have access to wi-fi."

"It turned out that Verizon dug an optic-fiber tunnel next to the bunker."

"Let me guess, should I go to Antarctica or something?"

"Nice try, Hitler."

"I'm not Hitler."

"Antarctica will be the perfect base in a few decades to launch a global domination campaign thanks to all the soon-to-be-discovered biochemical properties of penguin fat."

"What are the alternatives?"

"There are no alternatives. I'm here to erase your memory so our organization can continue to diligently sabotage every single one of your efforts in life until you die of natural causes."

"I can't stand it anymore! If you can't kill me, just put me in a coma or something!"

Nicoletta stood still for a moment. The robot was processing a new variable that it had not taken in consideration until that moment. And then, it spoke: "Coma seems like an alternative that will minimize the risks to the fabric of time that your eventual death by either murder or induced suicide may cause. And my hardware possesses a device that can cast such a state upon your body."

"I see, are you gonna hypnotize me? Or maybe use a chemical from the future?"

"I will hit you really hard in your head."

"You know what? Fair enough! I'll take it!"

"Very well," said Nicoletta, "Whenever you are ready."

Terri stared at the last rays of sunlight being refracted in the waters of the river, as he felt his eyes getting teary. But before he gave Nicoletta leave to bludgeon him, a plume of water suddenly rose up from the river and splashed both the robot and Terri. When Terri had a chance to dry his eyes, he noticed a rectangular device clasped to Nicoletta's neck that generated a cascade of sparks and electrical current. The robot seemed to be stunned although, for some reason, it hummed "I wish I was in Dixie."

"We don't have much time," said a voice behind Terri, who turned around to face a scrawny man with a long, ginger mullet and a jittery grin. Of all the agents he was the only one that could pass as a local.

"Oh, great," said a distressed Terri, "Are you here because the coma will make me control ferrets telepathically and use them as an army that will wipe the world?"

"That'd be rad, but no, *Mein Führer*," said the ginger.

"I'm not Hitler! I told it to all the other agents—"

"I'm not with these dorks! And I was just joking, you ain't like Hitler at all!"

"Well, thank you!"

"You are much better than Hitler, sir!"

"About that ... I'm not really into that racism stuff and—"

"It's not about racism, it's about ethics in work force hiring."

Before Terri could react, he frowned as he could smell a stench. A familiar stench.

"Did you ... fart?"

"Yes, sorry about that. I have this issue and ... you were ... I mean ... will be the only one who will take me seriously despite my ... flatulence. Since the start you knew I was much more than a farty hick from Louisiana who—"

"Were you the one who farted in the vegan restaurant?"

"Yes, I reckon I got some bottled farts teleported in there, but to help you, sir! That job would turn you soft."

"I needed that job!"

"You can do better, sir!" said the ginger, as he handed a business card to Terri. "Here, send your resume to these guys. They are our people. Once you get there it will be a safe space for you from these snowflakes that keep messing up your life."

Terri glanced at the card. It had a contact for the HR division of MASKKKULON Cryptocurrency Investments LLC.

"I ... I'm afraid."

"Of what?"

"I don't want to be Hitler."

"Don't worry, the psycho barker with the shark tank under the trap doors is gonna be your boss. You'll be the cool guy in the middle who throws surprise birthday parties and is always there with a mug of spiked hot cocoa when we feel the blues."

"So, I'm ... I mean, I will be your friend?"

"Heck, no! Don't get creepy on me, sir!"

"If I'm not the top guy why did these agents say that I was like Hitler?"

"Because snowflakes think that evil people are all the same, they don't get that we have different shades of darkness. Also, you are gonna punch the top guy to death and toss his body in the shark tank when he announces that he's stepping down and calling for democratic elections."

"Wait, are you saying that I'm gonna kill future Hitler?" asked Terri with a glimmer of hope.

"You are gonna replace him, boss!"

"I'm not a leader, I'm a doer."

"I know, your first decision as overlord will be to convene the

HR department to select a new overlord. That whole process will stress the hell out of you. You are gonna pack on even more weight and punch half of the HR personnel to death until they select someone."

"That's not me! I don't punch people ... I mean ... not on purpose ... I mean. ... Sometimes I do, when people get me mad, but I stopped being a bully in high school—"

"That was the problem, you should never have stopped doing something you're good at. But it's okay, you are gonna get back to using these three hundred pounds of brawn and these ham-sized fists for good, I mean ... for evil."

"I shouldn't do something just because I'm good at it."

"Why not?"

"Because I want to be normal!"

"Not sure about you, sir, but all the normal people I know are normal precisely because, given the opportunity, they do things they like and are good at."

"I can't."

"You will," said the ginger, amid a guffaw that showed a mouth with no more than three teeth, all of them broken, "And you're gonna like it."

Terri frowned, not only for the sight of the toothless mouth, but at the guffaw. He'd heard it before. It was the boisterous one that had been waking him up in the middle of the night. The ginger could only be his neighbor. Terri suddenly coiled his big fist and readied it to punch, only to realize that the damage in that mouth had already been done.

"You know where to find me and my teeth, boss," suggested the ginger.

Illimani Ferreira

Illimani Ferreira is a science fiction writer currently living in LSD (Lower, Slower Delaware), where he is trying to figure out if, as a person who grew up in Brazil's central savannas, he is a beach person or not. His humorous science fiction novel *Terminal 3* was released in 2020 by Möbius Books. This is his first professional short fiction sale. You can find Illimani on twitter (@ifscifi) or contact him through his website www.ifscifi.com.

COUCH QUEST

ERIC D. LEAVITT

Jim felt ridiculous.

"Lana, do I actually have to wear this?"

"Yes!" his wife said, looking down her nose at him. A nose that was now three times longer than his full standing height. "You're Lego-sized. What if you run into something in there? Like a spider?"

His knees wobbled. Spiders. The embarrassing armor his crafty wife had made out of soda cans and cheap toys from Wal-Mart went from too much to not enough.

"I'm not scared of spiders."

"Uh-huh. And that time at the park—"

"Fine! Fine. I'll wear it for you. It's just, couldn't you make it look, I don't know, less like it's from one of Daisy's stupid fantasy books?"

"They're not stupid!"

Her voice shook the table Jim stood on like an earthquake.

"Oops, sorry," she whispered. "They're not stupid. It gets her reading. And they can be pretty good! I'd know, since I've actually read some of them, unlike anyone else in this basement."

Jim rolled his eyes. "It's just a bunch of fake nonsense!"

Lana crossed her arms. "Jim, an alien flew by Earth blasting out shrink rays at random until other aliens stopped it. They apologized, told us it was drunk, that the effect would wear off, and to forget it ever happened before they flew away at faster than the speed of light."

"Well. Yeah. But that actually happened."

Lana's sigh was a gust of coffee-scented wind. "Jim, I know you've had a rough couple of days—"

"Rough? Lana, I have a nano-dick!"

"It's microscopic, not nanoscopic. Don't sell yourself short."

Judging by how much she was laughing, she'd been holding onto that one for a while.

"Yeah. Short. Hilarious. Lana. Lana!"

She covered her mouth. "I'm, I'm sorry! But your cute little face looked so angry, it was adorable! And your itty-bitty voice—"

More laughter. It was getting hard for Jim to stay insulted. Lana's laughter was near the top of the list for reasons why he fell in love with her.

"Lana, please! C'mon!"

"Okay! Okay." She wiped away tears large enough for him to drown in. He shuddered at the thought.

"Can't we look for the ring when I'm back to normal?"

Lana shook her head. "You'll be fine! Look." She reached down, her hand the size of a small house. "I made you a shield." A soda bottle cap that she'd whittled down. "And here's your mighty sword!" A sewing needle. This was so emasculating. Lana continued. "I'm positive it's in the couch. We looked everywhere else, right? It probably fell through one of the holes Scrappy put in it."

When the alien shrink ray hit, Jim was sitting on the gargantuan, ancient couch in the basement, watching TV. The only thing that shrunk was him. Everything he'd been wearing had stayed the same size. They'd accounted for all of it, except one very important thing: his wedding ring.

"The ring isn't going anywhere. Lana—"

"Jim." Lana rested her hands on either side of him. "If your mother finds out that I let you lose your grandfather's wedding band, she will never forgive me. She's bringing Daisy back for dinner and she is going to ask about it." She leaned back and placed a hand on her belly and the small bump there. "If we can't find it, we'll have to name our only son after him to make up for it. Do you want that? Do you want to do that to your child?"

His grandfather's name had been Kermit. Might as well name the kid Punching Bag. He raised his hands in supplication.

"Alright, alright. I don't understand why we'd have to do that, but alright." He swung his "sword" and his shield over his back with the bit of string she'd attached to them and tied them tight. "Let's do this."

Lana smiled, a bit smugly. "My hero." She laid her hand in front of him, palm up.

A minute later, he was attached to a length of fishing line suspended above one particularly large hole in the couch.

"Okay," Lana said. "I'll be right here the entire time. Just shout if you need help."

"If you could even hear me," Jim mumbled. His throat was sore from how loudly he'd been speaking. For his wife, he gave two tiny thumbs up.

Jim entered another world along a beam of light, courtesy of the basement LED can-lights. Everything else around him was dim, or cast in deep, dark shadows. As his eyes adapted, the couch structure became visible. Infinite rows of humungous wooden beams and massive metal brackets, disappearing into the shadowy world beyond his column of illumination. His heart thumped madly in his chest. He tried to take a calming breath, but instead sucked in a piece of dust as long as his forearm. He jerked to a stop.

"You okay?" his wife asked from somewhere above him.

"Peachy!"

"What?" she asked.

"FINE!" he said at the very top of his lungs, which sent him into another coughing fit.

"Should I keep lowering you?"

Jim looked down. Logically, he knew it couldn't be more than a couple of feet, but it looked like hundreds.

"YES." The descent continued.

What did all this remind him of? Oh. The Mines of Moria. Jesus, how many times had he watched that stupid movie? Probably hundreds. It was the only thing that kept Daisy occupied and quiet when she was two. He could recite it line by line. He blamed Lana.

As he neared the bottom, the basement's rug floor started looking like a forest. The old, plush carpet pile was taller than he was.

And there was, oh god, hair and dust and grime all over it. If he fell into that–

"Lana! Stop!" Nothing. "LANA!" Still nothing. Shit. There was a wooden support to his right. He'd have to swing for it. He started rocking as hard as he could. The carpet grew closer and closer, zooming back and forth beneath him. How did Lana not feel this!

This swing! He reached with his feet. The tips of his toes grabbed the edge. And slipped.

"Crap!" He swung back, the dust and hair covered rug grabbing at his legs. He hiked his knees up to his chest. He reached the apex of the back swing. He wasn't going to make it. He rushed downward, back toward sure death.

Adrenaline like he'd never felt pumped through him. And the memory of middle school gym class where he embarrassed himself by not being able to climb that stupid rope tied to the gym's ceiling. The fear of death was more effective encouragement. He hoisted himself up, hand over hand, as fast as he could. He hit the rug. His momentum slowed as dust and ancient dog hair pulled at him.

Hand over hand. Hand over hand. Hand over–his back hit what felt like a brick wall, his makeshift shield taking the brunt of it. In the clarity of mind that only oncoming doom could provide, he realized it was the wooden beam. He spun, reaching out with one hand, and found the edge.

He pulled himself up and flopped over onto the wood, a cloud of stringy dust wafting up in protest. Jim covered his mouth and gasped for breath through his hand.

"Holy. Crap. Holy. Crap."

"You reach the bottom yet?" came Lana's voice, like distant thunder.

"I'm down!"

"Honey?"

"Damnit." She couldn't hear him. He rolled around, untied the fishing line and tugged repeatedly as hard as he could.

"Got it! I attached the string to a little bell. Just tug and it'll ring when you're ready. Okay?"

"Sure. Only just nearly drowned in—"

Something crawled on his arm. He squealed, swatted at it, and jumped to his feet. The column of light from above only barely shone light on the platform he was on. All around him, things moved.

Jim froze. What was it? Oh, god oh god oh, wait.

He leaned over, inspecting the pile of dust near him.

"Dust mites?" Jesus, they were everywhere. His skin crawled and he swiped vigorously over his whole body. At least they were still small, like a beetle. But, they don't bite. Right? They eat dust. Wait. Wasn't dust mostly made from human skin? He was made of human skin.

He needed to find that ring and get the hell out of here.

"If I were a ring, where would I be?"

He walked quickly along the wooden beam, looking while also trying not to step on any of the mites or particularly large piles of dust. A few paces distant in any direction though, the space became dark and hazy.

"Shoulda brought a light." Except he didn't think they made lights small enough for him. Maybe one of Daisy's toys?

Jim decided he needed a better vantage point. Something higher up. There was another wooden crossbeam above him that looked good, but how to get up there?

There. A metal spring that wound up into the darkness. Why the hell would there be a spring?

"Wait! This thing reclines?" He had no idea! He'd never seen any levers! How many football games had he watched sitting up-right like some kind of peasant? He needed to figure it out.

The spring worked like a ladder. Very easy to climb, so long as he didn't look down. Once he stepped onto the second level, he continued tracing the spring up with his eyes. It was hard to tell. Was there a button up there? Or a mount? He didn't see a hinge anywhere.

Creak.

Ice ran down Jim's back. He spun. Nothing but quiet, dusty shadow in every direction. Spiders. Cockroaches. Swarms of fire ants. His mind raced at the possibilities. He swung his shield and sword off his back and braced his feet and his bowels.

Nothing. Silence. Then a gasping sound.

Jim looked up. There, peeking over the edge of the next level of wooden beams, was an alien's face. Like, a stereotypical, little green Martian alien face.

Jim screamed.

The alien screamed. It produced what looked like a cheap, sci-fi raygun you'd get at a Halloween store and aimed it at him. Jim lifted his shield on instinct. The non-monkey part of his brain reminded him that it was literally a bottle cap. The monkey part of his brain shrieked in terror.

There was a sound like a zipper being zipped too fast. His little bottle cap shield lit up like the Sun and disintegrated before his eyes, leaving him standing there holding a cloth strap and no hair on his left arm.

Jim looked back at the alien. The alien made another screaming noise. The raygun lit up. Monkey-brain pulled the next lever in the monkey self-defense arsenal. Run away! He bolted left. Again, the zipper noise, but this time followed by a pop.

Jim looked over his shoulder and skidded to a halt. The alien lifted the gun in front of his face, shook it, then looked down at Jim. Even though it was an alien, Jim knew terror when he saw it.

"Um," the alien said in a high-pitched, nerdy voice. "I come in peace?"

Monkey-brain turned into gorilla-brain. Gorilla-brain said MURDER IT UNTIL IT IS DEAD.

Jim let out a war cry and charged toward the spring. He slapped the sewing needle between his teeth and started climbing up faster than he'd ever climbed anything before. The alien squealed and leapt on the spring, too, climbing up and away. But Jim was faster. When the alien jumped off on the fifth wooden support beam, Jim was heartbeats behind, needle in his hand the second his feet touched down.

Flying Saucer. Both the monkey and gorilla sides of Jim's brain broke at the sight, letting normal human Jim's thoughts return.

He'd been chasing an alien through a couch armed with a sewing needle. What the hell was he—

Flying Saucer. There was a Flying Saucer perched on the wood not ten paces from him, about the size of his wife's hand. The alien was frantically slapping at what could've been a door panel at the saucer's center, where it was nearest the ground.

"Wait," Jim said, out of breath, with the experience finally catching up to him. "You speak English?"

The alien turned. "Uh. Yes?"

"Holy shit."

"Please," the alien said, holding up both hands, now empty. "I didn't *want* to kill you."

"You tried to vaporize me!" Jim brandished his sewing needle. "Seemed pretty intentional!"

"Well. Yes. But only because I can't be seen by you! If it's found out I've interacted with a native, I'll be fined!"

"FINED? You were going to kill me over money?"

The alien tilted his head. "Oh. Well. When you put it like that, it does seem like poor reasoning."

"IT IS POOR REASONING!"

"It's a lot of money though, and I don't really have any. I'll be in debt for life!"

"I'd have no life! I'd be dead!"

The alien shrunk back. "But—But I have important work to do!"

"Beneath my couch?"

"No. No, I'm just hiding here."

Jim put two and two together.

"Wait. Those shrink rays that shrunk everyone, shrunk me, were some kind of transporter beam?"

The alien rolled its eyes. "It's not like *Star Trek*, but yes if it helps you understand."

"You've seen *Star Trek?*"

"Yes. I'm a social scientist studying the evolution of primitive sentiences. I have to imbibe your media, especially those with visions of your future."

"You watch our sci-fi?"

The alien nodded. "And read it. And play your video games. It's a lot of work!"

"Yeah, I bet."

"But yes, those 'shrink rays,'"—the alien did literal air quotes with two of his seven fingers on each hand—"brought me and some of my comrades to the surface of the planet. Those of us lucky enough to escape before our vessel was captured. Your shrinking was unforeseen. We didn't believe it would have the same effect on your biology."

Jim rubbed at his temples. "So, let me get this straight. You're some kind of anthropologist? Who cares enough about anthropologists to want to hurt them?"

The alien looked aghast. "Anthropology is a critical field!"

Jim nodded. "Yeah, totally. Look, I'll forgive you for trying to vaporize me if you turn me back to normal."

"Ah. I can't."

"What? Why not?"

"I don't have the necessary equipment! But don't worry, without a maintainer, you'll return to normal size in ..." It checked its wrist. Jim didn't see any watch. The hell?

"Honestly," the alien continued, "You should've returned by now. Maybe there is a difference in your biology's response. Interesting. It should be any moment now."

"Oh." Jim scratched at the beard growing on his face. He hadn't dared try to shave and it wasn't quite over the itchiness hump. "That's good, I guess."

Wait, why was he here again? Oh! "Hey, okay, how about this. Have you seen a ring about ..." He held up his finger, paused, then stretched his arms as wide as possible. "About this big?"

"Yes." The alien said, curtly. Jim's eyebrows raised.

"Can you tell me where I could find it?"

"Yes."

The pause was deafening. "Jesus, what are you, a child? Will you tell me where to find it?"

"I ... can't."

"Why not?"

"Because you can't go to where it is. You're not allowed."

Jim glanced above the alien. "It's in your ship, isn't it?"

The alien flared his arms wide as if to block Jim. "No, it isn't!"

"Wow, you are bad at this."

The alien made a pained expression. Surprisingly human. All that TV maybe?

"Listen." It said. "I need—"

Creak. Scritch.

The alien's green hue went cool blue.

Jim whirled, raising the needle. "What was that?"

The alien didn't respond. Jim glanced over his shoulder to see it pawing at the base of the saucer again. It looked like there was a small keypad there. It cried out. "No! That was the right code!"

"Yo! What was that?"

"Stupid thing! No! I don't have fifteen minutes! No!"

"ALIEN!"

"My name is Xorbix! Doctor Xorbix! And that noise was some kind of horrible monster that lives in here and I'm going to die because of my stupid ship's security system!"

A blur of motion caught Jim's eye. He started backing up. "Oh god, oh god, what is it? Some kind of spider? A roach?"

"No! It's—"

And then Jim saw it. Legs, too long and too many, curling around a bracket to the left of the flying saucer.

"A house centipede!" they screamed in unison.

Jim nearly shit himself. He turned and ran full tilt. The alien squealed.

"No! Please, help! Ah!"

Jim looked back. It was huge. Twice as long as he was tall, and it was racing along another spring toward the alien, lightning fast. It pounced onto the saucer. The alien ran in a circle beneath the saucer, screaming the entire time as the centipede ran along the outer rim of the saucer after him.

Run, Jim told himself. Damn it. Run! It tried to kill you! You've got kids and a wife! It shrank you! You have a nano-dick because of it! Damn it, run!

Jim ran. Back toward the saucer.

"Keep going!" The alien needed no encouragement. It dodged and juked beneath the saucer as the centipede lashed out with its mandibles from above. The creature noticed Jim a moment too late for it to dodge his first needle thrust. It made a horrible shrill noise as the needle stabbed through its carapace. It curled and rolled off the saucer, terrible ooze coming from its side.

Jim held his needle up like a sword. "C'mon you bastard. Come on!"

It leapt at him. Jim closed his eyes and braced the needle. It hit it with a sickening *schlick* noise. The impact sent him to the ground, weight pinning him down. Its arms beat at him with incredible force, biting with dripping mandibles. Oh, shit. Were they poisonous? Wait, venomous? Whatever! Jim screamed in terror.

A length of hair, it looked like his wife's, lashed around the thing's neck and yanked. It bucked like a bull, twisting and writhing.

"Kill it!" the alien shrieked. Do centipedes have hearts? He didn't know. Jim decided on quantity over quality and stabbed blindly

over and over. It thrashed, slapping Jim into the air. He hit the wood beam once, then there was nothing beneath him.

He whipped his free hand out, barely catching the edge of the beam.

"Oh crap! Help!"

His hand slipped and was then engulfed in a fourteen-finger death grip.

"I've got you!" The alien strained against Jim's weight. It couldn't lift him, but it was enough that Jim was able to pull himself up. They flopped onto the dust-coated beam, both gasping for air.

"The centipede?" Jim asked.

"Dead."

Jim lifted his head. The centipede was curled into a ball to his right. He'd slayed it. Damn.

Fifteen minutes later, the alien walked down the ramp of his ship with some kind of tricorder looking thing.

"It's not a tricorder," the alien said. It passed it over the scrapes and bruises Jim had sustained. The cuts knit; the bruises disappeared.

"Looks like a tricorder," Jim said. "And thanks."

"Tricorders can't heal."

"Wait. Can't they? I swear I saw that once."

"Medical tricorders are used to scan the patient for later healing."

"I think you've watched too much *Star Trek*, bud."

The alien flipped the little device shut. "Heresy. But I must thank you. That thing has been hunting me since I got here. That weapon I cobbled together was meant for it, not for you."

"Ah. Makes sense."

Another pause.

"I apologize for your situation, but I really do need the ring."

"Why?"

"The platinum. I'm using it to amend a part of my size maintainer. When we escaped to this planet, we didn't have time to prepare. Without it, I'd grow back to normal size in a matter of hours."

"And that'd be bad?"

"Oh, yes."

"How bad?"

"If your government gets me? My people would be forced to atomize the area to prevent unnatural cultural contamination."

"Um, really?"

"Worse." The alien continued, "If my people find me, I'll be forced to give up my other comrades. It's a war out there."

"Jeeze." Jim rubbed his eyes and resigned himself to his fate. "My wife is going to kill me."

"I should be able to move along in a week or so. I'll leave the ring here when I go."

"Alright, alright. Kermit really isn't such bad name. Classic, really."

"Kermit? Like, the frog?"

Jim waved it off. "Sucks to go back empty-handed. Can you give me some idea or tech or something? I wouldn't mind becoming a billionaire."

The alien shook his head. "I'm willing to answer some questions, but I can't interfere with your development as a species."

Jim leaned back. What did he really want to know? He snapped his fingers. "Got it!"

AN HOUR AFTER he entered the couch, Jim rode the fishing line back up to the outside world. His armor was dented and covered in monster centipede goo, as was his sword. Dragon Slayer. Eh. Centipedes don't breathe fire. He'll have to talk to Daisy about a good name for the needle. He was definitely keeping it.

The glare of the basement can-lights was blinding. So was the relief on his wife's face.

"God, I was worried sick! I was about to start cutting into it!" Relief turned to disappointment as she lifted the rest of the fishing line out of the hole.

"No ring?"

Jim opened his mouth to reply. The strongest feeling of vertigo he'd ever felt rushed over him. The world spun.

Suddenly, he was upside down, feet stretched over the edge

of the couch. He was normal sized again, his needle sword now tucked into a crease in his palm. It took everything in his power not to vomit.

A blanket, reinforced with his wife's arms, engulfed him.

"Oh, thank God! How do you feel? Are you alright?"

"Ugh. Yeah. What a rush."

She checked him over. "All your fingers, toes, and other bits check out."

"No longer microscopic!"

She chuckled. "Cold though?"

"Yup!"

"I'll go make you some soup."

"Thanks. Sorry about the ring, no luck."

"It's fine. I was already thinking about how I could go with a Muppet theme on the baby room," Lana said, running a hand through his hair and tugging at the beard. "I'm just glad you're back to you."

"Yeah. But hey! Check this out!" Jim reached down beneath the couch and pulled a hidden lever. Instantly, the seat leaned back and Jim's feet raised into the air.

Lana's mouth gaped. "It reclines?"

Eric D. Leavitt

Eric D. Leavitt is a fiction writer and an engineer for a NASA contractor on the International Space Station program, living and working in Florida's Space Coast. He has a Bachelor of Science degree in Aerospace Engineering from the University of Central Florida and has worked in the aerospace and manufacturing industry for seven years. He is a multi-year Writing Excuses Retreat alum and a member of the Write of Passage writing group. This is his first published story.

PET CARE FOR THE MODERN MAD SCIENTIST

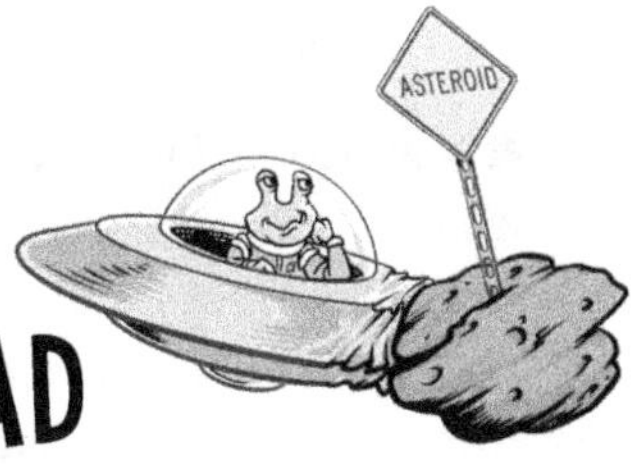

MICHAEL M. JONES

The second I got home, I knew my girlfriend had done something foolhardy, ill-advised, and quite possibly contrary to all the laws of nature and man. That's one side-effect of dating a mad scientist, after all. Instead of getting upset, I merely rolled my wheelchair over to the closest intercom, and hit the button. "Daphne, my love, did you clone the cat, even after I expressly told you not to?"

"Camille! You're home early!" she chirped back. "No, no, don't worry. You said no more cloning, and I haven't cloned anyone or anything in ages!"

"Then why," I replied, tone even, "am I looking at not one, but two identical versions of Mr. Farnsworth?" Indeed, Mr. Farnsworth was staring at me, in all his white, fluffy, snub-nosed glory, from two different spots in the room—one on the couch, the other perched on top of the cat tree, tails twitching almost in sync with one another.

"That's not cloning!" she replied. "It's—hold on, sweetie, I'll be right there. I just need to stabilize this compound before it gets to the explosive stage." The intercom clicked off, leaving me and our two cats to eye each other dubiously.

"I'm not sure I want her to elaborate," I confided to the Mr. Farnsworth on the couch. "Daphne's explanations tend to give me a headache, and I'm always afraid I'll be asked to testify someday."

The cat yawned at me, showing off his fangs, and promptly stretched, turning upside-down to show off a fuzzy belly that had a roughly 60/40 chance of being a trap. I rolled my chair over to the couch so I could stretch out a hand and risk it. The belly was soft and warm and not a trap; I was rewarded with a low rumbling. The Mr. Farnsworth on the cat tree watched jealously. "So, if you're not clones, what are you? Alien parasites? Protoplasmic doppelgangers? You guys both seem too natural to be robots."

"Wrong on all counts!" Daphne said, emerging from a set of blast doors at the far end of the room. I'd insisted she install them when we moved into this new space, if she was going to insist on working from home. That way, my stuff stood less risk of being caught in fire, flood, or explosion. She bounced over to drape in my lap, momentarily distracting me with her curvy blonde exuberance and cheerful kisses.

I returned her affections for a moment, before giving her a playful shove away. "Augh! What's that smell? No, don't tell me. Explain the cat, please."

"Oh, don't worry, I was just—"

"Cat," I pressed her.

Daphne laughed, kissed me again, and then flopped on the couch, next to the cat in question. "Okay, so you know how we agreed that Mr. Farnsworth needed a friend, but he's not really fond of other cats? Well, I figured that he certainly couldn't object to himself." She ran her fingers through his fur, and he purred like a rusty motor. The other Mr. Farnsworth, apparently upset that no one was paying attention to him, leaped from the cat tower to the couch to my lap, where he started kneading possessively, fixing his counterpart with an even blue stare. Daphne went on. "So, I combined dimensional variance theory and temporal mechanics to exploit a cat's natural probability uncertainty—"

"You're losing me," I warned. Daphne Watson hailed from a parallel dimension with a much more liberal view toward scientific disciplines, and, as a result, had a shaky grasp of what could and should be possible. She was the sort of mad scientist who'd make Jeff Goldblum weep and run for the hills. I was a grad student with a long history of changing majors to avoid leaving school. I often had to remind her to simplify it for me. On the bright side, she was the reason my wheelchair now had hover capability, built-in lasers, GPS, and voice integration.

"I put Mr. Farnsworth slightly out of sync with himself, so what you're seeing is a copy separated by a split second in time."

"Huh," I said. We each had a cat. So far, so good. "And you're sure nothing can go wrong?"

"I swear to Tesla, the math on this one was solid."

The Mr. Farnsworth on the couch hiccupped, and suddenly we had a third cat.

"Oh, no," Daphne and I said in unison.

"I'm going to go and recheck my math," she said, hopping up.

"I'm going to make nametags to keep them straight," I replied. The three cats meowed, all slightly out of sync with one another, like the world's worst a capella group. "And then I'd better feed them."

"Great plan!" Daphne said. She bent down to give me a kiss, before heading back to her lab. "I'm sure this will be an easy fix."

THREE DAYS AND more than a dozen Mr. Farnsworths later, we had to admit that it wasn't an easy fix. There were cats everywhere I looked, occupying every available surface, from the couch to the cat tower to our bed, and while they mostly got along, turf wars broke out with increasing frequency, leading to hissing, spitting, flying fur, and hurt feelings. I'd ordered cat food and litter in bulk, but it was hard to plan for the growing number of cats.

Daphne spent most of her time in the lab with the cat she claimed, without a shadow of a doubt, was the original—now designated F1 with a helpful collar tag—trying to reverse the process which saw him splitting off new versions. On the bright side, at least he was the only one generating copies, but according to Daphne, there was no actual rhyme or reason to when it happened.

"If this keeps up, I'm going to lose my mind," I told her as we grabbed a quick bite for dinner. "It's hard to study when I've got a dozen cats all demanding attention. And bless you for inventing a litterbox that eliminates messes with lasers, and automatically refills itself, and my God, that thing's going to make us rich as soon as you find a non-nuclear power source, but it's going off constantly like some kind of awful rave. Lasers everywhere, and it still smells funny. I think we're going to need several more, and quickly."

Daphne twirled pasta on her fork, and sighed. "I'm sorry, sweetie. I should have known better than to mess with cats and physics. Now I understand why that line of study was so heavily discouraged back home." She shook her head, ruefully, before brightening again. "Of course, I ended up studying Trans-Dimensional Physics, and we saw how that turned out ..."

"Living with a girlfriend who inexplicably loves you even if you violate causality and sanity on a regular basis," I agreed. I stabbed a meatball with my fork, and lifted it to my mouth, while F3, F8, F9, and F12 all stared from their various vantage points around me. F12, who was precariously perched on the arm of my chair, lazily reached out a paw as if to help himself. "Not even, furball," I said, giving him a shove so he was forced to leap down. "By the way, I caught six of them working together to get into the cupboard where we keep the treats."

Daphne blinked, and hastily swallowed her mouthful of pasta. "Oh no," she said. "They're forming a collective."

"A clowder," I replied. "It's a clowder of cats."

"No, no, no," she shot back, standing up. "This could be bad. I mean, okay, they're all technically the same cat, right? But they act like individuals. We basically have a dozen or so versions of Mr. Farnsworth. But if they're working together, linking up, we may be at risk of them developing a unified consciousness, which could lead to heightened intelligence ..."

"So, our cat becomes smarter," I said. "Is that bad? Maybe then we could teach him to be more useful."

Daphne's eyes grew wide, and she shook her head. "Imagine a cat with human intelligence and multiple bodies. This would be worse than the time I artificially augmented an octopus."

I shuddered, remembering the way Daphne had inadvertently

sowed the seeds of an octopus uprising. Sooner or later, that one was going to come back to bite us. "Okay, so how do we stop this?" I asked.

Daphne frowned. "I'm not sure. I've been working on several theories on how to reverse the process, but so far, no luck." F5 stropped her legs, meowing, and she bent down to pet him. Immediately, F2 and F11 joined the swarm. "Easy guys, I only have two hands. Wait your turn." She laughed.

I stroked F13, who'd curled up in my lap during the discussion. "We're not going to have to shoot them into space, are we? Because we can't keep getting rid of our problems that way."

She shook her head. "Not an option," she reassured me.

"Good. I'd feel bad, inflicting our cat upon the universe."

After dinner, Daphne returned to the lab, to study the original—F1—under controlled circumstances. I went to work on my latest cosplay outfit—a version of Entrapta from *She-Ra* with remote-controlled hair—and found it difficult indeed with eight cats all trying to help, all batting at my tools, trying to steal important components, and generally being nuisances. "Give that back!" I screeched at F4 after he pounced a piece of wiring. I prayed Daphne'd find a solution soon, before all hell broke loose.

That night, all hell broke loose.

We were both ripped out of sleep by blood-curdling screams, crashes, thumping, and shattering glass. "Oh shit, it's the airship pirates!" yelped Daphne, sitting straight-up, hair frizzled every which way. "To the escape pods!"

Someday she was going to have to elaborate on these airship pirates.... I blinked blearily. "No," I moaned, "it's just cats." And I was right. We exited the bedroom to find that the common room was now a wreck. "What even?" I asked. The cat tower had fallen over, the couch was a shambles, the television was on the floor and shattered ... and every single one of our fuzzy bastard, all fifteen or so by this point, was fully poofed and bottle-brushed, glaring at each other and growling.

"A cascading failure of diplomacy, I'd say." Daphne sighed.

"Typical cats," I grumbled. "Fix this, or the next failure of diplomacy will be mine. I'm about ready to start rounding them up and shipping them to every cousin and distant friend I haven't spoken to in years."

Daphne frowned. "I ... don't know how to say this, love, but ... I'm out of ideas. I've tried everything from quantum disentanglement to temporal compression, and they just won't go back to where they're supposed to be. I'm honestly wondering if Mr. Farnsworth doesn't want to be fixed."

"You're saying he can influence the process?" I asked, furrowing my brow. "How's that possible?"

"How is any of this possible? We're talking about cats here! And not just any cat, our cat! He's already been exposed to exotic radiation, experimental cat food, and stray elements in the atmosphere, and I should have taken all that into consideration before doing anything like this! I'm sorry, Camille, I screwed up and I don't know how to fix this one." Daphne threw up her hands in dismay, blue eyes wide and watery with the beginnings of tears, and it startled me. I'd almost never seen her lose her composure to such a degree.

I reached out, fingertips on her arm. "It's okay, hon. We'll find a solution." All around us, cats were slowly relaxing, fur returning to its normal level of fluffiness, tails lowering, growls dying down. Something struck me. "Maybe we've been going about this all wrong. We've been encouraging them, giving them reasons to multiply—food, attention, love. Mr. Farnsworth's been getting fifteen or so cats' worth of pampering, and he's soaking it up. What we need to do is encourage him to reintegrate himself."

Daphne unconsciously leaned into my touch, untensing even as she looked thoughtful. "So ... ignore the extras, spoil the original?"

I nodded. "Round them up, shove them all in the same space, and show Mr. Farnsworth the benefits of being an only cat again."

"But won't that reinforce his sense of superiority?"

I arched an eyebrow. "He's a cat, what do you think?"

Daphne nodded. "Good point, it's not like it can get much worse. He already thinks he rules the place."

So that's what we did. We herded F2-F18 into an enclosure in Daphne's lab—and I'll gloss over the details about that process, which took several hours, and cost us both remnants of our sanity.

At long last, we let F1, the first, the original, the baseline, out to roam the apartment, sole king of his domain. And he prowled, and yowled piteously, calling for his other selves, and they yowled back like a chorus of the damned, and we did our best to ignore those yells, giving them a little food and water because we weren't monsters, after all.

"Can't I go pet them?" Daphne begged. "I feel so bad!"

"No," I insisted. "Not unless you want a Farnsworth collective capable of conquering the world."

Instead, we spent the next few days spoiling the hell out of the one cat, giving him good food and lots of love, forcing him to stay in the moment, and finally—

Pop!

Just like that, Mr. Farnsworth pulled himself back together, swished his tail, and stalked off toward the litterbox. He'd had quite enough of this whole mess, and enough of us, thank you very much.

"That went well," said Daphne after a moment.

"And what have we learned?"

"No more experimenting on the cat."

"And if we want another pet?"

"Adopt, don't shop?"

"I'll allow it," I said. I gave her a kiss. "But let's be happy with the one we have for the time being."

The lasers in the litterbox flashed as Mr. Farnsworth finished his business and exited. Then there was a soft buzz, and a red light came on. "Containment breach imminent ..."

"Oh, no," we both said in unison.

But how we averted that crisis was another story, and another reason for which I will someday have to apologize to yet another government agency.

Michael M. Jones

Michael M. Jones lives in southwest Virginia with too many books, just enough cats, and a wife who keeps encouraging him to get more of both. He has edited several anthologies, including *Scheherazade's Façade,* and *Schoolbooks & Sorcery.* Camille and Daphne have also appeared in respectable venues such as *Broadswords & Blasters, Mad Scientist Journal,* and *Robot Dinosaurs!* where they have never destroyed the world. Yet. For more, visit www.michaelmjones.com, or find him on Twitter as @oneminutemonkey.

THE PUNCTUATION FACTORY

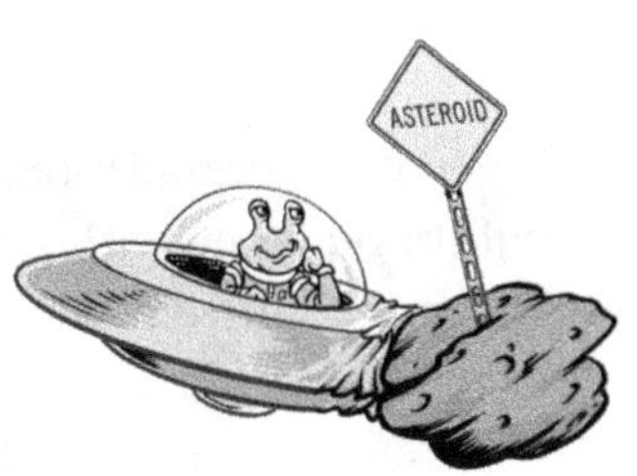

BETH GODER

Bernice clocked in at exactly 8:00 A.M., using the correct amount of cardinal numbers, capital letters, periods, and colons. She had worked at the Godwin Punctuation Factory for twenty-two years, starting out on the factory line producing commas, working her way up to floor manager, then office manager doing quality control for hyphens, until she had been promoted to the illustrious position of head of the Exclamation Department.

She thought today she might finally quit.

Bernice found Albert slumped over his desk, forlornly poking at wilted exclamation points.

"Did you see the memo?" he asked. She could hear the droop in his question mark, appended to the end of his sentence as an afterthought.

"Which one?" She kept her question mark crisp, as a point of pride, but she couldn't hide the tired lines under her eyes. Her blue scarf hung down like an exclamation mark without its point. Bernice herself looked somewhat like an exclamation mark: narrow legs encased in black slacks, arms boxed into a grey jacket, hair a black bob.

"Stewart left us to join Swindon's Grammar. He's already gone."

Bernice groaned. Stewart was the last employee in the Preservation Department. He made sure the punctuation marks were free of rot, degradation, and ink ticks. It was going to be difficult to get along without him, but Bernice supposed they would manage until someone else could be hired. She said as much to Albert, but Albert shook his head.

"They aren't planning on hiring anyone else," he said.

Bernice let out a sound best described as: !

Albert let out a sound best described as: ...

"Who do they expect to do all of Stewart's work?!" She was distraught enough that an interrobang just slipped out. She paced in front of Albert's desk, knocking over some stray commas.

"The idea is that we will all become generalists. There will be no individual departments. Instead, we will exist in a utopian efficiency."

"You mean, our director thinks we are going to magically acquire the specialized skills of all the departments, without hiring anyone who actually has the requisite knowledge or experience?"

"So it appears," said Albert.

"Great," said Bernice, wishing there was a punctuation mark to convey sarcasm. She jotted down a note to bring up a sarcasm mark at the next quarterly meeting, but then she remembered she was quitting. Probably.

As she made her way to her desk, she noticed the lid on a container of semicolons had come loose. Again. The Preservation Department oversaw the containers. There would be no one to fix it now.

Bernice pushed the lid, trying to force it closed, but the darn thing was stuck. Inside the container, semicolons hummed. Carefully, she pried the lid up, putting her hand over the opening. The semicolons tickled her palm like nibbling guppies. As she maneuvered the lid, her hand slipped. The box clattered to the floor, unleashing a flood of semicolons.

It had happened again; the semicolons were on the loose. Bernice buried her head in her hands; this was just what she needed today. A horde of semicolons made their way across the office; jumping; sliding; gliding. Onto papers; into mouths. They ran like ants; the floor was black and swirling. Chaos; chaos; chaos.

Bernice made a sound best described as: #@$&*!

The director stormed out of his office. "Who let the semicolons out?!?!" he roared. The director always used more punctuation than was needed. It bothered Bernice to no end.

It took her the rest of the afternoon to round up the semicolons, and eight were still missing.

She took out a blank sheet of paper and wrote, "I QUIT," using an obscene amount of capital letters. From her desk, she drew out a fine exclamation point she had been saving for just such an occasion, the black lines crisply drawn, almost glimmering.

When she looked down at her paper, it read:

I QUIT;

A semicolon had snuck onto her paper!

She couldn't leave her message incorrectly punctuated. She wasn't the director, for goodness' sake.

She appended: at least we all tried our best.

It was true. The Godwin Punctuation Factory was full of dedicated workers who knew the value of a job well done. Full stop. It wasn't their fault that the leadership couldn't tell the difference between an em dash and an ellipsis. She wished them all well.

Never one to slink out, Bernice strode into the director's office and handed him the paper. "It's my official resignation."

"After all of these years. What about job loyalty—or dedication—or at least the decency to not spill a crate of semicolons on your last day!?"

The director's proclivity for dashes made Bernice want to cover her ears. It was like listening to a violin bow scratching against strings. "Did you know we have a very excellent comma department?" she said.

The director, oblivious, went on. "I suppose it doesn't matter. The Exclamation Department will be reorganized shortly." He often used the passive voice to avoid responsibility. "Don't tell me that you're going to Swindon's Grammar." He said that last with particular venom. They'd lost a lot of employees to Swindon's.

Bernice hadn't thought much about what she'd do next. Maybe she would travel. She'd always longed to see the use of Spanish exclamation marks. What would the weather be like in Chile this time of year?

After, perhaps she'd see if Swindon's had an opening.

"Watch out for those semicolons," she said.

The director grimaced, revealing that he had a semicolon stuck in his teeth.

Before leaving, Bernice put the excellent exclamation point on Albert's desk, the crisp lines gleaming. She hoped he would find some use for it.

She walked through the doors of the Godwin Punctuation Factory for the last time, her smile like an upturned parenthesis.

Beth Goder

Beth Goder works as an archivist, processing the papers of economists, scientists, and other interesting folks. Her fiction has appeared in venues such as *Escape Pod, Fireside, Flash Fiction Online,* and Rich Horton's *The Year's Best Science Fiction & Fantasy.* You can find her online at bethgoder.com.

ONE BORN EVERY MINUTE

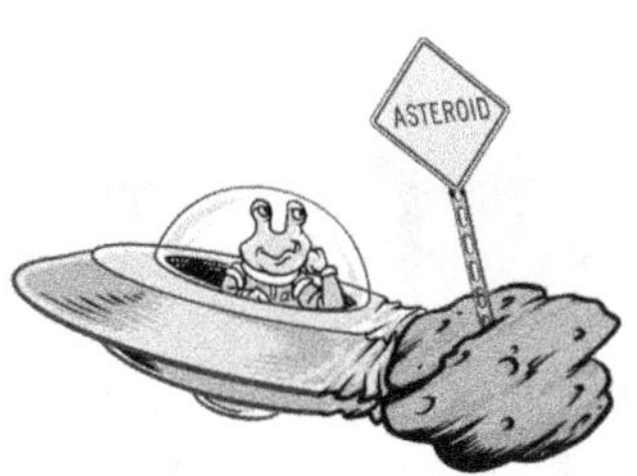

C. FLYNT

My brown-bag lunch was the most exciting thing to happen on that sleepy Moonday morning. I'd just taken the first bite of my sandwich when my orb flared.

"New client," she announced.

I dumped the sandwich into an empty drawer and straightened my nameplate. It read HIERONYMOUS GLYPH, ALCHEMIST AT LAW in discreet purple flames floating above an emerald-green crystal.

I smiled as a young woman slid into the room. "Good afternoon, how can I help you?"

She twisted her brown hair around a finger and glanced left and right. I guessed her age at sixteen, but the woeful expression on her face made me raise the estimate a few years. I seldom see a happy face—people only visit alchemists when they have problems—but hers was particularly despondent.

"I think I need a will," she whispered. "Right away. Today, if you can."

I raised an eyebrow. Kids her age don't usually worry about wills.

She took a deep breath. "I heard a banshee cry last night. This morning there were buzzards in the tree outside my window. I told the guys at work, and my foreman said to get a will as fast as I could."

"Banshees and buzzards are certainly dire portents," I agreed. Given her age, I doubted she had anything to protect. "Do you have a list of assets and beneficiaries?"

She shook her head. "I just graduated and moved here. This is my first job, and I haven't even gotten my first paycheck. I can't pay you." She raised her eyes hopefully. "But, I can will you my first paycheck, if that's enough. ..."

Her voice trailed off as she sniffed. I was afraid she was going to cry, but she pulled back her shoulders, thrust out her chin and looked me in the eye, displaying bravery in the face of impending doom.

I took pity on her.

"I'll tell you what, I'll witness a generic will for you. Bake me some cookies after you get paid."

My orb floated in and buzzed. "Name, please."

The girl spun and smiled at the orb. "Lizzie Islingtin."

The orb pulsed and a sheet of paper materialized on my desk. Lizzie glanced at it and signed while the orb hovered overhead. As I counter-signed, I noticed how she dotted each "i" with a cute little heart.

My orb announced, "Recorded and filed," as the paper faded away.

That was that. I never expected to see Lizzie again.

On Tiwsday, she was back, once more interrupting my lunch.

"I'm really sorry, but I need to buy a life insurance policy and I don't know who to talk to," she said. "The foreman told me I should have done that yesterday, instead of getting a will. He says insurance companies never pay a benefit until you've paid them more than you'll get. They'd go broke, otherwise. So, he says an insurance policy will protect me from the banshee and buzzards."

I swallowed the bite of sandwich I'd been chewing and slid the sandwich into the drawer. "You still don't have any money, right?"

She stared at the floor, twisted her fingers and peered up at me through her bangs.

"Um, can I make you the beneficiary? So you'll get paid after I die."

I tapped my nameplate. Today it was a black obelisk. Below my name it read PROVIDING LEGAL AND FINANCIAL SERVICES INCLUDING WILLS, CONTRACTS, AND INSURANCE.

"I represent Mutual Life Assurance. They offer a no-questions-asked policy with a one-month grace period for the first payment. I suggest the minimum coverage. You can expand it when you need more protection."

I conjured a stack of forms for her to sign. Once again, she dotted each "i" with a tiny heart.

The next day I ate my sandwich early. At five after noon, she was back.

"What now?" I asked. "A magic amulet? A charm?"

"How did you know?" she gasped. "I didn't tell anyone I was coming."

"No, but I'll bet your foreman talked about them this morning."

She nodded. "Everybody on the shift has an amulet. They hold the record for most days without an accident. He said the banshees and buzzards know I'm unprotected."

I sighed. I'd played along with the joke when it didn't cost her much and was a worthwhile investment. But amulets are expensive. The joke had gone far enough.

"You lived in the city until you moved out here, right?"

"Why, yes." She swiped her pink-polished nails across her bangs and appraised them. "Does it really show?"

"You've never heard a coyote howl, have you?"

"Coyote?"

"They sound like a banshee. At least, they do if you've never heard a real banshee. Hearing a coyote howl doesn't signify anything."

"But the buzzards! Right outside my window—"

"Where they roost every spring. We're on the migration route. Look, your foreman is playing you. You don't need a will, life insurance, or any charms."

"I don't need life insurance?"

I grinned. "As a registered agent, I'm required to say that everyone needs life insurance, but really, it can wait."

She crossed her arms, tapped a foot, and glared at me.

"You mean, you've been taking my money and laughing at me?"

"You haven't paid me anything. If anyone is laughing at you, it's the guys you work with."

She stamped her tapping foot and stormed out of my office faster than she came in.

I was surprised to see her the next day.

"Don't you ever eat during your lunch hour?" I asked her.

She shook her head. "I get breakfast and supper at the boarding house. I'll eat lunches when I have money."

She swallowed, stared over my head, then at my nameplate. Letters of smoke over glowing coals reminded clients PAYMENT DUE AT TIME OF SERVICE.

She twisted a strand of hair around her thumb. "I'm really sorry I've been wasting your time. I should have seen what was going on right off. I mean, I'm a college graduate, not some stupid kid. Right?"

I wasn't convinced "college grad" and "stupid kid" were mutually exclusive.

"I mean, I want to apologize." She shifted her weight and spread her hands. "I can't pay you yet, but can I do something for you? Maybe run some errands? The foreman says I'm the most reliable person on his team. That's why he's sending me to withdraw a bucket of steam from the bank. He said that whenever he sends one of the guys, they spend half the day in a bar, but he trusts me to be back before they need more steam," she blurted, without ever pausing for breath.

I shook my head. Fetching a bucket of steam is one of the oldest pranks in the book. "I don't need anything right now. But trust me, I'll remember you if I ever need any extra steam."

She grinned and dashed off, eager to finish her task.

I pulled my half-eaten sandwich out of the drawer and chewed thoughtfully. If her picture wasn't next to the definition of "gullible," the dictionary needed to be updated.

By now I expected her to interrupt my meal. On Friggday, I didn't unwrap my sandwich until after the union lunch hour. When the City Center clock struck one, I decided she wasn't coming. She must have finally learned.

I managed two bites before my orb flashed.

"New client," she announced.

I shoved the sandwich into the usual drawer, and barely had time to shake the crumbs off my tie before the door slammed open.

"Good afternoon." I smiled. "How can I—"

A workman who might have been half-troll filled the doorway.

"I'm here from the union," he growled. "We got a grievance issue, and I think you know who it's with."

I shrugged. I never know *who.* It's part of the alchemist-client privilege.

"Perhaps if you explain the issue?" I suggested.

"You been seeing a kid."

"I have many clients," I told him. "Can you be more specific?"

"Yeah, the girl gettin' a bucket of steam."

"Was there a problem? Did she get the wrong color?"

His face got red. I half expected to see steam flow from his ears.

He finally realized he was in an office, not a tavern. He shifted his feet and pulled off his cap.

"Look, I'm her foreman. Did she tell you what she's doin' at the plant?"

I shook my head as he glared past me.

"She's a cantrip-checker. Fresh out of school, and she hires in at the top pay grade."

He plopped two hands the size of dinner plates on my desk and leaned close, his face barely a foot from mine. I refused to back down as he glowered at me. I don't have to please anyone who hasn't paid me, and after the way he'd been treating the kid, I felt absolutely no desire to please him.

He exhaled garlic and onions. "Look, that slot's easy work. It's a reward for the guy with the most seniority. A guy who's put in his time and knows the ropes. We don't let no kid fresh out of school, and 'specially not some girl, take that slot."

"And, in your mind, that justifies harassment?" I asked him. "If someone treated your daughter like that, you'd have no problem with it?"

He stood up and had the grace to look embarrassed. He twisted his hat in his hands.

"Okay, I been riding her." He glanced at the ceiling, then back to me. "Maybe more than I ought to, but it's for her own good. If she can't take it, she should learn and get out fast, not waste everybody's time. Hers and ours."

"Has she filed a grievance?" I wouldn't have recommended one, but she had grounds.

"Naw, she's too green to know she could." He shook his head. "Here's what she did. She come back from lunch with a bucket of water."

I raised an eyebrow.

"So, I railed into her about being too stupid to know the difference between water and steam and how did she graduate so dumb."

"Good thing you're bigger than she is. Fights on the shop floor are dangerous."

"Yeah, one of the guys would'a slugged me. Anyhow, I barely got started when she tossed a red-hot salamander into the bucket. Boiled it dry in a half a second. You couldn't hardly see across the shop floor for the steam."

The foreman squinted as if the steam was in my office.

"Must have been exciting," I observed. "Fire elementals hate water."

"You know it! Damn thing jumped out quicker'n it went in. Landed on my boot." He raised his foot. The leather was burned through to the steel toe.

"Are you filing a grievance? I wouldn't recommend it."

"Naw, I only file against management. But let me tell you, steel conducts heat real good. I thought I was gonna die. Anyhow, I jumped and landed with one foot in the bucket, lost my balance and really did kick the bucket. I kicked it clear across the plant floor."

I raised my other eyebrow and repressed a chuckle.

"Did it hit anyone?"

"The plant manager."

"Is *he* filing a grievance?"

He shook his head. "Naw. Lucky me, with all the steam, he didn't see where it come from. Not every day I get to pull off something like that. I'm still laughing."

"So, who *is* filing a grievance?"

"The salamander. Salamanders don't do wet work. It's in their contract."

I grimaced. A salamander's boilerplate contract is ironclad and a pretty hot deal. I felt sorry for Lizzie, but this problem was more than a generic will or free advice.

The foreman twisted his hat and produced a wad of bills.

"So, me and the boys took up a collection. We want you should represent Lizzie so she don't get fired."

The bills fluttered onto my desk, and Lizzie's problem shrank to a manageable size.

"That grievance would get her out of your hair." I cocked my head. "Are you sure you want me to defend her?"

"Yeah. Anybody willing to deal with a salamander for a payback prank. Well, she's got ba—what it takes."

I swept the bills into my sandwich drawer. A few more jelly stains wouldn't hurt them.

"I've negotiated these issues before. I'm certain I'll work something out."

"Do what you can." He offered his hand. "I was plenty hard on her, but after that prank, I like her. I think she's gonna work out."

We shook hands and he left.

As he limped out the door, I admired the sign on his back. It read 'Kick Me!' with a cute little heart over the "i."

C. Flynt

C. Flynt is the husband-and-wife writing team of Clif and Carol Flynt. They share their house with one dog, two cats, and countless computers (several of which work). Clif developed Editomat (and many other computer programs) and is a technical book author. Carol has followed multiple careers, retiring as a freelance bookkeeper. They amuse their pets with interminable arguments over plots, themes, characters, grammar and whose turn it is to write the precarious first draft. They write science fiction, historical fiction, fantasy, romantic suspense, and (mostly) query letters. They thank Hieronymous Glyph for his role in gaining them SFWA membership.

SHY AND RETIRING

ESTHER FRIESNER

Shame crept from the soles of Ranwys's feet to the base of his thickly muscled neck. From there it spread over his face in a wash of red. Every sinew of his mighty form quivered with disgust over this—this *weakness* unbefitting a warrior and a shield lord.

"Toad," he snarled, launching the barque of bitter scorn upon a sea of self-flagellation. "Worm-cast. By-blow of a leprous cockroach. Dare you call yourself a champion? Puddle of rat drool that you are, there is no excuse for such frailty. If it were your first sight of this abomination, some might excuse you. But this is no fresh shock to your eyes! You knew the beast awaited, and still you cringe like a virgin tavern wench. And yet—" His tirade faded to a whisper. "—may the gods bear witness, that thing is *creepy*!"

Tiny eyes, black and chill as the deepest winter's night, met the shield lord's gaze. Ranwys could not look away from that flabby gray face set atop a bulbous, inhuman body. Sour sickness mounted in his throat.

"Avert your unholy orbs, foul beast!" Ranwys channeled his fear into false bravado. He reached for the sword that hung from the leather baldric across his bare chest. "The only reason you stand unslain is not my mercy, but my mission. Clearly you are dear to *him*—as dear as any creature could be to one whose heart is pure obsidian. I would not estrange him, but do not push your luck! Twice already has he turned me away. Know that if he refuses me this third time, your head will pay the price for his obdurate—"

"Why are you yelling at my mailbox?"

Ranwys froze. "*You*," he snarled at the tall, bearded, gray-haired man who had interrupted him in mid-rant.

"Last time I checked, yeah," came the reply, offered with a smile. "You know, I get that you didn't know what the hell to make of old Chubs here the first time you saw him—" He patted Ranwys' nemesis, a cement manatee gracing the curbside in front of a modest Mediterranean-style home. The creature held a black metal mailbox between its flippers. "—but I explained him to you then. How come you keep forgetting? A young, fit guy like you shouldn't have a memory problem. Have you talked to a wizard? Or better yet, an elf master-healer? They smell better."

"I have no need of healers, fragrant or otherwise! My mind is as hale as my body. It is the passage through the portal from the Realm Luminificent that affects it thus. Thanks be to the High Heirs of Paurul that the only harm done to my splendid intellect by this journey is forgetting the true nature of this—this—" He gave the manatee a major dose of stink-eye. "—this *offense* against nature and good taste. A sacrifice I make willingly if it means that I never lose sight of my sacred task."

He struck a moderately heroic pose, lifting his chin with that defiant little twitch made popular by doughty champions who couldn't *spell* "doughty" on a bet.

The older man laughed so vigorously, his Hawaiian shirt popped a button. He retrieved it and tucked it into the pocket of his Bermuda shorts.

"*Tsk.* Damn. Better sew this back myself or Kitty'll kill me. Worse, she'll say I'm getting fat and try making me go keto with her. Hey, listen Ranwys," he added in a reasonable voice. "I'm sorry you don't like my mailbox. Real talk? Neither do I, but Kitty's a sucker for manatees and this is Florida. I think they've got a law somewhere on the books that says if you don't own at least one manatee-themed *tchotchke*, you've got to move to Missouri.

"Tell you what: you've come a long way; you could probably use a drink. Let's go inside. We've got a nice wet bar on the pool lanai, good bourbon, I can rustle us up some mini tacos ..."

His voice trailed off. He gave Ranwys a quizzical look. "Why are you staring at me? Did I grow another head? Again?" He palpated his shoulders up to the base of his one-and-only neck. "Whew! What a relief. Don't scare me like that or no tacos for—"

The shield lord's sword flashed from its scabbard and the point froze level with the older man's nose. "Accursed creature of evil, you will not turn your vile sorceries upon me. I see through your scheme, embedding uncanny spells in your speech, each casting a thread over me until they form a noose around my neck. Desist or die!"

"What the actual *hell*?" The gray-haired man made an impatient sound. "It's like you don't even know me anymore. Put down that stupid sword and come inside like a civilized barbarian."

"Not until you undo your half-formed wizardry. Call back your mystic words!"

"My who the what now?"

Ranwys rattled off a protective cantrip before reluctantly articulating: "Wet bar ... bourbon ... keto ... taco ... lanai—" He sucked a fortifying breath and fairly spat: "*—tchotchke*!"

"Oh my aching head. When did you get to be so paranoid?"

"Paranoid! There's another one!" Ranwys shouted. His rage caused his sword to shake almost imperceptibly. Unfortunately, the tiny tremor was just enough to have the razor-sharp tip of the blade nick the other man's nose.

"*Now* you've done it." A voice at Ranwys's back took the shield lord by surprise. He made the rookie mistake of diverting his attention to the pretty, platinum-blond woman *d'une certain age* who had spoken. His eyes widened at the sight of her flamingo-pink blouse and body-hugging leopard print capri pants just as a wave of black oblivion crashed over him.

"HI, FEELING BETTER?"

Ranwys blinked up at the smiling face of the woman who had distracted him the instant before he was struck senseless. There was something unearthly about her. The youthful pink of her cheeks and lips belied the crow's feet at the corners of her eyes and the sagging skin of her neck. Her eyelids glittered purple. Perhaps it was the mark of a powerful seer?

"Are you—" he began. His lips were dry. "Are you a minion of Lord Maltoxigrym?"

"Who the what now?" she replied. It was the second time Ranwys had heard those words and wondered if they, too, were part of some spell of binding, banishment, or generic bane.

"Lord Maltoxigrym," he repeated, slowly sitting up. He found himself on an overstuffed couch upholstered in stripes of sickly apricot and bilious green. "Master of the thousand demons of shadow, enslaver of kingdoms, destroyer of all who rise against him, he whose face the gods themselves dare not behold lest his malevolent eye sear their immortality from their bones and that he, in his unreasoning wrath, devour their very *souls*!"

"Oh. *That* Lord Maltoxigrym." The woman slid from her perch on the arm of the sofa to land on the cushions. Dimples showed when she smiled. "He asked me to call him Malcolm. And you must be Ranwys. I'm Kitty." She offered the hand of friendship. He regarded it with the hesitancy of a debutante being asked to pet a hagfish, but before he could overcome his qualms, she jerked it away.

"Ooh, sorry, I almost forgot: Malcolm said not to let you touch me. I don't know why—maybe it's a germ thing?—" She put the width of one entire sofa cushion between them. "—but I guess he knows best."

The shield lord knew the real reason behind his nemesis's order: A spell could be like water, soaking you with so much magic that if you touched another being, a conduit would open, the floodgates would breach, the dam would break, and you'd both be soggy with the power of enchantment. Keeping his distance suited him just fine, for he had a plethora of misgivings as to the amount of epic magic with which this seemingly innocent creature might be imbued. One could not be too cautious where the Dark Master's work was concerned.

"*You* are Kitty?" he said. "You are *human*?"

His question amused her. "Last time I looked. What did you think I was?"

"A demon-cat in damsel's guise summoned from the fire-pits of Nizzelthoth to serve Lord Maltoxigrym and seduce the warrior who proves frail of will and purpose. You know, a *kitty*."

"Oh my goodness, you're *precious*." Kitty clasped her hands in delight. "I'm so glad I finally got to meet you. Malcolm told me about you, but I was always out running errands when you came by."

"He spoke of me?"

"Gosh, yes."

"In apprehension? In the bluster that so poorly conceals trepidation? In tones that bespeak his grudging yet inevitable admiration for a worthy foe?"

Kitty bit her lip. "Um ..."

Ranwys's fists struck his thighs so violently that the report made Kitty squeak in distress. "What. Did. He. Say."

"I—I—No offense, but, um—" She spoke rapidly, as if hoping speed would rob her words of their sting: "He said that you're okay, for a shield lord, but he can't wait for you to give up making a pest of yourself, go home, stay there, quit trying to turn a sitcom into grand opera and—"

Ranwys recoiled in the face of this fresh witchery, for who knew the depths of horror into which a properly employed *sitcomgrandopera* spell might thrust him?

"—and that you need to lighten up," Kitty concluded.

"*Lighten* up?" The shield lord scowled. He made a great show of trying to pinch any vestige of fat at his waist and of finding no purchase. "Calumny!" he declared.

"No, hon, he meant—"

"Then in what other way am I to lighten up? What, would he have me learn spells of levitation? Of illumination? Bah! The purview of lowly mountebanks and wizardly wannabes!"

Kitty's brows knit. "You understand *wannabe*, but not *lighten up*?"

Ranwys snorted. "I am a shield lord *and* the son of the despoiled and o'erthrown High King Corovir, not a dullard. I picked up *wannabe* the last time I came to beseech Lord Maltoxigrym to return with me to the Realm Luminificent and do his duty as Dark Master of our world." He cast suspicious looks to left and right. "Speaking of dark masters, where is that ageless fiend? Why did he strike me senseless only to abandon me? And to do so while my back was turned– Ah, perfidy incarnate! Cheat! Coward!"

"Don't you diss my Malcolm," Kitty said fiercely. "You were the one who stabbed him in the nose. He had to sort you out and then put Neosporin on the cut, but we didn't have any, so he went to buy some."

"A mere excuse. He fled, like the dastardly milksop he—*Ow!*"

Kitty slapped the shield lord right in the chops.

"He is *not*." She leaped to her feet and glared at him. "And you—you *deserved* getting KO'd. Shoot, you got off easy. You could've really hurt him. Malcolm's just too nice for his own good. If it'd been up to me, you'd be sleeping with the fishes. Oh, in case you don't get it, 'sleeping with the fishes' means—"

"I know. I gathered from context." Ranwys touched his cheek tenderly.

"Well, what I *don't* know is why you want to drag my Malcolm back to your stupid Realm Munificent. What kind of a name is that for a decent place to live, anyway? It sounds like something out of Marvel comics. If he's all Dark Master and whatnot, it doesn't sound like he spent his time there baking cookies and playing with kittens."

"Baking kittens *into* cookies, more like it," Ranwys muttered.

Kitty's shriek of horror was a sonic ice pick thrust through his ears.

"I did not *mean* that, woman!" he shouted. "It was merely a fortuitous gibe. Lord Maltoxigrym's fondness for felines is renowned through the Realm *Luminificent*. My father met his doom when his treatment of cats drew the Dark Master's wrath."

"What did your dad *do*?"

"Stole into Lord Maltoxigrym's fortress, seized the Dark Master's favorite—Jupiter, but he calls her Jupie-kins, and dressed her up in a unicorn costume that—" He nearly choked on the appalling revelation. "—that he crocheted himself."

"Awwwww. That's *adorable*."

"Oddly enough, that was exactly what Lord Maltoxigrym said after he destroyed the High King's stronghold, had him drawn and quartered, and then caught sight of Jupie-kins playfully juggling my father's spleen." A wisp of afterthought made Ranwys add: "You know, aside from all the blood and the screaming and the whole fortress burning down around us while my faithful old nursemaid was spiriting me away to safety, that cat really *did* look kind of adorable. Heh. Well, who *doesn't* know the old saying about cats and spleens?"

"Me," said Kitty. "And I also don't know why you keep coming after my Malcolm. Last time I asked, he said it didn't matter because you'd only have three chances to try and you'd had two."

"That is so." Ranwys' eyes were flinty slits. "When the duration of the spell that sent me hither this time expires, I may return no more. My quest will fail."

Her plump shoulders rose and fell. "I can't say I'm sorry. I don't want to lose my Malcolm, so I'm glad whatever you've been offering him if he returns to the Realm Whoozis isn't anything he wants."

Anything he wants.... The words sank sharp claws into Ranwys's brain. He fingered the edge of his baldric as he mulled them. A calculating look came into his eyes. He had a cunning plan.

"You might not be quite so glad if you knew him as I do," he said solemnly. "Oh, the tales I could tell! Perhaps it's best you remain ignorant, for were I to recount this forbidden knowledge, his deepest and most dire secrets, the possession of them would give you mastery over him for the rest of your lives together. *Tsk-tsk-tsk,* how awful *that* would be. I do well to say no more."

There followed a spirited back-and-forth of passionate wheedling on Kitty's part and badly acted reluctance from Ranwys. Throughout this exchange, he did his best to suppress a smirk. More than a shield lord, he was also a skilled angler who had learned one key life lesson from his pastime of fish-bothering: Success was all about using the right bait.

"So be it," he said at last. "I will reveal all, but as I value my life—and yours!—I must speak most ... discreetly."

He beckoned her closer. Kitty leaned in, all memory of Lord Maltoxigrym's warning gone from her thoughts. But when her ear was within whispering distance of the shield lord's lips, he wrapped his arms around her in an embrace of steel, pressed her to his chest, and shouted the spell of Return vouchsafed him by his family's bonded wizard, Palhag. The air crackled, the magic permeating the shield lord likewise engulfed his captive, they vanished together, and the sofa was left in need of a severe reupholstering.

"OKAY, RANWYS, YOU sneaky little pissant, you got me." Lord Maltoxigrym stood lone and resplendent in the heart of Castle Gallant, refurbished stronghold of warrior-kings. "Here I am, back in this jerkwater world when I'd sure as hell would rather be getting my senior discount at Waffle House. Come out, come out wherever you are, asshole."

Ranwys appeared in an archway, accompanied by a scrawny codger in rune-embroidered garments. Lord Maltoxygrym uttered a scornful snort when he saw them. "I should've known. Hello, Palhag. You're looking well, for a rodent."

The oldster dove for cover behind Ranwys.

"By the gods, Palhag, if you can't act like an almighty wizard, at least act like a man," the shield lord said, disgusted.

"I used up my finest shielding spells on you, m'lord," Palhag said in a quavering voice. "You're safeguarded from the Dark Master's rage; I'm not."

Lord Maltoxigrym's laughter shook dust from the tapestries. "Better have him cast another spell, Ranwys, one to protect your floors when he wets himself." As if on cue, a faint trickling was heard and Palhag's face went crimson. Ranwys's lip curled.

"Get out," he growled. Palhag didn't wait for a second command. He scurried from the great hall, the hem of his robe sweeping a faint, moist trail behind him.

The Dark Master's mirth ended abruptly. He folded his arms and glowered. His garb was a far cry from how he'd looked the last time Ranwys saw him. Gone was the Hawaiian shirt with its pattern of lurid green tikis. Gone were the khaki shorts, the scuffed sandals, and the white crew socks. His close-trimmed beard had burst into waist-length magnificence, and his steel-gray hair was now a thundercloud. Indeed, his unequaled sorceries sent arcs of lightning leaping through those unbridled tresses, a dramatic effect he'd chosen to underscore his blazing wrath.

"All right, Ranwys, let's get down to it. What have you done with my girlfriend?"

Ranwys was undaunted. "Wouldn't *you* like to know?"

"Well, *d'uh*," said the Dark Master, not caring if Ranwys added this to his list of *Eek-is-that*-another-*Eeeevil-spell?* words. "Try to keep up, boy. Just hand her over and we leave, no one gets hurt. I mean, it'll break my heart to disappoint Jupie-kins, not giving her a fresh spleen to play with, but this time I'm going to take *her* back with me, too, and see if she'll settle for all the catnip mice she can disembowel instead." A brief gesture, and a capacious cat carrier appeared at his feet, awaiting its precious passenger.

Ranwys defied him with an insufferably smug look. "If you want your woman so badly, *behold*!" He pronounced a single magic word, obviously taught to him by Palhag, and a vision appeared in the air between shield lord and Dark Master. There was Kitty, newly clad in a filmy rose-red gown that clung lovingly to her ample curves. She sat disconsolate upon a throne made of polished antlers and ornamented with the skulls of eagles, her wrists confined in golden manacles.

The Dark Master's hair sizzled with renewed fury even as a low, appreciative wolf whistle escaped his lips. His hands reached out for her.

Ranwys snickered scornfully. "You cannot touch her. She is pent far from here, beyond the range of your powers, wrapped in ten layers of the mightiest concealment spells gold can buy."

"Wow. You snatched her, what, less than an hour ago and you managed to set up all *that* before I came after you? Busy little shit, aren't you. So, you think you've got me because you've trapped her somewhere I can't—can't—" He paused. "Just a sec."

Ancient enchantments tumbled from the Dark Master's lips. Green smoke shot from his fingertips. Waves of sorcery radiated from his body.

Nothing happened.

"Damn. Okay, as I was saying, you think you've got me because it turns out I *really* can't find her, but you're wrong. You have reckoned without my command of the Sons of Ravenbloodwolf, my elite legions of trolls, orcs, ghouls, fiends, and murderous mortals who await a single word from me to scatter over the Realm Luminificent and use pure brute feet-on-the-ground force to discover her hiding place. They will rampage from cottage to castle, putting to the sword any soul who fails to give them the information they seek. They will be an unstoppable army, waging war in my name, leaving behind nothing but desolation, making fires rage and blood flow until she is returned to me."

Ranwys's face lit up like a toddler's on Christmas morning. "*Yes*! O gods, yes, yes, *yes*! Summon them, unleash them, have your troops wreak swaths of terror and destruction throughout the land! Embrace your ash-hearted devotion to tyranny once again, so that your name reclaims its rank as the nightmare of nightmares! Bring back the good old days!"

"You just bet your loincloth I will!" the Dark Master shouted. He whipped out a gleaming palm-sized oblong from his sleeve and flicked his wrist. The arcane device flipped open and he gazed at it with searing intensity.

Absolutely nothing happened.

"Whoops," said Lord Maltoxigrym. "No signal. Looks like I'm out of my cell coverage zone." He chuckled. "Honestly, Ranwys, did you really think I'd fall for your stupid ploy? It was fun watching you have a herogasm, but let's be real: You've got the subtle manipulation skills of a dead possum. Do or say what you want, it changes nothing. I'm finished with all this take-over-the-Realm-Luminificent-and-establish-an-empire-of-evil-2.0 crap. I'm *retired*; accept it."

"No, *no*, it cannot be!" the shield lord protested. "Change your mind, or *her* life will be forfeit." He pointed dramatically at Kitty's hovering image.

Lord Maltoxigrym shrugged. "I'm a single senior guy living in south Florida with my own house, my own teeth and hair, financial security, and a valid driver's license. You want to know how fast I'll find another girlfriend? Before you can spell Tinder. And that's if I even get the *chance* to check out the market. The minute some of Kitty's gal pals hear we broke up due to irreconcilable death, they'll be on me like—"

"Like *what*?"

The great hall shook with a rumble and blast fit to dwarf Vesuvius blowing its stack. The shield lord yelped and sprawled. The Dark Master stumbled sideways over the cat carrier and landed on his rump. Armed guards came charging to Ranwys's aid and collided en masse with an invisible barrier that sent them caroming back down the corridor with an audible *boiiiiinnnnggggg* familiar to cartoon coyotes everywhere. They took the hint, turned, and retreated at speed.

Lord Maltoxigrym clambered to his feet. "Hey, honey. What took you so long?"

"Don't you 'honey' *me*," a suddenly *there* Kitty shouted at him. She now stood a good twenty feet tall, every inch jam-packed with an inferno of indignation.

Ranwys stared open-mouthed. "Who is—?"

"You know how the Sword-Sisters who rule the eastern Dales of Martyn say that every woman's a goddess?" the Dark Master replied. "Well, sir, sometimes that's *not* just a metaphor."

"What is—?"

"I'm not sure. Probably fertility. She doesn't have any worshippers left ... except me. Heh."

"How did—?"

"Book club. First she joined, then I joined, then we—er, moving on."

"But—but if she's a goddess, why does she live in—?"

The Dark Master spread his hands. "*Everyone* retires to Florida."

"You selfish *creep*!" Kitty yanked his attention back by stamping one titanic foot and shattering the flagstones. "Weren't you even going to *try* negotiating with this jerk to save me? Oh, no, *you* couldn't be *bothered*. Just cut your losses and move on to the next little chippy who can warm your bed and help you cheat at mahjong, that's you all over."

"Aw, baby, you don't think I meant any of that, do you?" Lord Maltoxigrym cajoled. "I knew my favorite goddess would be listening in so I said something guaranteed to make you mad enough to manifest. Now, let's wrap things up with Conan the Boobarian here and we can go home. You never needed me to save you."

"What I *needed* from you was the truth." Her eyes turned a disquieting shade of crimson. "Why'd you never tell me the whole story? All you ever said about Ranwys was, 'Oh yeah, this guy I used to know dropped by. Nice enough, but kind of a tightass. He needs to—'"

"—lighten up," said the tightass in question glumly.

"I'll bet that if I was an ordinary woman and couldn't have noticed the leftover smell of cheap magic in the house, you wouldn't have told me *that* much," Kitty went on. "I do not appreciate being kept in the dark by my own stupid boyfriend!"

"Didn't *he* tell you anything?" the Dark Master jerked a thumb at Ranwys.

"Yes, while he was locking me up in *these*." She brandished her wrists, still encircled by the golden manacles, the chain between the cuffs now but a melted memory. "He said that after thousands of years of your dire dominion, all the different clans and critters defeated you with a military package deal. Then you ran away—"

"*Retired.* Ree. Tie. Erred."

"Whatever. Except Ranwys learned where you were and came after you because he wanted you *back* here to villain it up again. I said wasn't that asking for trouble and he said 'I hope so.' It didn't make sense. But you know what? The real question is why *you* didn't tell me what was going on. Don't you trust me?"

"I didn't want you to worry your pretty little head," the Dark Master replied smoothly. "We were nearly rid of him—two visits down, one to go. It was just a matter of waiting him out. There isn't one damn wizard in all of the Realm Luminificent with the power to send the big lug on an interdimensional commute more than three times. Not like *my* magic," he said with pride. "I can cast a spell three *hundred* times. Three *thousand*. Three—"

"Well, woo-hoo for you and your abracadabra Viagra," Kitty snapped.

Undiscouraged by his lady's sarcasm, the Dark Master persisted: "I was also afraid you'd get mad. You know what you're like when you lose your temper. Remember Atlantis?"

The lovers' quarrel might have gone on from there, except that both parties were distracted by a most unusual sound: Ranwys was crying.

The shield lord sat hugging his legs, teary face pressed against updrawn knees. He made such a pathetic figure that Kitty forgot all about her literally towering rage and dwindled back to a reasonable height.

"What's wrong, sugar?" she asked, kneeling beside him and patting his back gently. "Tell Kitty."

Ranwys sobbed and raised his head. "The one thing—" he said in a broken voice. "The one *teensy* thing I was trying to do was to make—to make the Realm Luminificent gr—gr—gr—"

"If he says 'great again' I will fricking blast his butt into next Tuesday," the Dark Master muttered.

"—grand and glorious as it used to be," the shield lord finished. "Once upon a time, all our kingdoms worked as one for the common good. Men, elves, dwarves, the women who ride the northern wastes, the dragon-masters of the south, the Sword-Sisters of the east, sea nymphs, halflings, tree sprites, titans, talking honey badgers, all of us bound together by a noble purpose. We were *heroes*! But now?" He laughed hollowly. "We're brats. We squabble over any little thing. Treaties dissolve. Alliances wither. Trade agreements that benefitted countless beings are trampled underfoot—"

"Instead of being trampled overhead?" Lord Maltoxigrym said sweetly.

Kitty gave him a hard look. "Put a sock in it, *Snark* Master," she said.

"No. He deserves this. He came to me *demanding* that I return but not once did he bother to say *why*. Just, 'Come back to the Realm Luminificent, Because Reasons!' Now he's bawling because this place is falling apart and I'm supposed to sympathize? Boo-hoo-*hoo*. This is no longer my circus and these ain't my goddamn monkeys!"

Ranwys flung himself at Lord Maltoxigrym's feet and seized the hem of his robe. "That's just it, my lord, that's the trouble! As soon as you were gone, so was any reason for our unity. Battling your insidious evil was all that kept us together. Make us your monkeys again, I implore you!"

The Dark Master plucked his garment from Ranwys's grip. "Why, so instead of going for each other's throats you can all go for mine? No way. I'm happy where I am."

"But *I'm* not. I'm supposed to be a hero, a shield lord, but without some really *big* foe threatening our world, that's just an empty title. Dad got to be *High King* by fighting you! They sing *sagas* about him."

"Yeah? What did the minstrels find to rhyme with *pussycat's hand-crocheted unicorn costume?"*

"Malcolm!" Kitty jabbed him with her elbow.

"All I want—" Ranwys sniffled. "All I want is the chance to do something with my life that's *bardworthy*." An afterthought occurred to him. "Oh, and to save the Realm Luminificent from falling to pieces. That, too." He stretched himself full length upon the floor and groveled mightily. "Great Lord Maltoxigrym, I beg you to reconsider. Give us the evil we need to coexist! I'll make it worth your while. I don't know how, but I'll think of something. *Pleeeeeease?"* His body shook with renewed sobs.

Kitty snuggled up to the Dark Master. "This is awful," she whispered. "I feel so sorry for him."

"So, for *him* to feel better you want *me* to move back into what's going to be a war zone," he said testily. "Okay, honey, I'll help you pack your bags because I am not doing this alone."

"Who, me? Move here? I love you, babe, but give up frappuccinos? And online shopping? And book club? Nuh-uh." She shook her head. "Can't you think of some *other* way to help him?" She toyed with his beard coyly, winding strands of residual lightning around her fingers. "For me?"

"For you doll?" He kissed her. "Anything." Lord Maltoxigrym closed his eyes, focused his thoughts, and searched his sweeping knowledge of unhallowed lore for the answer. And then ...

"Aha!" He disengaged Kitty's hands from their mischief and nudged the prone shield lord with the tip of his shoe. "Get up, gorgeous," he said. "You'll get your realm-wide unity and your very own heroic fa-la-la epic, and this world will get the Big Bad Evil Macguffin that's coming to it."

Ranwys sat up, overjoyed. "Huzzah! You will return to us!"

"Huh? Who says 'Huzzah' anymore? And no."

MALCOLM, THE ONCE and done with it Lord Maltoxigrym, lounged on the lanai and contemplated the vision he'd conjured on the side of his Bloody Mary. It displayed the impossibly vast throne room of his ancient citadel, restored to its former glory by a grateful Ranwys (on the down low, of course). There stood the loathsome legions known as the Sons of Ravenbloodwolf, along with a miscellany of lesser minions of malevolence. All awaited the commands of their new master, Trichechis the Omnipotent, the conqueror who had come out of nowhere to swiftly dominate the Realm Luminificent and fill the niche vacated by Lord Maltoxigrym. (Indeed, some claimed Trichechis had filled that niche after filling his belly with Maltoxigrym's bones.)

The Sons' commander, Hth'ar'v'fyz'x the Unpronounceable, addressed the throne: "Hail, Lord Trichechis! How may we serve your terrifying majesty this day?"

Malcolm sighed. "That's my cue. No rest for the proxy wicked." He took a long pull of his drink and traced a few mystic signs in the air.

A metallic groan as might issue from rusty hinges echoed through the throne room.

"My master summons me!" A crone dressed neck to feet in speckled snakeskin emerged from the shadows. "Heed now the Tongue of Trichechis," she intoned. "Know the will of our horrific lord."

She glided toward the throne and prostrated herself, then rose and bowed deeply to the massive presence there. "By your leave, O exalted destroyer." Her hand trembled as it stretched forth to reverently push down the little flag that had popped up on the doom-black box that never left Trichechis's grasp. The enigmatic figure, who had caused all benevolent inhabitants of the Realm Luminificent to re-band together for his eventual-but-not-ASAP overthrow, fixed soulless eyes upon his servant as she reverently withdrew a glowing scroll and read aloud its dire message.

Malcolm pulled the celery stalk from his drink and munched loudly. He didn't need to hear the Tongue of Trichechis read the scroll; he'd sent it. He'd sent it just as surely as he'd sent the Realm Luminificent's new Villain-in-Residence to take over the role he no longer wanted.

"I do good work," he murmured with pride. "Rid of the Realm, rid of Ranwys, and best of all, rid of *you*." He raised his glass to the vision: "*Hasta la vista*, Chubs."

The cement manatee on the throne maintained its dreadful silence.

Esther Friesner

Nebula Award winner Esther Friesner is the author of over 40 novels and more than 200 short stories. Educated at Vassar College and Yale University, where she received a Ph.D. in Spanish. She is also a poet, a playwright, and the editor of several anthologies, including the Chicks in Chainmail series.

Esther is married, a mother of two, grandmother of two, harbors cats, and lives in Connecticut. She also spends time in Florida and has actually seen the mailbox described in this story.

Repeatedly.

The horror ... the horror ...

THE DANGERS OF SUBURBAN DEER

JAMIE LACKEY

Garret stood and brushed dirt off of his knees, then stepped back and surveyed his progress. He'd planted his beans in a pentagram and dedicated each seedling to the dark lord.

Any deer or groundhogs or rabbits that nibbled on them would have a greater power to answer to.

He put his shovel away and went inside for some nice tea and cake, feeling greatly pleased with himself.

The next morning, the beans had been eaten down to their roots, and an angry imp sat in the center of the carnage, glowering.

"These creatures are shameless! Shameless!" it shouted when Garret approached. "They have no fear!"

Garret nodded sympathetically. "Suburban deer are the worst."

"I have failed you. Name your boon and the dark lord will grant it."

"I suppose a gift card to buy more plants with would be welcome."

"It is done!" the imp shouted, then disappeared.

Garret found a one hundred dollar gift card in his wallet, and used it to buy replacement plants and some smelly deer repellent to sprinkle around.

His second pentagram was a bit bigger, and he interspersed some tomatoes and broccoli with the beans. It rained that night, a lovely steady rain that would be wonderful for his garden.

He found a damp greater imp sitting despondent in his garden the next morning, surrounded by devastation.

"No luck?" Garret asked.

The greater imp sighed. "There were too many, and they were too powerful."

"The deer?"

The greater imp nodded solemnly. "The deer. And at least one enterprising groundhog. Would you like another gift card as your boon?"

"Sure, that'd be great."

This time, the card was for five hundred dollars. Garret bought some raised beds and trellises and topsoil, and spent the day arranging it all into a glorious pentagram. He added a couple squash plants and a cucumber into the mix.

The next morning, he found a demon with a fiery sword standing over his one remaining tomato plant. "I will grant you another gift card, and I will place some of my essence into this plant," it said. It brushed one finger against a tomato blossom, the yellow flower went red under its touch, and the leaves turned dark, glossy black.

Seven hundred-fifty dollars later, Garret had more dirt and some mulch and new gloves and a rain barrel and a truck full of hearty heirloom seedlings. He even picked up a couple of apple trees.

The next morning, the dark lord himself met him at the garden gate. The king of demons looked exhausted, its eyes shadowed and its red skin dull.

The plants had survived, for the most part, though there were a few bite marks here and there.

"I will grant you one last boon," the dark lord said.

"I'd be grateful if you could do anything to help," Garret said. "These deer are ruthless."

The dark lord handed him one last gift card. "Buy yourself a fence, for heaven's sake."

Jamie Lackey

Jamie Lackey lives in Pittsburgh with her husband and their cat. She has over 160 short fiction credits, and has appeared in *Daily Science Fiction, Beneath Ceaseless Skies,* and *Escape Pod.* Her debut novel, *Left-Hand Gods* is available from Hadley Rille Books, and she has a novella and two short story collections available from Air and Nothingness Press. In addition to writing, she spends her time reading, playing tabletop RPGs, baking, and hiking. You can find her online at www.jamielackey.com.

BODY DOUBLE

JODY LYNN NYE

"Stop it," Detective Sergeant Ramos whispered to Detective Sergeant Dena Malone as she sailed along the designated walkway through the echoing concrete cavern of Soundstage Two in her ornate floatchair. "You're drooling."

The young, brown-haired woman dashed a hand to the side of her mouth.

"I am not! But, oh, my God, I still can't believe it! I'm on the set of *Android Star*! Neal is going to be so jealous!"

Her heart pounded with excitement. On the way into the glamorous grounds of MOJO Studios and the reported crime scene, they had passed the actual Android Jet, the transport the studio used for special events. Next came a row of fancy trailers flashing neon images of the video stars who occupied them. Tyrone Chen, who played Doctor San! Dori Sanchez, the heroic captain of the *Star* itself! And, of course, Emmaline Hariyama, who had the biggest and fanciest of the private housing. Her character, Commander Lisbet Dao, had everyone swooning at her capable and mysterious feet. Dena practically dislocated her neck trying to spot the actors among the myriad of people. Makeup artists in smocks, effects technicians with heavy belts jangling with tools, and people ranked in importance by their clothing heading into the massive wardrobe room on one side of the studio. The shabbier the garments, the higher up in fame the people probably were. It was all so intense that Dena was in danger of falling into fangirl overload.

"The starship is most disappointing," K't'ank observed, as dozens of robots and pieces of equipment rushed past them in both directions in near silence. "On the screen it appears to be intact and airtight. It seems to have exploded into many fragments!"

As busy as they were, some of the passing humans turned to stare at the very pregnant woman in the floatchair, wondering if her baby was the one speaking in a cultured baritone.

"I'm hosting a Salosian," she explained as she went by them. "I've got a Salosian." A few nodded, wide-eyed. Those certainly had heard of the Alien Relations program between Earth and Salos that implanted the skinny pink creatures in the abdomens of suitable volunteers. The abdomens approximated the saline seas of Salos. K't'ank's voice came from the big, chunky platinum bracelet on her wrist. She was impressed at having impressed *them*, the ones who worked in this hall of wonders. They wouldn't be so amazed if they knew the tedious day-to-day reality of having someone she couldn't shut out commenting on everything she did or said. She dropped her voice to a near murmur. "That's so they can move the walls out and bring in the video equipment to record scenes and do special effects. Keep your voice down, or I'll have to switch off the bracelet."

"Do not cut me off!" K't'ank said, now in a loud stage whisper. "I must have a chance to address one of the actors! It is most interesting how the illusion is worked. I must analyze this. Memory, as you may know, is fragmentary. What one observes is necessarily only a minute amount of what is occurring around one."

"Thanks, Doctor Science," Dena said, dryly. "But you're right. There's a bunch of illusion going on here. We just have to work out what and why."

A short, gray-haired man in a white, open-necked shirt and worn khaki trousers beckoned to them. He jumped out of his canvas sling chair to shake hands.

"Detectives Malone and Ramos? I'm Carson Nerata, the executive producer." He looked down at the bracelet on Dena's wrist and addressed it. "Dr. K't'ank, hi! I'm a big fan of your work."

"And I of yours," K't'ank said, sounding pleased to be

acknowledged. "I wish to ask you many questions ... "

"Not now," Dena said, with an apologetic smile for the producer. "If he gets started now, we'll be here all day. We've got a case to investigate."

"Right!" Nerata's face split in a boyish grin. "Hey, we'll do lunch soon. When all this is over. I'd love to hear your take on the show."

"Make the date, Malone!" K't'ank shouted, hammering her ribs from the inside with his tail. "This is most exciting to query the inner workings of the televised illusion!"

"It's a promise," Dena said, as her heart threatened to leap out of her chest in further paroxysms of delight. She *had* to figure out a way to work her husband Neal into the invitation, or he would just die. The two of them never missed an episode of *Android Star.* In fact, if Dena admitted it, they re-ran whole seasons on their days off with the sound down so the neighbors wouldn't think they were complete geeks. Which they were.

Nerata grabbed Ramos's arm and dragged him along another branch of the painted path toward a long, boxlike modular office against one wall of the huge chamber. "We can talk in here." He yanked open the door, ushered them inside the surprisingly roomy space beyond, and gestured to a couple of chairs. "I'm ready to cooperate." He threw a pair of miniature drone cameras into the air. They hovered, one facing him and the other pointing toward Dena and Ramos. "Do you mind if I record this? My lawyer wants a video, and I want it just in case I can make a documentary about it later. The fans will eat it up!"

"That's not how we ..." Dena began. Ramos cut her off with a finger across his throat.

"No problem, as long as we get to be in it," he said.

"Sure! We can always dub your lines," Nerata said, with a gesture of dismissal. Dena felt annoyed that he assumed they couldn't speak for themselves. "My assistant will be here in a minute." He pulled a personal datapad from a hidden breast pocket and touched the screen. In less than a minute, a young woman with her mousy brown hair in a bun scrambled through the door, followed by three other people.

"Mr. Nerata, I called in Bud, Liesl, and Tony, too, since their departments might have been involved in the accident. I mean, it was an accident, right?"

"Thanks, Bonnie," the producer said, sitting back in his chair. "Detectives, over to you. Are my Evelyns under arrest?"

Lithe, muscular Bud turned out to be the stunt coordinator. Middle-aged, matter-of-fact Liesl was the makeup department head. Tony, an older white man with a long, sharp chin and bushy eyebrows that made him look like a disgruntled parsnip, was the executive in charge of special effects for *Android Star.* He fidgeted, very much upset at having been summoned.

"We just came from the crime scene on Soundstage Three," Dena said, trying to look as serious as possible while Ramos all but mugged for the floating cameras. "There were no signs of break-in or other intrusions on the security cams. What we saw looked as though one of your Evelyn clones got clobbered in the explosion staged for a run-through of one of the scenes. When we looked at the footage of the accident, it all looked pretty normal—"

"Really exciting!" Ramos added. Dena gave him an exasperated stare.

"—But when they cleared the set, an Evelyn was lying there unconscious under a heap of wall sections. The studio doctor said she wasn't knocked out by the falling props. She showed signs of having been gassed with apolomene."

Nerata goggled. "Apolomene! Knockout gas? Like in building alarm systems? Bonnie, check and see if any of the alarm systems went off."

"No, sir," the assistant replied, after a quick glance at her pad.

"Whew! Is the kid okay?"

"Yes," Dena said. "She's going to be okay, but there's a problem: the others say she's not one of them."

"What do you mean, not one of them?" Nerata asked. "They sent me that video of the girl on the floor! She's got to be one of those clones."

"They counted off for me," Dena said. "All eighteen of them." It had been a surreal experience to meet the stuntwomen who worked on *Android Star*. A host of identical people about Dena's height, all with short black hair, heart-shaped golden faces, and long brown eyes, all dressed in pale blue tunics over dark blue pants and nondescript deck shoes, speaking in identical voices, with identical expressions of concern for the fallen woman. "It was like a scene from the show, especially episode nine of season three, 'All Hands on Deck,' when Captain Sanchez called for volunteers to save Emmaline Hariyama trapped in an airlock with that giant robotic predator, and dozens of crewmembers showed up, willing to sacrifice themselves." Now that she thought about it, there had to have been seven Evelyns in that scene. Maybe even more.

"That was an enormous litter!" K't'ank exclaimed. "Malone's torso is almost overwhelmed carrying one fetus. How could one female bear them all?"

"They don't," Dena said, for the second, or third, or sixth time, but K't'ank just couldn't seem to get past that fact. "They're gestated in incubators. Is that ethical, Mr. Nerata? They said you had them bred eight years ago just for this program?"

Nerata waved a hand. "Standard practice in video, Sergeant! You have no idea how much money goes into a program like this. A bevy of clones is nothing. We could commission a new *planet* for what it costs to produce an episode."

"How much of it gets passed along to the talent?" Ramos asked, with a winning smile for the cameras.

"Plenty," Bud said. "The eighth season starts in a month. We're doing post production on the first three episodes now, so we've been working our butts off. Four of the Evelyns do stunt work for the star, Ms. Hariyama. This season's got a lot of action. They had to sleep-learn all the moves I choreographed out for them, and they nailed every one of them. They'll knock your eyes out, Detectives! All the firing weapons are fake, but the Evelyns are damned good with swords and knives. They're one of the most valuable assets of the show. And they make fantastic money."

"But, if effects are so realistic," K't'ank asked, "why is it necessary to have real Evelyns? Why not have one and reproduce her multiple times with computers? That one could be made to look like Emmaline Hariyama."

"Viewers like to see real people," Nerata said, shrugging. "Believe me, we tried it the other way on another show. It was a flop. You could hear it hit the ground right through the vid screen. The Evelyns are popular. At first, I thought Bud was pulling my leg when he said to get eighteen, but we use all of them. I'm almost sorry that we didn't order twenty."

"Did *you* order an extra clone for any reason?" Dena asked the stunt coordinator.

"Me?" Bud gawked. "This has nothing to do with me! I don't have that kind of money in my budget. Ask Tony."

"Wasn't me," the parsnip insisted. "I thought it was kind of overkill. Did you, Mr. Nerata?"

"No!" Nerata said, then glanced uncertainly at his assistant. "Did we order another Evelyn, sweetie? I thought Evelyn Seven recovered from that, uh, unfortunate incident with the laser cannon."

"She did, sir," Bonnie said. "The new leg is working perfectly. She can do stunts on it."

"For what we paid for the operation, it ought to let her fly! So, no, Detectives. Just the original eighteen."

"But, where did she come from, and how did she get onto the set?"

A loud argument erupted outside the office, with numerous voices shouting accusations. The bang of bodies or other heavy objects hitting the outer wall of the office put the two police on immediate alert. Ramos unholstered his sidearm and held it barrel upward in both hands. Dena turned her floatchair toward the door. She didn't have to reach for her stunner. The arms and top of the chair issued by Alien Relations concealed some pretty potent firepower that would go off automatically to protect her ... well, K't'ank.

The door slammed open, and a cluster of humans all but fell inside, the aforementioned Evelyns grappling with blue-uniformed security guards.

"All for one!" an Evelyn called out.

"And one for all!" the others chorused.

Dena watched as the first of the small females flipped a male twice her weight, then used his belly as a launch pad to jump another man who had his arms wrapped around one of her sisters. The security forces grabbed stun guns from their holsters. An Evelyn kicked the weapon out of the first one's hand. It popped into the air and straight into the hands of another Evelyn. Before any of the guards could fire, she potted five of them. They slumped in surprised heaps. The stunt women wrestled or bounced around the remaining security officers.

"Surrender never!" the first Evelyn shouted.

"Victory ever!" the others echoed.

"They are most proficient!" said K't'ank. "But where are the action music and sound effects?"

"That doesn't happen in real life," Dena said.

"This is real life? But it is happening in a video studio!"

"Nice," Ramos said, watching as one burly guard hurtled through the air and hit the wall over the producer's head. The uniformed man dropped out of sight. "Couldn't have done it better myself."

"That's for sure," Dena said dryly.

"Good brawl."

"I know! I almost wish we didn't have to break it up."

"Yeah, I hate being a spoilsport." But Ramos sprang into action, like someone out of *Android Star.* He jumped up onto the armrest of Dena's chair and somersaulted into the middle of the melee, landing with his hands up and flattened. Dena grinned. That flip was his party piece. He liked to do that with street gangs, who would be so taken off guard by his antics that they would stop fighting to watch him.

The Evelyns, though, were used to choreographed distractions. While the rest concentrated on disabling the security guards, five of them engaged him. In the great tradition of martial arts movies, they formed a circle around him, and attacked him one at a time. They waited their turn until he had exchanged a flurry of blows with each. They were too nimble for him to actually connect with a solid punch. Ramos grunted with frustration, trying to hit somebody, anybody. Dena rolled her eyes and urged her floatchair forward into the midst of the crowd with her speakers turned on high.

"All right, break it up!" she announced. Her voice echoed off the walls, making the small room vibrate. The Evelyns clapped their hands to their ears. The guards, no longer under attack, slumped against whatever wall was handy. "Back up and stop fighting!"

"Awww! We were having fun!" The Evelyns looked disappointed. So did Ramos. Dena gave him an impatient look.

"That's right," Ramos said, recovering his attitude of authority. "What's going on? When we left the soundstage, you were worried about the spare clone knocked out on your floor. What happened in the last hour?"

"The EMTs said she'll be fine." By her take-charge attitude, Dena recognized the speaker as Evelyn One. At least, she assumed it was Evelyn One. "Then, we got a message from our landlady. She said she didn't get our rent today!"

"Don't you have monthly expenses on autopay?" Nerata asked, his brows raised.

"We do! We checked our accounts! They're *empty,*" stated the Evelyn beside the leader. "All of them. What did you do?"

"What happened to our money?" another Evelyn demanded.

"We paid you," Nerata said. "Sweetie, we paid them, right?"

"Yes, sir," the assistant said, frowning at her datapad. "You were paid yesterday for the week," she said. "Every credit was transferred directly, like always. Salary, reimbursement of expenses, and bonuses for stunts."

"Then why did you take it back?"

Nerata looked puzzled. "Your money?"

"It's missing!" Evelyn One said. "Every credit. Why did you take it out of our accounts?"

"Our accounts are empty!" another Evelyn said, indignantly. "Our landlady wants to know why we stiffed her."

"We checked. The transfer to her company bounced," added a second.

"She's threatening to start the eviction process," yet another clone said. "Do you know how hard it is to find an apartment for eighteen?"

"Honey, baby, best friends," Nerata protested, looking from one implacable face to another. "We had nothing to do with it."

"What does the bank say?" Dena spoke up. They turned to look at her. "Well, didn't you check with it?"

"Of course, we did," Evelyn One said, blowing her straight black hair out of her face with an exasperated puff. "They said the withdrawals were authorized by someone who has access to the account. That has to mean *you*." She aimed a finger at Nerata.

"So, why did you do it?" Evelyn Two demanded.

"What did we ever do to you?" Evelyn Three asked. "We've always worked hard for you."

"Kids," Nerata said, seriously, looking from one identical face to another, "the studio can't withdraw money from you. Anyone can deposit it. Let me tell you, I would have pulled back payment from some pretty disappointing people if I could–and I've never been disappointed with you, I swear!"

The Evelyns looked mollified for a moment, and fell into a huddle. Evelyn One frowned. She turned to Dena.

"I want to report a burglary," she said. "Wire fraud. Bank robbery. Whatever! We want you to find out who stole our money."

"Well, all right," Dena said, raising her skinnypad to record. "What precautions do you take to make sure no one can get their hands on your financial records?"

In unison, the Evelyns turned over their hands.

"Like everyone," Evelyn Six said. "We don't share our numbers or passwords with anyone."

"We use one-time credit numbers when we make purchases," Evelyn Twelve said.

"We have to approve any debit amount over fifteen credits."

"Twenty," Evelyn Five argued.

"Ten!" Evelyn Four insisted.

"C'mon, what can you buy with ten credits?" Evelyn Sixteen said, shaking her head.

"But, how do you communicate with your bank?" Dena asked. "How do you keep security on your account?"

In unison, they chorused, "Facial recognition software."

Ramos scoffed. "That's ridiculous. You all look exactly alike!"

"No, we don't," Evelyn One said, giving him an exasperated look. "Evelyn Eight has a scar on her left eyebrow. Evelyn Sixteen has a more turned-up nose than the rest of us. On her left cheek, Evelyn Three has a mole—"

"It's a beauty mark," Evelyn Three said, hurt.

"Yeah, whatever. So, we're not completely identical," Evelyn One went on. "The bank software can identify everything down to extra hairs in our noses—which we don't have."

K't'ank interrupted them. "What about this extra clone? Why does she exist?"

"We don't know," Evelyn One said. She heaved a big, wistful sigh. "She was perfect."

"Yeah," Evelyn Four said, her eyes dreamy. "I mean, not a single feature out of place. Completely symmetrical."

"None of us got that." The others nodded ruefully.

"But, why a nineteenth one of you?" K't'ank insisted. "And where has she been in the last eight years?"

The Evelyns frowned at one another.

"We don't know," said Evelyn One. "We've got enough problems keeping track of all of us as it is!"

"This reminds me of the episode in season one—no, season three," Dena said. "Episode seventeen. The one where Captain Sanchez's long-lost sister came to the space station, and everyone kept thinking she was the captain." She snapped her fingers. "'Doppleganger,' that was it!"

Nerata regarded her curiously. "You know the show's history better than my continuity director. You want a job?"

Dena couldn't help but go starry-eyed at the offer, but Ramos poked her hard in the shoulder. She cleared her throat.

"No, thanks, I like what I'm doing," she said. "But K't'ank is right—why was this Evelyn hidden for so long?"

"I dunno," Nerata said. "We'd have to check with Another You, the cloning facility. We only ordered eighteen Evelyns, so maybe they blew the count and ended up with an extra." He snapped his fingers at his assistant, who tapped on her datapad screen.

"That does not explain her presence in the studio today," K't'ank pointed out.

"It must have been her who stole the money," Evelyn One said, disgust making her face wrinkle. The others echoed the expression. Dena felt as though she was in a hall of mirrors.

"But, she couldn't. She doesn't have any kind of mole anywhere on her face," Dena said. She brought up a three-dimensional image of the nineteenth Evelyn, flat on her back on the floor with her arms spread out amidst a scatter of prop debris. She enlarged the head. "This is exactly how we found her."

The other Evelyns let out a deep sigh.

"Have you questioned her?" Nerata asked.

"We can't yet," Ramos replied. "She's still unconscious from the apolomene gas. She ought to have woken up by now."

"Not if she got hit by apolomene," Evelyn Four said. "We're allergic to it. If we inhale any, we can be down for a week."

"Our landlady uses the same system. We've asked her to replace it, but she says it costs too much," added Evelyn Nine, glumly. "Now it won't matter, because we're going to be out on our butts."

"The studio will advance your rent money," Nerata said, waving a hand at Bonnie to make a note of it. "You can pay it back when you straighten out the problem with the bank. After all, it's the same bank the studio uses."

"We can push that a little," Ramos assured them. "When we check the files, we'll remind them they don't want to risk losing your business."

"They won't give out details, even to the police," Bonnie said.

"We'll get an Insta-Warrant," he said. He pulled out his skinnypad and pulled up the Auto-Justice menu. "Which judge's AI clerk do you think will sign off on this one without us having to send in documentation?"

"Judge Forrester," Dena said, without hesitation. "Her AI's a little off-kilter. If they ever fix its programming, we're toast, but in the meantime, hit her up for one."

"Gotcha." Ramos dictated the details of the alleged crime into the microphone, and the form filled itself in. Within seconds, GRANTED appeared in large green letters diagonally across the document. "Okay, Ms. Evelyns, all of you. We'll get back to you."

"INSIDE JOB?" RAMOS asked, as they left the studio.

"Has to be," Dena replied, steering her chair past the pieces of a massive robot that were being carried into the building on a floating flatbed. "Who else would know that the Evelyns are allergic to apolomene, and when they get paid?"

"Everyone in the studio," Ramos said. "Unless one of the Evelyns wanted to cut the others out."

"Oh, come on!" Dena protested. "They're sisters!"

"My sister would cut my throat for a wad of gum."

"That's because it's you," Dena said, with a grin. "The Evelyns are professionals. And they seem to like each other."

"Thanks," Ramos said, grimacing.

"The clone is the key," K't'ank said. "The existence of a heretofore unknown Evelyn is a most interesting facet of this case. It suggests extreme preplanning on the part of the perpetrator."

"Yes," Dena said, tapping her teeth with her skinnypad. "It had to be someone in the studio."

"We should enquire as to how a clone was diverted from the original stock," K't'ank said. "Whether anyone has information about her location all this time. I did not think that humans were capable of planning so far ahead. Your attention is taken by so many small things. Unlike Salosians, you do not see what lies behind."

"We're not that bad!" Dena protested.

"He's got a point," Ramos said. "The phrase 'Ooh, shiny!' came from Earth, not Salos."

His skinnypad made a chuckling noise, followed by a loud ding!

"The bank sent over the scans from the withdrawals," he said, handing the device to Dena. "It's like looking in a mirror, only it isn't my mirror."

Dena thumbed through the files. Eighteen short videos, all with the identical face and password.

"I am Evelyn."

"I am Evelyn."

"I am Evelyn."

"I am Evelyn."

"I am Evelyn."

"I'm going to hear that in my sleep," Dena said, handing it back. "Okay. Next stop, Another You."

In the luxurious, silver-and-gray boutique, Tenth Ramapuchan stroked the screen of Dena's skinnypad with loving hands. "Ah, yes, the modern Evelyn! One of my finest creations." The female, tall and slim, with teak-colored skin and deep brown eyes, smiled fondly. "So very nearly perfect."

"Why didn't you send her with the other Evelyns eight years ago?" Ramos asked. Ramapuchan fluttered her long eyelashes.

"Oh, why, because she didn't exist then! She was a special order. Very recent."

"I will not say I told you so," K't'ank said, smugly, his voice surprising the technician into arching her fine eyebrows. "But understand that I am thinking it."

"Well, thank you for your restraint," Dena said. "How recent, and where did the order come from?"

The technician raised a slender hand. Another Ramapuchan appeared at her side at once. Dena looked from one to the other, then shook her head to clear it.

"More identicals!" K't'ank crowed.

"Sixth, when did we get the order for the new Evelyn?" Tenth asked.

The newcomer pulled a holographic invoice out of the air and ran a delicate finger down its length.

"Three months ago. MOJO Studios sent the order. From the special effects department. We assumed they wanted her for some kind of special event or promotion for *Android Star.* We are all such fans."

"A promotion?" Dena blinked. "Does that happen very often?"

"Oh, yes!" Sixth Ramapuchan said, smiling. "Calca-Cola just picked up their order of twenty-four Cola Cals, every one of them tanned, rested, ready, and oh, so handsome. It's their hundredth anniversary, you know, and they're sending out mascots across the inhabited worlds and space stations for media specials."

"We bred the first Cola Cal sixty years ago when the original human got too old," Tenth Ramapuchan said proudly. "Our original was the technician who created Cal Two. Imitation is the sincerest form of flattery, you know." She paused, no doubt seeing the horror on the faces of the officers. "Is the new Evelyn not giving satisfaction?"

"THIS IS STARTING to make sense," Dena said, as they floated toward the section of the building where Tony was working. Dena had called for a forensic robot accountant from the precinct to meet them at MOJO Studios. TI-42, puttering along behind, looked like a shiny combination between a department store mannequin and a giant calculator. "If he had money problems, he could have used the new Evelyn to fool the bank."

"How?" Ramos asked, walking on her right. "She doesn't have any of those little flaws that set each of the others apart."

"Computer effects! She's like a blank slate on which they can be superimposed," Dena said. "That's what they did in season four, episode ten. The episode was called 'Missing and Presumed Dead.' The ship had to create a fake Commander Dao because she had been kidnapped, and they had to try to convince the Koromogi who was demanding a ransom that she had escaped by herself. It almost failed when they had a power drop and the signal got scrambled a little, but the Koromogi went to where they had her stashed. The crew followed them and saved her. The battle was awesome. I counted at least nine Evelyns in it."

Ramos shook his head. "Your geekdom is catching. I even remember that episode."

"Why not computer-generate an Evelyn to begin with?" K't'ank asked. "I believe that you are trying to fool your own minds."

"No, I get it now! I bet the bank software picks up on things like microexpressions, pulse, twitches, even blood flow through the capillaries in their eyes," Dena said, urging the floatchair in between two massive gray fake boulders. "You have to have a real person to pin those on. Tony obviously used her, then callously discarded her, like some of the stuff they use in the special effects. He had to know apolomene gas would knock her out, maybe even kill her. That's cold."

"Fire in the hole!"

Dena's chair reacted before her own reflexes could. A meshed metal canopy sprang out of the ornamental back and flung itself over her like an umbrella, shutting out all but a faint glow of light.

Boom! Crash!

An explosion rocked her chair. Dozens of objects struck the canopy from above, denting it like hail. Dena flinched back into the upright cushion, her arms and body shielding her belly. Shrapnel, or something, pattered down on the chair like a massive thunderstorm.

"What is happening?" K't'ank demanded. "Are we being attacked for seeking the truth?"

"I don't know!" Dena said. "Ramos, are you all right?"

She heard moaning from outside the shelter, but it wasn't coming from the right side of her chair. The canopy withdrew suddenly. Beside her, Ramos rose from a crouch, pulling a green plastic leg off his shoulder.

"Wow," he said, with a whistle. "Look at that!"

Dena looked. The four of them were in the center of a ring of mannequin parts. Disembodied heads, arms, and legs in every color of the rainbow lay scattered for ten meters in every direction.

"Cut! Cut!" Tony ordered. The special effects chief stalked toward them, tearing at his shock of white hair. "What are you doing in there? It took my 'bots hours to set up that cascade! We'll have to do it all over again." He turned to a young male technician in blue jeans and a pressed white shirt. "Reset the effects. Let's get it all back up into the catwalk."

"It's too bad," the tech said, presenting a large tablet to his boss. A brief video ran, showing Dena and the others moving into camera range just as the rain of artificial body parts began. Dena felt her cheeks burn with embarrassment. "The rolling eyes turned out awesome!"

Tony groaned again. "We've been working seventeen-hour days for three weeks to get this episode done!"

Not three meters away, Dena spotted the great Emmaline Hariyama. "Commander Dao" relaxed her tense stance and strolled a few steps away from her mark. Dena waited, heart pounding with excitement, hoping that the beautiful actress would look up so she could smile at her. Instead, the star beckoned to Liesl, who rushed to her side and began dabbing at her face with sponges and brushes. As soon as she was finished with Hariyama, the makeup artist started repairing one of the Evelyns' faces. The clone wore an identical uniform and had her hair arranged just like the star's. Today's stunt double.

"What's this going to be in the show?" Dena asked, eagerly, as the stagehands and 'bots moved in to gather up all the limbs and heads.

"Are you a fan, Sergeant?" Tony asked, with a grim smile.

"Of course!"

"I'm afraid your warrant doesn't include the right to ask us about proprietary information regarding upcoming episodes."

Darn, Dena thought. *So close.* Ramos shot her a sympathetic look.

"What is it you want, Officers?" Tony asked, sighing. "I'm trying to get this done before tomorrow."

"Sorry to interrupt," Dena said, trying her best to figure out what was going on around her. It looked as if a thousand technicians were putting together pieces of a giant jigsaw, one that concealed small black boxes blinking with red and green LEDs. "We've just learned that *you* authorized the purchase of the new Evelyn. We suspect that she got involved in the emptying of their bank accounts by the one who created her. Why did you do it?"

Tony groaned again. "I didn't! Look, Detectives, I don't have any stake in ripping them off. I like them. I work with them. Do you know what I get paid? As much as it cost to breed all eighteen of them put together. Without me, you don't get any hyperspace jumps or flying blue monkeys. My budget alone is half the show. Every time Dr. San winks at another woman, that twinkle in his eye comes out of my computer."

Dena was devastated. "His twinkle isn't real?"

Tony clicked his tongue. "Honey, it might have been in the early episodes, but he's getting worn out. Anyone with his love life ought to be in a hospital. Or an asylum." He shook his head. "How exactly do you think I'm supposed to have pulled off the robbery?"

Dena showed the images from the bank to him on her skinnypad. "You can see the woman looks almost but not completely identical. Each of the Evelyns have small features that are different from one another. You—or someone else—obviously used special effects to make those little changes, hoping it wouldn't be noticed."

"No way," Tony said, flatly.

"What about one of your staff?"

"Nope."

"Why not?"

"Because all special effects are logged in the computer system," Tony said, with a weary sigh. He handed her the tablet. "You can go over my entire database. None of us have time or money to waste on putting a mole on a stuntwoman's face. Or breeding one, for that matter."

"She said it's a beauty mark," Ramos said. Tony shrugged.

TI-42 extruded a jointed cable that plugged into the top of the tablet. "Downloading." The accountantbot's lights flashed on and off. "Line 561, dated four months ago, payable to Another You. Approved by Anthony Stinson. Confess! You are responsible!"

Tony clutched his hair again. "Oh, my God, I did. I mean, it's in my budget, but I don't remember doing it!"

"You did. But no record of effects regarding subtle alterations to the faces of Evelyns is in here," TI-42 said.

"That doesn't make sense," Ramos said.

"All things are logged," K't'ank said. "But what is not logged? What would not be noticed?"

Dena looked around her. The plastic body parts had almost all been gathered up. A few were broken, so they were tossed into a rolling bin that passed among the stagehands, vacuuming up scraps. Dena was tempted to take some of the trash home to Neal. Even discards from *Android Star* would be a treasure to him. The bin came near Liesl and sucked up sponges and pads that she dropped on the floor.

"Makeup effects aren't logged," Dena said, thoughtfully. "You could do little changes with putty and color."

"Not my department," Tony said, at once. "Someone ordered a clone on my dime, but I didn't do anything with her. I've never *seen* her."

"Sounds like someone's been ripping you off, too, brother," Ramos said. "Who has access to your accounts?"

"Nobody, really." Then, Tony looked embarrassed. "I'm wrong. My *girlfriend* did, our makeup artist. I was swamped helping to pitch the new season. She offered to help. I gave her my codes. We broke up not too long after that." He blanched. "I didn't change the codes!"

"Her?" Dena pointed toward the woman in the pink smock, who was now working on one of the Evelyns. "Liesl is your ex-girlfriend?"

Tony waved a dismissive hand. "No, no way. Liesl is new. Frankly, she's not quite as good as my ex-girlfriend. Marie created some creature effects that would knock your eyes out. A real head for detail, but she got kind of psycho. Nerata had to fire her."

The Evelyn that Liesl was making up was clearly eavesdropping. She beckoned to some of the others. Before Dena realized it, they were surrounded by a circle of clones, listening to their conversation.

"Did Marie have something to do with this?" Evelyn Four asked.

"I never liked her," said Evelyn Twelve.

"She wasn't too bad," Evelyn Seventeen said.

"This makes sense," K't'ank said. "Malone is correct in her comparisons with the show. The lessons of fiction can apply to reality. I recall the engineering assistant who made a machine that stole credit chips from passengers, but it had no identifying marks to prove where it came from. The machine exploded, removing all clues. 'Quo Vadis,' season two, episode sixteen."

"That was my favorite episode!" Evelyn Five said, coming closer to the detectives.

"You mean someone made another one of us just to rob us?" Evelyn One asked, joining her.

"And then discard her?" Evelyn Eighteen asked, her brown eyes furious.

"Like trash?" Evelyn Two asked.

"That's not right!" insisted Evelyns Sixteen and Four.

"K't'ank might be right," Dena said, suddenly surrounded by clones. "I think that's exactly what happened."

"Gotcha," said Ramos, aiming finger guns at Tony. "Where do we find this Marie?"

"We know where she lives," Evelyn Two said, her small face set in a firm grimace.

"Come on!" Evelyn Eleven said. "We'll take the Android Jet. I'll hotwire it!"

"I'll pilot it," Evelyn Four said.

"I'll serve drinks," Evelyn Nine said.

As one, the clones turned and strode toward the main exit.

"Wait, this is an official investigation," Dena called after them.

"Whatever," said Evelyn One, turning back. "Are you coming with us?"

"Are you kidding?" Dena said, urging her floatchair to catch up and out into the brilliant sunshine. "I wouldn't miss a chance like this for the world."

"Malone! Explain. Is this real life or is this part of the show?" K't'ank asked, as the hatch lowered on the huge and gaudy transport. The Evelyns poured on board, followed by the two detectives. Ramos was grinning like a kid at his own birthday party.

"Right now," Dena said, "It's a little hard to tell."

"I'll get onto Judge Forrester again," Ramos said. "We'll need another Insta-Warrant."

DENA WAS BREATHLESS from the G-forces the Android Jet pulled, but it got them to Marie's apartment building in nothing flat. The craft went into hover mode beside the balcony door on the sixty-third floor of the tall steel structure.

"Now, wait until we serve the warrant," she cautioned the Evelyns, who mustered near the hatch, blood in their eyes. "We have to do this right. Ramos and I go first." She drew her sidearm.

"Forget it," Evelyn One said, slapping the hatch release.

"This is personal," added Evelyn Fifteen.

"Last one in is a rotten potato!" Evelyn Six cried.

"Wait!" Ramos yelled.

But it was too late. The identical females hurtled out of the jet. They disabled the exterior alarm and blocked the security camera with duct tape. Four of them somersaulted onto the balcony. In moments, one of the enormous glass doors had been removed from its framework and set to one side. The rest of the Evelyns cartwheeled, leaped, or sprang into the apartment.

"Shouldn't there be exciting music to accompany this fight scene?" K't'ank asked.

"It would be appropriate," Dena said. She steered her chair inside.

The Evelyns hadn't wasted a second. A woman with dyed brown hair was tied in a chair with cables, belts, and scarves. Beside her, two suitcases stood, their electronic locks engaged.

"What did you do?" Ramos asked.

"Marie tried to leave," Evelyn One explained.

"She was all packed and everything!" added Evelyn Nine.

"Let me up!" Marie screeched.

"We have a warrant to search the premises," Dena said, presenting her skinnypad. The woman glared at her.

TI-42 rolled to the screen attached to the desk and extruded its cable. The monitor lit up and document after document scrolled. Then, images of the clones popped up.

"I am Evelyn."

"I am Evelyn."

"I am Evelyn."

"I am Evelyn."

"I am Evelyn."

"Her bank account has received a deposit that was routed through nine hundred and fifty seven intervening gateways," TI-42 said. "But the sum is precisely what is missing from the Evelyns' accounts."

"That's it," Ramos said to her. "You're under arrest for larceny, bank fraud, kidnapping, uh, unauthorized use of a clone, and about sixteen other charges."

"Confess!" TI-42 insisted, pushing its shiny metal head toward her face. "Explain your actions!" She glared at it.

Ramos aimed a thumb at the 'bot, making it back up. "We'll do this. Thanks."

TI-42 grumbled. Dena grinned. It wasn't the first accountant who fantasized about being a detective.

"Give us one good reason why we shouldn't treat you the way you treated our new sister and give you a lungful of apolomene gas," Evelyn One demanded.

"You can't," Dena said, pushing her chair in between the woman and the Evelyns. "Because otherwise you won't be the good guys anymore."

"Awww!" But they retreated.

From Dena's bangle, the *Android Star* theme music issued at top volume. Dena clutched her ears.

"Turn that off!"

"No, Malone, it is necessary!" K't'ank protested. "We have solved the case, and she must be brought to justice with the correct sounds."

Dena shrugged. "Well, I suppose you've earned it. Okay."

Accompanied by the stirring march, they walked the makeup artist toward the jet with the Evelyns following, their heads held high in triumph.

AFTER SENDING THE perpetrator to Central Booking, Dena and Ramos and the Evelyns went to visit the new clone in the hospital. The young woman was awake and sitting up, staring at the sea of identical faces in wonder.

"So, who are you?" Dena asked her.

"My name is Evelyn," the young woman said. "I'm three and a half months old. I was created to be an actor on a new show. It's really exciting. We've been rehearsing for weeks. I am very curious about this city, but the crew kept saying I would be able to see and learn more after post-production wrapped. Everybody was kind to me. I worked very hard. I was sleep-taught lots of dialogue and skills. The director was wonderful and very detail oriented. I thought I looked great, but she was always fiddling with my face between takes. I wondered why a person who was the director also did makeup."

"How do you know what the hierarchy is on a stage set?"

"Oh, that's part of the sleep-teaching," the new Evelyn said blithely. "The 'Know Your Place' lecture was one of the lessons I got every day. I can recite the whole chart, from the executive producer down to the gofers. Do you want to hear it?"

"Yes," Ramos said.

"No," Dena said. "Do you remember logging into a bunch of bank accounts on a computer?"

"No!" Evelyn said, alarmed. "Nothing like that. The director had me sit down in front of a console and say my name—I thought it was really nice of the writers to give my character the same name as mine. We did about twenty takes. In between, she kept touching up my makeup. Then, I smelled something weird that made me feel weak. The next thing I knew, I woke up here with everyone looking down at me." She couldn't stop staring at the other Evelyns. "You're all just like me!"

"No," Evelyn One said, with dreamy admiration in her eyes. "You're perfect."

"So, she's not involved at all," Evelyn Seven said.

"She didn't do anything wrong." Evelyn Two was adamant.

"No," Dena agreed. "We're not going to bring charges. Evelyn, what are you going to do now?"

"I don't know. I guess I'll have to find a different job. And a place to live." She looked as though she was going to cry.

Evelyn One put her arm around the girl's shoulders.

"We're going to get Nerata to hire you," she said. "You'll be part of the family. You'll be Evelyn Nineteen." All the others nodded.

"You're going to come on the show with us," Evelyn Four said.

"I'll be an actor?" Evelyn Nineteen asked, in delight.

"They paid for you, so they ought to hire you," said Evelyn Sixteen.

"How are you with a sword?" asked Evelyn Eight.

"Pretty good," Evelyn Nineteen said, modestly.

Evelyn One smiled. "You're going to be better."

"Is this a reality?" K't'ank asked, as they watched the young woman making future plans with her newfound family. "Or fiction that has become reality? Or reality that draws from fiction?"

"I don't know," Dena said, smiling, "but it has a happy ending."

"Then it deserves theme music!" K't'ank declared.

"Nope," Dena said, taking off her bangle and shutting it in her purse. "It really doesn't need any."

Jody Lynn Nye

Jody Lynn Nye lists her main career activity as "spoiling cats." She lives in Georgia with her current cat, Jeremy, and her husband, Bill. She has published more than 50 books, including collaborations with Anne McCaffrey and Robert Asprin, and over 170 short stories. Her latest books are *Rhythm of the Imperium* (Baen), *Moon Beam* (with Travis S. Taylor, Baen), and *Myth-Fits* (Ace). She also teaches the annual DragonCon Two-Day Writers Workshop. Visit her pages on Facebook, Twitter, and her website, JodyLynnNye.com.

ACKNOWLEDGMENTS

We'd like to thank everyone involved in making this book possible: associate editors Cyd Athens, Frank Dutkiewicz, James Miller and Tarryn Thomas, copyeditor Elektra Hammond, book designer Melissa Neely, graphics designer Jay O'Connell, cover artist Tomasz Maronski, illustrator Barry Munden, and many others whose talent and hard work made this a better book.

ABOUT THE EDITOR

Alex Shvartsman is a writer, anthologist, translator, and game designer from Brooklyn, NY. He's the winner of the 2014 WSFA Small Press Award for Short Fiction and a two-time finalist (2015 and 2017) for the Canopus Award for Excellence in Interstellar Writing.

His short stories have appeared in *Analog, Nature, Strange Horizons, Intergalactic Medicine Show,* and a variety of other magazines and anthologies. Most are collected in *Explaining Cthulhu to Grandma and Other Stories* (2015) and *The Golem of Deneb Seven and Other Stories* (2018). His fantasy novel, *Eridani's Crown,* was published in 2019.

In addition to the UFO series, he has edited *The Cackle of Cthulhu, Humanity 2.0, Funny Science Fiction, Coffee: 14 Caffeinated Tales of the Fantastic,* and *Dark Expanse: Surviving the Collapse* anthologies. His website is www.alexshvartsman.com.

The Unidentified Funny Objects Series

An annual collection
of humorous science fiction and fantasy.

UNIDENTIFIED FUNNY OBJECTS 3

Edited By

Piers Anthony - Robert Silve

Kevin J. Anderson - Tim Pratt

UNIDENTIFIED FUNNY OBJECTS 4

Edited By Alex Shvartsman

George R. R. Martin - Esther Friesner - Piers Anthony - Neil Gaiman

Jody Lynn Nye - Gini Koch - Tim Pratt - Karen Haber - Mike Resnick

The Unidentified Funny Objects Series

An annual collection
of humorous science fiction and fantasy.

UNIDENTIFIED FUNNY OBJECTS 7

Edited By Alex Shvartsman

Esther Friesner - Mike Resnick - Seanan McGuire - Gini Koch
Laura Resnick - Zach Shephard - Shane Halbach

CPSIA information can be obtained
at www.ICGtesting.com
Printed in the USA
LVHW040534150920
665954LV00004B/4

9 781951 064013